MERRY BELLES

A BLUESTOCKING BELLES COLLECTION WITH FRIENDS

BLUESTOCKING BELLES   ELIZABETH DONNE

CERISE DELAND   ALINA K. FIELD   SHERRY EWING

JUDE KNIGHT   RUE ALLYN   CAROLINE WARFIELD

Cover Design by Dar Albert

eBook ISBN: 978-1-965509-05-0

Print ISBN: 978-1-965509-06-7

THE ANGEL'S ANNOUNCEMENT, A HOLIDAY HOMICIDE

CAROLINE WARFIELD

THE ANGEL'S ANNOUNCEMENT, A HOLIDAY HOMICIDE

BY CAROLINE WARFIELD

They found the shepherd eight days before Christmas. Dead. Sybilla and Seth are thrown together to solve the murder, to care for a small angel with a broken ankle — and to face the hurt between them. Sibby has no idea why Seth left nine years ago without a word. Seth believes that Sibby knows he did not leave of his own free will. Can a small angel work some Christmas magic for these star-crossed lovers?

CHAPTER 1

Suffolk, December 1821

THEY FOUND the shepherd eight days before Christmas. Dead.

Sybilla Somer gazed on the man with horror. Sometimes she thought it would be better to be a wilting sort of female rather than the one the estate and half the shire relied upon. This was one of those times.

She stared at the old man, pushing aside her memories of him, concentrating on the condition of the corpse in front of her. He lay on his back, his head twisted at an angle. She saw no blood. Frost covered the ground in the early morning, but had not formed on the body, cold though he was to the touch. She saw no obvious signs of violence, but something didn't feel right.

A whimper brought her attention to Jack Cramer, who'd found him and run to fetch her. The boy was no more than nine but already working as a shepherd. He was, in fact, the deceased's grandson.

"Jacky, we should fetch the magistrate." Visions of Sir Whittleby dragged from his cozy breakfast room, blustering and complaining, filled her. He would glance at the body, bark a few orders, and leave as soon as he could. He would miss the details entirely. She dreaded the alternative, but had no choice.

"Wait, Jacky," she called, raising a hand. "Go ask Mr. Caulfield, the surgeon, to come. We'll notify Sir Whittleby later."

The boy ran off as he was told, relieved, no doubt, to be away from the grim sight. Sybilla pulled her thin cloak around her against the wind. She had sold her warmest wool last winter for fuel. Viscount's daughter she might be, but she had come on hard times since her father died.

She stiffened her back. Seth Caulfield would come; of that she had no doubt. She heaved a sigh.

I knew I would have to face him eventually.

Seth had been back in Astburn for three months, and she had avoided him the entire time. Foolish that. What lay between them was buried in the past, and her life had changed in more ways than she could count. His too, no doubt.

She dragged her thoughts back to the problem at hand. Old Mr. Cramer must have been at least seventy. Jacky had told her the herd was short one ewe when they brought it in the day before. The boy's grandda had broken his fast while it was still dark and set out to find the missing animal. Was it possible he simply fell over and the cold killed him? She doubted it.

She paced to keep warm while she waited for Caulfield—Seth— leaving a circle of footprints in the frost. The shepherd lay in a wide clearing in the shrubby area beyond the fields, just before the woods rose along the river, a sort of island among the various rivulets leading to the brook and the river itself. She spent several minutes in prayer and tried to keep her mind on Mr. Cramer rather than her encounter with the surgeon, reviewing the details she saw over and over. She needed a second pair of eyes.

Jacky returned more quickly than she had hoped, Seth trudging at his side. They must have run. Seth glanced only briefly at Sybilla, crouched down, and began an intense scrutiny of the body.

"What is it you want from me?" He didn't look at her when he spoke.

"An objective examination." She twisted her hands together to keep them still.

He nodded. "Young Jack here says the man left the croft long before dawn. There's no sign of frost on him. Still, he's cold enough for it to form. No blood. No sign of violence. Rigor is setting in."

"What does that mean?" Sybilla studied his back as she spoke. The navy had broadened his shoulders. Toughened him, she suspected.

"It means he's been dead at least three hours, likely more. His position is awkward. Have you moved him?"

"No. I haven't touched him. I thought a second witness should be here."

He glanced up at her then. "Wise. But you always were clever. Shall I turn him over?"

"Please." She swallowed hard to calm the flutter his quick glance planted in her belly.

Seth—she still could never think of him as Mr. Caulfield—calmly did as he proposed, gently taking Mr. Cramer by the shoulder and turning him over.

All doubt fled. The back of Cramer's head had been bashed in.

Sybilla gasped. "Still no pool of blood. He was murdered elsewhere."

"Clever as always. Yes. And not long after he went out, judging from the frost all around. Still, there should be some sign of him being dragged."

He began to examine the surrounding area without so much as another glance her way.

She swallowed her pride. *What did you expect? An invitation?*

Jacky needed her. He had vomited into the bushes.

Seth Caulfield would manage on his own. He always could.

SHE HAS CHANGED. *How could I have expected otherwise?* It had been nine years since Sibby's father and brother drove him out, horsewhip in hand, with shouts of "bloody presuming bastard" ringing in his ears.

They had him bound and delivered to press gangs in Great Yarmouth. Since his return he'd avoided any mention of the viscount and his daughter.

Seth ran a shaking hand through his hair and paused for a deep breath to clear his head before continuing. There would be time to consider Sibby Somer later. For now, there was a murder to solve.

He took a slow walk, circling the clearing. Instinct told him that, if Cramer had been killed near the village or the Somerton estate, the perpetrator would likely have dragged him to the cover of the trees rather than leave him in the open. It seemed more likely the trees hid evidence of the crime.

He hadn't gone far when impressions on the ground caught his eyes. Not drag marks. Not footprints—at least not a man's.

What would Sibby make of this? He cursed himself for running off without her. She had a great mind for detail.

He followed the marks, realizing in moments that he followed a child's footprints. Ones too small to be Jacky Cramer's. Twenty yards later he heard a faint sound and sped up.

The footsteps led into the edge of the woods and came to an abrupt end at a deep depression where the ground fell away. Surrounded by undergrowth, the drop wasn't obvious at first. He inched closer to a ditch full of broken plants and branches, and peered down. Whimpering came from a crumpled pile of white; he had no doubt it was a child.

He stepped down carefully and knelt by a small girl he quickly recognized as the Holdens' precocious seven-year-old, Becky. She lay on her back, her white gown muddy, her curls held by a silver ribbon around her forehead, and some sort of wood apparatus on her back.

She shrank away from him at first; but her eyes went wide with recognition. "I hurt my leg, Mr. Caulfield."

"May I check to see if it is broken?" He kept his voice conversational, as if they met in the church yard on a Sunday.

She bit her lip, but she nodded.

He explored her limbs and detected no sign of fracture, but her badly swollen knee had no doubt had a bad wrench. Based on her recoil, so had the ankle of the same leg.

"No break. I'm going to carry you to my surgery. Will that suit?

She nodded again. "Mama will be angry."

There would be a surfeit of emotion, but he doubted if it would all be anger. "What is this device on your back?"

She treated him to the disgusted look of a child amazed at the ignorance of her elders. "My wings, of course."

"Of course. But they'll have to come off so I can carry you." He set action to words and unbuckled the straps holding the wooden frames covered with white cloth to the girl's back.

She started to tear up. "They got all broken up, and Christmas is in eight days. I'll never be able to go."

The light dawned. He had just rescued a crumpled angel, a refugee from the village pageant. He handed her the wings and lifted her into his arms. "We'll see if we can fix both you and your wings before then. Don't you trust me?"

The depression appeared lower on one side, and he climbed out that way. He stopped in his tracks, however, when she replied. "Of course, I do. You're a doctor. Not the man with no face. When you found me, I was afraid he had come back."

He didn't say more until he had them both back on level ground. He began to stride toward the clearing where he had left Sibby.

"What man with no face?"

Becky turned her face into his coat. "The scary one what was carrying the shepherd."

Seth could only hope Sybilla Somers had developed skills with children since he knew her. Becky's description of a man with no face would require careful questioning. He could manage children's bones. Their minds were another matter.

Look at it this way. Sibby won't be able to avoid me until we solve this.

When he reached the clearing, Sibby appeared to be sketching in some sort of notebook. *Wise that.* She glanced up, and her eyes went wide. "What on earth?"

"It seems we have both a shepherd and an angel who have come to harm. Should I look for one of the magi? Or perhaps a donkey? We have plenty of sheep in east Suffolk."

Sibby ignored his nonsense. "You need to get her to her mother."

"I'm taking her to my surgery where I have my things. It is closer, and she is getting paler and quieter." From what Seth had seen of Becky Holden, she was rarely quiet.

"But of course, your surgery is better; do hurry. I'll have someone notify the Holdens."

"I need you to help me question her closely. She saw someone."

Sibby's brows rose. "Good! Jacky has gone to the magistrate. I'll stop at the Fox and Badger, send someone to the Holdens, and follow you as soon as I am able."

Seth was halfway home before he thought to wonder why she hadn't called the magistrate first.

CHAPTER 2

By the time he reached his surgery, signs of shock were his first priority. He lay the child on the table covered with a soft pallet that he used for examinations, wrapped her in a blanket, and spoke soothingly to keep her awake. He needed to take another look at her injuries but feared causing pain or distress until the shock subsided.

"I hurt. I need Mama." Her eyes drifted around the room.

"I know. Miss Somer is sending for her."

The little eyes drifted shut. "She will come then. Everyone does what Miss Sybilla wants."

His housekeeper, Mrs. Duncan, who hovered closely, chuckled. "That they do. Folk admire Miss Somer. Since the Viscount died, she's the one what cares for folks, no matter her own problems. Shall I make the child tea?"

"No. She's had a shock and needs to rest." *Since the viscount died... How long has it been? What are these problems? And why is she still unmarried?* He had taken much for granted while he avoided facing Sibby.

The girl jerked as if remembering, and her eyes flew open. "The black man. Will he come back?"

"The Black Man?" Seth asked.

"The one with no face. What if he finds Miss Sybilla?"

Seth's heart froze in his chest, an event contrary to any medical knowledge he'd gained either at university or in the heat of battle. *Sibby could be in danger.*

"He will, won't he." Becky's faint cry brought him back to the problem at hand.

"No. And don't worry about Miss Sybilla. She can handle herself." *She can, Caulfield. Get a grip on yourself.*

"Shall I fetch you that tea, Mr. Caulfield? You appear as if you could use it."

Seth nodded to his housekeeper. "Tell me about the Christmas pageant," he said to distract the child.

"We made a stable, but it has no roof. Miss Sybilla says so we can see the altar behind it. Nan Potter is going to be Mary. Miss Sybilla says I'm too young this year but, in a few years, I'll have a turn. Miss Sybilla says the angel is very, very important."

So it went, he knew not how long, Sibby at the heart of it all. Miss Sybilla thought Becky's palm tree was as nice as John Martin's even though it was small; Becky's speech was lovely; and the wings Becky's papa made were perfect. Sibby apparently also believed that Paul Jones could keep the real donkey from causing trouble, that a real baby was not a good idea, and that even the blacksmith's boy could be a shepherd on Christmas.

If Seth had had any doubt about whether or not Sibby Somer was the heart and soul of the shire, it would have faded in the onslaught of adoration pouring out of Becky Holden. He had no such doubt.

After a while the little girl's color improved and her hands felt warmer. "When is my mama coming?"

"As soon as Miss Somer can get word to her, she'll come running. How does your leg feel now."

Becky's lip quivered. "It hurts."

Seth couldn't wait for the parents. He stepped into the hall and called for Mrs. Duncan. "I need to take a closer look at Becky's injuries. Will you please sit with her while I do?"

No sooner had he said it than there was a knock at his door, and Sybilla arrived on a breath of cold air and purposeful energy. "How is Becky? An ostler from the tavern has gone after her parents." Her gaze skittered about as if searching for the girl, avoiding his face.

"Come into the surgery. Her shock is abating, but I need a woman's presence when I examine her." He turned back into the room.

Curt though it was, Sybilla took his words as an invitation. She approached the little girl and took her hand, stunned to receive a wan smile instead of Becky's normal torrent of words.

Seth spoke not a word while he gently probed the girl's belly. When she assured him that it didn't hurt, he muttered. "No sign of internal injury," as if to himself.

He lifted the girl's white "angel" gown and began to feel down one leg, competently examining a badly swollen knee.

"Why didn't you examine her injuries sooner?"

He still didn't look up. "It was more vital to treat her shock and cold. Both shock and hypothermia can kill."

"How did you learn all this?" She asked.

He barked a laugh, without pausing his work. "I learned many things in university in Edinburgh, but I learned boatloads more about injuries shipboard."

The reminder of her discovery, two years after he left Astburn, that he had found a place in the Royal Navy, stabbed her. But university? She'd had no idea.

Becky winced when he reached her ankle. So did Sybilla at the sight of the purple swelling. He had hardly touched it

He came around across from Sybilla and smiled down on the little one. "I'm afraid this next part will hurt, but I will have to examine it closely. You must keep your gaze on Miss Somers while I do. Perhaps you can practice your pageant speech."

Without a word or glance at Sybilla, he returned to the foot of the table, all professional.

Becky whimpered but bravely began, "B-b-behold I bring…" She groaned and swallowed, never taking her gaze from Sybilla. "tid-tide… What comes next Miss—Ow!"

"That's my brave girl," Sybilla soothed. "Tidings comes next. What kind?"

"Great," Becky said, gritting her teeth. "Joy."

"Very good, my love. How will you know when it is your turn?"

"Jacky will tell the sheep to sit…and the curate will shine the lantern on me."

Suddenly her pallor deepened, and she moaned. Sybilla glanced at the end of the table. Seth had her heel in his hand and probed the ankle with his long gentle fingers. He set it down as carefully as a precious jewel and covered it again.

"You are a brave angel indeed, Miss Becky. Rest for a moment." He gestured to Sybilla to follow him to the far side of the room.

"How can you stand to do that? It was horrific for her."

He sighed, but showed no other emotion. "No help for it. I'm afraid I was wrong. Her ankle is broken. There isn't much I can do except immobilize it and keep her off it."

"You're certain?"

"Until someone invents a way to look inside at bones, I can only rely on touch. Certain? No, but I believe so. I must do my best to give the ankle a chance to heal properly."

Sybilla studied his face, even as his eyes darted to a place over her shoulder. His confidence and skill were impressive. Whatever he'd been doing these past years, his work would be a blessing to Astburn. "How?" she asked.

"I'm afraid immobilizing the ankle will cause more pain than before."

"You will wrap it tightly?"

"That does more harm than good, but I'll wrap the knee and use ice to bring down swelling. I'll let her rest tonight. Tomorrow I'd like to try *plâtre coulé.*"

"What on earth is that?"

His confident smile reassured her. "It is a technique for encasing the injured part in plaster. I witnessed it a time or two in Germany," Peering at her expression he added, "I was permitted to try it myself. If we keep it to the ankle and lower leg, she'll have more movement while she heals."

Sybilla bit her lower lip and nodded. She didn't doubt him.

"I'm going to have to dose her with laudanum, both to keep her quiet tonight and tomorrow during the procedure."

Sybilla scowled. "Vile stuff."

"It has its place," he said offhandedly, distracted by a disturbance in the hall. The parents had arrived.

Sybilla soothed the mother before they allowed her into the surgery, while Seth stressed the importance of calm. Mr. Holden, tight jawed, viewed Seth skeptically. "My daughter is not one of your seamen."

It took a while for Seth to explain Becky's situation, and his plan to treat the girl's injuries. Sybilla kept a tight hold on Mrs. Holden's hand while she added simplification where needed and supported his plan.

The mother bravely held back tears at her daughter's bedside, and the father stood tall with his arm on his wife's shoulder. When Becky told them about the "faceless man," however, her father jerked upright and stared at Sybilla as if to question her.

Sybilla took Mr. Holden aside, whispered a brief overview of the murder, and suggested he keep details from his wife and take her home where four more little ones needed her, but he started for the door announcing he would "go after the monster what done this."

Seth managed to stall him before he popped back into the surgery to explain he planned to go with Holden to trace the trail back to the trees. "There is nothing I can do until morning, anyway." He didn't wait for Sibby's reply. She had words with Mrs. Holden instead.

The men were a few steps outside the door when Sybilla joined them, slamming the door behind her. "Did you really think you could leave without me? Becky's mother and Mrs. Duncan will sit with Becky until we get back.

Seth's stern expression was that of a man about to object, but she brushed past. "Let's get on with it."

Holden shook his head. "No one tells Miss Somer what she can't do," he muttered.

CHAPTER 3

Seth stepped lively to catch up with Sibby—or Miss Somer. He had struggled to think of her as anything but Sibby until she marched ahead of him, leading the way. She had become a force to be reckoned with in the time he was gone.

Sir Whittleby's grooms were finishing their work when Seth and his companions reached the place the shepherd had been found. They had wrapped the corpse in blankets and were loading it into a wagon.

"Old Cramer," Holden sighed. "What kind of animal would do this? Do you think my Becky saw it happen?"

Seth shook his head. "From what she said, she saw him carrying the body and ran. She called him 'the black man,' probably from his clothing, and 'the faceless man.'"

"He sounds an ogre." Holden shuddered.

"Likely a masked brigand of some sort," Sibby assured the man. "Human and therefore fallible." She turned to Seth. "Where shall we start?"

He pointed toward the east. "I found Becky that direction, but I saw no footsteps from an adult. Whoever did this had covered his footsteps around the clearing."

The Deber River was lined with thick woods along this section from where he had found Becky and on south past the tributary from which Astburn took its name. Rivulets and swampy areas crisscrossed the space between the clearing and the wooded area. It would make tracking almost impossible.

"There's no easy way. Shall we spread out from here south and go forward toward the woods?" Seth suggested. "Miss Somer, please stay with me."

Sibby opened her mouth to object to being ordered about, but closed it when he went on, "You have an eye for detail and know this area better than I. I've been gone too long." That seemed to mollify her. The truth was he needed her close.

Moments later, picking her way carefully through patches of wet ground, she spoke without looking at him. "A very long time," she murmured.

He had no response to that. It was a simple fact.

She stopped and peered directly at him. "Why did you come back?" Her words were sharp.

Seth swallowed. The answer was complicated, and there was no time now. "It is home," he said. He knew it was inadequate. From her expression, so did she. She turned and kept moving.

Holden stayed in eyeshot, and after a frustrating half hour with no clues they reached the tree line. Things changed quickly after that when the call of a great horned owl sounded.

"That's Frank Holden," Sibby said. She took Seth 's hand and pulled him toward the call. The feel of her hand in his, mittened though it was, sent all thought from his mind. He had to force himself to remember their mission.

"Are you sure?" he whispered, concerned.

Her response was a scathing glance.

They reached Holden quickly. He pointed to crushed twigs and one firm footprint at the edge of the brook that flowed into the Deber. Crossing it would take a man farther from Astburn, which lay beside the brook a half mile away. They started over it, using the same stepping stones as their prey obviously had.

In the middle of the brook, cold wind whipping Seth 's cheeks, memories surfaced: Sibby in that very place on summer days letting her hair down, laughing over turtles and frogs, and somewhere on down this direction, an ancient ruin of a fishing shack. He pushed happy memories down and focused on the little building in his mind, convinced it was their goal.

He glanced up to see Sibby studying him, most likely thinking similar memories. He hoped so. She turned to follow Holden.

Seth pushed himself forward, ahead of Holden. "Softly now," he said. "We can't be sure where or if he still lurks."

Small signs led them toward a more worn path along the river. Seth urged them into the brush, to remain hidden from the path, in the direction he was increasingly certain was their goal.

They reached a spot from which the old shack on the river was clearly visible through the leaves. All three understood the need to pause and watch without Seth needing to speak, for which he was grateful. Holden pulled himself up into a tree, giving a sign he had an excellent view.

When Sibby moved to their right, Seth grabbed her sleeve. She frowned at him and made hand motions indicating they needed a view of the other side. He let go, but he followed her. It was well they did. A small boat had been pulled up into the underbrush and hidden with branches. They could just make it out.

Seth glanced back at Holden who shrugged and slid down. "No one," he said when they reached him. They approached the shack with care, but it was obvious Holden was correct.

The place was more weathered, half tumbled down on one side and dirty, not at all the happy refuge Seth remembered, much like the rest of his life in Astburn. He glanced at Sibby. Maybe not all of it.

"Nothing," Holden said.

"Foul smells, dirt, and look there, some sort of pallet. The blankets are filthy, but someone has been staying here," Sibby pointed out.

"Long enough to need a fire," Seth said, kicking charred remains at the edge of the river.

"Bones," Sibby said. "Whoever was here ate well."

Frank Holden snorted. "Well for sure. Those are sheep bones. Maybe time for him to cook the whole thing."

Sibby picked up a fluff of fleece. "Cramer's missing ewe, I'll bet. If he saw, he would have been furious.

"They were here long enough for old Mr. Cramer to see something vile enough to get him killed. But what?" Sibby asked.

"Smuggling most likely. The boat seems to indicate he'll be back," Seth said.

Holden appeared ready to explode with rage. He wanted the man that terrified his Becky.

"We need to have the place watched, Frank. You can't do it alone, and your family needs you. I'll report to Sir Whittleby and prod him to send watchers—and yes Frank you can be part of it." Sibby turned to Seth. "Right now, Becky needs you. Return to the surgery to sit with her until you and Maud can see to your other children. I'll check in after I speak with Sir Whittleby."

That, Seth thought, *is that. With awe-inspiring efficiency.*

They put everything back where it had been, returned down the path, and walked along the brook toward Astburn.

When Holden trudged on ahead of them, Sibby gazed up at Seth. "Why *did* you come home, really?"

You were here. He didn't say it out loud.

"Talk to me Seth Caulfield. You disappeared nine years ago without a single word. It was two years before I even knew you were in His Majesty's navy. The wars ended six years ago. You never came back. Why now?" Sybilla's long simmering anger with the man got the better of her. She blurted out what had been eating her since he appeared in Astburn three months ago.

He peered over her left shoulder, and she thought he might not answer. He turned to walk on. "There isn't time for this."

"Six years, Seth." She'd waited, hopeful after Waterloo. It took months before she gave up.

Still walking he didn't look at her. "China. India. Java. The navy didn't cease operations after the Corsican was confined. No fighting, thank God, or very little, but we soldiered on. The Neptune sailed to the east via the Cape of Good Hope. My last voyage took three years."

She longed to hear about those places. "But you left the navy."

"It was time. Will you stay with Becky tonight?" He kept walking.

"It is hardly proper for me to stay at your house!"

"Not my house, my surgery. Don't be a goose. Mrs. Duncan can stay over to lend propriety. Take Holden with you to see Sir Whittleby." He turned toward Astburn.

"If I come to the surgery, will you tell me the rest?" She was speaking to his back.

He gave a jerky nod and went on.

Sybilla made short work of her confrontation with Sir Whittleby. The old fusspot complained about the needed coroner's hearing, claiming he had no time to deal with a ratty shack.

"Send to Woodbridge for constables. Let them handle it," he sputtered. "I have no—"

Taking in the sight of his rotund form in a well-padded chair, slippers on his feet, and comfits at his side, Sybilla snorted. No time, indeed.

Frank Holden quickly set him straight, threatening to round up men around the village, and giving Sybilla visions of mob rule.

"Surely, well-respected as you are, Sir Whittleby, constables will come quickly at your request," she said. *That and a clear report and letter from me.* "I'm sure your housekeeper can bring pen and paper now."

At a stern glance from Sybilla, the woman, who had been hanging around by the door, scurried away. Sir Whittleby sniffed. "Best to get them here quickly," he said.

"Still, it will be two or three days. The villains may return before then. Perhaps your game keeper might work with Holden to set a watch." Sybilla held her breath, waiting for his approval.

The writing utensils and a lap desk arrived, and the languid magistrate scribbled off a note, encouraged by Sybilla's offer to send it, sparing him the trouble.

Holden and Sybilla found the game keeper, and she impressed on both of them the importance of not interfering with evidence. She slipped some coin to one of the grooms, offered her own mount—far more fit than Whittleby's tired horses—stabled at the Astburn livery and sent him on his way to Woodbridge with the magistrate's note and one of her own. She left the men planning and set out for the surgery and Seth.

You will talk to me, Seth Caulfield. You will not avoid me again.

CHAPTER 4

Only because Sybilla agreed to look after Becky personally—and Mrs. Duncan agreed to stay over to provide chaperonage—did Mrs. Holden agree to leave her younger daughter behind.

A sigh of relief wracked Seth; he needed Sibby here. Before he could think why, Sibby herself bustled in, all energy and pink cheeked from the cold.

Mrs. Holden heard her, came to the entryway, and grabbed both her hands. "Thank goodness for you, Miss Somer. I don't know what the shire would do without ye', that I don't," she burst out. "Mr. Caulfield told me ye'll stay with my Becky, so I can see to my others. I thank you; I truly do."

Sibby shot Seth a reproachful look. She'd only agreed that she would "look in," not stay. He felt no guilt for manipulating her. He needed her, and he had promised Mrs. Duncan would be there if she stayed.

The mother gazed at Sibby trustingly and Sibby melted. "Of course, Maud, of course. We'll take care of your little one," she said.

Seth cleared his throat. "I'll speak to Mrs. Duncan. The both of you could use some good hot tea."

Frank Holden arrived moments later, and in the excitement that followed, a flurry of news, explanations, and concerns, the tea was forgotten. He announced that he would take his Maudy home, and go back to the shack at dawn for his watch. Now confident her daughter would be well cared for, Maud Holden wrung Sibby's hands. "What will happen with the pageant? My Becky has dreamed of little else."

Sibby made short work of the concerns, promising the pageant would go on and ordering Holden to help his wife repair the costume.

"We'll do our best to have her in church for the Christmas Pageant," Seth added, and with that, they left, Holden carrying the damaged angel wings.

Seth closed the door behind them and leaned against it with a sigh, dreading the reprimand he expected from Sibby.

It didn't happen. She peered into the surgery. "Where is Becky?"

"She couldn't stay on my examining table all night. We moved her into the little hospice across the hall that I set up for patients when there is need to keep a close eye on them."

Sibby glanced up at him skeptically. "I've not heard anything about that."

He tried to control his smile. She had avoided him, but she paid attention to his doings in Astburn. "Becky is the first to use it."

He opened the door steps away. The space inside, once the bulk of his grandfather's sundry store, had been made over with three narrow beds, a small table, an equally small cabinet, and a rocking chair. Two beds were empty; Becky slept peacefully on her back on the bed closest to the door with bricks placed around her injured leg to keep her from moving it, and ice around her knee and next to her ankle.

"We have to take care she doesn't roll over or move that leg more than needed," Seth explained.

Sibby nodded, studying the little room and empty beds. "I can stay here, but where do you stay? You said your house. Where exactly is that?"

Seth colored and turned away to light two candle sconces on the wall, keeping his eyes on the task. "It isn't exactly a house," he admitted. "I dwell upstairs in my grandfather's old apartment. For now." *No point in telling her I have an agent searching for a house.*

He glanced around to meet her scowl. "Mrs. Duncan will have tea ready by now and supper soon after."

He quit the room quickly, heart pounding. He wasn't sure if he dreaded or looked forward to the conversation that he had promised her.

COWARD. Sybilla glared at his retreating back. She had little time to consider it because Mrs. Duncan came immediately after, bearing the promised tea. "Don't you worry, Miss Somer. I'll be staying over." She busied herself arranging a fine cup and teapot on the little table. "I sent over to the dower house and Ellen brought your things. Wrapper, night rail, and clean linen. Even the book on your bed stand."

It seemed everyone except Sybilla was certain she was staying at the surgery, even Ellen, her companion, housekeeper and friend.

"I'll be sleeping in the alcove off the kitchen, right nearby, where the housekeeper bided when Mr. Caulfield was a boy," Mrs. Duncan went on. "Dinner is almost finished. Now you enjoy your tea and look after our little Becky."

She was gone before Sybilla could say a word, leaving her to sit in the comfortable old rocker and sip her tea, wondering if Seth planned to come back. She was almost sure he would not an hour later when the door opened and Mrs. Duncan pushed in a laden tea cart.

She was wrong.

Just as Mrs. Duncan pulled the narrow table from the wall, Seth entered carrying two straight-backed chairs.

The housekeeper left them with a tureen of heavenly smelling stew, a loaf of bread warm from the oven, and a jar of pears preserved from summer. Seth lit a candle in a holder and set it to the side of the table before sitting across from her.

He picked up the ladle to serve stew. "How did it go with Sir Whittleby?" he asked, without meeting her eyes.

"You manipulated me without shame, using Maud Holden, Esther Duncan, and Ellen Miller, and, now that you have me here, all you can speak of is Sir Blasted Alfred Whittleby?"

She glared across into his green eyes, once bright with life, now filled with pain. "Not even close," he rasped. "But I don't know how to start."

CHAPTER 5

"Why did you come back?" Sibby demanded. She had asked him that three times now. He choked on an answer and filled her bowl with stew. Hungry as she was, she licked her lips and stared at it, sending a frisson of desire through him.

This isn't the time for that, Caulfield.

"Slice that bread, if you please, Sibby. There's a bigger question than the one you asked."

She did as she was asked, her brow drawn up in a question. She didn't speak.

"You never asked me why I left. Maybe we should start there." He accepted a plate with slices of warm bread she had slathered with butter. It ought to be delicious, but he had never felt less like eating in his life. Considering some of the things he had endured, that was saying much.

Sibby waved her spoon in the air. "You disappeared. I went to the fishing shack the afternoon after the one when we, erm, enjoyed each other, expecting to see you, but you never came."

Her face and tone made it a bald accusation of desertion. They had been young, so very young. Seth opened his mouth and closed it again.

"All right, then why. Why did you disappear without a word, and why did you reappear?" She put her spoon down and glared.

"Why not ask your brother?" he retorted.

"Samuel? What does he have to do with it?"

"You really don't know?"

Suspicion flooded her expression. "Tell me," she whispered.

He sank against the back of his chair. "I went to Somerton Hall to ask your father's permission to marry you."

"You felt honor bound." Sibby didn't appear pleased by that notion.

"I loved you desperately," he shouted and drew in breath to calm himself. "I wanted you so badly I went, hat in hand, like a damned fool and offered to marry a viscount's daughter and live with her over a store." He shook his head at the innocent he'd been.

"He threw you out, and you ran. I'd have run with you if you had asked." More accusation laced with hurt echoed in the words.

"Oh no. Your father was shrewder than that. He knew you were young and obstinate enough to try it. He beat me with a horse whip and turned me over to Samuel."

"Samuel? My brother always resented you. You were smarter than he for one thing. Did he beat you as well?"

Seth grunted. "Samuel and the stable master were none too gentle when they hogtied me, bound me over a horse, and took me to Great Yarmouth. They gave me to a press gang."

Sibby blinked, and her chin quivered. "Press gang? *Forced* into the navy?" She put her serviette on the table and swallowed. "No one told me. I don't believe your grandfather had any idea either. I went to him the next day, and he said only that you had gone, he knew not where. He said the same every week for some time until I stopped asking. He grieved, Seth —*grieved*. It was two years—two full years—before he shared your first letter to him. You were serving on a ship off the coast of Portugal. You didn't say how or why, and you didn't mention me."

"It would only have hurt him if I told him the whole truth. Nothing good would have come of knowing. His letters were full of you, though. Baffling."

"Baffling?"

"You were seventeen and due for a Season when they took me. I had assumed you had gone down to London soon after and were flooded with offers."

She shook her head. "No Season happened. The first year he said I was too young. Before the second year, Samuel married, and father claimed the estate needed him. By the third year, he was ill and I cared for him. There were no offers, and I wouldn't have accepted."

"Why not?"

Her gaze, angry and full of accusations of stupidity, pinned him. "You, you lackwit. In those years I held out hope you would return. Father died just before Waterloo. The navy began to pull ships out of service, I was almost of age, and I hoped—oh how I hoped—you would come home. You didn't."

Seth stared down at his cooling meal. So much misunderstanding. So much separation. So much grief. His throat felt tight. "I had no idea you felt that way. Grandfather died that year as well."

"You didn't even come for his funeral."

"I was on my way down the coast of Africa by then."

She nodded. "That explains much. Why didn't you sell his store?"

Seth glanced around the familiar room where shelves filled with the sundry needs of the villagers once stood in rows. "It didn't belong to me. Grandfather rented from the Earl of Clarion. My father."

"The Earl of Clarion?!"

Seth nodded. "Didn't you realize? You knew my mother was never married. She brazenly insisted I have his surname, Caulfield."

"I never cared," she replied

No, you did not. It was one of the reasons I loved you.

"In any case, I assumed he would find a tenant or sell it. I forgot about the store," he went on.

"Then why? Why did you come back."

Seth blew out air from his cheeks and stood. "It's complicated. Our dinner is cold. Let's go see if Mrs. Duncan will heat it for us. Perhaps you can explain why you never married and why you live in that dingy dower house." He scraped their untouched stew back in the tureen and picked it up.

Sibby rose to follow, looked over at Becky and paused. "As you said. It is complicated."

SYBILLA SAT BACK DOWN. Her hands shook. She had eaten nothing since breakfast and was far from fortified for the conversation that had just passed.

There's more to come Syb. You best eat. She picked up the crusty bread, suddenly ravenous and ate it.

Becky stirred then, a faint whimper. Sybilla went to her.

"Miss S'bla? Sleepy. Did you see th'angel?"

Damned laudanum always brings strange dreams. Better angels than monsters.

Sybilla brushed Becky's hair back. "She is here to keep you safe. You best sleep."

Becky nodded, her eyelids drifting shut. Sybilla straightened the covers and gave them an affectionate pat. She liked children but had given up hope of having one of her own.

She turned at a sound to see Seth watching her from the doorway, a strange look on his face.

"She woke briefly, but I think she's sleeping peacefully."

He carried the tureen covered in flannel against the hot bowl, and set it back on the table. He also carried a bottle under his arm. He uncorked it and poured two glasses. "We best eat this time," he said.

She sipped her drink, pleased to discover a fine claret. They ate in silence for several minutes. Sybilla broke it. "Samuel rented out Somerton Hall with the specification that I have the dower house for my use." She swallowed another bite taking old resentment with it. "He gives me an allowance." *When he remembers.*

"The Hall looks empty." He continued eating.

"A person from the manufacturing industry up north rents it. They come in the summer and bring their cronies. Folks are relieved when they leave."

"What happened to the tenants?"

"Some remain. Samuel's factor collects rents, denies their requests, and ignores their complaints. Ignores me. We're glad when he leaves, too."

"And Samuel? Does he come? Does he bring you to London?"

Sybilla scraped her bowl clean, finished the last bite, and put her spoon down. "Samuel and I don't speak. He prefers to forget I exist, which suits the horrid woman he married as well as it does me."

"Is it entailed? Would he sell it?"

"Yes. He can't. So he lets it go to ruin." Familiar grief joined her confusion of emotions.

"What of the dower house? Could he sell that."

"He would have if he could. Shall we return to the real question? Why did you return? For that matter, when did you part from the navy?"

Seth refilled their glasses.

"You said its complicated," she prodded.

He nodded. "First of all, word reached me on the return voyage that my father had left me something in his will. We finally docked in Portsmouth in March 1818."

"Three years ago." Sibby frowned at him.

"Three and a half. I was released then, with back pay in my pocket. There was nothing for me there, so I went on up to London to see about this inheritance."

"What was it?"

"As you see." He indicated the building around them.

"That was all?" The earl had been a rich man.

"Not quite. I was blessed—or cursed—with an interfering brother. In fact, a few of them. The old reprobate named a list of bastards in his will. Left us all something. Some more than others. Society—something I have little experience in and less interest—calls us the Clarion Bastards."

"Still, three years ago, Seth."

He nodded. "I'd been lucky on my first ship. When the captain realized I could read and write, he ordered me to be the loblolly boy—the surgeon's helper. The seaman who'd been helping went back to crew gratefully. I was needed, and raised to Surgeon's Mate a year later. It was a blessing, considering they'd dragged me off the docks hogtied. I was eventually warranted as Surgeon."

She glared at him. "You're making a meal out of a simple question."

He sighed deeply. "I had some prize money. Not much. Some. My newfound brother David—the new earl—and his equally persuasive countess urged me to go to university. Edinburgh is best for medicine. To Edinburgh I went. I had enough for fees and to eat on. The course took two years."

"And then?" Sybilla wasn't going to let him off the hook. Not now.

"I spent some time at Clarian Hall in Ashmead, astonished to have family. David and his countess dragged me to house parties full of coxcombs, prigs, and gossips eager to pick over the bones of my origins. When they tried to bring me to London. I retreated to their home in Ashmead, a pleasant enough place."

"But." She fixed him with her firmest gaze. He would answer her original question.

"My new-found family were still strangers, and I did not want to live off their charity. Ashmead already had a decent physician. I needed my own practice. I had this place, the building and its contents. It had been locked up for six years by then. It took me a month just to clean the place up and create space to see patients. By then gossip had spread and they began appearing. That's it."

She waited. There had to be more. He swallowed and added, "Ashmead wasn't Astburn. It wasn't home."

"And so, you came home?" She reached across and lay her fingers over his hand. Their eyes held.

"I had to come and face... erm, everything. My past."

Me. You had to face me. He didn't say the words but he will. Oh yes, he will.

She watched him pile the dishes on the tray and brushed his hands away. "Let me do that." She leaned in to fill the tray, but he didn't move. She could feel his breath on her neck, and heat pooled in her belly. When she turned to look at him, she curled into his arms.

"Sibby, I—" Whatever he meant to say disappeared in the maelstrom that engulfed them.

His kiss, fierce and full of unspoken need, annihilated her breathing and took coherent thought with it. When he broke it off, she staggered back and reached for the chair to steady herself, searching his face for she knew not what.

He stood in place, as unsettled as she was, before dropping his eyes. "Sibby, I'm sorry. I—I need to retire for the night."

He turned and strode out the door forgetting the tray. She raised a trembling hand to her mouth and stared after him.

CHAPTER 6

Thoughts of Sibby and the revelations of the evening haunted Seth; elusive sleep came and went. He rose once to open his window letting the icy air cool his heated body. Tossing and turning, he twisted his covers and pounded his pillow. Regret filled him, though whether for leaving her nine years ago or for mauling her that evening, he couldn't say.

When he heard cries from downstairs, he leapt up naked, lit a candle, and scrambled to dress. In trousers and a loose shirt, he stumbled down the stairs in bare feet and flung open the door to the sick room to stare at the child's bed.

His patient's condition, thrashing and moaning, took a moment to come into focus, so distracted was he by the body of the woman leaning over the bed. Sibby held the girl down, keeping her injured leg still. As he watched, Becky stilled and settled.

Sibby rose and turned to him. "It was a nightmare. I think I kept her leg still. I gave her a few drops of laudanum to settle her."

Her glorious chocolate-brown hair hung loose around her shoulders, its honey gold highlights flickering in the candle's light. The night-rail, plain, modest cotton, clung to womanly curves that would haunt him for the rest of his nights. His jaw sagged open, and speech remained impossible. One thought echoed through him. *Mine. She's mine. She always was.*

In the face of his silent study of her person, Sibby dropped her eyes and scurried to put on a wrapper. His gaze dropped to the dainty toes he could just make out in the shadows beneath her clothes. *I should go back upstairs.*

He didn't. He walked to the table and set down the candlestick. He cleared his throat and swallowed hard. "Tell me," he said, his voice thick, "What happened."

Sibby hesitated, still in shadow. "As I said. She woke up in a nightmare. Her cries must be what you heard. She's fine now. Go back to sleep."

He nodded. "Thank you for sitting with her. Your actions were perfect." *You are perfection itself.*

"Thank you," she whispered.

"About my behavior earlier… I have no justification for my brutish—"

She rushed forward and put a hand to his mouth. "Don't. Please don't apologize." Her brown eyes bore into his. "It was…it was…" She swallowed and tossed her head, her hair floating up in a cloud of lavender-scented air. "We need to talk again, but not now. Not like this." She dropped her hand and touched his shirt where it hung open. "Not dressed like this. Not here."

"Talk," he repeated, holding her eyes. "Yes. Later."

She took a step back, and he lifted his candle, gripping his self-control by a thread.

He kissed her. Swiftly. Simply. Chastely. He fled the room.

SYBILLA ROSE from bed as soon as light showed under the window shades and checked her patient. Becky's breathing was even; she lay still, her leg still between the bricks. The child had slept through the night. Sybilla had not.

She dressed in what she wore the day before, her head throbbing and her belly complaining. She decided to go to the kitchen and make coffee.

Humming to herself she set the drink to brewing and located day old sweet rolls.

"The girl I knew nine years ago would have been lost in a kitchen. She certainly wouldn't brew her own beverages."

Seth leaned on the door frame. Unlike last night, he was fully dressed in a brown suit, waistcoat, white shirt done firmly at his neck and a neatly tied cravat. He had even shaved, whereas Sybilla had not yet done up her hair. She blushed and pulled it back in a twist.

"I've learned many skills in those years. So have you," she said.

He bit into a sweet roll. "I didn't expect to find you here. I thought I would go over to check on the watchers by the shack while Becky slept."

"Would you like some coffee?"

"That would be heaven on a cold morning," he said, his voice oddly hoarse.

They sipped in silence until Sybilla could no longer stand it. "Becky will awaken soon. I need to get back." She stood and gazed at him for a moment. "I think you should try that procedure, plat... plat... whatever you called it."

"*Plâtre coulé.* I plan to."

"First. Before we let ourselves be drawn into the murder. Becky's family will take over once you immobilize her ankle."

"You're right, Sibby. You usually are," he replied, gazing back at her. "We need to care for her and then deal with our murderer. We will talk after that."

Talk. She heard the echo of her words in the night and could only nod. Seth appeared as frustrated as she felt. What lay between them needed to be—what? Laid bare? Embraced? She forced her feet to move toward the door.

Mrs. Duncan bustled in as Sybilla left the room. "Y're both up so early. Some broth for the little one, Mr. Caulfield?"

Behind her, Sybilla heard him giving instructions and agreeing to eggs and a proper breakfast after they treated her.

Seth is right, though. We should check on the investigation as soon as the procedure is done. Sir Whittleby is worthless, and Frank could go off on a tangent. Sybilla approached the sick room. *That's what we will do.*

In the end, they didn't have to. The investigation came to them.

CHAPTER 7

Frantic banging on the door brought Seth out of his absorption in the work. It had gone well. He had constructed the tiny box and gathered the ingredients for plaster while Sibby helped Becky with her needs and allowed her water and a bit of broth. After, he carried Becky back to the surgery and laid her down with her leg encased in the box with her ankle properly positioned and gently wrapped in gauze, Sibby kept her still with amusing stories while he prepared and poured the plaster. Becky would have a plaster boot halfway to her knee while the ankle healed. Once firm he would shave the rough edges.

The mixture had just begun to set up, and Sibby had Becky laughing at some nonsense about an owl and a squirrel, when the knocking came.

It was Frank Holden, bursting with excitement. "Sum'un came like you said, Caulfield. We have him!"

"Where…" Seth stuttered, but he didn't need to finish. A stranger stood at his doorstep, one of Whittleby's grooms, he suspected, holding on to another person who had been tied and gagged, someone built way too slight to be their culprit. He urged them in from the cold, though he was at a loss how to deal with the situation.

Sibby was ahead of him. Behind Frank's back she urged Mrs. Duncan into the surgery to sit with Becky. "Now what is all this?" she asked, projecting her lady of the manor voice.

Frank yanked his hat off and repeated that they had caught the man at the shack. Sibby glanced at Seth and studied the prisoner. She reached up and pulled down his gag.

"Tweren't me," the prisoner shouted. "I never killed anyone. Must o' bin—" he clamped his jaw shut, and his eyes darted at all those staring at him.

"Who?" Sibby asked.

"No 'un."

"Help us, and we may help you," she said.

The prisoner snorted. "Ye'll need to do better. If I talk..." His chin came up defiantly.

"Put his gag back on," she ordered. "How did you find him, Frank?"

"He rowed downstream and pulled up at th'shack like we figured. Found him rooting around in there. Had this in his hand when we got 'im. Right shocked he were." Frank handed Sibby the bag. She passed it to Seth.

"Coins? Payment obviously, but was he paying or receiving? Are you going to tell us?" Seth demanded.

The prisoner's eyes, still defiant, but, Seth thought, frightened, glared back. He shook his head. They didn't bother to remove the gag.

Sibby addressed the groom holding on to the prisoner. "Take this vermin to the Fox and Badger. Tell Ned I said to lock him in his cellar until we can have him tried for murder."

The prisoner's brows rose, and his eyes went wide, panicked. He shook his head from side to side.

"I'll inform Sir Whittleby, Frank. You'll want to stay here with Becky," Sibby said as calmly as if she sent a man off to trial for his life every day.

The groom yanked the prisoner along by his arm, and Seth shut the door after them.

"You don't really believe that man is Becky's faceless man, do you?"

he asked. "He's too small. I don't believe that one could have carried old Cramer from the shack to the clearing."

"I don't either," she replied. "I'm hoping a night or two in that cellar will give him time to decide to tell us who he meets there."

"Good thought," Seth said. "I thought of asking her to look at him, but it didn't seem worth upsetting her. If it comes to a trial—"

"My Becky doesn't need—" Holden sputtered.

"If it comes to a trial, she may have to give witness, Frank. It is too early for that, though," Sibby assured him. "You stay here and help Se —Mr. Caulfield finish up with Becky. Can Frank take her home?"

"Once the plaster dries, he may. I'll have some instructions for you, Frank. Come and see what I've done." Holden looked torn, but concern for his daughter won. Frank turned toward the surgery, Seth's hand on his back.

SYBILLA HADN'T GONE two steps before Seth came out without his greatcoat and tugged her by the hand to the side of the building behind a shrub that hid them from the street.

Swept off her feet and into his arms, she had no time to think. She didn't want to think. What began as a sweet kiss, a confirmation of something settled without words, quickly flared into passion.

Seth pulled back and studied her face, as if he was searching for words, searching for answers, searching for permission... Before Sybilla could pull any of those together, he pulled her closer and resumed kissing her as thoroughly as a woman could be kissed, his lips sliding to the space beneath her ears and down her neck, before returning to her mouth. Sybilla responded with fervor she didn't expect and didn't regret.

He pulled away, setting his hands on her shoulders, and leaning his forehead to hers. "You said not to apologize. I thought then that I needed to make my intentions clear."

"You mean, sometimes we don't need words?" she sighed.

"Precisely." He stepped away then. "Off with you to the magistrate, to make sure they keep up the guard on the shack," he whispered.

She gave him an amused salute. "And that he doesn't cancel the constables."

CHAPTER 8

Two days later the magistrate sent for Becky Holden. Sybilla saw little of Seth those two days, but she floated through them on his unspoken promises. Promises she trusted.

She sat in Sir Whittleby's second-best drawing room and listened to his catalog of complaints and discomfort while they waited for Seth and the Holdens, who had all been summoned. Sybilla longed for all to be over. She needed to have that conversation—using words or not —with Seth without injuries, murder, and mystery hanging over their heads. Besides, she had a pageant to prepare in three more days.

It had taken all of Sybilla's diplomatic skills to convince Sir Whittleby not to have their first prisoner dragged up to Woodbridge and cancel the search. "Bird in hand and all that," the old fusspot had proclaimed waving his handkerchief and taking a bit of snuff.

Now they had another prisoner, much likelier and much sooner than Sybilla expected. This one wasn't just tall; he was built like an oak tree with broad shoulders and a blacksmith's beefy arms. This one had required two constables and one of the grooms to force him to the dower house for her perusal. At her command they moved him on to Sir Whittleby's manor. She was sure they had the right one; calling in constables had been the right thing to do.

Noise at the front door caught her attention. She just prevented herself from darting out to see to it. It was, after all, the magistrate's home.

"Shall I take care of it? You needn't bestir yourself, sir," she said through a tight jaw, waiting for his nod.

It was Seth and the little man they'd held for two days, much cowed and dirty from the basement. She nodded to a nearby footman who had already received instructions.

"Best to keep them apart at first," she told him.

"You really think we have him this time?" Seth asked.

"Yes, but we need to be sure. Sir Whittleby won't worry about the niceties. He just wants someone, anyone to be sent off to trial and far from his jurisdiction."

"We need it over, too," he said, his warm gaze examining her face as if it held the secrets of the ages.

She gave him a quick kiss and stepped back when he tried to pull her closer. "Do you think Becky will manage a confrontation?"

Seth sighed and ran his hand across the back of his neck. "She's a plucky little chick. I saw her this morning. Holden made her a crutch, her knee is better, and she's hobbling around with her new 'boot.' Yes, I think she can handle it," he replied.

"Come to the kitchen," Sybilla said, tugging him in that direction.

The new prisoner, a great bear of a man, sat tied to a chair guarded by two armed constables. He was dressed in unredeemed black. He also had new bruises.

She gave the constable a sharp look. The man shrugged. "He didn't want to give us a name. Took convincing. Calling himself Alfred March."

"He's had little to say," Sybilla told Seth.

"Where did you find him?" Seth asked the constables.

"The fishing shack, like last time," one of them said. "Rooting about the same too, only this time no purse."

"Money's mine!" Alfred March shouted. "Told you. Owed me."

The butler interrupted them. "Miss Somer, the Holdens are here."

"Excellent. Almost ready. You wait until we call you."

The Holdens sat nervously on a settee in the second-best drawing room, Becky on her father's knees.

"Becky, tell Sir Whittleby what you saw that day." Sybilla spoke softly.

Becky knew how to spin a story now that she felt better. She started with sneaking out in her angel costume to practice flying which drew a sharp frown from her mother. "I was pretending to fly and chasing bunnies when the black man came out of the woods," she said.

"Black man?" Whittleby huffed.

"Was he an African or wearing black clothing?" Seth asked.

Becky shrugged. "Clothes maybe. But he had no face."

Whittleby grunted. "Stuff and nonsense. No such thing."

"Think hard, Becky. What did he look like?" Sybilla asked.

"No face. *That* I know for sure."

"No face at all?" Sybilla asked.

"Just eyes. Mean eyes."

"What happened then? What did you see." Seth asked.

"He had Cramer the shepherd over his shoulder. Want to know how I know?" Becky peered around, enjoying her audience. "The back of Mr. Cramer's coat has a pink patch. I always thought it were funny. And the black man slung him over his shoulder. I could see the pink patch."

"Then…" Sybilla prodded.

"Then the man with no face yelled at me, and I ran and ran and ran. I fell."

Sybilla went to the door and gestured to a footman. Moments later constables brought the big man in. He glared around the room, his fierce visage designed to intimidate. It came to rest on Becky, and his eyes narrowed. She burrowed her face into her father's shoulder.

Sybilla went and knelt next to the Holdens. "Becky, was this the man you saw? Be brave now; take a good look." She held the girl's hand.

Becky peeked once, then twice. Then she sat up and studied the man glaring at her. "This one has a face. He can't be."

Sybilla gestured to the constable who pulled a piece of black cloth from his coat. They had taken it from the prisoner. He tried to put it over the man's head, but the prisoner tried to resist. It took three of them to wrestle it on, even though his arms were bound. Finally, the constable pulled the mask down. Of a soft knit cloth, it covered his entire head and face except for his eyes.

"That's him," Becky shouted. "The man with no face. The one that had the shepherd! It is him, Miss Sybilla! The one I saw."

Sir Whittleby laughed. "No face. Girl was right. Good one. We done now, Miss Somer? Almost time for my tea."

"Not quite, sir. Let me escort Mr. Holden and his family out, and we'll finish up," she said.

Laying a hand on Seth's shoulder, she whispered. "Get him into a chair, and we'll see what his accomplice has to say." He put down the note pad where he had recorded Becky's testimony and complied.

Sybilla hugged Becky at the door. "You were very brave and spoke well. You're going to be an excellent angel."

"We got him this time," Frank Holden said.

"That we do, Frank. He won't wiggle out. We'll see to it he's bound over for trial. You just get those angel wings repaired."

The other prisoner waited at the door when she returned. When they entered Alfred March tried to stand and run, but they had lashed him to a chair.

"Now," Sybilla said sweetly, "Perhaps one of you would like to tell us what you've been doing and why you killed Mr. Cramer. What did he witness?"

SETH WATCHED HIS SIBBY, erect and powerful as a duchess, stare down their prisoners. The answer would be smuggling, of course, this close to the coast. The trade had flourished after the wars ended, times were hard, and taxes rose.

The little man ignored Sibby and stared at March, quivering in fear. "He can't hurt you," Seth said. "We already have him for murder.

If you don't want to be held as an accomplice to that, you better speak, now."

"I n-never hurt no one," the little man stuttered, pulling his gaze from March. "I just took the goods and passed them on."

"What goods?" Sibby asked. Seth had no doubt about the answer.

"Brandy, gin, tobacco, tea. 'Specially tea. Sells well in Ipswich and Ely."

Sibby glanced at Seth. "All goods with high excise taxes."

One of the constables spoke up then. "We found eight crates of tea at the scene. We'll be notifying the excise men."

"Explain the money flow," Seth ordered.

The little man shrugged, careful to keep his gaze from Alfred March's hateful glare. "Dunno what March pays for goods. I suspect nothing. Brings 'em here. I pay what he asks. I sell for a bit more. Still less dear than taxed goods. Folks appreciate my service, they do."

Seth chuckled; a sound more cynical than amused. He recorded the conversation in his notes before peering up at the magistrate who was busy plucking at his lace cuffs. "Well, Sir Whittleby. Your shire has provided a convenient location for the transfer of smuggled goods. That could make you complicit." Seth wasn't sure that was true but it got the old windbag's attention.

"We'll burn that foul shack to the ground," the old man shouted.

"Lay boulders along the shore so they can't pull in boats," Sibby suggested.

Whittleby ignored her. "Ship these, these, malefactors up to Woodbridge with the constables. And you go with them Caulfield. You have the notes. Get them locked up tight." With that, he rose and left them.

Seth sighed, dreading the loss of time with Sibby. He knew he couldn't wiggle out of it. An idea occurred to him just then, however, and the trip began to feel like a good idea. He had an errand of his own to run.

CHAPTER 9

A day without Seth left Sybilla downcast. How had she endured nine years? When the second day dawned, she dressed and ate early. There was much to do at the village church with Christmas Eve now one day away. Work and hope sent her out the door.

Astburn lay a brisk thirty-minute walk from the dower house. She reached the surgery first and hesitated. It would take no time at all to check on Seth's trip. A few days ago, she would have feared being forward, but that feeling was long gone. She knocked.

No one answered. Mrs. Duncan, of course, didn't live in, and the morning was early. Perhaps… She knocked again, hoping to rouse Seth. Again, no answer.

"Oh Miss Somer, the doctor isn't home yet. I waited late last eve, but he never came." Mrs. Duncan, a loaded market basket over her arm, hastened to the door and unlocked it. "I confess I popped in before I went to market. He's not back. Will you come in for tea?"

He must have stayed over in Woodbridge. It is only a half day away. He shouldn't be long. She had loaned him her horse to speed his journey.

"Thank you, but no. I promised the vicar I'd be over early to set up the stable, the risers, and the props. The children will be coming in the afternoon to practice."

She hummed a carol and went about cleaning the church and directing the men setting the stage for the pageant. Her heart was full of joy in the knowledge that Seth would surely be back that day. Practice went smoothly even though her heart raced, expecting him to come at any moment.

He didn't. Nor did he come during the night. When she inquired mid-morning on her way to church to prepare on the morning of Christmas eve, there had been no sign of him. Old memories and old fears, ugly and depressing, curdled in her belly. She chided herself not to be a ninny. He wouldn't leave her again without notice. The first time hadn't even been his fault. He wouldn't. Would he?

Farm hands brought a cart full of evergreen and holly, and news that Sir Whittleby's folks had burned the old fishing shack to the ground.

She didn't have time to dwell on the magistrate or Seth's absence. The women's committee scurried about hanging garlands and tying bows.

Paul Jones lumbered into town with his donkey pulling a small cart loaded with straw. "M' ma said as you might need some."

They did. She directed Paul to tie his animal beside the church until his grand entrance, and asked him to carry the straw up front to the makeshift stable.

When Jacky Cramer arrived herding two sheep, her heart broke. His sister had come down from a farm near Ipswich as soon as she heard about their grandfather. A sensible girl, she'd organized a funeral and assured Jacky he had a home with her and her husband. They were taking the sheep with them. Jacky created a loose pen on the other side of the church away from the donkey.

All was ready by late afternoon, when growing darkness reminded her they were in the shortest days of the year. The pageant would be in a few hours, and still she saw no sign of Seth. She went to the vicarage with leaden feet and heavier heart to change her clothes and have a light supper.

The children began to arrive early as she had ordered. Becky Holden beamed at her in her cleaned gown and new white wings. The

Holdens would be in want of sheets this winter. She hugged Sybilla and hobbled to the front on her crutch. Frank Holden had contrived a platform for her to sit on to the left and slightly back from the stable in front of the altar. He would lift her up before they started. In the candlelit church she would be in shadow until Frank and the curate lifted raised lanterns on hooks on either side of her to light her announcement.

The curate lit candles; the vicar stood at the door greeting parishioners. Sybilla stepped out into the street and peered down at the surgery. It was dark. Her heart sank even further. It was time to start. Without him.

Sybilla sent the children playing townspeople down the side aisle, went out, and found Nan Potter, dressed as Mary, squabbling with Paul Jones who would take the part of Joseph and manage his donkey. They quieted at one word from Sybilla who helped Nan sit on the beast. Paul led them to the door.

The children began to sing and the pageant was on. Sybilla spared a quick prayer for Seth and sent Mary and Joseph down the aisle. Jacky hovered at the door in the dark with his sheep. The blacksmith's boy, also dressed as a shepherd, stood with him. Three boys dressed as magi stood behind them.

Sybilla took a deep breath. It all went well. Nan gracefully removed the doll from under her cloak on cue, the donkey behaved, and the two junior shepherds started down the aisle with two sheep.

Sybilla leaned against the wall at the back of the church and wiped away a tear. It was perfect, and not at all what she had hoped.

But then, her hand was gripped in a familiar hold, and Seth slipped in to stand next to her against the wall, while the children sang about the shepherds. Candlelight glinted off his hair, but his face was in shadow. He wore his greatcoat and had obviously come directly from the road.

"Where've you been?" she hissed, keeping her eyes on Jacky parading toward the front. "I was becoming afraid."

"That I wouldn't come?"

"That you were hurt somehow." She poked him with her elbow.

"I went to Norwich."

She glared at him then. "Why on earth?" she whispered.

"I bought a gift. For both of us. I would have been back sooner, but the bishop did not take kindly to being disturbed so close to a holy day."

Sybilla blinked rapidly trying to decipher his meaning. *Bishop?*

He reached into his coat and took out a sheaf of paper, handing it to her.

She tipped it so she could read it.

"It's a marriage license!" People turned to stare. She put her hand over her mouth.

"A common license. We can be married in a week." Seth kept his voice down.

She stared at the paper, overcome.

Seth's voice cracked. "That is, if you want to. Did I presume too much?"

Suddenly, lanterns lit up the front.

Sybilla put her free hand around his neck and pulled him into a fierce kiss.

"Is that 'yes'?" he mouthed, his lips on hers.

Becky's voice boomed through the church. "Behold I bring you tidings of great joy."

Sybilla kissed Seth with determination. They missed the rest of the angel's announcement. Only when the bells began to ring at the conclusion of the service did they break apart, smiling with great joy indeed.

The End

If you are intrigued by the infamous will and the Clarion Bastards, you will enjoy Caroline's series, *The Ashmead Heirs*. You can find them and all her books here: https://www.carolinewarfield.com/bookshelf/

ABOUT CAROLINE WARFIELD

Award winning author of family centered romance set in the Regency and Victorian eras, Caroline Warfield has been many things. She reckons she is on at least her third act, happily working in an office surrounded by windows where she lets her characters lead her to adventures in England and the far-flung corners of the British Empire. She nudges them to explore the riskiest territory of all, the human heart.

Website http://www.carolinewarfield.com/
Good Reads http://bit.ly/1C5blTm
Facebook https://www.facebook.com/groups/
WarfieldFellowTravelers
BookBub https://www.bookbub.com/authors/caroline-warfield
You Tube: https://www.youtube.com/channel/
UCycyfKdNnZlueqo8MlgWyWQ
Bluesky: https://bsky.app/profile/gma-roddy.bsky.social

SINGLE BELLS

ELIZABETH DONNE

SINGLE BELLES

BY ELIZABETH DONNE

Dedicated to Violet D. and Cecilia S.

For Violet Hughes, this Christmas does not ring in a season of good cheer. One friend betrays her confidence and tells a certain gentleman Violet has feelings for him, while another begins her own bold pursuit of the very same gentleman. When Violet decides to fight for what she wants, she is thwarted deliberately at every turn. Who among the single belles is her secret enemy? Violet will have to foil their plot to have her Yuletide wish come true.

CHAPTER 1

"Hic," said Violet, as the carriage hit another bump in the road. She looked mournfully at her brother. "I don't remember the journey to the Blaynes taking this long before. Surely two hours have passed?"

"They have," answered Donovan, "but the weather has required a more moderate pace from the horses. We'd rather arrive in one piece than on time, don't you agree?"

Violet folded her arms and glared through the window at the threatening sky. She dared it to send any more snow. The whole point of these weeks with the Blaynes was to have pleasant company while winter played havoc outside. These had always been the best of times. Since Mr. and Mrs. Blayne had been blessed with only one child, it was a joy to invite family and friends of their son's own age several times a year to bring light and laughter to an otherwise overly quiet, rambling estate.

As was the case each winter, the holiday gathering began on Christmas Eve and lasted until Twelfth Night, dancing and feasting and games brightening days that would have been merely cold, dark, and quite possibly snowed in.

To miss even one hour of these festivities and conversation with their favorite companions was a loss indeed. Add to that an aching back from too much sitting in the carriage, as well as toes that were frozen due to a warming brick that had long since cooled—not to mention a stomach that felt hollow and neglected—and Miss Violet Hughes was in a sorry state indeed.

All at once, as if the heavens felt she had suffered enough, the clouds shifted apart and allowed a ray of cheering sunlight to descend. The bright beam pointed, like a rainbow to a pot of gold, at a signpost that Violet recognized. It indicated their imminent arrival at the village of Hamptonlea. And just beyond this pretty village, with its rose gardens in summer and strangely immutable medieval ruins, was Hamptonlea House, home to the Blayne family.

More importantly, it was home to Mr. Victor Blayne, a man as dear to her as her own brother. The three of them had been inseparable as children, when their parents had enjoyed similar gatherings. Now, however, the older folk preferred to remain near their own hearths and left the younger generation to brave the elements in search of entertainment.

"Are you going to make up with Cecilia?" Donovan asked suddenly.

Just like that, Violet's mood sank once more. "I don't know. She hasn't even apologized to me."

"And what, dear sister mine, was so terrible about what she did? You know how she likes to jest. It was all in good humor."

"Hmph," answered Violet. "It's easy for you to say. You and Mr. Blayne are friends, and no one doubts those are the limits of your acquaintance. She had no business declaring that I had feelings for him. What if he had taken her seriously? It would have been extremely awkward."

Donovan stuck his chin out and scratched his neck. "It's really odd to hear you use so formal a name to refer to him when you have called him 'Victor' our whole lives. You don't think you might be overreacting a bit?"

Violet gave him a pointed look. "Thanks to his cousin, who found it humorous to tease him about an affection I had not expressed, I no longer have the ease and privilege to use so casual an address. I shall have to be more wary of my manners around him until I can be certain he has not taken her words to heart."

"And if he has?" her brother cocked his head at her. "Would you mind so very much? I have always thought the two of you to be an excellent match."

Despite the cold, warmth crept up from Violet's throat to her cheeks. Victor was a lovely man. But they had been friends for so long, a romance between them had simply never occurred to her. Now Cecilia, who should be her best friend, had awoken the possibility in everyone's thoughts. It was humiliating. As if Violet was some lovesick pup pining for Victor and his eyes, gray-blue like the sea.

Their color was exactly like hers. "Like looking into a mirror," Victor had murmured once. To which his cousin Cecilia had responded, "*You* don't have hair the color of dishwater," and cackled at her own joke, her freckles glowing and her boyish frame shaking with mirth.

Violet had not minded that jab as much. Her blonde hair *was* regrettably dull. And the dishwater joke had been made so often it was almost expected by now. Such playful banter did not bother her. No, the thought that mortified Violet was that Victor might have believed there to be a kernel of truth in Cecilia's most recent teasing comment and *did not return the feeling.*

"If such inclinations existed in Mr. Blayne's heart, he would have spoken of them by now," she told her brother.

"Perhaps." Donovan dusted an errant crumb—a remnant from an earlier sandwich that Cook had packed for their journey—from his lapel. "Then again, some men hope for a little encouragement before they risk everything."

"Encouragement? What would he have of me? We have known each other since we toddled across his parents' lawn together. He knows me as well as you do. We have always liked, nay, loved each other, as much as two people can."

Donovan shook his head. "You are surprisingly naïve for such a bright young woman, Vi. It is exactly because you have been a dear friend for so long that he would not want to chance losing the friendship."

Violet leaned back against the leather upholstery. "And how, pray tell, would he be putting it at risk?"

"By declaring himself without knowing beyond a doubt that you also wanted more."

Did she want more? Violet had never considered this an option any more than she would have considered her own brother for the role of sweetheart, charming though he was. The thought of Victor taking her in his arms was, well, strange. But, thanks to Miss Cecilia Isaacs and her penchant for pranks, that might now be exactly what he was hoping for.

"Do you know," she said, leaning toward the window and watching the long winding drive up to Hamptonlea House grow shorter beneath the wheels of the carriage, "I don't think I will be forgiving Cecilia quite yet."

CHAPTER 2

Williams, Violet's lady's maid, had gone ahead with Donovan's valet to unpack their belongings and prepare a warm bath for their arrival. The butler at Hamptonlea House had ushered the last two guests in and engaged a footman to take them straight to their rooms. Violet was deeply grateful for a chance to freshen up both her person and attire.

When she descended the stairs, feeling much more herself again, she found no one about but the servants, who were hurrying to decorate the public rooms in addition to their usual domestic duties, while the kitchen was, in all likelihood, equally busy preparing the Christmas feast.

Violet peered into several areas that had already been elegantly draped in boughs of greenery, but no sign of her hosts or the other guests was forthcoming. Eventually, she entered the large drawing room, only to sidestep quickly as two footmen came struggling through the doorway with a very large log. They headed straight for the hearth, carefully lowering the timber into the space that had been cleared for it, dusting off their palms and arching their backs with their hands on their hips to stretch as they straightened.

"I seem to have misplaced the entire household," Violet told them. "Where is everybody?"

"Mr. and Mrs. Blayne are resting before dinner," said one whose curly blonde hair was the exact golden shade Violet had always wished for herself. "The young master and his guests are outside collecting holly and ivy to decorate the rest of the drawing room."

"Oh," said Violet, disappointed. She was in no hurry to go outside, having just grown deliciously warm from her bath. "Will they be long, do you think?"

"I shouldn't expect so, miss. They'll be bringing what they collect inside as soon as they have enough. If you wait here, they should be along presently."

Violet looked dubiously at the unlit hearth. The room was chilly and uninviting. Her cashmere shawl did little to ward off the cold.

To her immense relief, the sound of familiar voices drew near, the usual merry tones of Cecilia and the melodious tenor of her cousin Victor among them.

Cecilia entered the room first, spotted Violet waiting there, and rushed forward to greet her. But Violet's restrained reception caused her to stop short, the armload of ivy tendrils remaining a barrier to their normally hearty embrace.

Next, Victor backed in through the doorway, chatting with eyes focused on the woman following close behind him. Violet did not recognize her, although there was definitely something familiar in her features. What captured Violet's attention far more was the way Victor and the unknown woman gazed unflinchingly at each other. The way she and he used to, before Cecilia made it all so dashed awkward.

"Mr. Blayne," Violet greeted him, hating the strange sound of such formality upon her lips. He spun around to face her, his face lighting up as he did so. Her heart made an odd sort of leap to see his attitude toward her unchanged. Or was it? Exactly *how* happy was he to see her? Happier than before? Had Cecilia's teasing words created a new expectation within him?

"Miss Hughes," he responded, and Violet's hopes were dashed. Was he, too, resorting to such stiff tones merely to match her respectfully? Or, could it be... Was he restraining himself from breathing her name too fondly?

"You remember Miss Thompson." He gestured with an armload of holly at the elegant young woman. "Bart's sister, back from her travels across the continent."

Violet knew she had seen that face before. Miss Pearl Thompson. Sister to Bartholomew, who was visible beyond the doorway, hidden behind a bundle of ivy that tickled his nose so that he wiggled it like a rabbit. She had changed so much that Violet hardly recognized her. Her blue eyes radiated the worldly experience of those who have seen more than just the English countryside. Her brown locks were piled on top of her head, tendrils hanging down past her rosy cheeks into her slender neck. Her manner had changed from the girlishness of one who had entered her first season to the sophistication of a well-traveled woman.

Miss Thompson, whose slender, milky arms carried nothing but a wrap drawn tightly about her, smiled warmly at Violet. "*Miss Hughes. Miss Thompson,*" she said with a light mocking tone. "Goodness! Victor seems to forget we are old friends. We used to hide under the wheelbarrow in the garden when it was their turn to seek. They never discovered our clever concealment. Of course, we were quite tiny then. With two braids each and white pinafores to keep our frocks clean."

The words were friendly and engaging, but Violet let them slip by, unnoticed. All that mattered was the realization that Victor had merely chosen to use formal terms for an introduction between them. And if Miss Thompson could call him by his first name after being away for more than a year, Violet was certainly not going to be left behind.

"It's good to see you, Victor." She said his name boldly, shaking off her earlier uncertainty. "And you, Bartholomew," she added, leaning past Miss Thompson to wave at the young woman's brother. "Good to have you back, too, Pearl. It seems we are a full *ensemble* again. That will certainly make matters easier for dancing. Three couples without anyone having to sit out. But where is my brother?"

"I believe he is arranging for some mulled wine to be brought to us," said Cecilia, who had been ignored until now. "We need something to draw the ache from our bones."

"You sound a hundred years old," laughed Bartholomew and pushed his way into the room to deposit his armload of ivy. Pearl had to scuttle forward to avoid his sudden lurching movement and ended up mildly crushing herself into the prickly holly Victor was holding.

"Bart!" she cried, "I am scratched all over. Look at my arms!"

Victor threw aside the vicious foliage and grabbed one of Pearl's hands, holding out her arm to determine the extent of the harm done. "Not to argue against the discomfort you might be feeling," he told her, "but your arm looks as lovely as ever."

Oomph. The strangest sensation, as if hit by a fist, ached in Violet's belly. What was this? It couldn't be. Was it... jealousy? Since when did she feel jealousy? She had no right to such emotion. Victor was not hers. He might compliment whom he wished. He had likely said many such things to herself over the years and simply meant them kindly. Yes. That was it. He was being kind. Pearl needed a little extra attention, being newly reunited with her childhood companions. Victor was a thoughtful man. Violet would not expect anything less of him.

But the green-eyed monster would not look away. It saw the gentle blush emerge upon Pearl's cheeks, noted the way she did not hasten to withdraw her hand.

And if she does like him, what is that to you, Violet Hughes? she asked herself. *They are both unattached. No doubt they would make a lovely couple.*

The ache in her belly twisted deeper. Why did Pearl have to look so *womanly*? How could poor Victor be expected not to notice?

Donovan arrived at last, rubbing his gloved hands together. "Is that the Yule log?" he asked, casting a glance at the hearth. "So, no fire here until tonight? That mulled wine is going to go down a treat then. What do you say?" He elbowed Victor lightheartedly, shaking loose the feminine hand that had, until now, been a willing captive. Violet decided, in that moment, that she had the best brother in the world.

"I've always wondered why the Yule log is in the drawing room," said Pearl, her attention still riveted upon Victor. But it was Cecilia who answered. She loved this house, having practically grown up in it. She knew every nook and cranny, including a secret passage she had shown only to Violet during one of their gatherings. Pearl had never shown any interest in the house's idiosyncrasies before, and Cece would therefore be jumping at the chance to feed any such interest shown. Violet could see the pride in her friend's eyes as she happily offered the details of her cousin's home.

"This house, like so much of Hamptonlea, dates back centuries. You know that much. Of course, the interior has been made more comfortable over the years. No doubt, you know that too. But the enormous hearths of the past that warmed large stone spaces were not all bricked up. This particular one stayed, perhaps because this drawing room is of an unusually generous size and needs a bigger fire to heat it. That is why my uncle and aunt have the Yule log in here every year. It is the only fireplace that can accommodate a log large enough to burn for 12 days."

"And thus ends the history lesson," said Bartholomew, who was always the most practical-minded of the group. "Let's get this greenery hung and withdraw to a warmer room where the fire has already been lit. Ladies, if you would be so kind as to make wreaths from the ivy, we will place them where you suggest and add the sprigs of holly. Our gloves are thicker than yours, which will prevent such calamity as has befallen my sister." He might as well have rolled his eyes at Pearl for all the subtlety of his comment.

Pearl glared at her brother. Violet had to stifle a giggle. Truly, Pearl's arm had barely a single scratch. It must have been more the unexpected sensation of the prickly holly than actual damage to her delicate skin that had made her cry out like that.

Violet caught sight of Cecilia in the corner of her eye. Unsurprisingly, she had an unconcealed grin spread upon her freckled face. Cece loved nothing more than a good joke, prank, or witticism.

Gently warring siblings were equally entertaining. She embraced anything that broke down the stifling expectations of what was proper. Cece was not one for artifice. She spoke plainly and laughed loudly. Although today, after the chilly reception Violet had given her, Cecilia was more subdued than was usual for her.

Violet's chagrin toward her best friend began to dissolve. After all, Victor had apparently not taken her joke about Violet's feelings seriously. No real harm done, then, despite her initial mortification. Besides, if Pearl was going to have him eating out of her hand, Violet reckoned it would be good to have someone by her side who would not take the newly-arrived competition seriously.

Competition. Now why had she chosen that word? She was not vying for Victor's attention. He would give it freely to all. Nevertheless, Violet's senses were on heightened alert. Which meant that, for the rest of the evening, all interaction, each gesture, every tiny nuance was noted and evaluated for evidence of a deepening connection between Victor and Pearl.

Her suspicions were aroused still further when the young woman, in a manner that seemed on the surface to be merely conversational, leaned over during the evening's carol singing around the pianoforte and asked, "Do you mind if I ask an impertinent question?"

Violet very much wanted to say, "Yes, I do mind. We are not well enough reacquainted for you to be in my circle of trust. Even Cece is sitting precariously on the boundary of it. What makes you feel I would like to answer a question you yourself have labeled impertinent?"

Instead, she nodded, her curiosity triumphing over caution.

"While I have been abroad, has there been...?" Pearl looked briefly at the floor. "How do I put this delicately?" She smiled sweetly as if to disguise the fact that delicacy was required. "Have you and Victor ... grown closer? Closer than friends, I mean. It's just that I notice he looks often in your direction even when you are not directly involved in the conversation."

"He does?" Violet's amazement was quickly replaced with a joyous thrill that shivered happily down her body right into her toes, the pink digits wiggling with hitherto-unknown delight. The beginnings of what must be an idiotically happy grin surfaced upon her features, and she fought to get her cheek muscles back under control. She tried to sound nonchalant. "I mean, does he? I had not noticed."

"Then the two of you do not have an understanding?"

Violet's toes grew still. Her mouth tightened. "No."

"Ah, that is a relief. I can tell you, then, dear Violet, that Victor is every bit as wonderful and handsome as I remember him. And I should be very grateful if he had such an understanding with *me*."

"I see." But Violet did not *want* to see. She certainly did not want such an image residing in her mind.

It was very perplexing. A few hours ago, she had been happy for her friendship with Victor to resume its normal course, grateful he had not been affected by his cousin's playful jibe. Now, it simply was not enough. If Victor was going to shift from friendship to deeper affection, it should be with *her*.

And yet, what right had she to claim anything? Moreover, what fault could she find with Pearl? Her beauty was refined, her manners pleasant. And she brought an element of novelty through her new experiences. Why would Victor *not* be drawn to her? If he *were*, she reminded herself, a true friend would be happy for them.

The evening grew late. The Blaynes and their guests made their way to the large drawing room where the Yule log lay waiting, nestled now in a bed of hazel twigs, dried pine needles and bark at its middle. A splinter from last year's log was produced by Mr. Blayne and lit by a footman before being buried within the nest of tinder. The smaller twigs quickly caught alight, crackling and snapping as the glow of flames began to shift to the smaller logs around the greater one. It took several minutes for them to build up enough heat to bite at the bark of the Yule log.

Once the bark was alive with fire, the family grew quiet. Each heart made a secret wish, one that might come true if the wood still burned in the morning. Violet's wish shamed her, for it was selfish, but she whispered it to the ether, nevertheless. Pearl could make her own request of the universe, and may the best woman win.

Bidding each other goodnight, the party of eight retired to their rooms, the servants likely just as eager to see their own beds after a very long day of unusually numerous tasks. Williams helped Violet change into her nightgown, brushed her mistress's hair, and turned down her bed. The door clicked closed behind her as she took a candle up to the attic, while Violet slipped under the covers and blew out her own candle's flame. She lay on her side, tucking her hands under her pillow as she prepared to sleep. Her fingers touched something cold and damp.

A moment later, Violet uttered a bloodcurdling scream, her bare feet taking her as far from the bed as possible, her heart pounding in her ears, her lips cursing the day she had ever chosen to befriend Miss Cecilia Isaacs.

CHAPTER 3

"It was a frog," Violet told everyone at breakfast the next morning. "One of Cece's little jokes." She grimaced. "I am sorry if my cries alarmed you. I asked Williams to assure you all that I was fine. Just a nasty fright. Cece sometimes forgets we do not enjoy her pranks nearly as much as she does." Violet pressed her lips together and glowered at the guilty party. Honestly! The tension between them had barely settled. Why would Cecilia think this a wise course of action?

The answer was, of course, that this had nothing at all to do with wisdom. Cecilia simply loved a good laugh. Violet could imagine her ensconced in her own bed, chortling into her pillow as her friend's cry of horror belted through the house.

"He was an awfully cute specimen," Cecilia said unapologetically. "I found him by the composting pile yesterday morning before the snow had started to fall, long before the rest of you arrived. Did you kiss him, Violet? He would have made a handsome prince."

"I most certainly did not! Williams summarily put him out the kitchen door."

"Oh! You didn't throw him out into the cold, you heartless creature!" cried Cecilia.

"That is where he came from. What would you have me do? Let him live under my pillow for the duration of winter?"

"Quite so," agreed Pearl. "I shudder to think of it. Is it not time you left such childish notions in the past, Cecilia dear?"

Cecilia, like her cousin Victor, had a fair degree of ginger in her family line. However, whereas Victor's rusty-brown hair was the only evidence of his heritage, Cecilia had the bright copper curls and temperament to match. She could laugh well enough. But she could scowl something ferocious, too. And, right now, she was treating Pearl to one of her best efforts.

"Not all of us wish to spend our time visiting one art gallery after another for months on end," she said in a huff. "Some of us less sophisticated specimens enjoy the countryside and simple pleasures. Likewise, games and humor are an essential part of me. It's who I am."

"But surely you would agree..." protested Pearl, only to have her brother tap her plate with his knife.

"Have you finished with the blackberry jam?"

Pearl looked at the little jar of preserves as if it had offended her. "No, I have not."

"Then perhaps you would like to finish spreading your toast instead of lecturing our friend so that others might enjoy some jam with their breakfast, too."

The look of contempt shifted from the jar to her brother, but Pearl reluctantly took a spoonful and dolloped it onto her buttery toast. She pushed the glass container across the table, away from her brother, and asked, "Would you like some jam, Victor? I would not like to be seen as claiming it all for myself."

"No, thank you," answered Victor, to Violet's immense satisfaction, a rejection of the offering being akin, in her eyes, to a rejection of the young woman. "*You* are fond of blackberries, Cee, I assume this will not go amiss." And he handed the now rather contentious jar to his cousin who was sitting beside him. She at once began slathering the contents all over her toast.

"Well," said Pearl, trying to regain her composure, "as long as someone is enjoying it."

Violet loved Cecilia. Her unwillingness to bow to convention. Her simple, unpretentious speech. But today, Violet was still sore about the frog. She might have laughed it off sooner when they were younger. Or if Cece had not already overstepped the mark quite recently. Or if Violet had not felt humiliated by screaming like a banshee while the elegant Pearl resided under the same roof.

So, while she smiled to herself at the battle of natures between the two women, mentally taking Cece's side, she would not be making peace with Cecilia today.

It was not the best attitude with which to head to church on Christmas morning. But her mood was greatly improved by the sermon. And the weather played along well enough for them to spend the afternoon delivering baskets to the needy souls among the tenants of the estate.

Violet had to hand it to Pearl. Despite her superior education and elegant dress, she was grace and kindness itself when handing out the parcels of food. Even the poor folk, wrapped in knitted shawls, their coats patched, their woolen socks gray with wear, took her gifts with as much awe as thanks.

It would be so easy to allow an envious heart to blacken Violet's opinion of her. But it would also be an injustice. Pearl might have some new views acquired during her travels that differed from those she had once shared with the rest of this group of friends, but she was not unworthy of admiration.

Nevertheless, Pearl still seemed to watch Violet anxiously whenever Victor engaged in conversation with her. No doubt she was desirous of having that attention on herself. She certainly claimed it whenever she could.

"Looks like you've missed your chance," said Donovan to his sister at the dinner table, between mouthfuls of savory mince pie. He tilted his head toward the two friends in question, who had now been seated next to each other, Pearl daintily slicing her roast goose into tiny bite-sizes to be nibbled discreetly, and Victor holding his glass of red wine for a small eternity, too enraptured by their conversation to take a sip.

Violet tried to shrug it off. "It would be poor show if this particular group of friends did not enjoy each other's company. Let them be."

"It's not too late, you know." Her brother pressed on. "At present, she is fascinating merely because she brings talk of new adventures. When that novelty wears off, she will become like the rest of us. But if she endears herself to him in these early days, he will never realize how ordinary she is."

Violet's mouth fell open. "You think she is ordinary? Come now, Donovan, Pearl is so much more than that. Her beauty, the way she carries herself..."

"Are all learned," he finished for her. "Do you think a man cares for these things when looking for a wife?"

"Why, certainly I do! You show me a man for whom beauty and poise are not attractive elements. I shall not believe it unless I see it with my own eyes."

"*Elements*, yes, dear sister, but not the essence of what he looks for. If Pearl had remained here with us, she would have nothing to offer him now. You and Victor, on the other hand, have always been kindred spirits. Take your love of riding, for example. The two of you are like centaurs, at one with your steeds. I cannot imagine Victor happy with a wife who is unable to ride with the same passion he does."

Violet fell silent at these words. There was so much of her kinship with Victor that she had simply taken for granted. It had formed organically over their entire lives, and she had never questioned it. Their closeness just *was*. She hadn't really considered how enviably comfortable they were with each other. It would certainly be a sound foundation for a life together. Goodness, some marriages never reached such solid connection, only enduring years of dull co-existence.

What had she been thinking, handing it all over politely to Pearl Thompson as if she had no claim of her own? She wouldn't just be losing the chance to be with Victor. She would lose the freedom they had to ride like two spirits unleashed. No more walking on his arm in the garden, talking of constellations, or lying side-by-side on the lawn, watching as clouds drifted by and trying to outdo each other for the most obscure image the floating shapes conjured up.

If he married someone else, he would have to be respectable. The dynamic in the group would shift. Their friendship would become a shadow-version of its former self.

Fear gripped Violet's heart with fingers that squeezed until she gasped aloud.

"Are you alright?" her brother asked.

"I... I don't know," she answered truthfully.

Donovan considered her in silence. Then, as if reaching a conclusion, he nodded his head slowly and smiled with satisfaction. "You understand at last. Good. Now, what are you going to do about it?"

Violet turned to Mrs. Blayne, who sat to her right, beaming at the collection of happy faces that graced her table. "Do we know if tomorrow promises weather much like today? It would be splendid to go riding together. I feel some rigorous exercise is in order after the feast we have enjoyed this evening."

"Oh, my dear," said Mrs. Blayne, "they haven't even brought out the Christmas pudding yet!"

"All the more reason," said Violet. "I am sure your horses would enjoy some freedom from the stables, too."

"Mr. Thompson," their hostess called as politely as possible across the table. "You are a man of practical talents. What do you make of the weather? Will it be good for riding tomorrow?"

Bartholomew pondered the question briefly before giving answer. "There is no suggestion that it will snow tomorrow. Neither should it rain, which is often a more dangerous consideration, since the ground may become icy. As for the cold, riding attire is a good deterrent, and exercise will do the rest. I should say it is an excellent suggestion, Mrs. Blayne."

"Oh," their hostess answered, "the suggestion was not mine, but Miss Hughes'. She is more at home in a saddle than I have ever been."

"That is very true." Victor turned excitedly to Pearl. "Do you still ride? I do not remember you being as enthusiastic a horsewoman as

Violet, but then few people are." His smile widened, and he offered it to Violet.

And there it was. The quickening of her heart. The giddy sensation of being noticed. The thrill of a compliment. And all of it occurring because the originator was Victor.

Foolish girl! Violet berated herself. *How long have you loved him like this and not realized? And you thought he was as a brother to you. How you have lied to yourself!*

Then she saw Pearl, and the envy with which she regarded Victor's smile, broad and beautiful, offered to Violet alone. "I do ride," Pearl said, her head tilted demurely, her lashes lowered. "Perhaps a little more sedately. As with my love for art, I am drawn to gentler pastimes. Perhaps I can offer pleasant conversation in the place of great speed. I remember Cecilia not being a great lover of chasing across the downs either."

"Me?" Cecilia seemed surprised to be drawn in as a collaborator for Miss Thompson. "I don't mind riding, but the horses won't have me. I think they sense that I am as wild a creature as they are. Being prey animals, they are easily frightened. They probably don't want someone on their backs who carries frogs in her pockets." She grinned at Violet, but the reference was more a bitter reminder than mutual joke, and Violet looked down at her plate instead.

"I can accompany you while my sister and Victor hare across the estate," Donovan volunteered. "I do not mind a gentle pace."

"That is very kind of you," Pearl replied, but her disappointment was poorly concealed.

"Well, then," said Cecilia, "I suppose that means you will have to watch me fight with my horse's reins, Bart. Unless you all plan to abandon me." She looked meaningfully at Violet.

"How are you with a phaeton, Cee?" asked Bartholomew. "There might be less resistance if you and the animals are separated. We could take turns at the reins and still enjoy a ride."

"As always," said Mrs. Blayne, smiling benevolently, "you are a pinnacle of practicality, Mr. Thompson. How lucky Victor is to have such a fine array of friends, each with their own excellent qualities." She gazed across the table. "Don't you agree?"

She had directed this last question to her husband, who had been dozing off from the heat of the room and the fullness of his belly.

Mrs. Blayne lifted the timbre of her voice and tried again. "I said, Thomas dear, don't you agree?"

Mr. Blayne's eyes flew open, and an involuntary snort escaped, followed immediately by an extensive exercise in throat-clearing. "What was that?" he said, smacking his lips as if to get them working again.

"Victor has excellent friends," his wife repeated.

"Goes without saying," he answered gruffly. "He's a fine specimen himself. Attracts the right sort of company. Don't understand why he hasn't yet found a wife."

It was at this point, Violet imagined, that Mrs. Blayne rather regretted having disturbed her husband and was possibly reminded of the wise expression to let sleeping dogs lie. It was too late, however, and Mr. Blayne proceeded to smile sleepily and affectionately at Violet, such that Pearl's ears turned quite pink.

The butler, who had endured many years with his employer's tendency to embarrass his family, albeit unintentionally, now leaned over and whispered in Mr. Blayne's ear. The gentleman perked up at once. "Ah, yes. Time for Christmas pudding! And not a moment too soon. I was starting to feel a little peckish again." He patted his ample belly and nodded at the butler. "You may have it sent up, Shaw. Chop-chop. There's a good man."

The pudding was indeed sent up, the brandy poured over it and set alight, the rich dessert devoured. Violet thought she would be waddling rather than walking to her room and felt extremely grateful that there were no further such banquets expected during their stay at Hamptonlea House. Games, yes. Dancing, yes. And tomorrow, wonderful, wonderful riding. Just herself and Victor with the wind whipping at her skirts, the ground a blur beneath their horses' hooves.

Everyone said their goodnights a little sluggishly this time, their beds beckoning them with the added allure of a place to stretch out their well-full figures.

Cecilia fell into step beside Violet. "You're not still upset about that little frog, are you?" she asked, her tone suggesting that it would be petty if she was.

"I don't know," replied Violet. "Is that going to be the last of it?"

Cecilia stopped and turned toward her. "You never used to be so thin-skinned about my harmless games."

Violet answered sternly. "But they're not always harmless, are they? And you don't consider anyone else, as long as you can amuse yourself."

Cecilia's coppery brows shot up above wide eyes. "You used to laugh it off. The amusement seemed mutual to me."

"You crossed a line, though. Did you ask yourself how Victor might take your 'harmless' comment about me? Whether he might think there was some truth to it?"

"Oh, pooh! You've never given him reason to think that. I never tease about things that could actually be true. That *would* be hurtful."

Violet said nothing.

"It could only offend you if it were true and you were afraid that..." Cecilia pulled up short. "Hang on. It's true? You *do* have feelings for my cousin? I didn't know! Why wouldn't you tell me? We're best friends!"

"Shh!" said Violet in an urgent whisper. "I don't need anyone else to know."

"I should think Victor would like to know. Why haven't you told him?"

"Oh, come now. That's not how it is done. Even a rule-breaker like yourself should know that, Cece."

Cecilia waved a dismissive hand. "Those rules are silly. And Victor is just blind enough not to see it for himself. Besides, Pearl Thompson doesn't appear to have any difficulty insinuating herself with him. If you don't tell him how you feel, he is going to end up in her web."

"That is not a very nice thing to say, Cece. Pearl is a lovely person in her own right. She is merely making sure she is noticed. She is hardly ensnaring Victor."

"Well, then, you should do the same. If you consider it acceptable behavior for someone as refined as our friend Pearl, then there is no reason you cannot also let him see you in that light. In fact, tomorrow is perfect. Riding is something that you and Victor have always shared in a way none of us have."

An impish grin lit up her freckled nose and cheeks. "It's a pity you can't ride like Lady Godiva. You would certainly have Victor's undivided attention then!"

"Cecilia Isaacs!" Violet threw her hands upon her hips. "The very idea!" She shook her head and let her hands fall free. "That's it. I'm off to bed. You are incorrigible."

"Sleep tight," replied Cece sweetly. Too sweetly.

Violet turned a suspicious eye upon her friend. "What have you hidden in my bed this time? It was bad enough that I looked the absolute fool last night. You would not want to give Pearl the advantage by embarrassing me two nights in a row, would you?"

Cecilia's eyes twinkled. "There is nothing in your bed."

"In my toilette?'"

"Nothing."

"If you have hidden something that will give me another fright, I swear I will never speak to you again!"

"Good ni-ight," Cecilia said in a sing-song voice, walking away and waving with her fingers over her shoulder.

Violet stood outside her bedroom door and considered her options. There wasn't much choice. Her bed was beyond the oaken frame. She could hardly sleep in a chair in the drawing room, although the idea was currently rather tempting. No, there was nothing else for it.

She slowly turned the handle, nearly jumping out of her skin when Williams' voice spoke right behind her."

"Ready for bed, miss?"

Violet sighed. "Ready as I'll ever be." And she opened the door.

CHAPTER 4

Violet had an unexpectedly good night's sleep, all things considered. It had taken her some time to settle. No frog or other unpleasant surprise having leapt out at her, she had finally accepted that Cecilia had just been toying with her.

She enjoyed a full and satisfying stretch, taking a deep, cleansing breath.

Her nose twitched suspiciously. What was that smell? It reminded her of… fish. Yes, fish. The odor was faint but unmistakable. Her room was too far from both the kitchen and dining room for either of these sources to offer an explanation for the smell.

Fully awake now, her curiosity piqued, Violet threw back her covers, swung her feet over the edge of the bed, and slid down to stand. The smell grew ever so slightly stronger. Taking a tentative step, she stopped and sniffed. Violet repeated this process until she identified the direction in which the smell was strongest. She took several more steps, ending up in front of her wardrobe.

Carefully, she opened the door just enough to allow her nose to experience the full insult of the cupboard's contents. She slammed the door shut again. Had a mouse died in there? But the smell was not musty. It did not reek of decay. Well, not that sort of decay. The odor had declared itself—as unlikely as it seemed—to belong to a very recently deceased fish.

Violet was ready to throttle Cecilia. Her pranks were really crossing the line of friendship. She returned to the warmth and relatively odorless safety of her bed and rang for her lady's maid.

A soft knock at the door told of Williams' arrival.

"Come in," said Violet. And then, "Prepare yourself, Williams."

Violet once again walked across to the wardrobe and pried its door open an inch. The smell celebrated its freedom and swooped out to assault their senses.

Williams, while not a lady, had a perfectly functional nose. "Heavens, what a smell! Is that fish? Why is there a fish in your wardrobe, miss?"

"I was rather hoping you might know," answered Violet. "It certainly wasn't there when I went to bed. Someone would have had to sneak into my room while I was sleeping. Would any of the servants have spotted them, do you think?"

"I can ask, miss. But the damage has already been done. I'm afraid that terrible odor will have crept into all your clothes. We will have to wash every single item, save the delicates that were in the chest by the window."

"What about the dress I wore yesterday?"

"It was already added to the laundry last night. It will be all crumpled. That is if the maids have not already begun the washing. Then it will be wet."

"Oh!" cried Violet as further realization hit her. "My riding attire! Everything was in that accursed wardrobe! I am going to give Cecilia such a talking to! She really has gone too far this time."

"May I suggest you retire to your bed while I remove the ... er, *item* from your wardrobe? Then I will send your clothing to be laundered. I'm afraid nothing will dry in this cold and damp for some hours. Perhaps one of the young ladies would have something for you to wear in the meantime?"

"I doubt that." Violet threw herself back on the bed in a sulk. "Cecilia is too short, and Pearl is too slender. Even Mrs. Blayne could not help. She is more well-endowed in the bosom area than I. Am I truly to be stuck in my room in my nightgown all day? And miss out on the chance to ride? It was my suggestion, you know. And now..."

Violet stopped before she declared her envy of Pearl to her lady's maid. There were some things she was not comfortable saying out loud, even to a trusted servant.

"I'm so sorry, miss." Williams seemed genuinely so. "I may have to speak to Mrs. Blayne about moving you to a different room. This cupboard will need to air. And it cannot do so while you are confined to the same room. It will be ... unpleasant. And we will likely need to open the windows, which will bring in the chill. All in all, it is not practical."

Indeed, it was not. To Violet's infinite embarrassment, the servants had to spend the morning preparing a new room for her, including starting a new fire, and moving the remainder of her belongings that had not been affected. They even had to bring her a breakfast tray upstairs because she could not dine with the rest of the guests. Her clothing alone became an enormous additional task for the busy maids and Violet could hardly look any of them in the eye.

So, when Cecilia popped in to check on her friend, Violet was in a particularly unreceptive mood.

"I suppose you're feeling very pleased with yourself," Violet said the moment Cecilia poked her head around the door.

"I don't know what you mean. I just came to see if you needed some company since you can't come downstairs."

"How noble of you." Violet pulled her shawl more tightly around her nightgown, the open door leeching the precious heat from the room. "If only you had been as considerate last night."

Cecilia frowned. "What should I have done last night?"

"I suppose it is more accurate to say what you *shouldn't* have done."

"What are you talking about?" Cecilia came inside and shut the door behind her. Violet did not bid her sit down, but she did so anyway.

Violet scowled at her. "I would have thought you would be having a good laugh at your success. But it was badly done, Cece. And now I cannot even leave my room, let alone go riding with Victor."

Cecilia leaned forward, concern etched upon her face. "It is a terrible thing to have happen to you, but I don't see what it has to do with me. I understand something has occurred to contaminate your clothing. Why would you associate that with me?"

Violet's scowl deepened to a glare. "You and your need to amuse yourself have hurt me twice before. And last night you as good as threatened me with a third 'little surprise.' Clearly you have nothing better to do with your time. Nor do you value our friendship."

Cecilia's trademark moody glower appeared, chasing concern from her features and replacing them with angry indignation. "I see. You think me capable of hurting you on purpose."

"Oh, no doubt you thought it would be hilarious. But you don't always think things through. I have to hand it to you. Waiting until I was asleep was clever. I had let my guard down by then. You must have struggled to contain your urge to laugh as you dropped the fish at the bottom of my wardrobe. I wonder if Cook appreciates her food being wasted for a prank."

"A fish in your wardrobe? That is not funny."

"Indeed, it is not. I am glad you see it now. It would have been so much better if you had realized it sooner."

"No, you don't understand. I would never find that amusing. It would be thoughtless toward you *and* the staff."

"Not to mention the temporary loss of my riding ensemble."

Cecilia's hands flew to her mouth. "Oh, *Violet*! Your time to connect with Victor! I would never rob you of that! I think the two of you are a splendid match. How could you believe I would betray your interests for a silly amusement?"

"You've done it before."

"But that was before I knew of your feelings for him! Good grief! What sort of friend do you think I am?"

Violet's conviction of Cecilia's guilt began to waiver. "If not you... Who else would do such a thing? It was clearly not an accident."

Cecilia barely hesitated before saying, "It could be Pearl."

"What?" Violet could not have been more astonished. "Pearl has no taste for your playful humor. She has said as much. Why would she engage in a prank?"

"What if it were not a prank but a tactical move?"

"I don't follow."

Cece shrugged. "Pearl has an obvious interest in Victor."

"What does that have to do with...?"

"And Victor spoke with great enthusiasm about riding with *you* today. He all but handed Pearl over to your brother. She would benefit directly from your entire wardrobe being inaccessible today."

"But she is a gentlewoman! Nothing about her behavior has suggested she would take such extreme action to secure Victor's affection. I think we can safely rule out such a thought. There must be another explanation."

"You discard her as suspect too easily," declared Cecilia. "She has been away for some time, exposed to who knows what influences on the continent. How well do we truly know her anymore? If she has set her sights on Victor and perceives you as a threat, she may very well reach for schemes she might not otherwise have considered."

"No," Violet insisted. "I cannot picture it. Pearl is not made of such devious stuff."

"And I am?"

"Well, yes." Violet waved her hand as she explained. "You are a born plotter, Cece. Perhaps you see in Pearl what you are able to conjure in your own mind."

Cecilia folded her arms and sat back, her lips squeezed into an unhappy pout. "I have the distinct impression I should be offended."

"I only say you have the skill for plotting," Violet added hastily. "I do not thereby mean you choose to use it for wickedness."

"*Hmph.* I suppose I should be grateful for such a testimonial." Before Violet could say anything in response, Cece added, "Here's an idea. Perhaps we could suggest another day of riding and see if a similar incident occurs to disrupt it."

Violet shook her head vehemently. "No, I could not bear another day trapped in my room. We must find a different way to determine whether Pearl is capable of such underhandedness."

"I shall think on it. I might as well put my plotting skills to good use." She threw a sulky glance at Violet.

"Oh, stop harping on it, will you? Would it help if I said I was sorry for doubting you?"

"As it happens," answered Cecilia, "it would."

"Well, then, I am very sorry for thinking you could stoop so low as to plant a fish in my wardrobe. "However," Violet added, looking down at her nightgown, "I think I have been punished enough."

"Then I shall stay and amuse you," declared Cecilia, her smile returning. "We shall send for tea and cakes and a pack of cards, and we shall play and talk while the others are forced to endure the cold. Even better, I believe Victor will sorely feel your absence. If this *was* a scheme by Pearl, I suspect it will backfire spectacularly."

This thought went a little way to giving Violet much-needed comfort. Being on speaking terms with her best friend again and having her bright mind working *for* Violet instead of against her was a great boon. The hours passed quickly. Cecilia only left the room when they heard the riders returning.

"You're deserting me?" Violet said unreasonably. The thought of Cecilia abandoning her to her own entertainment was unbearable.

"Only temporarily," said her friend. "I want to see how the outing went and get a feel for what success, if any, Pearl has had with Victor. I'll be back shortly."

"*Shortly*" ended up being more than an hour later, each minute during which Violet felt the room grow smaller, not helped in any way by the winter sun sinking low in the sky particularly early.

Cecilia had not yet returned when a gentle knock on the door caused Violet to lift her head. She rose and walked across the wool carpet, thinking perhaps it was a maid coming with a new tray of refreshment. Instead, a folded sheet of paper was slid in under the door, followed by the sound of footfalls disappearing down the hallway.

Violet reached down, cautiously pinching the page at one corner.

She had had enough of pranks. If this note was another form of torment...

It was not.

As Violet gingerly lifted the fold of the single sheet, three words swam into focus.

"You were missed."

Beneath this simple statement, Victor's name was scrawled in his distinctive hand.

For a moment, Violet doubted the note's authenticity, but the writing had the narrow loops and closing curls that typically marked Victor's written words.

Violet threw herself onto the bed, reading and rereading the short sentence, its warm sentiment burrowing deeper and deeper into her heart. She crushed the page and its precious words against her bosom. He had missed her! Enough to write and tell her. It would have been quite natural for him to express this amicably in conversation, but her current sojourn in her nightgown made that quite impossible. He must have felt the loss of her most strongly to have committed it to paper. She sighed happily. He had missed her...

In that moment, Cecilia came bounding into the room, almost slamming the door closed behind her in her haste to ensure their privacy.

"You should have seen Pearl's face!" exclaimed Cece. "It was a proper thundercloud! Apparently, Victor did not ride with her in your absence but chose to gallop off with Bartholomew! It seems your brother had promised her his company, and Victor said it was not his place to upset their arrangements! Ha! And then, when they entered the stable yard, Victor thanked Bart and said it would only have been more enjoyable had *you* been there. I thought Pearl was going to have some sort of quiet apoplexy! And *then*, Victor said, since you had been denied an adventure today, we should all go for a walk to the ruins tomorrow. And if none of your dresses were dry in time, he would lend you his shirt and trousers. *Ha ha ha ha ha!*"

Cece wiped tears of mirth from her eyes with the heel of her palm. "I think it is safe to say that Pearl is now truly apprised of where his affection lies. And if she was the one behind the fishy nonsense, her plan has failed beyond our wildest hopes."

Cecilia suddenly stopped and stared at Violet. "What are you doing on your bed? Were you resting? Did I wake you? If I have, I think you will agree it was worth the disturbance."

Violet shyly passed Victor's note to her friend, who read it and immediately waved it about triumphantly before jumping up onto the bed too. "He actually wrote and told you he felt your absence! There is certainly no doubt now—nor should there have been—that Victor is yours. Tomorrow, you should show him that his feelings are reciprocated. It would be unkind, nay heartless, to leave such a gesture from him unanswered."

"I think," said Violet, sitting up to retrieve her treasured page from Cece, "Victor's words have given me courage. Tomorrow I shall not be timid. If Victor shows any encouragement, I shall give him the same."

"A Twelfth Night engagement!" Cecilia cried with delight. "And you and I to become cousins! Yes, I find this all most agreeable. And I promise not to put any amphibians in your wedding shoes." She grinned.

"You are too hasty with your conclusions," replied Violet, but she was beaming. This day had morphed from being one of the worst she had ever experienced to one filled with delicious promise. And tomorrow. Ah, tomorrow. She could hardly wait.

CHAPTER 5

As soon as the sunlight framed the curtains of her new room, Violet was awake and ringing for Williams.

"I need to wear something to shield me from the cold today. We are off for a walk among the ruins after breakfast," said Violet, hardly able to contain her excitement.

Her lady's maid, however, wore a less than encouraging expression that sent a warning chill up Violet's spine.

"I'm afraid none of your garments are dry yet, miss," said the hapless Williams. "Between the cold and the damp, there is little one can do about it. I have taken one of your lighter gowns and laid it over a chair in front of one of the fires, and it may well be ready by the afternoon, but it will not be suitable for the outdoors, I'm afraid."

"You can't be serious! Am I to spend another day cooped up in my room?"

"I am very sorry, miss. I don't know what else to do."

Violet remembered Victor's offer of his own garments and wished such a brazen idea could be implemented. The thought of being inside his linens would certainly heat her up quickly! But it was beyond propriety, even in such desperate circumstances.

"Could I borrow one of your dresses, perhaps, Williams?" asked Violet, no other solution having sprung to mind.

"Oh, *no*, Miss Hughes! My attire is too lowly for someone of your station. What if one of the villagers cross your path? They will assume you are a servant."

"Rather a servant than a prisoner," grumbled Violet, but she did not insist further. Bother the many rules a young lady had to follow!

It did not take long for the rest of the household to become aware of her situation. Violet had been eating her breakfast alone once more when Williams knocked on the door and, upon being bade to enter, did so with a woven wool garment over one arm and a coat over another.

"Your friends have come to the rescue, miss! This dress is from Miss Thompson. She says you can keep it. It is no longer a good fit for her as it is too loose about the bodice. She apologizes for not thinking of it yesterday, but the ladies made an effort this morning to search among their clothes for something you might use. Miss Isaacs sent her spare coat. It will likely be too short, but it is often fashionable to show one's hem a little. By tomorrow, several items from your own wardrobe should be ready. The maids will make sure of that. Even if it means hanging the gowns in front of the kitchen fire once dinner is done."

Violet jumped to her feet and grabbed hold of Pearl's dress. It was a deep blue, better suited to its owner's darker looks, but Violet did not mind. It was incredibly thoughtful of Pearl to part with it at all. Violet knew Cecilia had been wrong about her. If Pearl had wished Violet out of the way, she would hardly have made it possible for her to join them on this walk.

Cecilia's coat was purple, a shocking clash with its owner's ginger hair, but then that was exactly the sort of thing Cece would want to do. She was not afraid of standing out. As for Violet, she cared little whether the items matched. They would only be worn for one day, and she was among friends. No one would speak an unkind word.

As it turned out, however, the shades of blue and purple were not an outright mismatch. So little of the dress showed that it would not have mattered anyway. Her pale gray hat and gloves had fortunately been kept in a separate box that had not been unpacked and were now whisked out by Williams, happy to dress her mistress and send her out into society again.

Violet descended the stairs as if she were arriving at a ball. There was a communal gasp of joy as she entered the drawing room where everyone awaited her. Cecilia rushed forward and drew her closer to the huddle of chairs where the rest of her friends sat smiling up at her.

"How do I look?" Violet twirled for full effect. "Ready for the ruins?"

"Definitely!" cried Victor. "May I offer you my arm as we walk?"

It was a gesture Victor had made countless times over the years. But today his broad smile and outstretched hand sent a shiver of delight and anticipation through her frame. She wrapped her gloved hand around his bicep, thrilling at the latent strength in his muscle.

The six of them, paired up and wrapped in their thick coats, set off down the drive and then turned into the lane that led to the village. The medieval ruins were just beyond the grounds of Hamptonlea House. A favorite spot for summer picnics. The wintry gloom, however, lent a romantic aura to the dark, neglected stones.

Her arm snugly pressed against Victor's, Violet felt the wool of Pearl's dress start to itch. She ran a finger along the inside of the neckline, but the touch only seemed to make it worse. The garment itself did not feel coarse, but perhaps the hems were, where the outer portion of the cloth folded in against her skin. Maybe that was why her wrists now began to feel ticklish too. The rest of the dress was held away from her skin by various layers of undergarments, for which Violet was very grateful as the urge to scratch the collar and cuff areas grew. She tried to resist it for as long as she could, but every now and then she had to give in and rub her nails across the irritation as much as her gloves would allow.

"Are you alright?" asked Victor when she had clawed at herself again as surreptitiously as possible.

She drew her hands back to a more demure position. "It would appear that, after one day without proper garments, I have grown unaccustomed to them. I find the cloth rough against my skin. I did not think myself such a delicate creature, but there you are." She tried to grin playfully, but it kept reverting to a grimace as Violet was forced to scratch once again.

"I've been meaning to talk to you about something," said Victor, slowing down so that the two of them fell behind the others. He stopped and turned to face her, steeped in the shadow of a battered wall overgrown with grass and ivy.

"Yes?" Violet tilted her chin up to him and tried not to think about how the collar of her dress shifted and tormented her skin. She was certain that welts had begun to form from her persistent scraping at the irritations.

"We've been friends a very long time."

"Almost our entire lives," agreed Violet, trying to imagine herself free of this dress and its perpetual discomfort.

"We have rarely argued."

Violet nodded, then gave in to the urge to scratch her neck.

"And our families are the best of friends too."

The itch crossed over into a sharp burning sensation. This was no longer a subtle annoyance. It was as if her body had grown allergic to the wearing of clothes, as ridiculous as that may sound. She wanted to claw them off. As such, she was barely hearing what Victor was trying to say.

He bent lower, so that his face reached for hers. In a voice that Violet vaguely recognized as unusually sensual over the screaming throughout her entire body, he said, "I think we could be happy with more. Would you like more, Violet?" And he cupped her chin so that his mouth might find hers.

In a wild panic, Violet cried, "I have to go!" She broke free from his otherwise welcome touch, scratching furiously at her skin, feeling the bumps under her fingers where welts had already formed. Grabbing her skirts, she ran, stumbling and gasping, back to the house.

In the growing distance, she heard the others call after her. Only Cecilia's nimble feet caught up with Violet's struggling form.

"What is the matter?" she cried, drawing level with Violet as they continued to run.

"Can't talk... Have to get this dress off... My skin is on fire!"

So little of it was visible, Cecilia was unable to see the rash that Violet could feel spreading across her wrists and collarbone.

As they approached the house, Violet tore off her coat and gloves, the icy air granting much-wanted relief from the sensory torment. Cecilia gasped as the angry red marks became visible beneath her friend's throat.

"What has caused it?" Cecilia asked, taking the discarded items from Violet so that her hands were free once again to scratch.

"I don't know," answered Violet before leaping up the steps and startling the butler as she burst through the front door. "Send for Williams. And warm water. And chamomile if you've got it." The instructions hung in the air as she tore up the next flight of steps and flew into her room, pulling the dress over her head and dropping it on the floor before even making sure the door was closed. Cecilia followed and closed it for her before pouring some water into her handbasin. She took a sponge and began to dab softly at the raised marks with the soothing cold water. Violet shivered. The relief was instant but short-lived.

Williams soon appeared with a bowl of warm water and a jar of homemade chamomile ointment. She worked quickly, washing off any irritation that may have remained on Violet's skin before gently applying the herbal lotion. Her efforts were gratefully received, and Violet was able to refrain from scratching at last, although the welts still sat stubbornly upon her wrists and neckline.

"I don't want to speak out of turn, miss..." Williams said after she had tidied up after herself.

"What is it?" asked Violet. "What do you want to say?" She hoped she didn't sound too irritable.

"It's just that Finch, Miss Thompson's abigail, has a similar rash on her hands."

Violet and Cecilia exchanged glances.

"Do you have any idea why?" asked Violet.

"No, miss. But she has been keeping to herself a bit since this morning. I didn't think anything of it until just now, when I saw how your condition is much the same."

"Send Finch up here at once," demanded Cecilia. "And don't mention what you have told us."

"Yes, miss," answered Williams.

When the two servants returned, Finch had her hands hidden behind her back. It seemed a simple show of respect, but Cecilia knew better. She immediately took charge "Let us see your hands," she said.

Finch's eyes grew large. She looked at Williams, no doubt realizing she had been called for this very reason. With a reluctance that was quite obvious, she brought her arms forward, the red marks on her hands at once recognizable as identical to Violet's, though the latter had covered hers in a shawl.

"What did you do to get that rash?" Cecilia wanted to know.

Finch was clearly very frightened, and said in a pleading voice," Please, miss, I didn't think it was so wrong."

"Explain yourself," insisted Cece.

"They were Miss Thompson's gloves. But she said they had been ruined, and I should throw them away or put them on the gardener's brush fire. I could see nothing wrong with them, so I washed them instead and thought to keep them for myself. I didn't see any harm in that. But soon after I had washed them, my hands grew very itchy and then these bumps came up. It looks like ivy sap. I've had that happen to me before, on my arm, in the summer. Miss Thompson must have realized she had touched the sap, which is still present in the stems even when the leaves have died back in the cold, and that's why she wanted to throw the gloves out. If I had known, I could have told her we could boil the gloves instead and they'd be fine. I could still do that. But I wasn't stealing. Honest, I wasn't!"

"Of course not," said Cece, and Finch sagged with relief. "But you will not mention this conversation to anyone. If Miss Thompson asks, you will say that you threw the gloves away and don't know what has caused the hives on your hand. Understood?"

"Yes, miss," said Finch, her demeanor greatly improved now that she was certain she had escaped any repercussions.

"Thank you. That will be all."

Finch turned and left briskly. Williams, who had stood in obliging silence, was the first to speak.

"Miss Thompson had ivy sap on her gloves, miss, and knew it. She must have handled your dress and yet not warned you. I call that a right callous thing to do, if you don't mind me saying, Miss Hughes."

"Indeed," said Violet thoughtfully. "That might not even be the full story. My guess is that Miss Thompson sought out the plant and administered it to this dress on purpose. That is why she did not tell her lady's maid to boil the gloves. She did not want to admit that she had come into contact with the plant that would cause this." Violet opened her shawl and looked down at her angry skin. "I'm afraid you were right, Cece. She must have been behind the whole business with the fish as well. And when that didn't reap the desired results, she tried again. Perhaps she thought I would be so uncomfortable and ashamed of my appearance with hives that I would confine myself to my room once more while she tried to dig her claws deeper into Victor. Well," she said, her voice growing stronger as she stood. "We shall see about that!"

"Hurrah!" cried Cece. "That's the spirt! We shall beat her at her own game. It's time we exposed Miss Pearl Thompson as the menace she is."

"Can I help, miss?" asked Williams. "I don't like that someone could do this to my mistress, right under my nose."

"Do you know," said Cece, a Machiavellian smile seeping into her features, "I believe you are the very person for the job."

CHAPTER 6

Violet and Cece shushed each other as they hid around the corner near Pearl's bedroom. Once everyone had been reassured that Violet was well enough and being taken care of, they had all retired to their rooms until dinner, the shock of another incident involving their friend casting a severe damper on the jovial mood.

Williams knocked on Pearl's door. She was a surprisingly good co-conspirator. She did not cast her eyes towards the whispering young women who watched her actions but stood straight and tall and ready to fulfill her duty.

Pearl opened the door, or she must have, because its frame now blocked the view so that the two women could only listen while seeing nothing.

"Yes?" said Pearl, an edge of surprise in her voice. "Did Miss Hughes send you?"

"No, miss. But I thought to bring you this." Violet assumed Williams now held out the tray with the small cake on it.

"A cake?" said Pearl. "That is very thoughtful, but I did not ask for refreshment."

"Cook—that is, Mrs. Cartwright—sent it for Miss Hughes," said Williams, "to cheer her up after the difficult morning she has had. But

I'm pretty sure it has almonds in it. And Miss Hughes is allergic to almonds. Not enough to do great harm. But she already has a rash on her wrists and neck. She does not need to have hives all over. I did not have the heart to tell Mrs. Cartwright that she had forgotten such an important detail. She meant well. So, I thought, instead of the cake going to waste, you might enjoy it."

"I see. Well, we certainly don't want Mrs. Cartwright to feel bad. Nor should you take a chance when poor Miss Hughes already suffers so. I will take the cake off your hands. And I will leave the tray outside Miss Hughes' room so that no one knows you brought it to me."

"Thank you, miss. That is very kind."

The door closed and Williams reappeared in the sights of the two inquisitive women. She walked down the corridor to join them.

"That was nicely done," whispered Violet.

"I can almost hear the cogs of Pearl's mind begin to spin," Cece remarked. "Now we shall wait and see how soon she makes her way to the kitchen to spin her web of deceit."

"Mrs. Cartwright keeps her finished cakes and pies in the pantry," said Williams. "It will be easier to sneak in there while the maids are busy preparing meals in the kitchen under Mrs. Cartwright's supervision."

"How will we watch her movements without drawing attention to ourselves?" Violet wondered.

"Oh, I have already spoken with Mrs. Cartwright," Cece said with an air of superiority. "That is one of the advantages of having a scheming mind." She grinned at her friend. "Mrs. Cartwright is going to make it really easy for Pearl to perform her dastardly deed. Then, at dinner, Pearl will see you are eating a slice with almonds in it and expect some kind of reaction, which she can blame on Mrs. Cartwright's supposed forgetfulness. But we shall teach her a lesson she won't soon forget."

"What are you ladies doing?"

Victor's voice made all three women jump.

They spun around, poor Williams looking as though she had seen a ghost. "If you'll excuse me," she said quickly and all but fled down the stairs.

"We're doing what women do best, Cousin," Cece said coyly. "Talking."

"Huddled on the landing?"

"Women are mysterious creatures, Vic. One cannot expect a man to understand."

"Well, could this man please borrow Violet awhile? Unless you have more huddling to do."

"She's all yours," said Cece smugly and immediately left the two to themselves.

Violet could not look at Victor. She was certain he had been about to kiss her at the ruins when she had fled back to the house. What must he think of her? How could he know that she would have savored that kiss when, instead, she had run from him, pell-mell?

Violet had a terrible suspicion that there may even have been an attempt at a proposal which she had quite disregarded in her haste to be rid of the dress. She owed him an apology at the very least. But how to bring up such a delicate subject?

Fortunately, Victor had similar thoughts on his mind.

"Shall we adjourn to the library?" he asked. "What I have to say is best said in private."

Violet nodded and followed him downstairs. The library's bookish smell set her at ease. It was her favorite room in the house—something Victor knew, and which was, no doubt, the reason he had chosen it for their conversation.

"Violet," he began at once. "I would like to apologize for my presumption earlier. I misread the closeness between us. I acted impulsively and fear I have hurt our friendship. Please say you will forgive me."

"Oh," said Violet, all other words escaped her as disappointment deflated her hopes. "Of course."

"Then our friendship is intact?"

The poor man looked so distraught that Violet could but nod and say, "Perfectly."

Victor exhaled deeply. "I confess my relief is immense. I promise I shall not speak of such matters to you again."

"Oh." Violet berated herself for being unable to find a more suitable response. She was going to lose him! *Think, Violet, think!* "Er... I was terribly itchy."

"Pardon?"

"At the ruins. The dress... from Pearl... it made me itch."

"Oh. Yes. I noticed you were scratching at your wrists several times."

"It became unbearable. A rash was forming." She folded back her shawl for him to see.

Victor's eyes grew large, and his manner switched at once to one of grave concern. "That looks profoundly uncomfortable. Have they given you some chamomile to offer relief?"

"Yes, and it has definitely helped. But when you were speaking to me at the ruins... I'm afraid I was... distracted. Certainly not myself. I could hardly think for the overwhelming desire to be shod of that dress."

In spite of the seriousness of the conversation, a smile twitched at the corner of Victor's mouth.

"Because of the *itching*, Victor!" she scolded, though the return of their comfortable manner lifted a weight from her mind.

"And now?" he asked. "Are you distracted now?"

Every single nerve in Violet's body stood to attention. "Not at all," she said, holding her breath.

"Might I be permitted to speak plainly then, as I did before?"

"You may."

Victor shifted his weight as if to prepare himself for what must be said. "Ahem. You know, Violet, we have always been excellent friends."

"We certainly have."

"And if I was to marry, I would value qualities like yours in a wife."

Violet's cheerful answers fell away abruptly as she readied herself for what was to come. Victor had actually used the words "marry" and "wife" in short succession! This was it!

"I would hope," Victor continued, "being such excellent friends, that you might find my qualities worthy of merit also."

Violet nodded silently.

"I am grateful that this is the case." Without the mysterious atmosphere of the Medieval ruins to aid him, Victor seemed to have ground to a halt.

"And our families are good friends…" Violet coaxed him gently.

He lit up at the reminder. "Ah, yes! That is so true! We are almost like family already. Er…"

"We rarely argue," she pointed out as his efforts of the morning began to surface in her memory.

"Indeed, that is something to be grateful for…"

Victor's hesitation started to eat at Violet's patience. "What shall we do with all these reassuring facts?" she said with some exasperation.

His head jerked up as if he had just remembered a salient point. "Why, we should marry, of course!"

Violet sighed. It was not the romantic proposal she had anticipated, nor did he reach down now to cup her chin in his hand as before. The hoped-for kiss eluded them. Instead, an awkward silence filled the void.

Before either of them could mend the situation, a head popped round the door.

"Hullo, you two," said Bart. "Fancy a game of charades? The rest of us are tired of sitting about. We need some shenanigans to brighten the day. And a good laugh wouldn't hurt either. What do you say? Will you join us?"

"Certainly," said Victor, no doubt realizing the moment had been fumbled once again and he was helpless, at present, to mend it. "Are you coming, Violet?"

Violet wanted to cry. How was it possible that she had been proposed to twice in one day and yet remained unengaged? She didn't want to play silly charades. She wanted Victor to kiss her! On the mouth. With her in his arms. And ask her to marry him properly so that she could say "yes." Then their friends would have plenty to smile and talk about.

Everyone, that is, except Pearl. If only she could tell Pearl the rivalry was over. That she no longer stood a chance. That there was no need to go to such extreme lengths to try and keep Violet from Victor's company.

"Is Pearl playing with us?" she asked suddenly.

"I'm not sure where my sister is," answered Bartholomew. "She may be taking a brief nap. I tried knocking on her door, but there was no answer."

Violet pictured Pearl furiously occupied in the pantry, watching over her shoulder to see if anyone was walking past. If Pearl was willing to go that far, her conscience unbothered at making Violet sick just to gain one more opportunity to win Victor over, then she must be exposed. She was not the friend she had once been.

"I will join you," she said at last.

"Excellent," Bart answered. "Cece and Donovan are already waiting for us. Although Cece was oddly agitated that I should be fetching you." He shook his head. "Women are a constant mystery to me."

Violet pictured Pearl slipping slivers of almond into a cake to subdue her rival, and declared, "Bart, you don't know the half of it."

CHAPTER 7

The battle lines had been drawn at dinner.

Violet and Pearl flanked Victor on either side. Opposite Pearl sat Donovan, who had been briefed as to the role he should play. He had been more than happy to assist in bringing Pearl's schemes to light. And, being the romantic he was, he was equally keen to facilitate a smooth conclusion to the brief, faltering courtship between Victor and Violet.

Beside him sat Cecilia, with Bartholomew to her left. Only Victor and Bart and their hosts had been left out of the discussion. Cece had not trusted them to believe Pearl capable of such immense subterfuge. The less they knew, the more smoothly the plan would proceed

Violet, having applied the soothing chamomile ointment again before coming downstairs, now struggled far less with the effects of ivy sap, but her emotions still played havoc with her peace of mind. She did not like secrets. Or drama. She felt certain that Victor must sense her internal squirming at what lay ahead. Then again, he might well assume her awkward silence was the result of his doubly-botched proposal.

Doubts crept into her already-disturbed thoughts. What if Victor defended Pearl when the truth came out? Might he be disappointed in Violet instead, because she had planned a ruse and created a scene at dinner? Such thoughts gnawed at her innards and deprived her of any appetite.

"You are pecking at your food like a little bird tonight, Violet," commented Victor. "Are the dishes not to your liking?"

"I am not that hungry," she replied, "but I still want to save a little room for dessert."

She tried not to look at anyone while she said that, afraid that she might give something away in her expression. *Don't think of cake. Don't think of cake.*

"That is just as well," Mrs. Blayne chimed in, "since Mrs. Cartwright has made your favorite apple pie." No mention was made of cake at all.

"I am looking forward to it," answered Violet, and waited.

Sure enough, Pearl turned to their hostess, her composure marginally askew. "Are we just having pie?" she asked. Realizing her wording must have sounded rather audacious, she quickly corrected herself. "I mean, Mrs. Cartwright usually spoils us with a variety of confections."

"Oh, *yes*, my dear," replied Mrs. Blayne, "you are quite right. I believe the menu allows for plum pudding and orange-syrup cake. Quite a fruity theme, but 'tis the season for it, after all."

Pearl relaxed at these words, her warm smile returning and her attention to Victor resuming.

Violet let her be. There was no need to assert her own claim over him. Besides, it really wasn't formally concluded, was it? Both attempts had been interrupted. She fumed inwardly. Bother the itchy dress and bother charades! Not to mention the show she still had to put on in front of all her friends. Cecilia would have been more comfortable in that sort of role, but it was Violet who had to create the performance of the night.

She fidgeted in her chair as one course after the other was removed from the table. Mr. Blayne had dozed off once again, though his wife had wisely decided to leave him to it this time. He snored contentedly, unbothered by the chatter around him. Even the arrival of the desserts did not disturb him.

Violet requested a small slice of each, making much of each mouthful of apple pie to please her hostess, while she felt Pearl's eyes upon her, willing her to move on to the cake.

Cece would likely have toyed with Pearl, slowly consuming the plum pudding second, savoring each bite and delaying the next one with a long, unnecessary conversation. But Violet's nerves were making her so uncomfortable, she feared her mouth would be too dry to swallow anything when the time came. So, she sank her fork into the shiny coating of orange syrup, prying away a section of cake and pretending not to notice the chopped pieces of almond or the way Pearl had frozen to watch the fork enter Violet's mouth.

She chewed slowly, for it was, in fact, a very good cake. "Surprisingly nutty," she said to Victor, and gave what she hoped was an unsuspecting smile. Violet was sorry indeed that she would not be able to finish the delicious treat. Instead, halfway through the enticing slice, she sat back and coughed politely. Then she coughed again, rather more forcefully, bringing her hand to her throat. She shook her head, as if shaking a worrying thought from her mind.

"Has Mrs. Cartwright put almonds in this cake?" she asked, trying to appear alarmed.

"I don't believe the recipe calls for them," replied Mrs. Blayne.

"Mrs. Cartwright wouldn't do that," said Donovan, right on cue. "She knows you are allergic to them."

"Violet isn't allergic to almonds," countered Victor. "Are you?" he asked, turning to her with a frown.

Violet's response was to add her other hand to her throat and widen her eyes.

"She only developed the allergy recently," said Donovan, casting a counterfeit concerned eye upon his sister. "But we warned Mrs. Cartwright about the severity of it. She wouldn't have been so careless. Not when it puts my sister's life at risk."

"What do you mean?" asked Pearl, looking genuinely worried. "She'll probably just come out in hives, won't she?"

"No" said Donovan, rising from his chair and rushing around the table to his sister's side as she pretended to gasp for air. "Her throat swells. If she has had more than even the smallest amount, she might stop breathing altogether."

Violet promptly rolled her eyes back and fainted.

Pearl screamed and jumped to her feet. "This is all wrong! She's not supposed to die!"

Victor grabbed Violet by the shoulders and shook her. "Violet, wake up! Breathe, Violet breathe!"

Tears were now streaming down Pearl's cheeks. "Why would Williams lie to me? I never wanted this to happen!"

Violet opened one eye at Victor, raised a finger silently to her lips, and promptly resumed her fainting spell. It was just long enough to see his abject expression of confused relief and chide herself for causing him even a moment's pain.

"What are you talking about, Pearl?" Donovan asked from behind Violet's chair, appearing rather callous in his apparent disregard for his sister's supposedly unconscious form. But he was clearly enjoying his role as co-conspiracist and trying his best to have Pearl confess. "What does her lady's maid have to do with this?"

"Never mind that," cried Mrs. Blayne, waving her hands at him. "We must help the poor child. Victor, try and breathe some life into her!"

Victor must have hesitated because Violet could hear Bartholomew throw back his chair and rush forward, saying, "Good grief, man, what is wrong with you? Help her!" Before Victor had time to react, Bartholomew had planted his lips on Violet's and forced a lungful of his air into Violet's throat.

She spluttered involuntarily and lurched back into a sitting position to the relief of all present who had not been privy to the plot.

All except Mr. Blayne. His peaceful snores punctuated the silence that reigned briefly at the table before chaos erupted.

"What was that all about?" demanded Victor. "Were you ill or not?" But his inquiry was cut short by Pearl rushing from her seat, throwing herself at Violet's feet, and weeping into her lap. "I am so sorry!" She sobbed. "I didn't know the almonds could kill you. You must believe me!" Her eyes were blurred with tears as she looked up woefully into her would-be victim's face.

"Is somebody going to tell me what is going on?" said Victor, the pitch in his voice rising dangerously.

"I think Pearl has something she would like to share with us," announced Cecilia, her voice hard and sharp enough to chop wood.

From where she was kneeling, Pearl stared up at the guests with horror. No doubt she dreaded the idea of declaring her schemes in front of everyone, especially Victor. "I don't know what you mean," she said, wiping the streaks of tears from her cheeks with both hands.

"Believe me," said Cecilia, "it would be far better coming from you. You would have a chance to explain yourself. If you do not tell the truth at once, I will do it. And I shall not be merciful."

"I..." Pearl looked from Victor to his mother to her brother, the only people in the room whose opinions of her would matter. All three stared at her, confused, expecting clarity. She slid to the floor. There was no escape. She must know Victor would never forgive her. She had lost all hope of winning his love. Mrs. Blayne would be unlikely to receive her as a guest again. Pearl had betrayed her trust.

Only her brother remained.

Pearl touched her fingertips to the floor and hauled herself upright. "Bart, please accompany me to my room. I will explain everything while Finch and I pack." Pearl looked miserably at Violet. "I really am sorry. You were kind to me and didn't deserve any of this. I just needed an opportunity to make my mark on his attention. But I realize now I never stood a chance."

Pearl flexed her hands, exhaled a sigh, lifted her chin, and exited the room with as much dignity as she could salvage in the chaos she had created. Poor Bartholomew watched her departing figure, gazed around the table at the multitude of mixed expressions, and ran his fingers through his hair. "I don't know what to make of any of this," he said. "I'd better go and hear what she has to say. But if she is determined to leave, I shall escort her home. Whatever she has done, she is still my sister." He exited the room in a rather less aloof manner than his sister had mustered, and Violet pitied him for the shame he would have to bear because of Pearl.

In the heavy silence that followed, Mr. Blayne's soft snoring continued, a strange rumble of contentment amidst a shattering end to the dinner.

CHAPTER 8

"Well!" exclaimed Mrs. Blayne, placing her napkin on the table, "I think you had better enlighten us, Cecilia. Victor, wake your father up, he should probably hear this."

Victor did as he was asked, patting his father on the shoulder until he awoke with a start. "Is the pudding ready?" he asked, looking expectantly at the table, only to find his plate empty. He looked about and five disconcerted faces stared back at him. "What has happened? Where are the young Thompsons? Is dinner finished already? Is it time for bed?"

"No, dear," said Mrs. Blayne, "but there has been a bit of an upset. Cecilia is about to explain it all to us now, and I thought you should be aware of what is happening under your roof."

"Ah, yes, well, certainly," said Mr. Blayne, sitting up straight and tugging at his dinner jacket before straightening its sleeves. "I am ready to observe. You may proceed, Cecilia."

"To put a very quick point to it," said Cece, "Pearl has been tormenting Violet with wicked schemes ever since Christmas. Her intention was to draw Victor's eye from Violet and focus his attention on herself. It was she who placed the fish in Violet's cupboard to prevent her from going riding with us, an outing she knew Victor and

Violet would bond over. It was Pearl who rubbed ivy sap onto the trim of the dress which she then offered to Violet to wear, causing Violet to once again be pulled from Victor's company."

"Wait a second," interrupted Victor. "These are terrible accusations against a good friend of ours. Do you have any proof?"

"Not for the fish incident, no," his cousin admitted, "although it is clear she was the only one who had anything to gain from such a mean trick. When you left her in the company of Donovan and did not ride with her, she tried again, hoping to incapacitate Violet with the ivy sap, which worked rather well until everyone, feeling concern for Violet, returned home to check on her and then withdrew to their rooms."

"And you have proof of this second incident being her doing?" asked Mrs. Blayne. "I must say, it would need to be very convincing. Miss Thompson is such a dignified and genteel sort of person. I find it difficult to conjure an image of her sinking to such depths simply to catch my son's eye. Besides, there would have been no reason to consider Miss Hughes a rival. She and Victor have been friends for a lifetime without any romantic developments. Surely Miss Thompson had a clear path to Victor's heart without resorting to such extremes?"

Violet and Victor glanced at each other and quickly looked away.

"I think," said Cecilia, "that Pearl sensed something you have not, Aunt. But Victor can tell you more later. To answer your question, we spoke to Finch, Pearl's lady's maid. She had handled Pearl's gloves and was rewarded with the same rash that afflicted Violet. That means Pearl touched ivy sap with her gloves, and very recently. The fact that Pearl tried to throw them away meant she knew she had touched the sap. There was nothing else wrong with her gloves to cause her to dispose of them. But she did not tell Finch. She would only be secretive if she had touched the ivy on purpose, then wanted to dispose of the evidence. Unfortunately, that is not the worst of it."

"You are saying that Pearl purposely affected Violet with ivy sap and that this was not the end of her plotting?" Victor shook his head. "I don't understand. She has given no indication that she is capable of such terrible things."

"I thought the same," said Violet. "So, Cee and I created a trap for her, to show once and for all that she would stoop as low as was necessary to achieve her goal."

"That's right," said Cece. "We had Williams mention to her that Violet was mildly allergic to almonds."

"But you're not," said Victor. "That was a ruse."

"Certainly," replied his cousin. "We couldn't exactly accuse her of anything until we were absolutely sure she would use any opportunity to remove Violet from what she perceived as a competition for your affection."

"We asked Mrs. Cartwright to keep an eye out for anyone that might interfere with the food," added Violet. "It wasn't long before she spotted Pearl meddling with the cake."

"Are you saying Pearl added almonds, believing it would make you sick?" asked Mrs. Blayne, her hand cupping her mouth, her eyes wide, her brows furrowed. "By all the saints, that is a very wicked thing to do!"

"You pretended to be choking!" said Victor. "Do you have any idea how you frightened us? You drove Pearl to tears!"

"Victor!" Cecilia scolded her cousin. "You are *not* going to take that woman's side! If she had had her way, Violet would now be covered in hives. All so that Pearl could get her scheming hands on you!"

"But I would never have given her a second glance," said Victor, amazed. "All this plotting was in vain. I could have spared you so much suffering." He reached across and collected Violet's hand between both his own, like a sacred flower. "Violet, my love, if I had known, I would have asked for your hand sooner. Made it clear there was no one else for me but you." He swallowed hard, his eyes growing moist. "I thought I was going to lose you. I have never felt so powerless."

Mrs. Blayne stared at her son. "You love her? And she knows this? How is it there have been so many secrets in my house? And at Christmastime, no less."

"I have *tried* to propose," said Victor, looking a little embarrassed. "More than once, in fact. But both attempts were bungled. I had hoped Violet might say 'yes,' but, to be fair, circumstances have made it difficult for her to answer." He looked at his beloved now, his feelings pouring forth in almost tangible waves.

"I am so sorry, Victor," answered Violet.

Her unfortunate choice of words made him shrink back, pulling his hands from hers. Had he thought she was rejecting him? Violet hastened to set the record straight. "I am sorry that we had to leave you in the dark. I wish I could have told you what we had planned tonight. But we had to catch Pearl in the act, so to speak. Like you, we had thought her a lady in every good sense of the word. It was a shock to realize what she was capable of. How could we expect you to partake in exposing her when she was so seemingly innocent?"

Mrs. Blayne, apparently having had no difficulty at all accepting Pearl's guilt under the circumstances, was far more interested in a different matter. "My son has proposed to you twice?" she asked. "Since your arrival?"

Violet nodded shyly.

"And you have yet to answer him?"

"Mother," Victor interceded, "Violet is not to blame. I asked her the first time while she was in the throes of the ivy sap's effects."

"Well, that was rather unwise of you, Victor," his mother replied pertly.

"He didn't know," explained Violet. "He thought I was just disinterested."

"And you're not?" asked Mrs. Blayne. "Disinterested, I mean."

Violet could feel the deep blush rising up into her cheeks.

"You are putting Violet on the spot, Mother."

"And what are *you* going to do about this unresolved matter, Victor?" Mrs. Blayne demanded.

Now it was Victor's turn to grow pink about the ears.

"She has a point, my boy," said Mr. Blayne, entering the conversation out of the blue.

Victor, apparently quite clear on the course of action needed, slid smoothly from the chair to his knee. "Violet Hughes," he said, causing Violet to grow weak with anticipation, and making her very grateful indeed that she was currently sitting down. "You hold within you everything I value: beauty without vanity, a sense of joy without being too giddy, an excellent seat on a horse, and indomitable integrity. If it is not too great a sacrifice, would you agree to marry me?"

A wave of emotion washed over Violet, her heart buoyant on its tide. "Yes! Oh, yes!" she said, slipping her hand back into his. "You are the best gift I have ever received. You," she added, smiling at Donovan and Cecilia in turn, "and the love of those whose loyalty have brought me safely to you."

"A toast!" called Mr. Blayne, who was once again in high spirits and ready to make a feast of it. He lifted his glass. "To Violet, a very welcome addition to our family. And to Victor, who has finally acted upon the feelings some of us have known were there all along."

But the couple did not join in the toast. They were locked in each other's gaze, their smiles only for each other. Every nerve in Violet's body cried for more of Victor's touch. His hand was warm, almost glowing within her palm. But she wanted to hold him fully, have him rain his kisses down upon her skin. She imagined the softness of his lips against hers, a current passing through her at the thought of his mouth exploring her body.

"We should call the banns at once," said Victor abruptly. His voice was rough, as if he, too, had pictured Violet in his arms, the wait for which felt suddenly all too long. He cleared his throat. "That is, if your parents approve."

"My parents would consider themselves blessed to have you as their son-in-law," insisted Violet. "But I shall write to them first thing and tell them our good news."

"Perhaps now they will see fit to join us at Hamptonlea House," said Mrs. Blayne. "We could extend your stay until the wedding. That is, if your brother does not have to return to London on matters of business."

Donovan bowed his head. "I am at your disposal. After all, it isn't every day one's favorite sister marries one's best friend."

"I am your *only* sister," laughed Violet. "But thank you all the same."

"Hooray!" cried Cece. "I can start planning what manner of

creature to hide in the wedding chamber." She grinned at Violet, but Donovan brought such chatter to a thundering halt.

"Now, Cee, that is not the sort of talk one wants to hear from a married woman. You will need to curb your playfulness somewhat, just enough to pass for a civilized lady."

"But I am not a married woman," she answered gleefully.

"Would you like to be?"

It seemed an innocent enough question, and Donovan had certainly phrased it in a very casual way. But something in his tone suggested he was saying so much more.

Violet had never seen Cecilia at a loss for words. Indeed, the entire gathering had been silenced by his question. But Cecilia was not one for quiet.

"Uhm..." she said and looked at Donovan as if he had grown a second head. "I haven't given it much thought. No one has ever shown that sort of interest in me."

The rest of the company, Violet was sure, had in one voice—albeit in their minds—said, "Not until now!"

"Perhaps you have been too occupied with planning your next prank to notice," Donovan replied. It was not a reprimand, but a declaration. *Here I am*, he was saying, *and I want you to notice me.*

"You are quite wrong, you know," Mr. Blayne said to his niece. "Young Mr. Hughes has been patiently in love with you since last Christmas. I distinctly remember that the mistletoe had run out of berries and that he produced one from his pocket to demand a kiss from you."

"But that was all fun and games!" Cecilia exclaimed. Then she turned a furrowed brow to Donovan. "Wasn't it?"

"If you prefer to leave it at that," he said softly, "I will honor your choice."

Cecilia sat and thought for a moment. "So, when you always walk beside my horse because we know it will try to throw me, that isn't just kindness."

"We all know you could take care of yourself perfectly well, my dear," said Mrs. Blayne.

"And… and when I was under the weather and couldn't go to the Spring Ball and you said you weren't going either and would keep me company, that wasn't because you were tired from too much sun?"

"When has my brother ever minded the sun?" Violet thought aloud, realizing, along with her friend, that she, too, had missed the signs. "You know how much he loves to dance."

"And you did," said Cecilia. "Here, with me, humming in my ear as we waltzed around the furniture in the library."

"Come on, Don," said Victor, "Ask her properly. She understands now."

Violet's mouth fell open. "You've known?"

"Well of course. Just as your brother has known of my feelings for you. Men are not quite as dull as you seem to think they are."

"Indeed not!" Violet answered, thoroughly amazed. "It seems it is we women who have been blind to everything around us."

Cecilia, meanwhile, had cocked her head to one side and was looking at Donovan with new eyes. Interested eyes. Eyes that said, "If you ask me, there is a very real chance I might say yes."

So Donovan did.

He did not kneel, because Cece would probably have giggled at him and told him she hoped the floor had been swept. At least, that's what Violet imagined. But he did take her hand. And it clearly drew a solemn response, for Cece neither smiled in encouragement nor pulled her hand away by way of rejection.

"Miss Cecilia Isaacs," began Donovan, only to be interrupted by a tiny, happy squeal from their hostess. He cleared his throat and started again. "Cee, I know you are fiercely independent, and I have no desire to tame you. I only hope you are willing to be fiercely independent *with me*. And that sometimes you will let me take care of you a little. I love you just as you are, even if that is a little rough around the edges. And I know you would prefer I speak plainly thus, for that is when you know you can trust what I say. I promise to make room for your many moods, if you will temper them a little out of pity for me. What say you? Is this agreeable? Could you marry me?"

"I think that is the best offer of marriage I could ever hope to get," she answered firmly. "Truly. I know you have seen me at my worst. If, in spite of that, you are willing to have me, I am happy to accept. For I have loved you as a friend my whole life. And being your wife grants me that friendship forever." She took a deep breath and exhaled it. "The answer, Mr. Hughes, is 'yes.'"

The dining room erupted in applause. Donovan and Cecilia blushed shyly at each other. To be honest, Violet believed it was the first time she had ever seen Cece do *anything* shyly. She rose from her chair and walked quickly around the table to her friend's side. "Not cousins, then, but sisters," she said and squeezed her joy into Cece's warm embrace.

"A double wedding!" cried Mrs. Blayne. "And, if all your parents are as happy as they no doubt must be at this news, we shall have our own friends here for Twelfth Night and prepare for your nuptials together. What a merry time that will be!"

"Does this mean I can kiss you now?" asked Cecilia, her impish grin returning. Donovan's answer was to pull her to him and kiss her without hesitation or ceremony.

Violet looked longingly across the room at Victor. She yearned for him to be as spontaneous as her brother had been. But it was not in his nature.

Nevertheless, he watched her thoughtfully. "I wonder," Victor said at last, "whether I might be excused to thank Mrs. Cartwright for her excellent dinner. And for her willingness to help bring an end to my fiancée's ill-treatment by Miss Thompson."

"Of course," said Mrs. Blayne, sharp on the uptake. "No doubt Violet feels exactly the same. Offer her your arm, Victor, and you shall find Mrs. Cartwright together."

Violet, who had already preened inwardly at being called a fiancée, recognized the opportunity being created and latched onto Victor's arm at once. "Thank you for a lovely dinner," she said to her soon-to-be-in-laws. "And for not holding our little scheme against us."

"Ah, but we can deny our new daughter nothing," said Mr. Blayne with a hearty smile.

Despite her eagerness to be away and in Victor's embrace, Violet leaned away from him briefly, reaching down and planting a kiss on Mr. Blayne's cheek.

The gentleman touched the spot as if it were magical and smiled at his wife. "Lovely girl," he murmured.

Violet clutched Victor's arm tightly as they hastened from the room and across the foyer towards the back stairs leading to the kitchen. But they did not descend. Not yet.

"At last," said Victor, his voice low and thick with longing. "I have wanted to kiss those lips for the longest time."

"Then what are you waiting for?" Violet found herself saying before she grabbed his lapels and pulled his head down towards hers.

Their lips met in a rush of warmth and softness before desire overcame their momentary inhibition. Victor wrapped his arms round Violet and drew her deeper into his embrace, his mouth opening to taste more of her. Violet's skin tingled and hungered for his. She slipped her hand around the back of his neck, spreading her fingers across the only heat of his body that she could reach.

Someone on the stairs cleared their throat. With a gasp, the couple pulled apart.

Williams blushed. "Sorry to disturb," she said, waiting to pass.

Violet tried to gather herself, but she could still feel Victor's touch upon her.

"Not at all," Victor lied. "We were just heading down to speak with Mrs. Cartwright."

Williams gave them a knowing look. "I'm sure she'll be very happy to see you. She will want to offer congratulations. The staff have all been rooting for you."

"Happy to oblige," grinned Victor. And taking Violet's arm once again, they took another step together toward the rest of their lives.

EPILOGUE

The Twelfth Night celebrations were the most joyous Hamptonlea House had ever known. The shadow that had been cast by the furtive departure of the Thompsons had faded. The arrival of Violet and Cecilia's parents rekindled the excitement of their children's engagements, though they professed they were not in the least surprised at the events.

The Blaynes had invited several neighbors to join them for an evening of dancing, as was tradition at this time of year. And having two betrothals to celebrate made the evening that much merrier. While the older couples nodded and beamed at their offspring, the more youthful guests lined up for the Scotch reel and even partook in the waltz, the Blaynes being more open-minded than many of their peers to allow such propinquity between the sexes.

Violet's dress swirled about her ankles as Victor guided her with both his hand and the gentle pressure of his fingers upon her back. They moved as one, evading other couples easily in the ballroom that was not nearly filled to the high season's capacity.

The music swept them along, as if they were skating on the winter ice. The notes told their feet when to move, but their north star was the love that pulsed between them, steering them towards their shared future so that even when the players stilled, their connection stayed.

A tinkling of spoon against crystal glass sounded.

"It is almost midnight," announced Mr. Blayne. "Time to tend to the yule log."

The small crowd filed into the large drawing room, the ladies' silk dresses rustling against the starched trousers of their partners. In the hearth, the fire burnt very low, really just glowing in the belly of what little remained of the once great log. Splinters of wood had snapped off in the continuous heat of twelve long days. Mr. Blayne now reached for one of these and lifted it for everyone to see.

"To light the fire next year," he announced. "This year's wood has served us well. May your Christmas wishes all have come true."

Victor lowered his head toward Violet's neck. "I know mine has," he breathed into her ear."

Violet's core lit up at his closeness, his words echoing her own thoughts.

A few feet away, she noticed her brother wrapping his arms around Cecilia, drawing her closer, no doubt to speak words of a similar nature. It only added to her own happiness. And she leaned against Victor to tell him so.

He smiled at the mention of their shared joy. "Ah, yes, soon our little group of friends will have no more single belles."

"I wouldn't have it any other way," murmured Violet into his broad shoulder. It was a shoulder she knew she could always lean on. And she knew she had a lifetime to do so.

If you enjoyed *Single Belles*, Elizabeth Donne presents **Sophia's Letter** for your further reading pleasure.

Inspired by the life of Elizabeth Barrett-Browning, **Sophia's Letter** is the story of a lonely poet with family secrets. Sophia has never expected to experience love, but a letter from an unknown admirer will change everything.

Find **Sophia's Letter** here:

elizabethdonnebooks.com/sophias-letter

Elizabeth Donne writes award-winning sweet Regency romance, a natural outpouring of a lifelong love affair with English literature. She has spent most of her life in Cape Town, South Africa. In 2015, Elizabeth moved to Iowa with her husband, their two children, two cats, and their African bush dog. When she's not writing, or discovering the secret wonders of the Midwest, she is enthusiastically introducing her visitors to the joys of drinking *rooibos* tea. With a biscuit, of course.

Social Media links:
Website: https://www.elizabethdonnebooks.com
Free Newsletter: https://www.elizabethdonnebooks.com/#subscribe
Facebook: https://www.facebook.com/profile.php?id=100093280712789
Instagram:https://www.instagram.com/elizabethdonnebooks?igsh=dW4wdmt6Y2g1d2xx
Goodreads: https://www.goodreads.com/author/show/35270040.Elizabeth_Donne
BookBub: https://www.bookbub.com/authors/elizabeth-donne

HIS MERRY HOUSEKEEPER

CERISE DELAND

HIS MERRY HOUSEKEEPER

BY CERISE DELAND

Novellette in *Delightful Doings in Dudley Crescent* Series

Lord Bettington in Number 42 Dudley Crescent needs a new housekeeper. Because his three raucous motherless sons constantly create chaos, he requires someone bold to tamp down his boys' hijinks.

But the earl wants so much more. He has ordered his young chatelaine, Miss Winifred Mathers, up from his country estate to take charge. Lovely Winn has won his heart.

But can he win her mind if Winn knows the *ton* will oppose her wedding the only man she's ever loved?

CHAPTER 1

December 16, 1821
No. 42 Dudley Crescent
London, England

Bettington stared at his three sons in dismay.

Roger, the oldest, licked crumbs from his lower lip, but had the presence of mind to look sheepish.

William, age five and next younger, gazed at his father with dazed eyes. He had no idea what he had done wrong, bursting out from the kitchen cupboard with a scream and scaring the cook and scullery maid to death. Tio, at four, wore the innocent expression of a child who had followed his older brothers and enjoyed the biscuits and pudding they'd found in the larder.

How did Bettington punish his naughty children when they had chased off two maids, their second governess, and third housekeeper in four months?

Returning to the servants', registry in Piccadilly was not a welcome option he relished. The last time, two months ago, when he'd applied for new staff, the owners of the registry had begun to look at him as if he were a ghoul. He was—when not besieged by errant children—a kindly soul!

He stood. Hands clasped behind his back, he strode around his desk. He did not like to intimidate his children. God knew, he had personal experience from his father that such show of force only withered a child's spontaneity. Ingenuity, too. His mother had left his belligerent father and lived in Brighton since his sister Ella had taken their father's prize thoroughbred and run away. They had never heard from Ella again. As for him, well, he had escaped much of his father's cruelty because a week after his mother and Ella left, his doting uncle, his father's younger brother, had taken him away and put him in Eton close to his own home.

Now his three boys needed the same empathy and structure his Uncle Hayward had shown him, and Bettington endeavored to imitate the man. But clearly he had not done well.

He sighed.

They needed a mother. Henrietta had passed away two years ago. But in truth she had left their three sons even before they were born. A self-possessed woman who took more time with her hair than her children, she had loved the marriage bed but hated pregnancy. Most of all, the hard painful work of birthing was her hell. The hours of that had turned her off her babies, their "wrinkled squinty looks" and certainly the very idea of nursing, let alone cooing to them.

Bettington frowned. In many ways he had been father and mother. Not the wet nursing of course, but so much else. Singing his children to sleep, reading stories to them, he even loved pushing them high in the garden swing.

But he couldn't make them behave. Pick up their toys. Obey their governesses. Or be polite to those in the kitchen.

"This will not continue," he said. "You three must behave. Roger," he turned and faced them before continuing, "after the holiday, you will go away to Jasper Font school."

"Sir?" The boy spoke up. He was tall for his age, keen about frogs and flowers—and roast "beast," as he called a good round of beef. "Where is that?"

"South of London. In Kent."

"I...I will sleep there?" His large sky blue eyes, so like his own, widened in shock.

"You will."

"But...but, sir, I—"

Bettington lifted his palm. "William, you will no longer sleep in the nursery, but move further down the hall into your own room."

The little boy's chubby round face fell. At five, he liked anything with sugar in it. Cookies, ices, berry pies and his brothers. "But...but Tio will want me."

Bettington winced. William and his youngest son Tio had often slept in the same bed whenever Tio had bad dreams. More often than not, he would find them hugging each other in the mornings, cherubic smiles on their lips. William loved his little brother. They had always made a good team. Too good.

A rap came at his office door.

"Come in," he called to his butler, Fox.

"My lord," the older man, who still wore chocolate pudding on his frockcoat, appeared calm as he met Bettington's gaze. "You have a visitor."

Bettington hoped it was the woman he'd been waiting for these past days.

"A lady?" He asked his man, hearing hope in his voice.

"Indeed, sir. The very one you spoke of. I have placed her in the drawing room, sir."

Winifred Mathers. Bettington sighed. Her very name filled him with renewed hope. "Bring her here, Fox."

The servant ran his large brown discerning eyes over the three young boys staring back at him. "Now, sir?"

"Now."

Roger, William and Horatio shot glances at each other. Roger grinned. William straightened his shoulders. Tio had no idea how to react, so he just looked at his older siblings and shuffled his little feet.

Fox closed the double doors and went to do his master's bidding.

Bettington needed Winifred Mathers. Her presence. Her person. Her firmness of mind…and he needed her this minute.

His body anticipated her arrival in a most inappropriate manner and so he cleared his throat once more, then folded his hands before him in a strategic place.

"My dear sons, you are about to meet our new housekeeper."

The three knew Winifred already. Had done for the three years she had served in that capacity at his country house. But Bettington wanted to instill a firmer respect for her in her new position.

After all, her ability to rein the boys in was one of the reasons he had asked her to come and serve him here. The other reason was… well, to be honest, not one he could put before three little boys.

"She is a fine lady from the country." *A beauty.* "She is a lady, educated and refined." *A treasure.*

"Does she play croquet, sir?" This from Roger.

"Indeed she does." He had watched her play with the staff last August in the country at Bettington Grange.

"Will she play with us?" Roger pursued his favorite topic.

"Not only that, she will teach you how to hold the bat correctly and to hit the ball gently." *So as not to break more windows.*

William scrunched up his nose. "I want to shoot arrows."

"You need to learn how to do that correctly, William." The boy had found the old archer's cache of arms in the back room of the garden shed last Monday and shot a maid in her bum. The results had not been pretty or delicate. The doctor whom Bettington summoned had taken a rueful assessment of Bettington and suggested William get ten lashes.

That Bettington would never do. No matter if William had put an arrow in the doctor's arse.

"Is she young?" Roger had hope in his dancing eyes.

"Our new housekeeper is—"

"Not an old creeper like Mrs. Hardcastle?"

"Roger, please. You will not speak ill of servants. Mrs. Hardcastle was a good lady." A bit stuffy and clumsy, but otherwise, a tyrant who screamed that she had nearly tumbled on a step that had wooden soldiers strewn about.

William chuckled.

Bettington scowled at him.

Tio sucked his lower lip, lost in this conversation.

Bettington gathered his wits. "Roger, you must be kind. Mrs Hardcastle did her best to—"

"She whipped me!" Roger said with venom.

"*What? When?*" No one could raise a hand to his children. Even if they were a bit…well, unruly. He would get that out of them, but not by pounding on their little bodies.

The boy shifted on his feet. His oldest knew that Bettington did not approve of physical punishment, and he had used that knowledge to gain favor with him. "Dunno. Last week."

"Why?"

"What?"

"Why did she spank you, Roger?"

He shrugged his thin little shoulders. "Don't remember."

Bettington sighed.

A knock came at the doors.

Fox did not wait for permission. The door fell open, and to the man's left stood the young woman Bettington had wanted in this house for years. Wanted but never had the right opportunity to place.

Not as his friend. Although she had been that for over a decade.

Not as his housekeeper. But now she would become exactly that, he hoped. She was a youthful sprite and witty, as well as sharp of mind and tongue. She was his last hope at a normal life. A woman whom he could look to each day with confidence that she could put sunshine in his day.

A murmur of approval ran through his three sons.

"Ohhhh, Miss Mathers." Roger beamed.

"Yay!" William grinned, showing the gap where he'd lost two teeth yesterday.

"Miz Mabbers!" Tio had problems pronouncing *ts* and *ths*.

"Boys! Please welcome her here."

Winifred Mathers was precisely what they needed. A woman of strong coloring, red gold hair and rosy cheeks, lush pink lips and eyes so green and brown that when Bettington looked at her, he thought he walked in a forest of delights.

"Miss Mathers." He strode toward her, his hands out to welcome her.

She took his one hand to purposely shake it, but she winced, uneasy.

What was he thinking? She was to be his servant. His employee. Not his friend. But so much more.

He cleared his throat. "I trust you had a pleasant journey from Bettington Grange." His country home in Kent was a mere hour's coach ride from his home here at No. 42 Dudley Crescent.

"I did, thank you. I appreciated you ordering the grooms to carry me here in your traveling coach. The ride was very pleasant."

She glanced at his three sons, who ogled her and clapped their hands in glee. Pretty women were not abundant in their daily lives. But this lovely one had been each summer. Furthermore, they knew her well. They had played games with her. One-legged races and apple bobbing contests. For his children, she was the leader of merry rounds of laughter. For adults, especially for Bettington, she played a harsh game of billiards and chess. And she always dressed in pastel gowns that showed her pretty oval face and ivory complexion to a distracting perfection. In fact, he'd often thought of her as a confection, like fondant or a strawberry ice. He also wondered what she tasted like. *Could he kiss her and learn?*

His mouth watered. "Allow me to introduce you properly as our new housekeepr. I have not yet told the boys of the change in our staff here."

"Sir, allow me to speak," she interrupted and captured his gaze."I have come out of courtesy."

What did that mean? "Of course, Miss Mathers."

"I—I accepted your offer and I have come in your carriage, for which I am most grateful, sir. But I must tell you I cannot stay. I must go."

"What? *Why?* Is it your father? Is he ill?" That man claimed every ailment known to the world. He could be a cantankerous old bugger, too. And Phineas Mathers carried an old grudge against the Bettington family. Heaven knew what it was, but the fellow groused about it every chance he could.

"No, no, sir. Not my father. He is well, thank you. But I cannot stay because I will not accept your offer of the position."

"You won't be our housekeeper?" Roger asked, disappointment wrinkling his little brow.

"I did accept," she said to him. "But, my lord," she faced Bettington, "I have come. It is only courteous that I do. You see, I cannot stay. I apologize for the inconvenience and the mixup. But I am only here to say I am sorry that I cannot remain to serve as your housekeeper."

Bettington stood before her, his stance wide, his feet rooting into the carpet. "This is highly irregular."

"It is, I know. And I do regret my inability to stay."

"What has happened that has changed your mind?" He fought frantically to find reason for her desertion. "Is the salary not sufficient? I can increase it."

"No, no, sir."

"My three boys have promised to behave." Perhaps servants here had written and told tales to those at Bettington Grange about his boys' latest antics.

She looked upon the three and gave them the giddiest of smiles. "I am certain they would."

Tio pouted and grabbed her hand. "You'll catch bubberflies with us."

She and the three boys had caught butterflies one day last summer. Bettington had taken them down from London in June. He grinned, recalling the madcap scene in his rose garden. Cherubs among the red and white roses, his boys happy as they should be, scampering about and giggling.

"We had fun," she conceded and bent to cup her hand to his cheek. "We did. But there are no bubber…butterflies in December."

"Angels!" William declared. "That's what come at Christmas. You said so!"

"Did I?"

"Angles!" Tio exclaimed. His youngest had trouble with *gs* too.

"Oh, my dears," she crooned. "I am so sorry."

Bettington saw that his little boys were tugging at her heartstrings.

But she dropped Tio's hand and shook her head. "I recall I did mention that."

"And fairies, too." William stuck out his head like a tyrant. An insistent little man, William would one day terrorize the world with his demands.

"All three of you know I would be most happy to do all of that and—"

"Live with us," Roger said as if it were an order.

"Yes, but you see, I simply cannot."

"Why?" asked William.

"Yes, why?" Roger looked crestfallen.

Tio shifted one small foot to the other. "I wantta do angles."

Hands on his hips, Bettington knew he appeared flustered and damn disappointed. "What then? What has changed your mind?"

He was frantic. *You always looked at me with those doe eyes, as if no man in the world could ever match me. You were kind, considerate to my wife when you were upstairs maid to her. Later when you were downstairs maid and she gave you the keys to make you chatelaine, you ordered our lives at Bettington Grange like an army sergeant. And your gazes at me became infrequent and secretive, but as hot and yearning.*

He took two steps forward and grasped her shoulders. "Tell me, Winn— Miss Mathers. Why can you not stay?"

She licked those lovely lips of hers and cast a look of apology to each boy. To him, she raised her chin and locked her luscious chocolate and minty eyes on his.

"All of you will leave us. Miss Mathers and I have much to discuss."

The three boys expressed their unhappy farewells and filed out the open doors.

Fox too lumbered away.

Bettington caught her hand. "I cannot let you go."

CHAPTER 2

Winifred cast her gaze to his hands, one on her shoulder, one on the other.

He let her go and cocked a long brown brow at her.

She blew out a breath of exasperation. "I came only to be polite."

"So you said. And?"

"This appointment is not wise." *You know it.*

"You have served as housekeeper at Bettington Grange for the past few years. You have experience. I have a need. Yes, you and I are friends. That should endear you to taking the position."

Endear me? I am too much endeared. She lifted her chin. He would not lure her to this outlandish proposal. He could not.

"I do apologize," she took another tack. "But my father needs me."

That was fibble-fabble. Her father had bid her go. "More money! Do it, girl!" The man favored money. He was the local barrister, retired, known for his stinginess. But he also had a mad desire to be regarded well, trying for higher status. She did not blame him. He had contended with the shame her mother had brought on them, trying to make up for it all his life and Winn's.

More reason why I cannot accept this position

Bennington flowed closer. His subtle cologne washing over her like ambrosia.

She would not retreat but held her ground. What a mistake to have come, to be so near, to tempt herself with the job, his scent, his magnificent shoulders and demanding mouth. But she had come, longing to see him once more before she would never be so near him again.

"Is he truly sick?"

"Sick? My father? No, no. But he grows older, more infirm. He needs me."

Bettington pouted. Pouted! His fabulous firm lips should do more noble things, even if she did adore his disappointment. "I need you, too."

Bennington gazed at her with such sorrow in his cerulean -blue eyes that she wanted to weep at her frustration.

"I cannot. It would not be appropriate."

"In what way?"

"Oh, do not press me!" He was like a dog with a bone, always tugging at her.

"What else can I do? I want you here."

"I cannot remain with you night after night under one roof."

"You have done so many nights in the country. Why not here now?"

"Do not show me your anger." She was miffed with him that he took such a tack. "I am not yours to attack."

"Attack! I would never do that."

"Cajole! Influence! Yes, and you have me here."

He stepped near, his shoulders so wide he blocked out the rest of the world. "I do," he murmured, his voice a resonant baritone. "And I am happy for it."

"Well, I am not."

"No?" he stepped closer, his breath mingling with hers. His fingers beneath her chin. "Look at me."

Ohhh, the man was going to kiss her. She could taste it, delicious as candy, hard and hot— but no. She dare not have it. She allowed herself one last longing look into his mellow blue eyes. "I must go."

"Don't leave me."

His words like rolling thunder on a far-off hill shook her insides. "I must."

"Why not stay and see if our friendship can grow?" He bent near and his lips were headed for hers.

She would give him the bald truth. "I know it can. I knew last summer when you kissed me."

He curled a finger around an errant curl near her cheek. "As I remember, it was you who kissed me."

"And I should not have!"

He brought her body so close to his, she closed her eyes to ward him off. But she failed.

"Stay. Please," he begged her in a ragged whisper spoken on her lips.

"I cannot."

"Why?"

She stared him down and gulped. "I...I have made a personal commitment which...which makes it impossible for me to take this position."

"What?" Bettington winced. "What kind of commitment?"

She set her jaw and prepared to go to battle. "I...I have accepted a proposal of marriage."

Of all the reasons in this world why this woman would not stay and work with him...or rather *for* him, Bennington had not suspected this! "To whom?"

She opened her mouth, confusion in her eyes. "That is not polite to ask, sir."

"Who?!"

She set her teeth.

"Very well. When?" he demanded.

"Last..last week, I accepted."

"Before or *after* you accepted my offer to come here?"

She stared at him, tears appearing in her eyes.

"Before or after?" he persisted, curling his fingers, holding himself in reserve, against his urge to gather her in his arms and kiss away those tears.

"After! *After* I got your letter."

"After you accepted me and sent off your agreement to me?"

"Yes."

He filled with shock, then sadness and finally a raw anger. "When do you marry?"

"Soon. Very soon. Next week."

"Next week?" He rocked back on his heels, as satisfied as a man who'd just won a thousand pounds.

"Indeed." She nodded her head.

He held back the smile that teased at his lips. "You can't, Winn."

She bristled. "Of course I can. *Sir.*"

"No." He refused to give way and he was certain the world stood firmly with him on this matter. She would be his. Just as he planned. "No one may marry during Advent."

She frowned.

"Do not mar your brow, my very dear Winn. You cannot marry next week. We are in Advent and no officiant of the Church of England will marry anyone until it ends."

"Oh."

She looked dejected. Had she forgotten that? Well, what a muddle. If Bettington knew anything true about her father, that man most likely had learned of Bettington's offer of a position and encouraged her. For the social advantage and for the money, too. Her sire was so greedy, he most likely demanded a share of her new wages for some fantasy project he had. A new carriage? A new roof? Now if she went home without the money she had promised to give her father, he would howl. He always did when money he expected did not come his way. Each client he'd ever had had learned to make firm contracts in writing on money matters. Winn often confided in Bettington that she wished her papa would stop. But he was her father and he had been a loving one, a caring one and kind, until her mother died. Then for a few years, he lost much. His reason and his clients. As for his parsimony, that he had always had. To her sorrow. But his humor had returned and his love for her had never wavered.

Bettington searched for a solution. "Stay through Advent."

"What? As your housekeeper?"

"Why not? You know the job, the house, the servants. You could bring much stability and peace to us in this Christmas season. Much happiness for the boys, too. We all need it."

She shook her head. "That is not wise."

"Why, Winifred?" Tall, bold, demanding, he was all man with that entreaty. All *her* man.

"You know why..." She had almost called him by his given name. *Walter. Walter. Darling Walter. How he had urged her to address him that day in the garden when she'd been impulsive and put her fingertips to his cheek and her lips to his.*

"We will be proper." He took both her hands.

She retreated. "I do not believe that."

"We have an entire household who will hold us to etiquette."

She swallowed a laugh and blushed as if she dare not trust herself to it. "This is serious business. I am engaged, sir."

"I will double your salary."

A smile curled her lips. She wanted to laugh. "My lord, no."

He wanted to chuckle himself. "Triple it, then! Call it a Christmas gift. I assume your father wants a goodly portion for some costly plan?"

She gave him a rueful eye. "He does."

"Fine. At triple your monthly salary, he will be satisfied you remained with me."

"But not my fiancé."

"No? Who is he?"

She huffed. "I do not wish to fight over this."

Bettington arched both fine brows. "Jerome Landers?"

She made a face.

"Ah. Not the smithy? Fine, fine." Bettington read her easily. But he stared at her, then his mouth fell open. "Do not tell me you accepted George Detwiler!"

She swallowed and glared at him.

"No, Winn. Not Detwiler of all people."

"The very one."

"The owner of the carriage inn! He's fifty if he's a day. When did he ask you?" He stepped toward her again. "He asks every June first. On your birthday. Every year since you were sixteen! And every year, you have refused him. Did he ask this past June?"

"He did."

He could see on her face that that was no lie. "And did you accept him then?"

"No." *The truth was not difficult to blurt out, was it, Winn?*

"So! He asked again, did he? Recently?"

She did not answer.

"Hmmm. I see not. So what then? You, my dear Winn, went to him after you got my invitation, after you accepted my offer and *you asked him* to marry you?"

She straightened her shoulders.

He loomed over her. "If you marry him, you will spend your life cooking and washing and cleaning for guests at the inn. You will die within two years, Winn. Just like his first two wives."

She fluttered her lashes at his insult and his continued sweet use of her little name. "He is a pleasant man. I like him. And you cannot tell me what to do."

"But I am even more pleasant. And you more than like me." He clenched his fists. "You cannot marry him."

"I will."

※

He ran both hands through his hair. He was done arguing with her! "Very well. Stay until Advent is over. Go back to him then. And take your salary. Give what you will to your father. I am sure Detwiler will be thrilled with a substantial bridal dowry."

She blinked, fuming. "He asks for nothing."

"I bet."

"You know, sir, you are not nice when you are angry."

He fumed. But he had her. "Remember that, unlike Detwiler, I am slow to anger, my dear."

She stomped her foot. "I won't accept your overblown salary."

"Detwiler won't like extra money?" he chided her. That man was as bad as her father looking for money in every cubbyhole.

"That's outrageous, Wal... *Sir*."

"I'll pay it, *Winn*. Stay."

He watched her as wheels turned in her head. Her father happy. Her husband to be, thrilled.

She scowled at him. "When it ends, I go then."

"Ah, really? On Christmas Day? It is so sad for anyone to travel on Christmas Day. I cannot let you go then." *If ever. But I see I must try to make my case in ten days.*

"I must go home. My father loves Christmas and I must be with him. Plus, I have to manage Christmas at The Grange."

"With your efficiency, I am certain they all know what to do without you, Miss Mathers." He took both her hands again in gentle warmth. His hold had her knees melting. "Stay with us. Celebrate Christmas."

She locked her dark gaze on his and he knew she looked for reassurance he would keep his hands—and his lips—to himself. "The day afterward, I return to Bettington Grange."

"Of course," he said.

But she narrowed her eyes at his tone.

She did not trust him.

And she shouldn't.

CHAPTER 3

Winifred hurried down the hall toward the kitchen from her the room at the front of the house's ground floor.

"Good afternoon, Bridgette," she bid the family cook with a huge smile and open arms. They had known each other since childhood, played together and worked together for most of their twenty-four years. Bridgette had come to work here in London for Bettington five years ago. Since a child, she had helped her mother who was cook in The Grange.

Bridgette dusted her hands on her large white apron and opened her arms as she ran toward Winifred. "You decided to come?"

"I did." Winn glanced around the large warm kitchen. Empty of others, the expansive room was heated by the huge open fireplace and well-lit by the sun streaming through glass dome of the ceiling. Filled with copper pans and cooking utensils, the kitchen was a marvel of modernity. It smelled of malt and cinnamon, cooked apples and roasting chickens. Bridgette had made it home.

"Everything looks so wonderful. You have kept them well fed."

"I have done me best, thanks to you recommending I come up from Bettington Grange. They look good, too. Those boys, I mean. As for his lordship, he's off his feed these days."

"I noticed."

"Why are you here?" Bridgette led Winifred by the hand to come sit in a comfy chair to one side of the stone fireplace. "At first you wrote you would come, then in another you said you would not."

Winifred took a moment to ponder her words. She had never breathed a word of how she cared for their master. Never gave an inkling of her foolish desire for him. She had buried deep her memory of that day in the Grange's rose garden when she had made the mistake to touch his cheek, commiserate with him…and kiss him.

She caught a breath. She must not recall those moments now, either. Bridgette knew her so well, if she blushed or dithered, Bridgette would ask questions. "I thought I owed it to him to give him my decision in person."

Bridgette tipped her head, a skeptical look in her eyes. "How did that work?"

She inhaled. "Not well. I am still here, aren't I?"

"Did he assign the housekeeper's rooms to you?"

"He did. I left my traveling reticule there and came here straight away to talk to you." At the sound of rattling in the far hall, she met Bridgette's gaze in alarm.

"It's fine. That is Fox, the butler, probably in the wine cellar. His hearing is bad. My two maids are off to the market. We are alone. How long do you stay?"

"I am here until the day after Christmas."

Bridgette opened her mouth at that news.

Did she have an idea anyway of her desire for the dashing widower who was their employer? "He trapped me."

"What?"

"I don't mean that to make him sound dastardly. But when I told him I could not stay, he asked why. The only thing I could think of was to say I was going to be married."

Brigette snorted. "So he objected."

"Like you would expect. He is used to getting his way."

Bridgette gave her a sarcastic look. "Ha! You can say that. Except for his sons, of course. They run him ragged. All of us, too."

"They are such good boys. Thank heavens they are kind and smart and—"

"And full of trouble!" Bridgette sniffed. "So if you told the master you were going to marry, what did he say then?"

"He asked when I'd take vows and I made the mistake to say soon."

Her pretty friend chuckled. "But it's Advent."

"How well I have forgotten," Winn mourned.

"Did he ask who you were to marry?"

"Detwiler," she said with a wince.

"Oh, dear me. Him! There are a hundred men in Bettington Grange village and nearby Canterbury who would give their teeth to carry you over the threshold."

Winn grinned. "No toothless man for me."

"But Detwiler? He's plain as a pewter mug and just as gray." Bridgette folded her arms over her ample chest and pulled back in alarm. "You are not really going to marry him? Are you? He'll work your fingers 'til they bleed. Not a kind man or…well, not a man to want in your bed."

"Bridgette!" Winn laughed, a hand to her mouth.

"Well, do you? Want that kind of man pawing you?"

"No, of course not. Why do you think I've refused him these many years?" She rubbed her arms. The man in her bed should be a blue-eyed man of thirty-five with chestnut colored hair, tall, strapping, with kissable lips. *And he should want only me.*

Bridgette seized both her hands. "Tell me true, Winn. Why won't you take this job?"

She stared into her friend's dark eyes. It was time to come to terms with what she had always wanted…and what she could not have. Bettington. The handsome, dashing Earl of Bettington.

She rose and stood before the fireplace, one hand up to the scorched brick. Fifteen feet high, it dwarfed her. So much about this house, this man and her affection for him did. She'd hidden her feelings, her aspirations, her daydreams of belonging to him. Now she had days in December to come to terms with who she was and why she could not ever be his.

She had grown up in the presence of the Earl of Bettington. Her father who met with the man often, took her with him to those frequent visits. She was a precocious child, dominated by her blustering father who, if he could help it, did not let her out of his sight.

From an early age, she was treated to the mellow resonance of Bettington's baritone voice. To his silent contemplation of issues. To his measured approach to problems. So unlike her father was Bettington that she saw the young earl as her ideal. Then as she grew to a youthful girl, it was Bettington who filled her nights, just as he often appeared in her days. She mooned over him until seven years ago when he married. Then she told herself she would cut him from her reverie. Impossible as that was, it became even more difficult when the new countess had trouble managing her households. That lady's frequent outbursts of temper and her disinterest in her own children created chaos at Bettington Grange and here in Dudley Crescent.

Winifred's unique ability to calm a difficult father and settle disputes among quarrelsome villagers meant her own father recommended her to Bettington as maid and later, at the grand old age of twenty-one, just before the countess died, Winn became housekeeper of Bettington Grange. She'd carried out that function for the past three years.

As such, she'd ordered Bettington Grange's staff in the main house and the gardening staff. Occasionally, she'd settled disputes among the grooms. But she became a presence to Bettington whenever he appeared for summer holidays. Since the death of his wife, he brought his three sons with him and it became a natural responsibility for her to hire and fire their governesses, order their meals, their days, and play with them. Catching bubberflies. Planting flowers and herbs. Swimming in the river. And teaching them how to dance.

Now Bridgette wanted her to share her most intimate longings with her. "I am the local barrister's daughter. The one who was his house maid, then his country house housekeeper. I am no countess."

"We have not discussed this, but I will say I understood that you took the maid's position to remain close to your father. But it was also to remain near *him*, wasn't it?"

"It was that or take a position as a lady's companion in Bath. I could not..." She caught back the tears that memory caused. "I could not leave my father."

"Or this man whom you admired."

"Or this man." *Whom I love.*

She heard Bridgette scrape her chair across the tiled floor. Her friend came to wrap her arms around her and hug her close. "Let's make the very best of this opportunity, can we, hmmm?"

Winn turned in Bridgette's arms and hugged her tightly. It felt good to share her secret with her. "Thank you."

"No need for that. Now, we begin with your welfare. I baked scones this morning. Or I have a good fish pie left from last night's dinner. You must be hungry."

"The pie would be grand." Winn followed her to the door to the cold cellar. Her mouth watered at the thought of flaky goodness.

As Winn finished her pie and tea, she thanked her friend and sighed. "I have to get on with this. Tell me what the major problems are."

"His lordship did not tell you?"

"He focused on the boys' needs." *A hint of his own.* "But I want to hear from you about all else. What do we need here?"

"Two new upstairs maids who do not faint at the sight of little boys being boys. A new footman who is strong enough to carry more than a feather. Also one who bears with Fox's poor hearing and does not yell at the fellow and scare us all to death."

"Two maids and a footman who are kind, strong of body and constitution. What else?"

Bridgette set her teeth. "A governess."

Winn rolled her eyes. "They are usually such a dry bag of bones." *And difficult to hire during the winter holidays.*

Bridgette pointed a finger at her. "The last one walked out bag and baggage, grumbling about the three of them."

"They are not bad boys."

"No, they are not. But she was a hag, having them up at six, washing in cold water, hours and hours of study and not enough fresh air."

"We can wait on that one until after Christmas...or well, no, I cannot. I am here only until the day after Christmas."

"Stay longer!"

"Bridgette, you know if I do, I get myself in trouble."

"So then, just avoid his lordship!"

"Easier said than done, my friend." *Especially when he presses so near and tempts me with his scent and his gaze and...*

"You can do it. Besides, there is much else here to cure."

"Like what?"

"I'd suggest a look at the household books. The last housekeeper was a simpering fool in front of the earl. But judging by the way she trimmed my budget, I think she had sticky fingers."

"Stealing from the earl's purse?"

"I have no proof, but she ordered me to spend less. That meant fewer produce from the greengrocer and no choice cuts at the butcher's."

"Did the earl catch her at it?"

"I doubt it. But he complained about my stew, so...he had an inkling of something amiss."

"Huh. Good riddance." She felt better about her stay here now that she had clear direction to improve the way the house ran. "What else?"

"Make playtime for those little boys."

"Playtime it will be." Winn smiled, wishing December weather could create bubberflies. "What else?"

"Playtime for his lordship."

Winifred burst out a laugh. "Absolutely not!"

"You know he needs it. He always has."

"Not with me."

"Why not?" Bridgette gazed at her, all soft with compassion. "You play a ruthless game of cards. I know because I've lost too much coin to you! Take him at cards."

Cards was not the play her friend implied. Nonetheless, the temptation sent a thrill up her spine. "I cannot."

"You can. Be good to him. That wife of his was an odd fish."

Winn often wondered how much of the countess's scandals had permeated the household servants' knowledge. She would not ask, lest she have to explain. She would not allow anyone to take her man for a fool.

"Winifred! You know that he needs a woman who loves him."

She glanced about, ensuring they were alone. "If I started...if I dared to show him any of...of my true feelings, you know that I would not be able to contain myself."

"Exactly."

She shrank back. "I cannot be his mistress."

"Of course not." Bridgette grinned. "Be his wife."

THAT WAS IMPOSSIBLE. Winn strode about her new rooms among the servants' first floor accommodations, murmuring to herself how she could never become Bettington's wife. Her father had often warned her against such aspirations. He had been the one to comfort her when villagers taunted her for her mother's scandalous behavior. She had always told herself that being good was its own reward.

Over the years, she had established a good reputation for herself, one that had blotted out her mother's behavior. She had rejected Detwiler every time he'd asked. She'd also refused one new resident in the village and two other farmers recently. She loved only one man and had consigned herself to spinsterhood, but taken his household position as housekeeper. None there in the country house suspected she cared for him. Having lived to twenty-four with no incidents to mar her spotless reputation, she was no longer ridiculed for her mother's mistakes. But her father had noticed that as a sixteen-year-old, her gaze was plastered to the local earl. He warned against any infatuation. Lest he or anyone see her longing for Bettington, she sought to keep her gazes impersonal in public. She had succeeded—or so she thought.

But after Bettington married, her father had erupted one afternoon after Bettington had invited her to participate in the family archery contest. "Never think it possible. You are not his family. He is too high born and if you try to be his friend, you will only be shunned. He, too! Abandon all hope!"

Winn had heeded his words. Oh, yes, she had a good education and a way with words. She was smart and happy to meet new people. She had manners and indeed, she could dance with grace. But she could never be a countess.

Housekeeper, yes. Substitute governess for a while, that too. But never Bettington's equal.

She had more sense.

She would simply stay out of his way these next few days. She'd care for his sons. Coordinate the staff. Ready the house for a Christmas reception.

Then go home. To George Detwiler and ask him to marry her.

CHAPTER 4

He could not suppress the warmth that suffused his entire body as he gazed down at Winn cavorting with his three boys on the back lawn. More snow had fallen last night and from its looks, it was sticky, powdery stuff to make excellent snowballs.

The idea to marry Winn was preposterous to so very many. It was against all the rules of high society. Bettington knew it. Had known. Debated it for the past two years since his wife's death. He'd even voiced his dilemma with his best friend, Wharton—and with his mother.

Wharton had said, "Society does not sit at your table, laugh with you in your parlor or rejoice with you in your bed."

His mother was even more adamant. "You love her? Then marry her. She cares for you? Even better. You have three sons, and we know they bring you joy. It is time you had a wife who does the same."

Bettington flinched at that statement. His mother did not mention that his wife may have given him his youngest child who was not truly his. Society had certainly whispered about the countess's wayward ways, but he had not cast her out. Wharton said he should have. Mama had turned a black eye to the woman who came to his bed to cover her own promiscuous ways.

He had refused to make a spectacle of their marriage and had allowed her to remain with him. But they were not a couple who appeared anywhere together. The last year of her life when she became so ill with her rashes and fevers, she did not wish to leave the house anyway.

Now she was gone. He had waited the requisite year during which he had rebuilt his own confidence in himself as a nobleman, an estate manager and as a man with ambition and a clear view of how to gain his happiness. He had spent the next year planning how to make a new life for himself. His first step had been to admit he did not simply fancy the old barrister's beautiful hazel-eyed daughter who was his country house housekeeper. He loved her. Biding his time, he had gone often to the Grange and innocently enjoyed her company. Most of that was spent discussing household matters, but increasingly, it had included their discussion of his boys. Then last year when they walked in his rose garden and she had spontaneously kissed him in the meadow, he knew she cared for him. He began to plan to ask her to marry him.

Save for the political matter this morning demanding his attention, he too would be wrapped up tight against the cold with the four of them out there catching snowflakes. Snow 'bakes.'

He chuckled. His youngest Tio would call them that. The little boy had such trouble with pronouncing words. But he'd grow out of that soon enough.

Bettington knew he himself would not grow out of his desire for the lady who danced like a sprite with Tio and his older two sons.

Would that he could persuade her to dance into his arms. *And into my bed.*

So, how, Walter? The lady doth protest so much. How will you do this?

CHAPTER 5

For three full days, the lady he desired found ways to avoid him, and he was determined to discover ways to remain near her.

So after a dinner taken disturbingly alone, he had Fox summon Winn to him in his small library. He sat in his wing chair and rose when she entered.

There, her hands folded before her, her gaze trained somewhere over his shoulder, she did a curtsy. He silently fumed. If he could rise for her, she took that to mean she should bob for him. *Blast it.*

He sought some cooler resolve and began to tell her of his decisions.

"Tomorrow you will take your breakfast with me and the children at half eight in the yellow room on the first floor."

Confusion struck her and she batted her lashes. "I...I don't understand."

"You will appear at half eight in the yellow drawing room. I have ordered John the footman to bring up a small table from the storage room. Fox will have it dressed for breakfast. The three boys will attend. So will I."

"But...why?"

"To eat."

She did direct her eyes to his then. "That is not done."

"It is now."

"Young children do not eat with any regard to their fingers or—"

"Like all else, they will learn more by example than warning."

She bristled. "Housekeepers do not dine with their employers."

"Mine does."

She narrowed those mesmerizing dark brown eyes and—yes, he heard her—she growled at him. "The boys will get ideas."

"I expect them to do so."

She twitched her nose.

Perturbed, was she? Good.

"If this is your way to—?"

"What?" *Make us a family?*

"Endear me to them."

"There is no need for that. You already are dear to them." He had to point that out to tug at her heart. "They speak of you constantly. No governess has shown them any spark of fun."

"That is not the role of a governess."

"It should be. Besides, they need it. You know it. Have provided it freely and in good will. So shall it continue."

She took a step toward him, shaking her head. "They must not come to expect that from a governess or a housekeeper. Servants do not give laughter or succor."

"But you have."

She drew herself up in umbrage. "I merely acted normal as if…"

"As if you cared for them?" He rose and took two steps toward her. She wore that scent of honeysuckle, reminding him of that summer day when she had reached out to him, her hands spread upon his chest, her lips melting upon his—and suddenly he had her in his arms. "I know you care for them. You cannot help it. Giving, consoling, celebrating is what you do. It is who you are at heart."

"But when I leave, they will be so disappointed." The look of remorse turning down her pretty pink mouth told him she would be sad, too.

It would be so easy to touch her, bring her close, enfold her and kiss those firm sweet lips. But he would not. Must not. He would instead show her all the reasons why she must stay.

"Then you must not go."

She scowled at him. "You try to trap me."

"Never! I had a woman who accused me of that. She did not wish to be with me other than in my bed. Now I see you as a woman who may wish to be with me not only in bed but out of it. And not just happy with me, but loving to my charming children."

He stood inches from her, the temptation to persuade her with hot kisses a force sweeping his whole body. "Tell me you don't want me and we will be finished here."

She fought for words, her mouth opening and closing as she formed thoughts.

"I see," he said with compassion for her torment, "you cannot lie to me. Another trait I value. A valuable trait I could never depend upon from my wife."

Fear suddenly flashed in her eyes.

He knew not why, but he would try to learn. "Go now. I will see you at half eight for breakfast."

AGAIN SNOW HAD FALLEN YESTERDAY. The weather was so cold and dreary, everyone in the house had remained inside. But this morning, one look out his dressing room window told him he was in luck today. He had bright sun and a crisp breeze.

Dressed warmly in grey wool trousers, a forest green frockcoat and a deep purple and green Scots plaid waistcoat, he had waived off his valet's attempt at an elaborate tie to his neck cloth and rushed out to the hall and down to the kitchen.

By the foyer clock, he noted it was twenty past seven. He knew his boys were not yet awake. Former governesses awakened them at seven. By one in the afternoon, they were always cranky. This later time and sweeter company would better suit them.

"Good morning, Miss Ferris." He smiled at his young cook who was elbow deep in flour rolling dough. She was Winn's good friend and she had always been agreeable as well as skilled.

She inclined her head. "Morning, yer lordship."

"I see you are already at work. I made a few changes for the house last night and I should have instructed Fox to inform you of them. But it was late and I urged him to go to bed."

"Mister Fox told me last night, sir, of yer new breakfast plans."

"Wonderful. I have come to ask a favor."

"'Course, sir. What can I do for you?" She wiped her hands on her long white apron.

"While I do not wish to disturb your progress, I wonder if you might be able to make something sweet for our first breakfast together."

She was a stocky woman, healthy and also up from his country estate. She had big smiles and when she bestowed them, she showed off her big white teeth. She did so now. "I've planned for scones, sir. Apple. Will that be good?"

"Excellent. You can add the regular oat porridge and prunes. Toast, too."

"And a bit of bacon?" She had a twinkle in her dark eyes.

"A fine addition. Thank you."

Winn appeared in the archway from the hall. She halted, one hand to the plaster, surprised to see him there. "I came to check on the breakfast menu." She glanced at her friend the cook and offered a faint smile.

"I have already done so," he told her. "Cook makes apple scones in addition to our usual fare."

"Oh?" One of her brows dipped as she examined both of them. "Do you need anything else, sir? Anything special?"

He stared at her. *Was she shooing him out of his own kitchen?*

"My business with Cook is done, Miss Mathers, but I will have more to discuss with you after we dine."

Bridgette folded her arms, her eyes dashing between them, as if she waited for an argument to erupt.

Winn turned for the hall. "As you wish."

"Wonderful, thank you, Bridgette." He strode toward Winn. "After you, Miss Mathers."

She harumphed, but swung away. "I'm off to see if the boys are dressed and ready."

"As you wish."

He proceeded to the small room, now transformed from informal sitting room into a room whose very center was a round intimate table for five. Fox had ordered the downstairs maid to dress the table in a bright berry red cloth with merry green serviettes. The children could enjoy their meal as they should without regard to white linens. He wanted his boys to find happiness in all they did. He had tried these past two years to learn them, their ways, their funny little intricacies and he had tried to be a good father, albeit a traditional one. But stuffy went only so far. From now on, he would ensure their happiness in new ways.

He took a chair, facing the door. Earlier, he had ordered Fox to deliver his newspaper to him in his room with his coffee. He would have nothing disturb his time with his family.

He heard them coming down the stairs, Winn urging them along.

"Good morning," he bid them all as they rounded the table. He rose and extended a hand toward the chair beside him. "Miss Mathers, this is your place."

Her gaze shot to him. Surprise gave way to a flash of anger and lastly, surrender. "Mr. Fox and the footman will arrive with our breakfast."

"Why do we have to eat here?" William scrunched up his little mouth.

Roger sat taller in his chair. "Will we be bad if we spill food on the carpet?"

"We doubt you will," Winn said to him, though she confirmed what she said with a sharp glance at Bettington.

"Papa?" William was not to be calmed. "I don't want the belt."

"William," Bettington sighed, "you will never fear a belt again."

Roger tipped back his head. "Never?"

"That is right."

"Why?"

"Roger, things are different in this household. We do not go by what others think or what they want. We order our lives on what we know is right. One fact to know is that hitting children with a belt or a hand is not right. If I had known of the practice of your governesses before, I would have stopped it."

Roger checked Winn's gaze. "Even...even housekeepers?"

"Even them," Winn interjected. "I do not find such actions necessary."

"Not for li'l kids with bows and arrows?" William asked.

"Not them," she told him.

"Not anyone," said Bettington.

Surprise had the three boys looking long and hard at both Winn and him.

Bettington forced himself to refrain from smiling at them, one and all.

Instead, he waited until Fox and the footman had come and gone, leaving dishes on the table to be passed and shared, just as he had instructed Fox last night.

When the bacon had disappeared, the porridge bowls emptied and the scones mere crumbly memories, Bettington pickled up his serviette, wiped his lips and put it to one side. "Now, I have plans for us today."

Four pairs of curious eyes met his.

"I have ordered the carriage brought round. At ten o'clock, we leave for a spot north of town where a small pond is iced over. Bring your pattens and your blades."

"We're going skating?" Winn asked him, her expression brightened by the prospect.

"We are." He stood.

All of them followed.

Winn began to curtsy and the boys started to incline their heads.

He put up both hands. "Here, we are in private. Morning meals, afternoon teas and dinners will be here. You will attend. Each of you. Among us, you will show no formalities. Only when in public. I wish to see instead impeccable manners. Am I clear?"

Tio, his mouth decorated in crumbs and berry jam, tugged at William's sleeve. "What's forma-bittles?"

"Bowing to Papa." Roger stared at him, struck by this new approach to life.

Tio appeared even more confused.

"Come along, boys." Winn took up the reins. "I will explain. We must go find blades."

THEIR CARRIAGE RIDE was a happy affair, the boys chattering about the wonders of snow and ice.

"Angles, Miss?" Tio flapped his arms wide as if he were in a snow mound. "We'll make angles!"

Bettington chuckled.

Winn thrilled to the fact that Bettington's youngest boy had one thing he loved doing with her and he had to do it soon.

"We will," she said. "I promise."

"Today? Please, pease, pease!"

"If we have good snow at the pond."

But the pond was surrounded by icing mounds of old snow. Two other groups of four each were also skating there, and they seemed proprietary about their stretch of pond perimeter.

"We will do that at home," she told all three when it was clear they should think only of skating not making angels.

"Tomorrow?" Roger and William were in on the chorus now.

"Tomorrow."

"Come," Bettington told them all, "let's get our skates tied on."

He did his quickly, helping Roger and William. Winn was still trying to get Tio's on him.

Bettington approached them as she bent before Tio. "You left breakfast before I could speak with you."

She could not care. She had work to do here to get these little boys on the ice. "I did. My apologies. I wanted to get the boys ready for skating." She raised her brows, triumphant in that, and avoiding him once more by trying to tie on Tio's blades to his pattens. "Tell me now. What else do you require?"

"We have a dinner party next week. The night before Christmas. I want you to send out the invitations."

Her mouth fell open. But she caught herself and went back to her work. "Surely, you are joking."

"Not a bit."

She looked like a snow queen in a pretty pale blue velvet bonnet trimmed in pale green piping. The blue matched her long wool coat. She was pretty as candy, but that color was all wrong for her shining golden hair with its vibrant red strands. She pressed her lips together, her anger burning color onto her already pink cheeks. "I will not do it."

"You can."

"Can but will not. Anyone who received such an invitation would either laugh and consign the card to the trash or—"

"Realize that I raise you up to a higher status." He smiled to himself. "Then they will happily attend."

"They will attend only if you write the invitations, sir."

"To you, I am Walter."

"To me, you are my employer. For six more days only."

He sighed.

She had to find some peace when she was with him. She focused on the boys. Roger was already spinning around like a top. William had fallen a few times, but true to his need for success, he made a go of a few long strides. Tio took baby steps onto the ice, laughing all the way.

As for herself, Winn was a disaster. She had never been good at this. Going along at a rate that even Tio could beat, she clung to an old rough log railing along the edge of the pond. Afraid to let go, she either waddled along on the toe of the blade or spent her time bending her arms in shapes they should not go just to keep hold of the rail. She is so ungainly, even a puppet could do better.

Bettington skated up to her, graceful as a bird and stopped before her with a flourish.

"Showing off, I see," she sniffed.

"Come dance with me." He offered a gentlemanly hand.

"We will both go down."

He merely arched his brows, indifferent to her prediction.

She wiggled her nose. "Very well. I warned you."

But he circled one mighty arm around her waist and urged her to put out one foot and glide with him. "Let me lead us where we're going."

Exactly what I must not do. To her surprise, she traveled with him. "You are not falling."

"I have you. You surrender well, and so we make a fine circuit."

His words seemed so prophetic that she grew uneasy. "How are you so sure of yourself?"

"In skating, I found my abilities early in life."

"I didn't."

He took her around in small circle, both her hands in his. "You did not go out to skate with your friends?"

"I didn't have any friends for many years."

He shook his head. "I am surprised. I did not know."

"You wouldn't. You were away at school and Cambridge."

"True. I did not notice the charming girl with regally gold hair and tawny green eyes until she looked at me when she was...what? Sixteen?"

He swept her along and she followed him easily, though she did not look at him.

"Winn?"

"Concentrate on not letting me fall."

"I am. Now tell me was I right that you cared for me when you were quite young?"

Oh, why not admit the truth? "Very young."

"Sixteen?"

"Precisely." She did not like this questioning. She tried to slow him down and only fumbled. "Stop now. I've had enough."

He kept going, leading her out in a long smooth sail in one straight line across the glittering pond. "I wish I had presence of mind to wait until you were older to explore your feelings and mine."

His? He had liked her when she was a youth? No. Impossible. Oh, why did they have to discuss the past? "You were on a path different from mine. What would a young girl's desire for you mean when you were meant for ladies more prominent than I?"

"I learned all too painfully what prominence merited a lady and a man."

"Society teaches you to stay within your class." Those were her father's words. He had drilled them into her. Whenever she rushed home crying from the cruelty of other children or once, from the vicar's wife who called her a tramp, her father would promise her relief in years to come.

"They will forget how your mother ran off with a duke's younger son," Papa would say. "They will learn how kind and smart and sweet you are. What's more, they will see how upright and moral you are. Your future will be grand, my girl. Very grand."

Bettington had brought them to a stop.

She took a step backward, wishing to end this topic. But she was not sure-footed without him. She started to rebuke him, whipped out a hand to catch the railing when suddenly her arms were windmilling.

He caught her to him, his body long and strong, and her heart pounding. "Listen to me, please, Winn. I saw that you cared for me when you were young. I was flattered and took it only as a feather in my cap. And you are right, I was told to look among certain others for a wife. But I have learned from my own experience and from those of a few of my friends, that staying within your class, merits you nothing if there is not mutual respect. Without that, there can be no love. No joy."

"I agree."

"For once, we find common ground." He gave her one of his glorious smiles.

She had to give him her own. "We do."

"Not just on ice."

"On ethics."

He hugged her close and they both chuckled.

Breaking apart, she cleared her throat. Looking around she was happy the other two groups had left. She was here alone within the arms of the man she adored—and they had stopped their arguing.

But she was not certain what peace had gained her.

CHAPTER 6

The next morning after breakfast, Winn excused herself from the table and told the boys to go prepare for their lessons. Their family conversation this morning had been easier than yesterday and she rejoiced at the lack of tension.

She was about to step from the room and leave Bettington to his coffee when he asked her to remain.

"Please, a moment of your time. What do you plan for today?"

"I examine the linen and china closets for service for your dinner party. I consult with Bridgette about whatever she may need for that and I pay the household bills to the greengrocer and butcher. Those two men have told Bridgette the bills are long past due and so, I see to them."

"Very good. I will send you the guest list for the Christmas Eve party."

"Sir, I should not do those invitations."

His blue eyes looked pained at her refusal, but she would not relent.

She had to explain. "It would be a point of gossip and I could not endure it."

He nodded but looked confused. "I will do it. I see it as a mingling mostly for family."

She was relieved he would not argue with her more about that matter. "Is that all, sir?"

He winced at her use of the formality. "Anything else you plan for today?"

"I will look at my tallies in the household records to see if my numbers are correct." She had told him at breakfast that she thought his last housekeeper had fidgeted with the funds. He said he wanted proof to inform the registry he had used to hire the woman. "I will come to you with my maths."

"Good. And the maid you interviewed yesterday here?'

"I like her."

"Then hire her. We need her and if you like her, she passes muster. Do you go out with the boys today?"

"I had planned only a short walk. The wind seems very sharp today. I will not risk their health. Why do you ask?" *Please do not say you come with us again. I cannot remain aloof when you are so carefree and charming.*

"A good idea. What time do you go?"

"Half past eleven, I think."

"Good to know. I will not join you today. I have meetings. The Duke of Wharton comes to talk with me here. He arrives at two. I want you to be in attendance to greet him. Pour tea. Offer whatever delicacies Bridgette offers up. Make polite conversation. Then if you wish you can remain or leave us to our talks."

No, no. He was exposing her to his colleague and doing so as a substitute for his wife, exactly what she could not do and would never become. "Oh, Bettington, please, I—"

"You provide a measure of respectable polish which this household desperately needs."

She straightened her spine. Affection for him had her wishing to give him the world, but she felt herself falling into his demand. "I am but the housekeeper."

"You are a lovely, gently bred lady. I need you to show the world I know quality when I see it. Come. Be my hostess. Ten minutes of your time does not shake the world."

Despite all against it, she knew he honored her to ask it of her. "I will. I'll see what Bridgette can create for you."

He stared down at her, his long dark lashes drooping over his large blue eyes, creating an impression of his gratitude. "I am glad we do not argue."

"As am I." She began to curtsy, but caught herself. "Until later," she said and began to turn away. But at once oddly brave and impetuous, she swung back around. "Would you answer a question for me?"

"Anything," he said with a verve that told her he truly meant she could inquire about any matter in the world.

"Did you hire me as housekeeper for the Grange because you knew I had once cared for you?"

"Once?" His mouth tipped up at one corner as he teased her with the word. "I wanted you there to bring your merry self to a household demoralized and disorganized. But now you are put off by me, and I am flummoxed. I do not know what to do to bring that happy woman to us here."

He was too charming, tempting her to throw away every rule she had ever formed to stay away from him.

She hurried away. That happy woman, as he called her, was scared to death to find herself in his embrace, defying every law that would save her from her father's despair and her own ridicule.

WINN THREW her head back to laugh as the three boys each fell backwards into mounds of snow in the Crescent green. They were all wrapped up tightly in wool coats and hats too big for them, their little necks wound about in their father's heavy scarves.

"Look at me! Look at me!" William yelled, falling once more and whipping his imaginary wings up and down in the powder.

"Angle! Angle!" Tio lay in a pile as he whipped his arms up and down. At once, he scrambled up and pointed to his impression in the snow. "A big angle!"

"It's an *angel*, Hore!" Roger, miffed at his youngest brother's mispronunciations, called him the name that Horatio had called himself when first he talked. They had all received the decree from their father that Horatio was now Tio. And so it was, on pain of a dressing down.

Winn went to Roger and took his hand. "Come now, I think all our works are lovely. Don't you, Roger?"

He pouted, recognizing her polite reprimand. "Yes, Miss."

"Angle, angle, angle!" Tio ran in circles around his newest creation, flapping his arms as if they were wings.

William had his hands on his hips as he glared at Roger. "We know, Tio. We know!"

Tio ran ahead, his little legs pumping, his arms churning.

"Wait, Tio!" Winn ran after him. She found him, falling backward into a fresh pile, his laugh like a tinkle of a bell...until he gave a cough. And then another.

She didn't like the sound of that cough and offered him a hand. "Do sit up, Tio."

"Good afternoon, Miss Mathers." The deep bass voice had her glancing up toward the dashing silver-haired Duke of Wharton. She had met him yesterday afternoon when he had come for his meeting with Bettington. He had been most gracious, indeed so gracious toward her that she wondered if Bettington had prepared the duke for a lady in the house. Or rather, a woman who was not a lady but who was receiving him nonetheless.

The duke continued his flawless behavior toward her and offered her his hand. His smile was generous to her and playful to Tio to whom he said, "Lovely angles, Tio."

The little boy beamed at the man whom he obviously knew. "Mmm-hmm. Big ones."

"I do agree, young man. Most notable." The duke gazed at Tio's latest and nodded. "I wish I could do as well."

Tio grasped his hand, tugging him toward a huge mound of untouched snow. "Do, do!"

"Oh, I cannot…"

But now Roger and William were joining the chant of Tio.

Winn contained a chuckle and spread both hands wide. "What will you do, sir?"

At which, he pursed his lips, frowned at each of the four in turn, then turned around and fell into a patch of snow.

His wings were, of course, huge, as were his applause.

"Wait!" Bettington came toward them all, grinning like a child. "I too must be an angle!"

"Yay, Papa!" yelled Roger.

After which, Bettington found a clear patch and fell backward. As he lay in the snow, the breath knocked from him, his gaze met Winn's, then his sons', followed by his friend's, and back to Winn. "I saw all of you and had to come."

Winn offered her hand to help him up. "Have you hurt your back?"

"Definitely not!"

"You do not move quickly, Bett." Wharton leaned over him, skeptical.

"I am fine. Fine, fine!" He rolled to one side, avoiding Winn's and Wharton's hand.

"It's a terrible thing to grow old," Wharton mourned as they all walked toward Bettington House.

"You should talk, Wharton. You are four years older than I."

Winn bit her tongue as the two men chided each other and all of them marched into the foyer. Immediately, Fox appeared to help them all with coats and hats and scarves.

Tio, to Winn's dismay, had begun to cough once more. It was a deep resonant cough that rattled his chest and her composure.

"My lord," Fox said to Bettington, "Your appointment is here. I put her in your office for the moment." Fox's chocolate brown eyes darted to Winn.

"Tell her I will be there in a few minutes." He ran both hands through his thick curls as he checked Fox's wary eyes.

Winn wondered who this lady might be, but she busied herself urging the boys to go upstairs to change their wet trousers.

"Wharton, could you please wait for me?" Bettington asked his friend. "I have a matter I must see to. Five minutes, no more. I apologize."

"Go to it," Wharton said, waving him off and turning for the main salon.

"Miss Mathers!" Bettington called to her as she took the stairs up behind the boys. "Can we speak for a moment?"

"Tio has a cough. I don't like it." Winn recalled that last summer the little boy had caught a fever after he fell into one of the fountains at the Grange.

"A poultice for his chest, then," Bettington frowned as he watched the boys scamper up the staircase. "Warm tea. Broth. I will come to see him put to bed as soon after I speak with Wharton and the lady in my office."

She nodded, prepared to turn away

He caught her forearm. "Wait, please. The visitor in my office is for you."

"Me?" She knew not who it could be.

"She is a dressmaker from Half Moon Street. Very accomplished."

"I do not understand. I know no dressmaker here in London."

"I have called for her for you. Her name is Madame Channard and I have asked her to sew for you four new gowns."

At first, her mouth fell open. "I am stunned. Furthermore, I cannot—"

"You *can* accept them."

"That is beyond—"

"No, it is not. You cannot wear the same dress for days on end."

Ohhh. She huffed. "Why not?"

"Well for one thing, you like to change regularly. And bathe, too. Always have."

Oh, why did he do this? She would like to look pretty for him. Smell good for herself, too. Even have him admire her in more than this plain robin's egg cotton. But she was no coquette, no diamond, no equal to his station. Nor was she a beggar, needing favors. "I cannot accept them."

He strode so near, she felt his determination roll off him in waves of heat. He lifted her chin with two fingers—and she rooted to the carpet, wanting his strength, yearning to merit his gift and hating his demand she take it. "Madame will do this. You will accept them. So buy them from the woman yourself or reimburse me from your salary at the end of our arrangement. But wear them."

THE NEXT DAY she dared not take the children out. Not only was it dreary and bitterly windy, but Tio was worse. She consigned him to bed. Taking the household ledger, she sat with Tio and reviewed her latest figures on the previous houskeeper's estimates. It was a good conclusion. Finished. Winn devoted herself to entertaining Tio again.

He grumbled, but promised to be a good boy after she promised hot tea and many biscuits. Still, it became a challenge to keep him quietly occupied. Reading to him finally put him to sleep.

Tucking the covers under his chin, Winn hurried from his room down to Bettington's library.

She knocked and Bettington called for her to enter. But she saw that he had guests. The same gentleman as yesterday, the Duke of Wharton, stood and gave her a generous smile. Beside him stood a slightly younger man, grey at the temples, and discerning cool grey eyes. In his gaze stood an interest she could only term salacious. If Bettington spied it, she could not say. But it repelled her, even as she knew she would not give any indication that she knew or that she found it disgusting and appallingly bad manners.

Bettington introduced her. "Miss Mathers, you have met his grace, the duke. And this is Lord DeVries. Both gentlemen are here to discuss the bill that the duke and I propose in Parliament."

She gave a small curtsy and a smile. "Good to meet you, my lord, and Your Grace, good to see you once more."

Bettington's face was lined with anxiety. "You come with news of Tio?"

"I do, sir. He is finally napping."

"His cough?"

She shook her head. "No better. I worry."

"I will have Fox call in the doctor."

"A good idea. But in the meantime, I will begin to apply a warm poultice to his chest. Bring up the fire in the room, too."

"Thank you. Pardon my intrusion." She promptly left them for her little charge.

BETTINGTON WATCHED WINN GO, taking note of Wharton's approval and of DeVries' sharp craven interest in her. Naturally, he would not hint at his recognition of the man's interest. DeVries' friendship was vital to Bettington to help with this bill.

"Please," he said extending a hand to their chairs. "Let us continue."

Both men settled in.

But DeVries, a widower with a reputation for enjoying himself with many women, shot his cuffs and caught Bettington's eyes. "Lovely lady. Who is she, Bettington?"

"My housekeeper."

"Is that so? I wish I could find one as pleasant. Devoted to your children, too. Where ever did you find her?"

He would keep this simple, precise—and formal. "The country. My village."

"Ah, so she is then your...?"

"Housekeeper, DeVries. My housekeeper."

BETTINGTON APPEARED in Tio's bedroom an hour later.

"Any better?" he asked her and bent over his son.

"No change, I am afraid." She noticed his eyes strayed to the household ledger on the nearby table. "I've been tallying the accounts as Tio sleeps. I have finished the books. It is true that the last housekeeper took money. Nearly eighty-four pounds."

"Dear God." He sighed. "I will tell the registry of her crime. I will not pursue the matter to regain the money. The woman is most likely gone without a trace. By the way, did the person applying for the maid's position appear for work?"

"She did. I like her."

"Marvelous. We have some order." He smiled at her in that slow warm way that told her he was happy. "Wharton likes you."

"And I like him. He seems a good man."

"DeVries likes you, too."

She arched a long golden brow. "So I noticed."

"You will tell me if he makes any untoward comments to you."

"So then, is he a rogue?"

"He is. But I would say it is because he has not yet met the right woman."

CHAPTER 7

Winn lifted Tio's head. "Sip this, sweetheart." He gazed at her with glazed blue eyes, but drank the tepid tea.

She eased him back to the pillows, then put her hand to his forehead. His fever had not broken.

She stood back. Dawn had not yet come, but faint light shown from the east. She had tended him all night long, dozing on the chaise longue in between ministering to the boy. But now it was time she went to get Bettington to tell him she had no good news.

If the little boy's temperature did not fall soon, he would have less chance of surviving it. She knew this from last summer, when they had consulted the village local doctor about Tio's fever and chills.

"A fever must break," said Hugh Carlin, "in early hours of the morning, or it can be fatal."

She whirled from Tio's bedside, heading for the door. In the hall, she ran down the stairs to the second floor to the master suite. There, she caught her breath, a hand to the door frame. She was dizzy from her night of constantly tending Tio. She widened her eyes, got her balance and knocked.

Bettington ripped open the door—his dark hair wild, his red banyan loose about his waist. "I was just coming. Tell me."

"He's not good."

Bettington seized her hand and strode with her up the stairs to Tio's room. When the little boy had become so ill yesterday, Bettington had moved William's bed into the former governess's room. He had stayed with Tio and her until wee hours when Winn had insisted he leave them and go to bed. He knew she did it also for propriety's sake. Reluctantly, he'd gone, making her promise to get him if Tio's condition changed.

Now as they both looked down on Tio, the little boy murmured nonsense. His forehead glistened with his raging fever.

"We should bathe him," they both said in chorus.

"I'll get the maid to bring us more warm water," she said to Bettington. The small bowl and cloths she had would not suffice for bathing all of his tiny body.

"I'll go," he told her. "You stay. Sing to him. He liked that when you did it last summer."

She tried to smile. "I will. Go."

Within minutes, he was back. In the meantime, she had removed Tio's sleep shirt and his stockings. He burned and she could not stop the trembling of her lips or the shaking of her shoulders.

Bettington covered her hands and held. "Shall I take his toes and you his head?"

"Yes, first let me give him a fresh poultice for his chest."

They worked, over and over again. Interrupted by the new maid who came with a pot of tea and another of coffee plus bread and jam, the two of them worked in concert. How long Winn did not know, save that the dawn had turned to a brighter day as Tio stopped his writhing and sank to a sound rest.

Then she laid the back of her hand over Tio's forehead and stared at Bettington. "Am I imagining that he's cool?"

"Not imagining at all," he whispered with a glorious smile and tears in his eyes. He put down the cloth he'd used to bathe his son and pulled the sheet and blankets up to his little boy's neck. Then he moved to Winn's side.

This time, when he came near her and pulled her into his arms, she went like a magnet to his iron embrace. His lips in her hair, he whispered that she was bone tired. He did not want her becoming ill.

"Come sit with me," he urged and picked her up in his arms and took her to the chaise longue. There he settled against the back and gathered her up against his chest. "Sleep. You need it. If he awakens, I will let you know."

She closed her eyes and snuggled near to his warmth, his strength, her friend and the only man she could ever love.

The room was very warm when she stirred. Realizing she could not sit up and that she was in Bettington's embrace, she sank back down. From this cozy cocoon, she could see that Tio still slept, his little mouth open, his arms wide. She did not move as the fragrance of lemon and sandalwood permeated her being. Bettington had always smelled of springtime and solidity. She ached to belong to him. Never wished to part from him.

She burrowed into his strong essence. Suddenly, his fingers were in her hair, pushing back her long tendrils from her cheek and her throat.

"My dearest Winn," he breathed against her lips, "this is how I have wanted you near me, so close one to the other, united in all we do."

Her head cradled in the crook of his arm, she did not move but, as once she had last summer, she crossed the distance that separated them and put her lips to his. Once again, she was met, not with his surprise this time, but with his fire and his fierce claim of countless kisses.

She did not stop but went, careless to the consequences, her nails clutching at the heavy silk of his banyan. He sent kisses down her throat, across the exposed expanse of her simple muslin gown. Ignited by his flames, she wanted only his possession.

He cupped her cheek. His sky blue eyes devoured her in a look of love. "Winn, my darling. I want to marry you."

This could make her life divine. To be his in word and deed would be all she ever asked for in this world. "Sweet man. That cannot be. You are an earl."

"That is a title granted to a distant man. Who knows if he ever wanted it or was even happy of it."

She pulled herself to sanity. "Whoever he was, whatever he wanted, you have it as your own. Rules come with that. Rules long standing among your peers."

His fingers in her hair, he did not look into her eyes. "My days are not consumed with the duties of my title. I live here in London, but the work I have done over the years to manage the land and the tenants is very good. I have ensured the prosperity of my estate. I now have time for politics for bills I know are important to Britain's integrity."

She shook her head. Confused.

"What's more, I have lived here in London but each time I go to the Grange, I have learned to enjoy my days more than I ever have before. I value you and each moment with you more."

"Impossible. You do not know me."

He seized her hand. "But I do. I know you like to read and dance. I know you carry a tune very well. You play the piano with a modicum of accomplishment."

"Don't be too kind." She grimaced at him.

He gave a laugh. "My darling Winn, I know you love your friends, like our Bridgette. I know you love my boys. I know you love children." A fond light appeared in his large blue eyes. "I want to give you many children."

Burning with a blush, she tried to rise.

But he would not let her go.

"That…that is risqué," she blurted, but a chuckle escaped.

He grinned. "You see? You want my babies. I know you do. I love you, Winn," he whispered. "I love your humor and your wit. I love your joy of living. I love your—"

She pushed up and away from him. With a frantic look toward quiet little Tio, she put up a hand to ward off Bettington and whispered. "I cannot marry you! My father will not approve. My reputation, after being here, will be questionable." She noticed he froze for a moment, pondering an aspect of what she had said.

"Why?" He frowned, advancing on her. "Why would that be?"

"My father did not want me to come."

"Ahh. That's because he knows I want you."

"What? No. No, he doesn't."

"But he does. When he discovered us kissing last summer in the garden, he took me aside later and warned me away from you."

Her mouth fell open. She snapped it shut and said, "That's why you left the Grange so quickly."

"It was."

"Ohhh. I thought it was because you were ashamed of kissing me!"

He stalked her. "My darling, how could you believe that?"

She was flat to the cold wall. Her body flooded with desire for him. When he leaned in to kiss her lips, she turned aside and he blessed her cheek instead.

"Please. Please stop. You do not understand my dilemma."

He backed away enough to put both hands to the wall. But he was still dangerously close. "Tell me then. Let's have done with this."

"My mother was our disgrace. When I was two or three, she took up with some fellow, a duke's younger son, and after a year, she ran off with him. My father was laughed at, ridiculed. So was I. But people forgot. Gradually my father became his good self again. And I was no longer the girl that others laughed at. But I remember what that was like. I never wish to live with such scorn again. I will not live my life ashamed of myself."

"All the more reason to marry me, sweetheart."

"I do not want to be ashamed of myself! To be your wife would mean I would be in society I do not understand! That I was not trained for!"

He blinked. Frowned. "I care not for society's wants. My God, Winn. My mother was frightened and disgraced by my father's belligerent nature. She left him. And it was noted in society. My sister ran away from home when she was seventeen because my father was cruel. She has never returned, nor written. We know not if she is dead or alive. All that was noted in society. My wife was promiscuous and brought great shame upon herself. It took me years to deal with my own emotions on the subject. And now, now I know what is the most proper thing to do. It is to rid the world of those who judge others by poor standards and who mistreat people because of their birth, their job or their gender. I propose a bill to fully limit the merchant business of selling humans to others. Powerful men oppose me. Do you think I could continue if I cared what others think of me and mine?"

Winn filled with pride in him. He was bold to fashion such a measure. "I did not know. But Rome was not built in a day. If we marry, you will feel the brunt of others' disapproval. And your activities in Parliament? They will wither. They will die. I will not allow you to suffer that! One success can lead to more. You must continue and not think of me."

"You refuse me?" His words were so broken that they shattered her heart.

She tossed her head against the wall. Tears burned her eyes. "Yes!"

"So you also refuse to love Roger, William and Tio?"

"Ohh, Bettington." Battered by his logic, she wiped tears from her cheeks. "I love them. Do not use them against me."

"Very well. But tell me one thing."

She swallowed hard on her desire to wipe the despair from his beautiful eyes. "What is it?"

"Do you love me?"

She stared at him as tears destroyed her vision of him. "Because I love you, I will never do anything to ruin you."

"But that is just the ticket, my love. You never could ruin me."

CHAPTER 8

That evening Winn took her dinner in Tio's room. She sent the new maid down with word of it to the dining room. She told herself it was best if she remained aloof from the dear man who had proposed to her and whose arguments still had a powerful sway over her.

But her supper was tasteless. She picked at it. That was not Bridgette's fault but her own despair. Bettington had suffered from his father's cruelty and society's sting. He had been hurt by his mother's remove to Brighton and the loss of his older sister. Bettington had suffered just as Winn and her father had suffered because of her mother's choices.

Her father had lived in such a way that people respected him in spite of rumors of the past. Winn, too, had outgrown the barbs from others and ultimately, they had abandoned them. She had established her own good character. She was proud of it. Was that not enough to equal a good stand in society? Beyond birth or title, gender or profession?

The rightness of that had her rising from her chair.

Tio slept on, peaceful, his forehead cool to the touch. Tio lived and she wanted him well care for, well loved. Roger and William, as well.

She wished the three little boys happy lives—and wanted to be one of the two who gave that to them.

She let her eyes drift closed. She yearned to accept Bettington's proposal. She wanted to be his wife, his lover. If he could be so bold as to love her, see her as his equal, could she also not ignore the rules he found so repugnant? Could she not stand with him to change how others thought of the constrictions of class, gender and race?

She could. She would!

She had to find Bettington and hoisted her skirts to take the stairs down at a run. No one was in the little dining room. They were finished. She paused. Where were they? She had not heard them upstairs. She clamped a hand to the newel and ran up the stairs, pushed open the double doors to the large front salon…and came to a halt.

"Oh…I did not know we had company."

The lady who sat in the upholstered crimson silk Hepplewhite chair flashed remarkable sky blue eyes at her. That color blue Winn knew and knew quite well.

"Forgive me." Winn pointed to the hallway. They had never met, she had never been introduced to the countess who kept to her townhouse in Brighton. Yet tonight, she was here. For the holiday, Winn concluded and saw it as a breakthrough. "You wait for Lord Bettington. I will leave you to it."

She would have gone, save the woman called to her.

"Do come back. I assume you are Miss Mathers? Miss Winifred Mathers?"

"I am, my lady." Winn regarded the lady who was the Countess of Bettington. When Winn was young, she had never seen the lady. But during the years she had served as housekeeper at the Grange, Winn had heard of the genteel lady who had left her husband and lived by herself in Brighton. Bettington, her son, had often gone to visit her and taken his children to their grandmother. "Forgive me for barging in on you. I was in search of his lordship."

"Who was here and does return soon. He is reading to his two oldest sons and putting them to bed."

"I see." She curtsied. "I will seek him out later."

The woman raised a manicured hand. "A word, Miss Mathers."

Winn caught a breath. Whatever this word was, the lady did not sound pleasant. "Of course. What can I do for you, ma'am?"

The countess narrowed her eyes, so blue and true as her son's and her three grandsons'. "I understand you have served my son well at the Grange."

Winn nodded. "I have endeavored to do that, yes."

"For three years."

"Yes."

"And in that time, you have endeared yourself to my grandchildren."

That sounded like a bone the lady wished to pick with Winn. "Yes. I like them very much."

"Do you?" She rose from her chair. Her stark white hair, perfectly coiffed, complemented her pristine complexion. The midnight blue of her silken gown attested to the countess's wealth, station and breeding.

Winn braced for the lady's words.

"I understand you have an education."

In the dead silence, Winn noted she was expected to reply. "I attended Canterbury School for Young Ladies, ma'am."

"And your father taught you much about the law."

"He did. I could not help but learn." She fondly recalled the hours in which Papa would comment on different cases.

"The law is precise."

"Mama, I took longer than I—" Bettington appeared and stepped toward Winn. "What is the matter here?"

His mother shot him a look. "Miss Mathers is about to tell me the nature of the law."

Winn gathered her pluck. "Indeed, ma'am. The law is precise, but also best adapted to time and use when it is fluid."

The lady strolled nearer. "As society is often not."

"This is also true." Winn had no idea where the countess led this conversation. Was she arguing against Winn's involvement with her son? If she was, she would lose that debate. Winn wanted him. Would have him. Enjoy him. Honor and keep him.

Now the countess stepped directly before Winn.

Beside Winn, Bettington seemed skeptical of his mother's direction of thought.

But Winn had an inkling. She faced her with a growing smile.

The exact height, the two ladies matched each other in build and unflinching intent.

The countess looked directly into Winn's eyes. "What do you suppose is required to sway society to be more fluid and useful?"

Ah, this Winn knew. Her father had preached it a thousand times. She had found hers time and time again. Upstairs, minutes ago, she had claimed the last portion of it that she needed in order to marry the man she adored.

"Well, Miss Mathers? Have you an answer?"

I do, ma'am. "Courage."

"For a woman who loves—and you do love my son, don't you, Miss Mathers?"

Winn stood her ground. "I do. Very much."

On a gasp, Bettington curved a strong arm around Winn's waist.

"Do you not have the courage to take and give what love you have for him and make your lives worth living?"

Winn turned her face toward the dark handsome creature who had stolen her heart when she was very young. "I hope, sir, you will forgive me for this, but—"

His features fell to dire despair. He caught her closer to his chest. "Winn, I will not let you go."

"Oh, no, my dear, dear man. I do not leave. I want you to know that I am not engaged to be married."

"How delightful," he crooned and bent, taking her lips in a ravishing kiss. "I need not go and challenge George Detwiler to a duel."

"What? No!" She chuckled as the man who embraced her kissed her lips once more. "You would not have. Would you?"

"To win you, my darling Winn, I would do anything!"

"Oh, that is wonderful to know. So then, tell me one thing, will you?"

"Anything!"

"I am asking you to marry me, sir."

"Walter," he demanded, an infectious grin spreading wide his firm mouth.

"Walter, then. Do you think you might marry me? Soon? Say... after Advent when an officiant of the church will allow us to say vows?"

He threw back his head to laugh. "I will get the first cleric who agrees!"

She kissed his cheek.

"Sir?" Fox was suddenly behind them. "Pardon me, sir. You have a—"

"Visitor!"

Winn and Walter stared at the burly little man whom Fox presented. The euphoria of Winn's decision and question equaled the surprise at seeing her father before them.

"You did not come home, girl!"

Her attempt to hug him was met by his scowl. She paused. "I know, sir. I wrote a note—"

"It was piddle. Pardon me, sir," her papa addressed her with sad eyes and a wave of his hand, "but, my girl, you cannot just send me one sentence."

"No, sir. Not good. But I want you to know—"

Her father reached over and pumped Walter's hand. "Thanks for your letter. I would not have had the gumption to come if you hadn't invited me."

"You invited my father?" Winn was aghast.

"I did." Walter nodded firmly. "He deserved to know."

"Know?"

"Know what you intended, sir. I worried about my beautiful girl." Her papa shook a finger at her. "You should have written me that he loves you, sweeting. Besides, I could not let you have Christmas without me! Nor get married for that matter."

He clapped Walter on the back. "Good man. You take care of her. Through thick and thin, illness and health. All that. Eh? Who's this? Oh, the countess! 'Course, it is! I recognize you, ma'am. Not over a day, I say. Lovely. Lovely. Do you approve of this between them?" He bent close to her, not taking any guff, his beady brown eyes hot on her blue ones. "I hope you do, ma'am."

For the first time here, the lady chuckled. "I certainly do, sir."

"Good. Good. Now, that means we can have a tipple to the couple, can't we?" He followed Walter to the sideboard while the countess embraced Winn and took her to a nearby chair.

"When is the wedding?" her father harangued Walter. "Soon? Better if it is, you know, sir. Talk among the nutters, not good. I brought my best frockcoat. I say, I went to tell old George Detwiler I was coming here!"

Winn froze. "Oh, Papa. George is such a gossip." If Papa told him she had come to London to serve Bettington or rather, Walter, George would think the worst and spread it around.

Walter was grinning at Winn. "What was George's reaction?" Walter handed him a small glass of sherry. "Mama, you would like one, too, eh? And Winn?"

"Yes," said the countess.

"Yes," murmured Winn.

"George took it in stride. Said he never expected our Winn was good enough for him. But he had to try. Didn't he? I say, hmmm. Good sherry. Got anything stronger than this?"

Walter had looked at Winn through it all. The twinkle in his eyes told her that he was glad she was his.

"Not here, Mister Mathers. But I will have my butler bring up a good bottle of brandy for us. After all," he said with tenderness in his gaze, "we forgive each other all kinds of weaknesses when we know we bring each other a bright new day." He came forward to hand Winn her glass. "Wouldn't you say so, my love?"

"I do. Every day." She clinked her glass with his.

Hours later, as she lay in his arms in his bedroom, she sighed, startled, thrilled and complete. She had told them the whole truth.

George had not proposed to her recently and she would have had to have gone to him to propose when she returned after Christmas.

"I knew he hadn't recently."

"No!" She pulled backward. "How?"

"You are a terrible liar."

She collapsed back into his arms. "Oh, thank God, you know. I do try to be good."

"You are. At everything."

"*Everything?*"

"Well, practice does make perfect. Shall we try again?"

CHAPTER 9

Eight days later the vicar of St. George's came to No. 42 Dudley Crescent to perform the wedding of Miss Winifred Mathers to Walter Frederick Charles Somerville, the earl of Bettington.

News of it had been announced in all the newspapers of credible and not so reliable import. Hints of either the bride's or groom's past were nowhere mentioned. Instead, due note was taken of the bride's education and her father's fine reputation. The earl was credited with advancement of many useful laws in Parliament and of one new bill which, while not favored by many members currently, showed signs that the earl was a progressive thinker who valued all men and women equally.

As for the bride, she stood serenely before her mirror in her assigned housekeeper's suite and admired the fine work of Madame Channard. The dressmaker had outdone herself not only with new gowns but with an additional order for a new full length coat and many new items of translucent silk lingerie for the bride. Of the four new gowns Channard brought the day before Christmas, three were day wear muslin, comfortable and pretty colors of the spectrum from purples to greens. The colors were at the request of the earl who demanded hues to complement his intended's red gold hair and earthy green-brown eyes.

This gown Winn had chosen for her wedding day, however, was a pale mint Luccan silk with emerald-colored ribbons worked in and out of the bodice and at the edges of the elbow-length puffy sleeves. Winn felt like a princess. She stared at herself, acknowledging that she would become more than she had ever hoped. She would be a lady of her own house and mistress of a large and happy country house. She would be a mother to three wonderful boys who cared for her and she for them. Better than all the rest, she would be the wife of the man she loved.

"Are you ready yet? You are late. Five minutes, Winn!" Bridgette urged her on with wide eager eyes. "You don't want the groom to leave!"

"He would never. He's spent too much time these past weeks persuading me to stay!"

They both giggled as Winn led them to the door.

But it burst open!

And there stood the worried groom! Dressed in formal dark gray morning frockcoat, elaborate cravat, cream and blue embroidered waistcoat, his sky blue eyes hooded with anxiety, he stepped toward her. "You are ravishing!"

"What are you doing—?"

But he swept her up into his arms and spun for the hall.

"Taking you to be married, Miss Mathers!"

She realized his problem. She had dallied for five forbidden minutes and he had rushed to her, suffering his old fear that she had left.

"You can put me down, my dear man."

"No."

"I do walk."

"That is what I am afraid of."

"Not away from you." She caught his cheek in one hand and said, "Stop. Look at me."

He did. Frowning still, he gazed at her hair, her ear, her throat, her bodice, her lips and finally, her eyes.

"I go nowhere without you ever again."

"You promise me?"

"With all my heart, my darling. I love you. I have all my life and I am the most honored of ladies that you love me in return."

"Excellent." He nodded, his brows unknitting. "Let's make that legal, shall we?"

So he took the servants' back stairs up as Winn held her breath that the two of them would not tumble back down and break their necks, single unto death. But he carried her into the salon like a pirate's prize where twenty-four guests, including Bridgette and all the house servants, gasped and grinned at their appearance.

Winn's father stood near the vicar, laughing at his soon-to-be son-in-law's jolly smile. Her dear papa had remained at the house for the holiday festivities.

The countess stood to the other side and smiled at her son's bravado and at his bride's chuckle. Roger and William stood by the vicar and clapped at the sight of their father and their soon-to-be-mother. Tio however broke away from his brothers and ran to the couple. He tugged on his father's frockcoat and demanded the man give over the lady in his arms.

When he surrendered to his youngest son's wishes and put Winn to her feet, Tio caught Winn's hand and kissed it. Never breaking his grip, he walked between his sire and his new lady and took them before the vicar.

Winn curled her fingers toward Roger and William. Roger took his father's hand. She took William's. Together as a family, the five of them stood as the bride and groom said their vows and turned to receive the applause and good wishes of their guests.

Breakfast was served in the formal dining room. There the earl and his countess visited with each guest.

The Duke of Wharton beamed at them and offered congratulations. "A fine couple. I wish you all the best in this world and many long years to enjoy it."

Next to him, Viscount DeVries also offered his best wishes. "I envy you, Bettington. Would that there were many to equal your new lady wife."

"I know there are many who are worthy," she told him.

He laughed, liking her words. "Help me find one, will you, my lady?"

"I'd be happy to do that."

An hour later, her husband and she were in his traveling coach leaving the city.

Wrapped up in her new winter coat of purple velvet with white fox at her collar and cuffs, she snuggled into her husband's embrace. The hot bricks in the floor warmed her toes, but it was her husband's embrace that filled her entire body with hot delight. She arched up and planted a firm kiss to his handsome lips.

"Where do we go, sir?" For days, he had refused to tell her where he planned their honeymoon.

"Not far."

She shivered. Each night since she had gone to him, she had lain in his arms and learned the physical joys of a true and earnest partnership.

"Cold?" He pressed her closer.

"Pleased." She let her brows dance in anticipation of what marital delights awaited her soon.

He let out a hearty laugh and hugged her madly.

"So, sir, where do we go?"

"A cottage by the Thames on Wharton's land near Richmond. An hour at most."

"Oh, I am pleased." She kissed him once more in the midst of a laugh.

"Eager, are you?"

"To be yours again?" She curled up closer to him. "Never have I wanted any other man. Nor will I."

"I am yours, my darling, always."

"As I am yours alone."

Hoping you have enjoyed HIS MERRY HOUSEKEEPER, and would like to read the rest of the *Delightful Doings in Dudley Crescent* series. Do begin with HER BEGUILING BUTLER.

In Number 10 Dudley Crescent, the widow Lady Ranford has a butler who is devilishly attractive. Too bad, he finds her fascinating.

Too bad he thinks she murdered her husband.

Get it here: **https://books2read.com/HerBeguilingButler**

Cerise DeLand is the USA TODAY Bestselling Author who believes love brings rich rewards from a life lived with honesty, valor—and a functioning funnybone.

She reflects that in her novels, accenting her two hallmark qualities: poetic elegance and accuracy of detail.

Please visit her website for more information: **https://www.cerisedeland.com**

LADY LOUGHTON'S LAST WAGER

ALINA K. FIELD

LADY LOUGHTON'S LAST WAGER

BY ALINA K. FIELD

When her son escapes school just before Christmas to attend a boxing match, the dowager Lady Loughton seizes the opportunity to avoid a holiday party encounter with the disreputable Lord Lindhorst who's been pursuing her. Arriving at the inn where the match was held, she finds her son isn't there—but Lindhorst is.

Knowing the frigid weather will strand them, Lindhorst seizes his own opportunity to convince the delectable lady he's not as bad as she thinks.

PROLOGUE

London, Spring 1824

"No, Lindhorst," Lady Neda Loughton said, replying to his murmured suggestion. "You will cease."

His hand at her waist, the other holding her hand... She took in a breath and ignored the creeping intimacy, willing away the feelings threatening to overtake her.

It was only a dance, she reminded herself, one in a series over the past few weeks of this season with this same persistent man. She straightened to her full height in a way that seemed to amuse him, though she had to lift her chin to see his lips quivering.

Egad, he was handsome, no quibbling there. Silvery strands laced through his ebony hair, his fashionable coat clung to muscled shoulders and arms, and his breeches—

She mentally flogged herself. Orson Sommerton, seventh earl of Lindhorst was physically a fine—very fine—specimen of British nobility.

With the usual inflated sense of entitlement, especially when he was after a lady. He'd been a regular on the society circuit for the last several years, charming, affable, and said to be always in pursuit of the latest widow.

This year, she was the rumored prey, and it must be true, given his actions. The next thing she would learn is that she was a line in the betting book at White's. Again.

Insufferable men. It had happened before at various times in her long marriage, and she'd weathered the whispers and in fact had never truly been tempted.

Until now.

"A ride in the park?" he asked, spinning her into a turn that left her gasping. "I'll wager you would enjoy yourself."

"No." She caught her breath. "I'm far too busy with—"

"I'll bring the barouche. Your daughter may come along and chaperone us."

That last came with a boyish grin meant to melt the resistance of his quarry.

Like the rest of the ton, Lindhorst knew that, after more than a year of mourning, she'd come to London for her youngest daughter Nancy's first season.

"I had rather she be seen riding in the park with a respectable admirer."

"Ah. Not her *mama's* admirer, not a bounder like me." He hitched her a half-inch closer. "You, on the other hand, my dearest lady, being a widow, and a respectable one, might find that your goodness reforms my badness."

Oh, oh, oh. If only he knew.

She *had* been good, all the years of her marriage. It hadn't always been easy though. She liked society—the routs, the parties, the dancing. And the gentlemen had liked her. "I fear it will take more than my so-called goodness."

No matter how attractive, desirable, and altogether virile he might be—*was*, no *might be* about it!—Lindhorst had much to answer for. His *badness*, as he jokingly called it, had caused her many sleepless nights a few years earlier. He unfortunately lacked the self-awareness to suspect it.

She'd like to take a switch to him, but the mere threat of that might entice him.

Since her husband Henry's death, Lindhorst had been making his interest known—inquiring about her with friends, and acquaintances, and even her son, George. Heavens, Lindhorst had promised support for the railway bill George was trying to see approved by Parliament.

From the distance of Loughton Manor in Leicestershire, the whispers were easily dismissed. When she arrived at the London townhouse though, so did Lindhorst's first bouquet of flowers.

He'd made it clear what he wanted. She was a widow, fair game by the standards of his sort of gentlemen—gentlemen like his father, whose reputation had been far darker. And what Lindhorst offered? He'd wager she'd enjoy it, he'd said. She feared he might be right.

No, as much as Lindhorst made her pulse quicken, after bearing ten children she'd planned for a measure of... rest from *all of that.*

It was a lonely sort of rest, to be sure, but hadn't she had months at a time of loneliness when Henry was in London helping to steer the country through years of war and the after-effects of war, as well as looking after his investments? Once her two youngest, boys of twelve and fourteen, were grown, she'd decide what to do with the rest of her life.

LINDHORST SAW the flash of annoyance on Lady Loughton's face turn into a faraway look that perhaps signaled a glimmer of grief. That wouldn't do.

"Perhaps you might, nevertheless, make the attempt at reforming me," he said, and was gratified to see her lovely blue eyes spark with ire.

He'd come along to this ball solely because the dazzling, but very proper dowager Lady Loughton would be in attendance. She was bringing out her youngest daughter, a tall, somewhat awkward lady of nineteen. Like the other young girls, Nancy Lovelace would be putting herself forward for marriage to a lord, young or old, single or like himself, widowed. Any lord might do for most girls; he imagined Lady Neda would be picky about who plucked one of her chicks.

He'd had a young bride like that once, all blooming beauty and smiling amiability and look how that had turned out. He had no interest in Nancy; it was her mother who held his regard, had done so for several hopeless years when she'd brought her brood up to town to join her husband.

Her eldest, Fitz, had introduced them. Lindhorst had been in his reckless years then. He'd found her cheerful and welcoming—to everyone else. With him, she'd been reserved and polite, a reaction that intrigued and challenged him.

She was the sort of steadfast wife who'd given the late Lord Loughton six healthy sons and four healthy daughters of indisputable pedigree. Pursuing her then had been impossible; despite rumors to the contrary, he didn't poach other men's wives.

Had she come to town after Loughton was felled unexpectedly by a fever, he might have approached her. But she'd remained in the country with family. Fitz's first wife, Alice, had died, and Fitz had remarried a less fashionable lady and distanced himself from old acquaintances. There'd been no particular excuse to descend upon Neda at her home in Leicestershire.

Besides, if he'd followed that yearning to appear at her door and invite her to form an *arrangement*, one of her sons would have called him out.

Things were different now though. Word had come from France that his own estranged wife had died. He'd long ago grieved the demise of their marriage, and the relief that he was free of the legal bonds had been, frankly, immeasurable.

During several months of mourning that his late wife in no way merited, he'd had time to think. Time to reconsider what a lady of true grace and true honor really deserved. Time to wonder what Lady Loughton might want for herself, for her life?

Might he convince her to want him? He had an insatiable itch to know. And to try.

The dance ended and Lindhorst lifted the delectable lady's hand and pressed his lips to the top of her glove.

"I am determined, you know," he said. "Someday—"

"No." Her expression was mild—certainly for the benefit of the onlookers, not himself—and her voice, when she spoke, was a soft, cordial murmur. "Speaking plainly, it will be a cold day in hell, Lindhorst, before you get me into your bed."

Stunned, he watched her take the arm of her next partner, the color rising in her cheeks.

The lady knew to hide her feelings from the ton, but still... there'd been a sparkle in her eyes, a quiver in her hand when he kissed it, and that color rising in her cheeks. She wasn't unaffected.

He was approaching fifty and age had taught him to be patient. She wasn't likely to begin a liaison with someone else, and he wasn't one to give up easily.

"Having any luck there, Lindhorst?"

The rumbling question was laced with humor and brandy-breath. Elliot Pickworth, eldest son of Baron Pickworth, was a friend from the wild days. He'd leaned too closely and spoken too loudly in this crowded ballroom.

"Luck? I haven't made my way to the card room yet." Lindhorst ushered the fellow toward the balcony door and to the balustrade. The night was bracingly cool and there was no one outside.

"Ah." A chuckle followed. "It's in the betting book at White's, you know."

It would be, of course. The fribbles had always gambled on Lindhorst's conquests, not that there'd been all that many.

Lindhorst brushed an imaginary piece of lint from his sleeve. "And who inscribed the offending bet? Do tell me so I may direct Fitz's challenge to the proper party."

Lady Loughton's eldest would be appalled. Might even call *him* out, though apparently Fitz's current happy marriage had mellowed his tendency to jump into a fight.

"Harmless fun," Pickworth said. "My wager's on the lady. She won't have you. Cold as ice—though bearing ten brats, one has to wonder…"

He paused, glanced around the empty balcony and then down at the low balustrade into the darkness below. The dolt.

"Sorry," Pickworth said. "I see the look in your eye. I'm brandy-bitten tonight. No need to throw me over into the garden."

"No," Lindhorst said. "We'll save that for another day."

CHAPTER 1

Loughton Manor, Leicestershire
December 1824

Two carriages sat waiting outside Loughton Manor, the elegant Palladian manor that was home to several members of the very large, very prosperous Lovelace family. Lord Loughton, his lady, and his mother, resided there as well as his remaining two unmarried siblings when they were not at school. A large wreathe of evergreens and red ribbons decorated the open front door, and more evergreen boughs coiled around the porch pillars.

While horses shifted in their traces, eager to finally be off on the sunny but very cold morning, Neda Lovelace, the dowager Lady Loughton, stood just inside, staring at a letter handed to her earlier that morning by their butler, Biggs.

Her eldest, Fitz, his wife, and their children had departed days ago for the family's Yuletide gathering. Neda's newly married daughter, Nancy and her husband, Simon the Duke of Swillingstone, were hosting the holiday party at their Derbyshire home.

Her two youngest boys were to travel directly from their school in Rugby, along with Arthur, Lord Glanford, the stepson of Neda's son George. It was something of a daring adventure for three boys alone, but at fourteen, thirteen and twelve, they were old enough.

Another last-minute guest had been added as well. She crumpled the offending letter carrying the bad news, wondering whether she should spend her Christmas at home alone and avoid being plagued, and worse, sorely tempted.

What sort of excuse could she make?

"I have your small case here for the coach, my lady," her maid, Barnham said. "Patrick has stowed the trunks and packages with the gifts on the baggage coach and—"

A bellow and raised voices from the back of the house had them both turning.

The look crossing Barnham's face said *that man again*, but the maid's thin lips primmed even tighter on the words. Barnham was a recent hire, and as stuffy a lady's maid as anyone could ask for. Perhaps too stuffy for the lively Lovelace household. Neda hadn't quite decided whether she wanted to keep her on.

With the slightest of frowns and a bow, Biggs, hovering nearby, excused himself and went to investigate the argument that had grown fiercer.

The voice was that of their new cook. Fitz had taken a notion to hire the histrionic Frenchman when their old cook retired. He'd done so without consulting the lady of the house—either of them, his wife, or his mother.

No delicate souffle was worth the upset among the kitchen staff. The current Lady Loughton hadn't had the heart to chastise Fitz for dabbling in her domain, and Neda had held off from interfering.

No longer, though. "Barnham, I must see to this. You go on ahead in the baggage carriage, and I'll follow in the coach presently."

Biggs might handle the immediate problem in the kitchen, but the new cook needed to be dismissed and replaced. Her daughter-in-law would thank her later for her meddling.

The role of chatelaine had been hard to relinquish when her

widowed son Fitz inherited and remarried. Sooner or later Neda must remove herself to the dower house.

She'd just dash off a note to the steward to handle the matter.

"My lady?" Barnham prodded.

Neda took the valise from her and shooed her on, then beckoned the coachman, Martin. An old family retainer, the sturdy fellow had put each of the Lovelace children on his or her first pony and had risen from groom to his current station.

"Squawking again, is he," Martin muttered.

She ignored his impertinence—he was impervious to corrections anyway. "Send the baggage coach on with my maid. We'll leave in a few minutes and catch up later."

He left, grumbling about the horses standing out in the cold too long.

She smoothed out the unwelcome letter from her daughter. The guest Nancy had added to the Yuletide party could only stay a few days and would leave well before Christmas eve. Dealing with the cook would not delay her departure long enough to avoid him. Perhaps she could take a longer route to Derbyshire or stay longer at each stop.

In the library, she took pains with her note for the steward, then returned to the hall, contemplating other ways to delay her travel.

Outside, the coach with the baggage had disappeared, but a rider was approaching at a gallop.

Bad news? Had some one of her children or grandchildren fallen ill? Had her daughter Nancy miscarried?

Alarmed, she stepped out, barely feeling the cold.

Biggs had settled the dispute in the kitchen and hurried past her to accept an express. He passed coins to the rider, who refused hospitality, lifted his hat, and turned back down the lane.

In the courtyard, Martin paced while a groom soothed the restless horses.

The letter Biggs handed her was addressed to Lord Loughton, but a glance at the seal showed that it had been sent a few days earlier from the school her two youngest, James and Edward attended. The letter had been misdirected more than once.

She breathed a silent prayer that neither of her sons was ill or injured, and with shaking fingers, cracked the seal and unfolded the paper.

Fourteen-year-old James had departed the school without permission along with a friend. Under close questioning, Edward had finally revealed the boys were traveling to witness a prize fight at an inn near Kettering.

Dear James. If he was in her clutches right now, she'd be tempted to birch him soundly, something she'd never done.

Perhaps she ought to have. What was she to do with him?

She beckoned Martin, thinking. Kettering wasn't far, but it was in the opposite direction of Derbyshire. If she traveled there to fetch James, and then went on to Rugby for Edward, she would certainly delay her arrival at the Yuletide party. Lindhorst would be gone before Christmas eve. She could dodge the pesky, flirtatious, too-handsome-for-his-own-good earl.

Too handsome and a full eight years younger than herself.

Well then; she'd gather up James and his unnamed friend, and then they'd fetch Edward at school, and travel on to Derbyshire and with luck arrive after Lindhorst's departure.

"What do you know about a prizefight near Kettering?" she asked Martin.

He lifted his hat and scratched his head. "Kettering?"

"Don't play stupid, Martin."

He had the nerve to chuckle.

Over the years, he'd snatched one Lovelace boy or another out of inns, rescued them from the occasional brawl before too much damage had been done, and covered up other indiscretions. He had his finger on the pulse of all the illicit activities a young gentleman might get into.

"Yes, Kettering," she said. "On the way there, I'll consult my copy of Paterson's Roads. We will ask at the inns along the way."

CHAPTER 2

Two days earlier, 13ᵗʰ December 1824
On the Rugby Road

"Now what?" Gordon Sommerton dusted dirt from his gloved hands and pulled at the torn shoulder of his coat.

"Stop complaining," said his companion and schoolmate, James Lovelace. "Another wagon will be along soon, and you'll see. This one will be an upstanding farmer instead of a bloody rogue. Did you see his eye after I planted him a facer?"

"At least you haven't lost your hat," Gordon grumbled.

"Ack. Don't forget this was your idea."

"And you're the one who said transport would be easy. I'm the one who has a place for us to stay. Do you suppose they're looking for us yet?"

"Mebbe. Edward promised to hold out under questioning as long as possible. But we'll make Kettering in time to see the mill before they catch up to us. At least then they'll finally agree to send us off to the army."

"My uncle will never allow his heir to join up."

❄

15ᵀᴴ Dᴇᴄᴇᴍʙᴇʀ, Rugby School

"Damn your foolishness, Edward. Mother is missing."

Fitzhenry Lovelace, Lord Loughton, gripped his younger brother's coat and gave him a shake.

"Missing?" Real concern shone in the freckled face, and his voice had resonated with the squeaky crackling of his twelve years.

The day had been a bloody confusion of troubling messages and hard riding. Accompanied by his brother-in-law, Simon, he'd left at dawn to meet up with his mother, the dowager Lady Loughton, and escort her from her inn to the Swillingstone estate. He'd been hoping to surprise her; instead, as only Mother could arrange, he'd been the one knocked off kilter.

He'd run into one messenger from his brother George, who had stopped at their younger brothers' school in Rugby, and then another from his loyal butler, Biggs who'd puzzled out that she was headed for the same destination.

Now here they were, in Rugby.

"Yes, missing," Fitz said. "She was supposed to be coming here to fetch you and James."

A maid appeared with a tray loaded with sandwiches, and George directed her to a cleared table.

"Fitz, Simon," George said. "Take some refreshments and let's think about how to proceed."

His brother George was always the steady voice of reason. He and his wife Sophie had decided to leave earlier than expected from their home in Lancashire to gather up his stepson and younger brothers instead of having them travel on their own by stagecoach.

Simon filled a plate and handed it to Fitz. "I'll warrant she went to Kettering to snatch up James herself. Woe betides him. Your mama is a formidable foe."

James and one of his good friends had departed school on Sunday, sneaking away to attend a mill.

Fitz shoved a sandwich into his mouth and washed it down with gulp of small beer.

"Well, then," he said. "I'm off to Kettering."

"It will be dark before you reach there." Simon shook his head. "I'm coming with you."

"I will as well," George said. "Sophie will keep a guard on Edward and Arthur at the inn."

"No, George, you stay here in case... just in case. Send a messenger with any news."

NEAR KETTERING

15th December

By the time her coach approached the decent-sized inn on the outskirts of Kettering, the sun had disappeared behind a shield of clouds as gray as the pall covering Neda's spirits.

The Hound and the Hare was the third inn they'd stopped at in this quest. Her polite inquiries at the others along the way had been fruitless. Martin and her groom, Jasper, had questioned the ostlers at each location. As to whether two boys of fourteen had passed through, he'd found no answers, but he'd learned that The Hound and the Hare was the inn closest to the farmer's field where the boxing match was to take place.

When they arrived, the yard teemed with traveling chaises, phaetons, and curricles, and they waited long minutes before an ostler approached.

Neda pushed open the coach door, and Jasper hastened to put down the step.

"This must be the place," Martin said. "Want as I should go in and ask, my lady, so as the young master isn't embarrassed by his mama snatching him up by his neckcloth?"

She shook her head, anger stiffening her spine. "He *ought* to be embarrassed." If she were a man, she'd thrash him. Perhaps Martin, as well. "And you're impertinent. Be prepared to leave immediately as soon as I bring him out."

"If they have a fresh change of cattle," Martin said. "Horses can't go on much further. Mayhap we can stay the night—"

The door of the inn opened, and noisy laughter poured out.

"My lady," Martin leaned in, "let me do the snatching up. No telling what…men in their cups—"

"No." Exasperation sparked in her, laced thoroughly with anger. "And we'll not stay the night here."

It had been a long day—a long year with her mischievous son. It was a wonder that Nancy's husband, Simon, would allow him into his home after the antics James had pulled at the Midsummer's Eve party that year. Itching powder in a duke's clothing, of all things.

Never mind that Simon had forgiven Nancy, who'd been complicit in the caper. That was different. Simon had made her his duchess, and now she was carrying his child.

"I'll see to this, Martin and then we'll leave. Do your best about the horses. There will be a quieter inn a little further along the road where we may stop before night falls."

Muttering and shaking his head, Martin turned and whispered to Jasper, who hastened after her protectively.

"I'll just stay close while you make inquiries, my lady," Jasper said.

The inn door was held open by a gentleman whose perfect waterfall knot had forked into two decidedly separate streams.

She drew her cloak tighter and set her face into a haughty mask. She was far past her prime, and a lady, and she'd managed to raise four spirited males to respectable manhood. She could do this.

As she reached the door, an older man with an apron—surely the innkeeper—rushed to meet her. "Let the lady pass, if you please, sir," he said, leading her inside.

At least he'd seen that she was not some doxy coming in to accommodate a room full of rowdy drunks. And surely such women were much younger. She might look well enough, but she saw the wrinkles in her mirror every morning.

A rush of distinctly warm air hit her as she stepped onto the stone floor of the entry hall, along with the odors of damp wool, masculine cologne, spirits, and horse.

Gentlemen had spilled out from the tap room into the inn's hall. As if running a gauntlet, Neda followed the innkeeper, conscious of giggles, whispers, and heated glances, while the proprietor chided the drunken oafs with gentle obsequiousness.

Christmas greenery festooned the doorways, adding the faintest woodsy scent to the atmosphere. As inns went, The Hound and the Hare would be a pleasant stop, if one could sweep out all the present guests.

He led her to a reception desk and bent his head confidentially. "I fear I have no rooms available, madame," he said. "Bedchambers or private dining rooms."

"Because of the prize fight?"

With a grimace and a frown, he sighed. "I had heard a rumor it was to be held, er, nearby."

Prize fights were illegal. He was probably running his own betting book on the match.

"A rum piece of work it was too."

She glanced over her shoulder at the speaker. A youngish man with glazed eyes had moved closer. More bosky faces filled the doorway to the tap room.

"Be assured," Neda said, "I'm not seeking lodgings, nor am I planning to call in the justice of the peace."

Likely the local justice of the peace had attended the fight, winking away any legal concerns.

"I'm looking for a very young man, traveling with another young friend."

"I'm young," the drunken lout said. "Will I do?"

Behind him, laughter erupted, catcalls, and other offers.

She corralled her temper and looked back at the innkeeper, lowering her voice. "My fourteen-year-old son, James Lovelace. Tall for his age, with blond hair. I don't know his friend's name. His brother, Lord Loughton, is very concerned."

The innkeeper blanched at the mention of a title. "God's truth, my lady, he's not here. I've been working the tap all afternoon and I would have remembered."

"Did you attend the fight yourself?"

The innkeeper's cheeks bloomed with color, and he hesitated.

"Please. I just want to find him."

"Not a big crowd today," he said. "Weren't any young ones there that I didn't recognize."

"MIGHT AT LEAST HAVE EXPECTED a second round," Lindhorst's tablemate grumbled. A middle-aged brewer from Kettering, he was one of a few men from the middling sort in this crowd of popinjays and Corinthians.

Better dressed though, and slightly more sober.

"Did your man win?" Lindhorst asked. "I barely made it in time to see the knockout punch."

When he'd finally reached The Hound and the Hare and hastened to the nearby field to survey the attending crowd, the fight had already begun. When it ended too soon, the rowdy crowd of disappointed men retired to the tap room to while away the day and drown their sorrows. He decided to join them before moving on to the next likely place.

The other fellow laughed. "That feisty Irishman is likely hightailing it back to Ireland before his opponent has the chance to die."

A commotion in the entry hall had heads turning and excitable men shoving their way to an attraction outside the barroom door.

"There's a well-rigged frigate asking about a boy," someone called.

"Send her in. I have a lap for her."

"A proper lady, a prime article, not a whore."

"Then why's she here?"

"I told you, she's looking for a lad."

"Is she pretty? Here I am."

"Pretty enough if you like them your ma's age."

Words and fragments of phrases reached Lindhorst, tickling his intuition.

"Blonde," someone called.

"No higher than a…"

"Son is Lord Lough…"

He tossed a few coins on the table, bid the brewer farewell, and strode toward the door, jostling drunken fools out of the way. By the time he'd elbowed his way through the gawkers, he found the innkeeper stepping back inside from the cold.

CHAPTER 3

"The lady," Lindhorst said, squaring up on the innkeeper. "Where is she?"

"She's just left, sir. Wouldn't wait for fresh horses."

"What was her name?"

"Sir, she's a respectable… Her privacy… I wouldn't want to…"

Lindhorst pressed a coin into the man's hand. "I'm Lindhorst," he said.

Though he himself hadn't been recognized, the Earl of Lindhorst was well-known in these parts, more for ill than good, though the ill days of his father were long past. Past, but not forgotten among the wary locals.

"And if the lady is who I think she is, her eldest son is a friend," he said. "He wouldn't want one of these louts molesting her."

The innkeeper looked down at the half-crown in his hand, his lips twitching as he came to his decision. "Lady Loughton," he whispered. "Looking for her son of fourteen. Left school with a friend to… to, er, attend the event. Though I didn't see the lad."

Nor had he. Either lad.

"Where was she going next?"

"I sent her on to The George," he said.

Lindhorst strode out, calling for his horse. Despite the lofty name, The George was two steps below The Hound and the Hare. Very few of these sporting so-called gentlemen would have gone there seeking shelter.

Would a pair of boys have ventured that far?

He knew Lady Loughton's son James, a lad only slightly more badly behaved than his own nephew and heir, Gordon Sommerton.

Gordon was James's friend and schoolmate and the named subject of the letter sent by express and stowed in his very pocket. He'd been silently cursing the lad for disrupting his visit to Swillingstone's house party.

Perhaps now he would thank him.

NEDA PULLED the carriage blanket higher, regretting that the hot bricks at her feet had grown frigid. Though it was still the afternoon, the gloom had thickened. There would be rain, or if it continued to grow colder, snow. With perhaps ice in between.

The tired horses had slowed to a mere walk and now stopped. She peered out but saw no evidence of an inn or other dwelling.

"Why are we stopping?" she called up to Martin.

A horse appeared next to her window, the rider swathed in a many-caped great coat, with a tall beaver shading his face.

The man brought his mount closer, and she lowered the window and strained to hear the words he exchanged with her coachman.

A shiver went through her, the low baritone setting her nerves on edge.

Jasper appeared at her window. "His lordship says The George ain't safe for a lady alone."

"Lord who?" she asked.

Jasper stepped aside and another face appeared. "Lindhorst, my dear."

Lindhorst.

Oh feathers, of all the gentlemen offering help, why must it be him?

"At your service, my lady. I happened to be at the inn you just left and learned from the innkeeper about your quest."

Nerves jangling, her mind raced with alarm and... questions. "You attended the boxing match?"

"I happened upon it just as it was ending. And no, your son was not there. I can also affirm that I did not see him among the crowd at The Hound and the Hare."

She nodded. "Martin, let's push on. Good day to you, my lord."

Lindhorst eyed her a too-long moment, and then his face crinkled in the dimpled smile that ladies found so charming.

Heaven help her—that she found charming as well.

He disappeared from her view and as the carriage rolled forward, she leaned back against the squab and pressed a hand to her chest, willing her heart to stop pounding, willing the warmth Lindhorst always incited to cool. Yes, she was charmed, and truth to tell, a bit relieved to have more than Martin and Jasper to help her. What if...

She squeezed her eyes shut. No, Neda Lovelace was, for heaven's sakes, respectable; responsible. She had children who were still young. She couldn't shame her boys by engaging in a mad fling. Couldn't and wouldn't, and that was that.

WHEN THEY ARRIVED at The George, Lindhorst dismounted and went to open the coach door before the groom could reach it. A few gentlemen's gigs crowded in with humble carts and wagons, and the sound of raucous laughter signaled that the crowd here might be even less refined than the one at The Hare and Hound.

He might have galloped ahead and talked to the innkeeper before her coach pulled into the innyard, but he knew that would win him no points with Neda. And he desperately wanted those points.

Lindhorst yanked the door open, and she edged forward on her seat.

"My lady," he said, blocking her exit, "will you allow me to make the inquiries while you wait here?"

"He's my son. This is my mission, not yours."

The inn door burst open, a roar pierced the air, and bodies tumbled out. Two men had stripped off their coats and begun thrashing each other, while a circle of others stood at a distance exchanging bets and calling encouragement.

She frowned and looked up at him. "This is just the sort of place James might frequent. Perhaps you could accompany me? If you'll but put down the step?"

Instead of dropping the step, he reached in and scooped her out, carefully depositing her on a dry spot in the innyard.

"At least they're not blocking the door," he said, ignoring her irate expression.

Setting a protective hand at her waist, he put himself between her and the informal mill, and they skirted the group of fighters and watchers.

Inside, The George was as he'd remembered it from previous stops, a sagging, half-timbered Elizabeth structure in need of a new roof and paint.

The innkeeper came around the bar to greet them. With most of the crowd outside for the fisticuffs, the only remaining patrons were passed out from drink or were wavering on the cusp of oblivion.

"Sir," he said, bowing. "Madam."

The innkeeper had assessed her attire and bearing and donned a measure of respectfulness. At least the man knew a lady of quality when he saw her.

"Well if it ain't Lindhorst."

The greeting came from one of a pair of young bucks.

Lindhorst sighed. Stewart Chaney lolled on a bench at a nearby table, next to another drunken lout, Horace Pickworth, much younger brother of the execrable Elliot Pickworth.

Younger sons of peers, they'd been let loose on the town to sow their wild oats until their fathers pulled in the reins and packed them off to the army, the church, or the inns of court.

Lindhorst turned his fiercest frown on them, the one he'd had occasion to use on Gordon.

Chaney, leaned from his seat, blowing beer breath and almost falling before righting himself. "Brought one of your doves," he said in a stage whisper.

Pickworth laughed.

Lindhorst, his hand still at her waist, felt Neda stiffening.

"Here now," the innkeeper said, turning on the two young bucks. "I'll not have you—"

"Allow me." Lindhorst cut off the innkeeper's rebuke, abandoned Neda to his care, and yanked Chaney out of his seat.

Astonishment lit the lad's face as Lindhorst steadied him. Pickworth, a hair more sober, wobbled to his feet, looking almost as surprised.

"Don't mind him, Lindhorst," Pickworth said. "He's spoony. Don't know what he's saying."

Chaney giggled.

Lindhorst gave him a little shake. "Does he have the wits to apologize?"

"He does. Don't you, Chaney? Tell his lordship you're sorry. I ain't in no condition to serve as your second."

"Wha-at?" Chaney teetered, almost falling backward.

"You are sorry you insulted the lady," Lindhorst said.

"Lady? Who?"

Lindhorst sighed and let go. Chaney staggered, clung to the bench, and tipped it over, before struggling to stand again.

Chaney's father was a high stickler, not a particular friend, but nevertheless they were on speaking terms. "Your father and I—"

"No, no, no," Chaney said. "Not the old man. Don't tell him. Please. Sorry. Sorry, my lord, madam."

Lindhorst felt a tug on his arm.

"Leave it," Neda said, turning to the innkeeper. "I'm looking for my son. He's a bit younger than those two," she waved a hand, "but I fear just as silly. Tall for his age. He was traveling with another lad to attend the prize fight. Have you seen him?"

He frowned, scratching his head. "No, madam. Even in this crowd I would have noticed them. Did you want a room, er rooms? I'm afraid mine are all taken, though mayhap some one of these fellows will give one up."

"Could they have gone somewhere else?" Neda asked.

"There's The Hound and the Hare—"

"We've come from there."

Her voice had taken on a strained note, and the innkeeper noticed.

"I'm sure there's no need to worry. Further down the road you'll reach The Wild Stag. But will you sit a moment and take some, er, refreshments first?"

Neda did look pale, but they wouldn't stay a moment longer than necessary in this place.

"Send hot drinks out for the lady's coachman and groom. Something hot for the lady, and a basket of food as well." Lindhorst leaned in, close to her ear. "I know the place," he said.

He tossed coins on the bar. "Those drinks and victuals right away, landlord. Come, my dear, before that crowd returns inside."

He hurried her to the coach and helped her in. A fine drizzle had started, the air had grown noticeably colder, and she was unexpectedly quiet.

Before he closed the door, she gripped his hand. "Lindhorst—"

"No. We won't worry yet. Or at all."

Frowning, she opened her mouth for what might be a tongue-lashing, but the innkeeper and a maid carrying steaming mugs interrupted them, promising to bring the food basket forthwith.

"Drink up. I daresay your lad is not so foolish that he can't find shelter." And there *was* shelter nearby. The boys would easily find their way there before freezing to death.

The fight outside had broken up, and curious eyes were turning their way. Worse, he spotted Pickworth approaching.

He reached in and squeezed her free hand. "I know another likely place to look," he said. "Please trust me." Closing the door, he signaled the coachman to wait a moment for the innkeeper's wife who was hurrying their way with the basket.

When he turned around, he found Pickworth at his elbow. "That's Lady Loughton," he said in a low voice. "You sly... Elliot told me about the wager."

Swallowing the urge to bash the lad, he leaned close until Pickworth's eyes stopped glittering.

Ah, the power of a steely glare.

"Yes. Hold your tongue, there's a good lad. When a lady needs assistance, a gentleman helps her. He doesn't gamble on her virtue. He doesn't slander her good reputation. If he *is* a gentleman."

He watched the color flash darker in the younger man's face and then drain under Lindhorst's merciless stare.

He hadn't noticed Pickworth there. Might he have also missed James and Gordon?

"There's no need for us to quarrel and be required to meet, Pickworth. You're the least knackered of any fellow I've seen today. Did you attend the mill?"

Pickworth rubbed his throat as if Lindhorst had actually grabbed it, and nodded.

"Did you see two young lads, about fourteen or fifteen in the crowd?"

"No." Pickworth's brows furrowed. "Not of the gentry sort, not that I noticed. Wasn't that big of a crowd that I'd have missed them though."

"And you're the sort to notice things. Well. Not a word about the lady, or her son. Or me, for that matter."

It was hopeless of course. Pickworth would tell his brother, and the news would be all over town.

Seeing that Jasper had stowed the food basket inside the coach, Lindhorst clamped his hat down tighter and strode to his horse, thinking. Perhaps they ought to have searched the stables at each inn to see if they'd taken shelter in the hayloft. But no, likely someone would have seen them there, and he couldn't imagine Gordon making do with straw bedding unless he absolutely had to.

The letter had been delayed. Perhaps they'd changed their minds and returned to their school or gone on to... where? Not Loughton

Manor, or else Neda wouldn't be searching. Not his own estate in Bedfordshire. There was a place much closer where they might have taken refuge, one he'd brought Gordon to during the school break.

A blast of rain stung his cheeks, driven along on a bone chilling wind.

Neda might not like it, but they'd have to stop, to spend the night under the same shabby roof, and without much in the way of staff to serve them. They simply couldn't go on in this weather.

LINDHORST'S MOUNT and buckskin-clad legs passed Neda's coach window, and she heard his rumbling exchange with Martin, though she couldn't make out a word of what was said. Perhaps he was giving directions to the Wild Stag.

Oh, but this was Lindhorst. Anything was possible with him. What was this other place he was talking about?

She pulled the carriage rug around herself and settled back—frazzled, fuming, and altogether frantic. Also freezing. She could read the weather signs—snow would be coming soon, but before the white blanket fell, this rain would turn to ice. And James was somewhere out there in it.

She sent up a silent prayer. James wasn't her worst-behaved son—that honor had been earned by her eldest, Fitz. The tangles Fitz had got himself into hurt her heart. His father had pushed him into a marriage at too young of an age to a very pretty girl who was completely wrong for him.

And before that, the drinking, gambling, and... She shook her head. He'd kept an actress as a mistress, a secret that all his brothers and even his sisters seemed to know about. During his first marriage, like the other fashionables, including Lindhorst, Fitz had dabbled in adultery. He'd neglected his first wife and baby daughter. It was no wonder Alice had cheated on him with a scoundrel.

Lindhorst had been part of the crowd Fitz ran with in those days. A much older member of the crowd, and a terrible influence. In public, she was courteous to him; in her heart, she'd never been able to forgive him.

Whatever help Lindhorst gave her today would no doubt come with unpleasant strings attached.

Or... What perhaps made her the wariest: those strings might not be unpleasant at all.

She'd been widowed for two years. Her vows to Henry had been her armor against temptation; but now he was gone.

Handsome, well-spoken, rich... and now widowed himself, Lindhorst was much in demand by society hostesses and mamas looking for husbands for their daughters. Mamas who had no thought to the wretchedness of their girls being mismatched with an older man whose inconsiderate neglect had driven his late wife to run off to Paris where she'd succumbed to a fatal illness.

The firmly muscled, buckskin-clad legs appeared in her window again, and she gritted her teeth. She wasn't indifferent to men; she just wasn't free yet. She had responsibilities to the two boys still left. Thank heavens her youngest, Edward was as sensible as...

She would have said Nancy, except memories of her youngest daughter's antics at the Midsummer's Eve party flooded her.

She leaned back again. Lindhorst had fixed himself by her window, the gentle gait of his mount keeping pace with the coach.

Her son George said that Lindhorst had changed. Was that possible? Might she trust him? In truth, she had very little choice now but to do so.

Letting down the window, she poked her head out and the freezing rain stabbed her. Martin and Jasper and the horses must be miserable. "Where are we going? We must stop soon."

"We will," Lindhorst called down. "Do not worry. I know this country."

She closed the window in frustration and huddled deeper into her lap rug. If only one of her sons, Fitz, or George, or Rupert, or Selwyn were here. If only it was one of them riding alongside her carriage and telling her not to worry.

The coach turned onto a lane and despite their slow pace the rear wheels skidded, the carriage body bobbled and then righted itself. The rain must be turning to ice.

They rolled on a bit further and with a loud crack the coach fishtailed and listed right. The horses shrieked, Martin cursed, she grabbed for the hand strap, and as if in a bad dream, heard herself scream.

CHAPTER 4

"Broke a wheel." Jasper called frantically.

Neda forced the door and slid easily to the ground. While Martin and Jasper struggled with the carriage horses, Lindhorst brought his well-trained mount closer in an effort to help soothe the distraught animals.

Mere feet ahead of them she saw the problem, and it sent her heart clacking and pounding. The loud crack had not been just the wheel. A tree, a huge elm laced with heavy ice, had fallen, obstructing most of the road.

Praise God that they'd been picking their way so slowly up the slick lane. A few moments faster and they would have been under that tree. She and her servants might have been crushed. Lindhorst might have been crushed.

She caught him glancing back at her and dismounting.

"Neda."

He hurried to her, and her heart lurched. Water streamed from the brim of his hat, his face rugged and grim, and as handsome as ever.

"Are you well?"

Sudden tears threatened—of relief, of gratitude. She swallowed them down. "It's a miracle we weren't under that…" She pointed at the felled elm. "Are the horses injured?"

"Not that I see. We'll know better when we get them unhitched."

"Martin and Jasper?"

"They did well, considering. No one took a tumble. Let's get you out of this rain and cold. Will you wait in the coach?"

"For how long? Will you go for help?"

He tucked her hand over his arm and nudged her along. "Wait here a few moments while I help them. Gather what you want to bring with you."

"You mean for us to walk in this weather?" She squeezed her eyes shut. "I'm sorry. I don't mean to be missish."

LINDHORST HELPED her into the coach, resisting the urge to kiss her.

He'd found another reason why he so admired this lady. She might have a wild hair that made her chase after her son foolishly, but she had the grace to apologize for getting them into this predicament.

"No apology needed. You've had a shock on top of all your worries and are entitled to be tetchy. Right now, we need to get ourselves and the horses out of this freezing rain, and quickly. I'm going to talk to your men and make a plan."

Pressing her lips together, she nodded.

She was putting herself into his hands reluctantly, he could tell. Ultimately, she wouldn't like where they were going, but it was better than any other alternatives.

Despite their frozen fingers, the two servants worked quickly and led the horses away from the downed carriage.

"Where to, milord," the coachman asked. "Got to get these fellows somewhere warm."

"We're halfway between the George and a manor house I know of. Take them back to the George. Have their feet looked at." He passed over some coins. "They'll make room for you in the stables. Lady

Loughton and I will go on to Pheasant Run and find safer shelter for her there."

"We're meant to go with her," the coachman said.

"Commendable of you to mention it. I know this place, and they're not going to have much feed, nor a farrier handy. And The George is no shelter for a lady right now."

The stubborn man chewed on the thought and watched the horses stamping, one of them favoring a leg.

"Lord Loughton won't like it."

"I know. I'll square it with him when we meet. And I'll see that she's safe."

He nodded. "Known the lady all me life. You'd best do that, milord."

Lindhorst blinked. He wouldn't normally take such cheek from a servant, but he had to respect the fellow's loyalty.

On the other hand, perhaps if the coachman had been a little more insolent, a little less loyal, she wouldn't be in this predicament.

The man beckoned the other servant. "We'll see to these cattle and find our way to Pheasant Run later."

Lindhorst nodded. "And get that wheel fixed once the weather clears. Don't you bloody freeze to death, or her ladyship will skin me alive."

NEDA SLUNG her reticule on her wrist, passed Lindhorst her valise and the basket, and then slid from the coach to the icy ground—and kept sliding until Lindhorst caught her neatly and pulled her close, wrapped in his free arm and his greatcoat. She was too cold and too grateful for warmth to object.

His horse stood nearby, and they picked their way to it carefully. She'd watched Martin and Jasper lead the carriage horses away, back toward that hideous inn. Perhaps the innkeeper and his wife would let her shelter in their own parlor, if they had one in their quarters.

In moments she was settled—awkwardly sidewise upon

Lindhorst's mount. While she clung to the saddle, he secured their belongings and flung himself up behind her. His arms came around her with more intimacy than was proper—though she supposed it was better than falling off. And warmer. Much warmer.

Tucking one leg up as if she rode side saddle, she faced forward, held her breath, and ducked her head against the turmoil brewing inside her. He'd nestled her closer and brought the capes of his greatcoat around both of them. It was gentlemanly, and lovely, and so far, innocent. Though the promise of more was certainly there. All she had to do was say yes.

She shivered, and he drew her tighter against him.

Must. Not. Shiver. The closeness was intimate and tempting. She tried to remember if Henry had ever held her thusly. No—he'd preferred to travel in a carriage when they were together.

Henry had been thorough and prudent in everything. The only exception, the only impulsive deviation, had led to their hurriedly called banns. That was a secret kept carefully from the children.

The unexpected touch, and warmth, and strength of a man—she remembered, and she missed it. How bad was Lindhorst, truly? Had he dispensed with his earlier wildness, as Fitz had?

Lindhorst tipped his head and water sluiced down on her from his hat brim, jarring her back to her senses and bringing forth an apology.

"I suppose my bonnet has completely deflated," she replied, shivering.

A cashmere scarf, warm from his body, redolent with his scent, settled over her head and she grabbed the ends of it with one hand, astonishment tying her tongue.

He was a scoundrel, wasn't he? If he wasn't, if he had reformed... Oh, she was in deep trouble.

"Thank you," she said, mustering speech. "If only we had an umbrella."

"It's all above ice on this road," he murmured, the deep baritone sending waves of heat through her.

The statement had been a non-sequitur if ever there was one; was he worried, or just ignoring her? Or perhaps, he was just as unsettled as she was.

"And we can't gallop," he mused. "It's not far though."

The murmur, the increased intimacy stirred her nerves to new heights of buzzing. Pride made her shove down the tingles, straighten her spine and curve it into a bow away from his chest... pride and a healthy dose of caution. She must remember his past reputation. Lindhorst would attempt to muddle her senses. To try her on as if she were... some opera dancer, or wicked widow, or... Heavens. The scent he wore she remembered from their dances in London—bergamot and perhaps a hint of cinnamon—now mixed with a faint and not unpleasant musk. Under the fine clothes he was muscle and brawn. He was fitter than Henry, who'd grown a bit portly and slack in later years.

But portly Henry had been older. His little paunch had not begun expanding until his late forties.

A muscled arm tucked her tighter, sending another, more intense wriggle of desire through her.

Oh, oh, oh.

Guilt stabbed her, as if she was being adulterous. She felt... unfaithful.

And flat-out silly. No matter how desirous he was, she wasn't going to dally with a younger man. She was old. More than a little shriveled. Though she was not quite dried up yet, her best years were certainly behind her.

He would be happy to amuse himself with her, but she didn't wish to be toyed with. In fact, it was downright offensive for him to do so as if there really was some wager in the betting books at White's.

Yes, certainly, that must be it. When they reached the inn...

She lifted her head, looked around, and panic rose, almost choking her. "This is not the way back to The George. Where are you taking me?"

❄

LADY LOUGHTON'S LAST WAGER

LINDHORST SWALLOWED AN UNGENTLEMANLY CHUCKLE. She was so petite, and fit so well in his arms, and she had no idea how alluring she was.

"Pheasant Run. It is a manor house just up this lane."

"Whose manor house?"

"As it happens, it is mine."

He couldn't tell whether the tremor that ran through her was excitement or worry.

"And who resides there?"

"The recently hired steward, who is supervising renovations, and his sister who serves as housekeeper and cook for now. Along with a couple of grooms. Though at present the only horses there are the steward's mount, a couple of draft horses, and a donkey or two. There is not an abundance of feed, nor is there a farrier there to see to that carriage horse's limp."

Her long angry huff did nothing to ease her stiff posture.

"Yes, it's true," he said. "We will be unchaperoned. At our ages, who will care?"

Her continued silence simmered between them.

"Do not worry, my dear. I'll get you there safely. There'll be a fire and warm drinks for us and more food than what we have in the basket, though I can't say the fare will match what is served up by The George." It might be better.

Farley, his new steward, had been an ambitious and reliable man at his main estate in Bedfordshire before being promoted to this new position. On Lindhorst's last visit to Pheasant Run, he'd brought Gordon, and they'd stayed at the nearby inn, visiting Farley to discuss the work underway and review the bills coming in for building materials, coal, and other necessities.

His father had used the estate for disreputable hunting parties that scandalized the local people. In the decades since, it had fallen into a drafty, leaking wreck with broken windows and sagging floors. The roof repairs had been completed by a crew brought in from his main estate, but Farley was having trouble finding good local workers for the rest. He was hopeful more would come around soon for good wages and a more respectable employer than the last Earl of Lindhorst.

It would be an expensive endeavor. No furniture would be ordered until they decided what could be salvaged from the attic and lumber room. Farley reported that he'd scrounged an adequate bed for the chamber Lindhorst occupied. It was the only room with a bed—the steward and his sister had a cottage a stone's throw away, and the grooms lived above the stable.

"I intend to use it as a hunting box until my heir comes of age," Lindhorst said. *And it might take those full six years to make it shipshape.* "After that, it will be his to manage."

A violent shiver went through her.

"You're drenched," he said. Her rucked-up skirt revealed one shapely ankle. The wet, heavy cloth of her carriage gown was starting to freeze like the ground under the horse's hooves. He had good cause to be grateful that Icarus was a plodder, and as reliable as a horse could be.

The gelding's foot slipped, and Lady Loughton gasped. The loyal fellow quickly righted himself and stepped on, but warily.

"We should walk," she said quietly.

While they'd talked the rain had turned to snow and was blanketing the ice beneath.

He reined up. "Can you manage it, my lady?"

"Yes, of course. He'll be no good to us lame."

No complaints about her drenched garments, how cold she was, or her boots which were certainly ruined.

He slipped from the horse and lifted her down, impulsively bestowing a kiss on her cheek.

She looked up in shock.

"It's just around the next bend. Stout Icarus here can carry our baggage that short distance. Come; we may find better footing on the verge."

NEDA SAT SHIVERING before the kitchen fire, cradling a steaming earthenware mug in her still-gloved hands. Tendrils of warmth rose from the drink that Lindhorst had presented, bidding her to drink and then leaving to confer with the young man he'd introduced as his steward. Perhaps it was her imagination, but it seemed that steam was also rising from her thawing boots and skirts.

She chuckled and, finally a bit warmer, looked around. Ribbon-wrapped evergreen boughs here and there signaled an attempt at holiday cheer. The tidy kitchen was evidence of a female presence—the mostly tidy kitchen; a few unwashed dishes perched on a sideboard near covered platters.

Where was the female who ruled this realm?

Though the steward's missing sister niggled at her, she was still too cold to fret much about her absence. Outside the hearth's circle of heat, the room was almost as cold as outdoors. She missed Lindhorst's warmth.

She shook her head and chuckled again. The cold must have addled her—she was well on her way to *liking* Lindhorst.

Touching her lips to the rim of the mug, the scent of the drink assaulted her. The scant portion of strong tea had been drenched with warming spirits, a healthy dollop of them. She sniffed and took a sip. It was a well-sugared gin, a spirit she'd only tasted once. Not often a gentleman's drink, at least at Loughton Manor; Lindhorst must have grabbed the first bottle at hand.

To warm her, or to render her easier to seduce?

She took another careful taste and reminded herself—alone with an amorous man who'd made his interest clear, she needed to keep her wits about her if she didn't want to succumb to temptation.

He'd been a gentleman so far. Despite the snow and the cold, the walk had been invigorating, even with Lindhorst's steady arm around her. Perhaps more so with his arm around her.

What a henwit she was, all because a handsome, desirable man had shown her attention. She might as well be that sixteen-year-old girl again casting herself at a fetching rogue.

Oh, yes. When she was honest with herself, she recognized that

Henry had been a bit of a rogue, one who'd later teased her that she'd managed to tame him.

But he was different than Lindhorst and she was different than that young girl of sixteen, wasn't she?

She shivered again. What if Lindhorst wasn't really a shallow, callow, scoundrel?

He'd been kind to his servants, even kind to his horse. Icarus, Lindhorst had called the beast, with surprising affection. Before they'd even reached the manor house, they were spotted on the road by a groom who'd hurried out to take charge of the mount.

Then Lindhorst had scooped her up summarily and carried her the rest of the way to this kitchen. He'd draped a blanket over her and busied himself preparing this hot drink.

She took a healthier swig, letting the warmth swirl around inside her. A new wave of shivers wracked her, and exhaustion swept through her, along with shameful self-pity, and fear.

She'd failed James and, in the process, let herself fall into the hands of the disreputable, womanizing, desirable man who'd help to ruin her eldest son's first marriage.

Where was James? She ought to be thinking of him, not swanning about in her head over being alone with Lindhorst. James might be out there in this, cold, hungry, perhaps losing fingers to frostbite, or catching a chill like the one that killed his father.

She drained the cup. Her son might die while she—

"Ah, good. You've drunk all of it." Lindhorst had crept in so silently his words tickled her ear. "Come with me, my lady. You need to change out of those wet clothes."

Praise be. He must have found the missing sister who could help her undress and loan her a dry gown.

She staggered to her feet, alarm bells clanging as Lindhorst swept her up again.

"Is Miss Farley—"

"Do not worry," he said, his voice gentle. He must have heard the embarrassment in her squeaking voice. "Ah, here is Farley. Is all ready?"

Farley was descending the stairs as they were going up. He edged to the side, allowing them room to pass. "Yes, my lord," The younger man said. "I'll fetch some dinner for you and more tea."

He bowed and passed them, his bootheels clacking on the uncarpeted stairs.

"I have no clothes. I..." Her small valise held only toiletries and a fresh chemise, probably drenched also. What was she to wear?

If this was a hunting box... many so-called gentlemen brought ladies to these places. Would he give her one of his mistress's castoff night rails? There'd be no warmth in that sort of negligee. What she needed was a thick, humble flannel.

Or... "Is there something of Miss Farley's I might borrow?"

"You'll be modest and warm," he said blithely.

"In one of your Cyprian's gowns?" The words had come out more waspishly than she would have wished.

Oh, why should she care if he thought she was waspish. She'd had a devil of a day.

Lindhorst paused before a closed door. "I have brought no Cyprians here before you, and there will be none after."

His solemn tone had her head spinning.

The room they entered, a small bedchamber, smelled of fresh plaster, paint, and a roaring coal fire, the flames jumping in the drafty space. She glimpsed flimsy shutters closed over a window opening, leaking in frigid damp air through a seam in the shutters and cracks in the casing and sill. Near the hearth there was just enough room for two shawl-draped armchairs and a small table. On a far wall stood a clothes press, and in a far corner an antique screen.

And of course, the room held a tester bed. The four posts and canopy had been hung with rich blue velvet. The bedding looked newly laid, the coverlet and blankets folded back and ready to receive the person destined to lie here, the person who may or may not freeze in his or her sleep on a night like this.

The beckoning bed was wide enough—just barely— for two.

Lindhorst set her on her feet and began whisking away her

garments. First the deflated bonnet, then the blanket he'd draped over her in the kitchen.

She gasped as he pulled the sopping mantle from her, tossed it aside and, turning her, began unfastening her redingote with its attached fur capelet. When his long fingers reached the level of her breasts, she clamped a hand over his.

That had been a mistake. He'd noticed her gloves, the once soft kid molded and stiffening. Pausing, he tugged at the leather with a look of fierce concentration.

First one glove, finger after finger, and then the other, and when they were both off, his large warm hands swallowed her icy ones in a clasp that made her want to weep.

It was because of the drink. The spirits were muddling her.

"I shall get the rest," she said. "You may go."

He opened his mouth, shut it, and looked pointedly at the top of her gown. "You are able to manage the gown underneath the redingote on your own?"

Oh. Botheration and blast it. She'd expected to have met up with her maid by now or at least to have found herself at an inn with a female servant who might assist her.

She could rip the seams of the skillfully sewn gown, but then what would she wear on the morrow?

A tap at the door brought the steward and his laden tray.

"Mr. Farley," she called. "Will you please send for your sister to assist me?"

The young steward shifted from one foot to the other, increasing her vexation.

"My lady, I'm sorry," he said, finally. "She's gone to Peterborough for our sister's confinement. I expected her back by now, but the weather…"

Chest tightening, she held herself very still trying to quell the jumble of emotions, the only sounds the whistle of the wind through the poorly sealed window, Lindhorst's quiet voice dismissing the steward, and the snick of the door shutting.

CHAPTER 5

Large hands settled gently on her shoulders, and she looked into his eyes so very dark, and so very close to her own.

"You're a sensible woman, Lady Loughton. You can't stay in these wet clothes. There are only Farley and the grooms to help you. And me. You *know* me."

"Ah, yes." She gritted her teeth. He didn't *look* as if he were ready to pounce. Perhaps he wouldn't need to. Perhaps this wasn't fear making it hard to breathe but anticipation. Perhaps she would know him much better very soon.

She squeezed her eyes closed. "I *know* you, indeed. Get on with it, please."

His large hands slid her redingote off, and the long fingers worked the hooks of her dress, moving down her back more quickly than ever her maid could do. Lindhorst had experience at this sort of thing. If rumors were true, he'd undressed countless opera dancers, actresses, and the widows of some of his fellow peers.

The gown slid to the floor, and he held her hand, helping her step out of it. Her stays came next, and she was left shivering in a wet shift.

Before she could tell him to get out, he'd yanked the shift over her head and settled a dry, warmed garment in its place.

Heart pounding, she clutched at the garment. The crisp linen, the long sleeves… it was a shirt, a man's shirt that fell to below her knees, with an open, flapping neck that peeled back to reveal her small decolletage.

Dear Lord, she'd been naked. He'd seen her naked. *Bare-arsed* the boys would giggle. It was mortifying.

Would he crow about it in the clubs?

A man's heavy velvet robe engulfed her. She pulled the lapels tightly and caught her breath. A mistake… Lindhorst's scent filled her, addling her as much as the nearness of his fingers and hands disrobing her.

"There now."

His voice sounded as shaky as her own quaking heart. This was madness.

LINDHORST TURNED AWAY and went to the table, giving the lady a moment of… not privacy. He supposed he'd thoroughly disrupted any chance of that.

He, however, needed to still his own racing heart. Neda Lovelace was no lady bird, no opera singer, no member of the demimonde, though he'd more or less treated her as one of those tonight—without actually touching more than her hand.

Though he'd certainly been tempted. She was a lady, a beautiful one who didn't realize how attractive she still was. Seeing her naked…

He ought to be ashamed of himself, but he found he wasn't. She was, at last, out of those wet frozen garments, and—he lifted the dish covers to find heaps of carved ham, pickled vegetables, sliced bread— she would soon be well-fed.

He glanced back and found her staring into the fire, clutching the robe as if she wanted to disappear into it. The heel of one sodden boot peeked out—those would have to come off—and the coil of hair on the back of her head had slid drunkenly sideways, pins hanging loose from tendrils of lovely golden hair.

On impulse, he went to her and began pulling out pins.

She put up a hand, pointedly halting an inch from his own. "Do stop," she said frostily. "You are not my lady's maid. I can manage my hair on my own."

"Nevertheless," he said, and carried on until her hair fell loose and messy well past her shoulders. "Somewhere around here is a brush," he said, "but I think we ought to eat first. I fear it's a cold collation that Farley has brought us, or if not, it will be soon. Please take a seat, and I'll make you a plate."

The robe tightened around her as she hunched closer to the fire.

"And because you are a sensible lady who I'll warrant has had nothing to eat all day, I presume you will eat at least a little."

If for no other reason than to fight off my advances. He swallowed a chuckle. Best not say those words. She wasn't in the mood for teasing. Plus, he wasn't sure he could honestly frame it as teasing.

Farley had brought wine as well as steaming water. He set himself to fixing her tea, heaping sugar into it before bringing it to her.

She eyed it askance.

"No spirits in this one. Just sugar. You must drink it before it cools."

Pursing her lips, she accepted it and sniffed, while he moved a small table between the chairs. "Please, do sit, while I fetch you a plate."

She refused to converse, but seated herself and sipped at her cup, eyeing the ham and bread on the plate he brought her.

When he dropped to his knees and reached for her booted foot, her hand paused over the plate.

"What—"

"I fear these are ruined," he said, struggling to keep his tone business-like. "And they must come off, along with the wet stockings." He'd found a pair of clean stockings along with the dry shirt, too large for her, but at least her feet would be warm.

A glance showed that her face was unreadable, but when he'd removed the sodden footwear and reached for her garter, she swatted his hand away.

"Please," she said. "Go and eat."

He sat back on his heels. Sliding his hands up her leg to the garter —yes he'd better not, just yet.

He stood and handed her the dry stockings. "I'll pour us some wine."

Watching her from the corner of his eye, he glimpsed a bare, still shapely leg, and quickly turned away.

By the time he'd devoured a quick sandwich and returned with two glasses, she'd finished and tucked the robe around her legs.

"Thank you," she said solemnly accepting the wine. She frowned into the red liquid a long moment and then set aside the glass, jumped up, and paced the room.

His own glass in one hand, the other hand perched on the mantelpiece, he waited.

"I'm worried, Lindhorst," she said, clutching her hands to her heart. "Where is my son? Traveling in this weather, with, heaven knows, perhaps very little money. He could freeze to death."

Not a tongue-lashing for the bold undressing, then. The lady continued to surprise him.

"Or he could be curled up in someone's barn," he said, "cold, but sheltering with livestock."

"You don't understand, Lindhorst," she said turning on him again. "How could you possibly understand? I've... I haven't lost a single one of my children. Oh, we had scrapes, and broken bones, and once a whole house down with the measles and... You can't imagine, Lindhorst."

Hands fisted, her eyes glimmered with unshed tears. "My James. Oh... there are times when I think, we ought to have stopped after Nancy, but James is delightful when he's not driving me mad. You can't imagine... the thought of losing..."

Pausing, she looked at him and then turned away.

The minutes ticked by before he could finally speak. "Because a father doesn't feel the loss as strongly as a mother?" he asked quietly.

"I... I don't know. My father showed no emotion when my brother and sister died." Her gaze fixed on him as if to ask, *did you?*

So, she'd remembered. He'd once had an heir and a spare and they'd both died within months of each other.

HER TONGUE HURT where'd she'd bitten off the words she wanted to hurl at him. Lord Lindhorst, known scoundrel and womanizer. He'd lost two sons, his only children. Had he felt anything? Or had he hidden a bleak grief under a proud mask?

Perhaps she'd been wrong about him.

"How did you bear it?" she asked.

He shrugged, setting the wine sloshing. "I drank and wenched heavily."

Cocky, self-assured, undignified. And yet, she suspected there was more underneath that swaggering exterior. She waited and saw his chest move as he released a breath.

"I can't bring them back. The schoolmate your son James left with? That boy is my nephew and heir, Gordon Sommerton. They're at school together, did you know? And they're good chums, and no doubt Gordy is as much a nodcock as James. But he's a nodcock who likes his comforts, and he would have found his way to shelter, dragging James along with him. I thought they would come here. He knows this will be his someday."

His nephew... his heir. He had as great a stake in the boys' safety as she herself did. Perhaps greater. And yet...

"Your heir is out in this weather, yet you don't appear very concerned."

He grimaced, set aside the glass of wine, and remained silent.

"Oh. I suppose nephews and cousins are thick on the ground for you," she said, prodding him, her own anger rising. "More heirs waiting behind Gordon. Is that why you're not worried?"

Some men in a temper lashed out with their tongues, some, she knew from tales told by her friends and acquaintances, with their fists. She'd been fortunate that Henry had never done more than hurl words, and that rarely.

For a long moment Lindhorst stared into the fire while she waited with bated breath for his reaction.

"I *am* worried," he said. "But I have faith that there is some common sense in the lad, and that he will find his way. He will be a man soon enough and if he spends one night shivering with a farmer's cows, he might learn to anticipate consequences. Since my brother's death a few years ago, I've become as fond of Gordy as if he were my own son." He picked up the wineglass and handed it to her. "Please. This will help you sleep. Please try not to fret."

How could he be so calm? The urge to rattle him more spurred her.

"As commendable as it is that you're fond of your heir, that you're even arranging this estate for him, it begs the question, Lindhorst: you lost your two boys years ago; why did you and your wife not have more children? She was young enough."

He stiffened and for a moment she thought she'd succeeded in stirring his temper. "That is a highly personal question, my lady."

"You have abducted me and carried me off to your hunting lodge. You've stripped me *naked*. I feel entitled to pry."

His eyes flashed with something like a warning. "And so, it follows, that if *you* see *me* naked, I may pry out your secrets?"

Heat flamed into her cheeks, and a stirring image of what he might look like under the coats and the linens sent her heart quaking.

Years of dealing with strong-willed Lovelace children carried her through, her gaze locked on his, her feet fixed to the floor until he finally grimaced and broke the contact.

"There is a night stool behind the screen," he said. "I'll return later to tend the fire. I'll endeavor to not disturb you."

The door closed on him, leaving her unsatisfied in so many ways. What, besides infidelity, had gone wrong in the Lindhorst marriage?

And what would Lindhorst look like under his coats and linens?

The answer to the first question was none of her business, and the second one…

She drained her glass, used the night stool and then turned down the lamp. Still wrapped in the heavy robe, she stretched on the bed and pulled even more covers over her, sending up a prayer, putting James and his friend Gordon into God's hands for safekeeping.

But sleep wouldn't come. Besides the cold wind whistling through the room so that she still couldn't get truly warm, she kept remembering the look in Lindhorst's face—his shrug, his cockiness, the grimace when she accused him of being unconcerned. And the warning thrust of flirtatiousness when she pried into his marriage. That had been a barrier put up to hide something. Some vulnerability.

And she'd rather not see him naked if he thought it might remove some of *her* barriers.

Shivering into the bedding, she closed her eyes, remembering how he'd warmed her on that short but very cold ride.

She must have managed to doze because when she opened her eyes, a gale force wind blowing icy bursts of snow had snuffed out the light and she saw a dark shadow fighting the flapping shutters.

LINDHORST KNELT at the bedchamber hearth stirring the fresh coal as stealthily as possible.

He'd awakened minutes earlier, shivering in front of the waning kitchen fire, his arse and back aching from the stiff wooden chair. He'd banked those coals and fled upstairs where he found another fire in need of fuel, plus a much softer chair.

One glance at the bed, and then he jerked his attention away. She'd left the lamp burning and in sleep, she looked younger, the worry lines softened, her golden hair loose on the pillow.

He was just settling onto the cushion when a loud crack brought a burst of icy air that doused the lamp and sprinkled snow across the wooden planking.

The shutters had sprung free, the brace holding them skittering across the floor. Uttering a curse, he hurried over, struggling to hold one shutter closed against the gale, while trying to grasp the other one.

"I have it."

Neda was there, wrangling the shutter to where he could reach it and slam it closed, and then bracing her back against it.

She was still swathed in her robe, soaked again, probably.

"There's no glass?" she exclaimed breathlessly.

"Can you fetch the bar? I think it flew near the—"

"I know where it is. I almost tripped over it."

In the dim light of the fire, he saw her dragging the heavy bar back. Working together they were able to heft it into place and secure all the latches.

"Won't the whirlwind knock the bar off again?" she asked.

She had a point. The blasted tools and nails had been cleared from this room. He'd have to find another way.

"Can you relight the lamp?" he asked. "There are spills on the mantel."

While she hastened to the hearth, he shoved and jostled the tall clothes press in front of the window.

The approaching light flickered in the draft. "That will help but a little," she said. "Perhaps the kitchen will be more snug."

"Or just more uncomfortable. At least here you have a bed. And if you will allow it, this chair is much easier on my backside than the one downstairs."

A long pause followed. He could almost hear her thinking.

"You're cold and your coats are wet."

"I've been colder and wetter. Before I inherited, I had a brief stint with Wellington in the Peninsula, with plenty a weak campfire." Not that he didn't prefer a warm bed. And with a warm lady in it...

He sighed, settling onto the chair and pulling a shawl around him. "I'll be fine, my lady."

She mumbled something and carried the lantern away. The bed ropes creaked, and the bedclothes rustled. "Lindhorst," she said, her voice soft. "I *am* sensible. Practical too. And very, very cold. I had to remove that wet dressing gown of yours. Whoever was meant to put in your windows ought to be birched. Now, there is just enough room here. You might as well shed the wet coats and get in this bed instead of catching your death in that chair."

He threw off his blanket and approached. "Are you sure?"

She lifted a hand and wagged it, eyes still closed. "It will be warmer for both of us. But no wet coats please."

He shed his coats and footwear, went to the other side, slipped under the bedcurtain and covers and turned on his side toward her.

Her back was to him. It would be easy enough to drape an arm over and draw her closer.

Instead, he rolled onto his back and stared up at the blue velvet.

The covers moved with what might be a chuckle. "Well, Lindhorst, it seems this is a cold night in hell. You have me in your bed."

"I don't recall that I ever said that I wanted you in my—"

"And I don't think much of your technique this night in achieving that goal. Go to sleep."

His technique? He supposed that being pursued by a man who everyone believed was a womanizer might make a lady think... Oh hell. He remembered what Elliot Pickworth had said after Lindhorst's dance with Lady Loughton: his pursuit of her was a matter for the betting book at White's.

Once she found out about that, all hope for something more honorable was lost for him.

"Thank you," he said. "Most unexpected. I shall not overstep."

Silence followed, and for a long time he thought she had fallen back to sleep.

He heard stirring and looked her way. She had turned on her side and was facing him.

"I am sorry," she said. "You may ask me prying questions if you wish, without disrobing. This is intimacy enough for me."

For now, it might be.

"Yours was a love match?" he asked, wondering what it would be like to be loved by this lady.

A long pause was followed by a sigh. "There was a strong attraction."

Not love, then. Perhaps he would have a chance, for he'd wager the lady felt an attraction for him.

"We grew to care for each other, though perhaps Henry's first love was business followed by politics."

The late Lord Loughton had been a keen man for investments and heavily engaged in the wartime parliament. He was very rich, and he'd taken a very rich bride.

"But you had a good and lasting relationship," he said. "You don't regret your marriage. You were an heiress as I recall. You might have had other choices."

"I miss Henry. I miss the companionship, the true friendship, as well as..." She waggled a hand. "Some things become less important over the years. As for other choices, I decided not to think about what might have been. Henry was a good husband and father. I was sixteen when we met. Henry... Henry was eight and twenty. Imagine? He always said I was older than my years, but I was not so old as to stop matters from getting too far one night in the summerhouse. But I didn't want to. Stop, that is. Fitz was a six-month baby."

"Was he indeed? I am shocked."

In truth, he *was* a bit shocked. Not at her, of course. He knew Henry Lovelace, Lord Loughton, as a personable, sensible, conservative man with no known vices except working too hard. Perhaps he'd had as wild a youth as many of his peers. How else could he have seduced a young girl and got her with child?

"Don't think badly of him. I was wicked then, and it was as much my fault as his. He was so rich I knew he wasn't after my money. My parents were dead. In fact, most of the family were dead, at least the male members, and the title had gone into abeyance, the entailed property returned to the Crown. But there were substantial unentailed assets, and those became mine. My guardian had investigated him and approved of him as a suitor. As for me, well, he was handsome and caring and willing to hold an intelligent conversation with a young girl. I was deadly tired of my guardian's tight leading strings. Had we not had that encounter in the summerhouse, we might have waited two years until I was eighteen. But we were both steady enough to make a go of it."

"And indeed, you did."

Ten children. Dare he ask about that?

"I'm told some women find childbirth easier than others. Did you?"

"My confinements were relatively short. I know I was fortunate, that it isn't that way for most."

"Yes. For my wife it was difficult."

He glanced and found her watching him.

"Ours was not a love match," he said. "Nor was there, to be frank, a strong attraction. After my two boys were born… I thought it best not to bother her. When they died, I thought…"

Ought he to say more or just shut his trap? A small hand settled atop his own.

"I wanted to reconcile and try for another child. She told me she'd given me an heir and a spare and could not help it that they hadn't lived. She said she'd fulfilled that part of the marriage contract and there wouldn't be any more."

The anger he'd felt then stabbed at him now, but the pain that inevitably followed seemed more bearable.

"As much as I tried, I couldn't woo her, and I wouldn't force her."

CHAPTER 6

How surprisingly honorable of him. Was it pride that held him back, or a guilty conscience? He hadn't bothered his wife, but he'd had other liaisons after his sons were born.

Though, as she recalled, there'd been little gossip about him the last couple of years.

"I'm sorry for stirring bad memories." She paused. "You might just as well marry again and try for an heir."

A twang of... regret surprised her. Lindhorst, with some young woman, when he could be *hers*.

You are mad, Neda. The intimacy is heating your brain as well as your toes.

"I have an heir, one who I think will make a rather fine Earl of Lindhorst. You see, I am free."

Free. Oh, if only... She must try again to talk sense to him.

"If the lad survives this bitter cold night. Really, Lindhorst, there are many good women of childbearing age who will appreciate being pursued by a handsome, wealthy earl. Even some widows."

"But not you?"

"At my age—"

"As I said, I have an heir already."

"Yes. I understand. You have an heir, and so you have no need of marriage."

"Do I not?"

She rolled away from him, confused. Surely, he wasn't interested in marriage. Everyone knew Lindhorst sought mistresses, not wives.

But of course, for the last many years he couldn't marry. He'd been a lusty man with an uncooperative wife, and the freedom to drink, wench... and lead astray younger men. Men like her son Fitz.

Lindhorst had something to answer for there.

"You harmed one of my loved ones," she said.

The bedclothes rustled as he propped himself up on one arm. She glanced back and saw him looking down at her.

"I did not, my lady. I... I admit, I came close to dishonoring a lady close to you, but I did not."

"A lady?" She sat up and glared. "What lady? Not one of my daughters?"

He shook his head. "No. And I don't wish to speak ill of the dead."

The dead. She let out a long breath. "Alice."

Fitz's first wife.

Alice had been a beautiful young lady of fine birth. Fitz had been taken with her looks, and Henry with her dowry. Neda had tried to overlook her haughtiness.

"Tell me," she said. "I would hear this story."

He fidgeted, and sighed, and finally spoke. "It was some years ago at a house party, not long after she and Fitz married. She was already increasing and had arrived alone and very angry. She approached me and made her intentions crystal clear."

Alice had borne Fitz only one child, a dear daughter who Neda had helped raise. Then Alice died a few years later birthing another man's child. They had all assumed that Fitz's old friend Glanford had been her first dalliance, embarked upon in revenge after she'd learned of Fitz's affairs.

But this story... "I would have heard this rumor," she said.

"Perhaps, but not from me. No one would have heard it from me."

She lay back, studying the shadows cast by the flickering lamp.

What was the truth? Had Fitz already taken up with a mistress then? Or, had Alice strayed first?

Early in his marriage to Alice, Fitz had fought a duel. It wasn't until much later that she'd learned of it, and no one would tell her what it had been about.

"Did Fitz know?"

"About me? I don't think so. He arrived at the party the next night and stumbled across her with someone else. He was late, and she was angry."

Lindhorst sighed. "Fitz arrived with one of your other sons. They'd been overseeing a problem at one of the Loughton properties. I gathered there'd been a marital spat over being late to the house party, and she'd refused to wait for his escort."

"I see." She fisted the coverlet in her hand. "They were a mismatch. I ought to have seen… I ought to have—"

"No." He stroked one long finger down the side of her face, the pad scratchy and more calloused than a lord's should be. "You can influence. You cannot control."

His touch sent a ripple of awareness through her interrupting thoughts of the various scrapes of her offspring, and Lindhorst's own ruptured marriage and his lost children.

"You've learned this the hard way, as well."

"Yes," he said, lazily, tracing her jaw with his thumb, drawing her gaze to his shadowed face.

"Lindhorst," she asked, summoning her courage, "What exactly do you want with me?"

"To know you," he said. "To truly know you, and for you to truly know me, and then if you care for me as much as I care for you, to marry."

"You want to court me?" She laughed, trying to fight off the little frissons of desire his touch was stirring, intoxicating and yet frightening.

"To truly know someone takes years and years of intimacy," she said, "and even then…"

There had been many hollow times with Henry, times when he was caught up in governmental affairs that he wouldn't discuss with her. Times when he was off traveling on behalf of the Crown. Times when she had to bite her tongue and squash her own feelings, for the greater good.

"I assure you, the Loughton I was acquainted with had no dark secrets," he said. "He was supremely sensible. Even in that tryst in the summerhouse when you were sixteen. He found a rare diamond and snatched her up."

A mix of emotions constricted her throat. With long separations, one always had doubts. She hadn't entirely trusted Henry, but she'd cared for him enough to ignore spurious rumors, and he'd never humiliated her.

"I wish you would marry me," he said. "But first, we must sleep, and then we must find our boys."

Our boys. The notion of sharing the burden with a man who had equal stakes in the worry sent tears to her eyes.

Grateful that he didn't seem to expect a reply, she squeezed them back and rolled on her side away from him. A large arm draped over her.

"Take my hand so it doesn't stray to where it shouldn't go."

She complied, most willingly, glad for the affectionate gesture.

"I fear this delay finding the boys will cause me to miss my stop at the duke's house party," he said yawning. "I must go and gather Gordon's sister from school before we go down to Bedfordshire for the Yuletide"

"Gordon's sister? You're raising a young girl?"

"She is thirteen now. Quite an intelligent lass. We are rubbing along well so far. Lacking a female relative in residence, I've sent her to school."

It was hard to picture Lindhorst raising a young lady. She turned his way. "Bring Gordon and his sister to our family gathering and stay through Twelfth Night. There'll be plenty of company and games and dancing for the young people."

In the dark, she could see his lips turn up, and she set a finger into his dimple. Of its own volition, her finger raked gently over his scratchy stubble.

A memory came to her: the night, so many, many, many years ago, when she'd first touched a man's scratchy beard.

Henry had invited her to meet him at the summerhouse late that night. He'd wagered with her that she wouldn't be able to dodge her maid and anyone else keeping Lady Neda in check.

The daring, the excitement, the intoxicating touch—feelings that had mellowed with parenthood, and responsibilities, and age, those feelings flooded her now.

Henry had been the only man she'd ever been intimate with. Until now.

"One kiss," she said and heard his indrawn breath. "Just to check whether I might like it."

"Of course," he said, cupping her shoulder. The blankets slipped back, and she barely felt the cold. "I shall endeavor to please."

When their lips touched, his hand slipped to the back of her head, and the other went to her waist, gently tugging her atop him.

Fierce desire shot through her. He was... aroused? Oh yes, and his lips were moving with hers, his tongue searching hers, sending currents of heat through every part of her.

It had been so long, so very, very long.

Gad, but the lady was passionate and lovely, and they had to stop while his brain still worked. In a bit, because the kiss was magical. Lord Loughton had been a lucky man.

Now her small fingers were working their way under his shirt, raking through the hair at the top of his chest. Her own shirt flapped open, and his control nearly slipped.

The shutter banged against the obstructing clothes press and an icy wind slithered over them.

He couldn't get her naked again tonight, and he wasn't about to make love to her the first time under layers of bedding.

There would be a time though, and soon. Perhaps Swillingstone would have a heated summerhouse.

He broke off the kiss and pulled her shirt closed. "Tonight, we must sleep."

NEDA RAISED HER HEAD. Light from the lamp flickered over his grim look of determination.

She snapped to her senses, embarrassment sweeping through her, threatening to swallow her whole.

He'd found her disgusting. A gentleman might bear the signs of aging and still kindle desire, but for a lady... He was tucking her collars together as if she were some errant child. Or perhaps the wrinkles on her neck had brought him to his senses.

Too stunned—embarrassed, mortified—to comment, she rolled away from him.

She was a fool. He was playing with her. The mention of marriage —bah. He was looking for a mistress, and he'd found her lacking.

There was probably a wager on it.

She was tugged close, into the warm circle of his arms, nestled against his long body.

"We'll sleep," he said, "Find the boys. And then we can marry and continue this."

Marriage. Could he possibly be serious?

"You're mad," she said.

"For you. You are my heart's desire, Lady Loughton. Now sleep."

Too astonished to comply, she lay quietly listening as his breathing slowed to a low rumbling snore that was, surprisingly, comforting.

Marriage to Lindhorst? What in heaven's name would that be like? Would he chase other women? Would he disappear for months at a time as Henry had done?

Women desired him, younger women than herself, and he might give in to temptation.

What sort of man was Lindhorst anyway? Even buried in the

country, she ought to have heard gossip of his recent escapades, but the only sordid matter was his wife's decampment to France. And he'd explained that. Still, marrying him would be a roll of the dice.

On the other hand, she would have her own home to manage again. Perhaps Lindhorst would be willing to take James in hand, while she helped to bring out Gordon's sister.

And she'd have a husband, a man who was handsome, virile, gentlemanly. In spite of all that had transpired this night, in spite of his past reputation, she couldn't help liking him.

NEDA WOKE, having slipped into sleep after all. The room was still dark and yet a hint of light glimmered around the window opening. Despite the chill in the room, warmth cushioned her, a strong muscled arm binding her close to the source of that heat.

Her heart beat a little faster as she remembered—she'd kissed him, like a wanton, like she'd kissed no other man but her husband, and that so long ago she'd almost forgotten how to go about it.

"You're awake." His voice rumbled over the top of her head. "What time do you suppose it is?"

She lifted his hand away and sat up. The blustery wind had died down. Had the snow stopped?

"It's well past dawn. Mid-morning, I'd guess." And she knew how a man might be in the morning after a cozy sleep. "I'm going to go find my carriage gown. Is it in the kitchen?"

"Wait," he said. "*You* kissed *me* last night. Let me return the favor."

"That was not well-done of me."

He was silent so long she turned to look at him and found him staring up at the canopy, a thoughtful look on his face.

"I didn't find anything wrong with it. I thought it was quite sublime. We need to try it again to be certain."

His cheek dimpled again, and she noticed that one of his teeth was chipped, and it did nothing to distract from his roguish appeal.

She couldn't help returning the smile.

He hadn't forced himself on her during the night, as a true scoundrel would have done.

"All right. Perhaps one more kiss will do no harm." She settled back on the pillow and pulled the blankets higher.

Lindhorst swept his thumb across her lips and gently turned her head toward him. His grin softened, his eyes glowed darkly.

Oh dear. She knew carnal desire when she saw it, and, heaven help her, *felt* it.

"One kiss," she said. "And then I'll go make us s-some p-proper tea."

He raised up and bussed her forehead. "I'll wager..." A soft murmur at her ear, "you'll forget..." His lips moved to her neck, "the tea."

The soft nibble set her afloat on a wave of pleasure, the tea completely forgotten.

THE LADY WAS SUPPLE, and experienced, and surprisingly quick to respond and throw off caution. He reminded himself that she wasn't sure of him—yet. His conscience yanked his hand back from where it was wandering.

You need her to trust you, the voice said.

He wanted her trust, wanted more than that. He wanted her love. Her generous heart. Her future.

While lust battled with conscience, voices outside intruded.

He tried to ignore them. The grooms wouldn't interrupt, nor would Farley.

"Where is she?"

The gruff shout raced up the stairs just before pounding footsteps.

He lifted his head and saw Neda's eyes widen as she struggled up.

"That's Fitz. Did you lock the door?"

CHAPTER 7

Her shirt had flopped open revealing the breast he'd been fondling. Her lips were swollen, her cheek grazed from his morning stubble, her hair a tangle of blonde curls.

He hastily buttoned her, just in time before the door flew open and four men swathed in greatcoats and heavy wraps jumbled in.

"*Mother!*" a creaky voice cried.

Not four men, but two men and two boys who were almost men. The blond-haired boy he recognized as James Lovelace. Jostling his way to the front of the group, the lad would have come closer, but the taller blond man behind him—Fitz, Lord Loughton—pulled him back.

"Lindhorst," Fitz said, his mouth tight. "Mother."

Behind Fitz stood Gordon, and, for the love of God, Neda's son-in-law, the Duke of Swillingstone.

He was in for it.

"Good morning, Loughton. James." Rising and reaching for the robe he'd tossed on the floor, he nodded to the two dark-haired arrivals. "Gordon. Swillingstone. If you will remain here, my lady, I'll take these four lads downstairs and fetch your gown from the kitchen where I set it to dry."

But she was already rising, swathing herself in the counterpane, tossing her hair back like a queen, as if her sons discovering her in a man's bed was a matter of no consequence.

She marched up and stood with him, confronting the four intruders.

James's gaze speared him, and the lad opened his mouth.

"You foolish boys," Neda said, preempting her son's scold. "I'm heartily glad to see you didn't freeze to death, as Lindhorst and I almost did, searching for you. What possessed you to leave school like that?"

"I-I'm sorry," James mumbled, probably not meaning a word of it. His lips were drawn as tightly as those of his eldest brother whose fierce glare was threatening pistols at dawn.

"Gordon." Lindhorst mustered a bit of sternness, "explain yourself."

His nephew frowned and mumbled his own apology, his gaze skittering to Neda and then jumping away again. It wasn't often a lad his age saw a beautiful lady in total deshabille.

"Mother," James said, "There's a wager... Lindhorst and..."

"A wager?" She'd gone very still, her tone as frosty as the chill in the room.

Hell and damnation.

That blasted wager. Pickworth's words came back to him: *It's in the betting book at White's, you know.*

He felt her gaze on him, her expression unreadable.

Shame washed over him. Unearned shame... Or, hadn't he always laughed at the wagers? His damned reputation preceded him. "Neda, this has nothing to do with—"

"James, Gordon, leave us," Fitz interrupted.

"No, Fitz." Neda shook her head and drew herself taller. "The boys will stay. I would hear what James and Gordon have to say about this wager."

As the boys remained silent, dread set Lindhorst's nerves on edge. Would he lose all hope with her?

Still, the words must be said, and he would be the one to say them. "There was a wager in the betting book at White's. I was told of it. I had nothing to do with it. It had nothing to do with... with us."

She sent him a long look and nodded, and a tiny flame of hope flickered.

"It was a wager that Lindhorst would make you his mistress," James said.

"And you know of this how, James?" she asked, her tone surprisingly calm.

James raised an imperious chin. He was a handful. More so than Gordon, another rebellious lad whom Lindhorst had more or less brought to heel.

No wonder Neda fretted about James. Fitz must be busy with his own growing brood and James was too old for a birching, as if that sort of discipline even worked on such a strong-willed lad.

Lindhorst took a step closer and glared. "Answer your lady mother."

James's mouth quirked and he finally blinked.

"One of the fellows." Gordon jumped in, a lad who knew when it was wise to confess. "His brother writes him and..."

He closed his mouth, uncertain about revealing more.

Lindhorst knew what would come next. So would Fitz and Swillingstone. There was always some fellow at school or in the officer's mess ready to organize his own betting book.

"One of your schoolmates is taking bets," Neda said, surprising him again with how much she knew about boys and men and their foibles. "*You*, my foolish son, what side of the wager did you take?"

Color rushed up the lad's cheeks. "Mother, I knew you would not... er, I *thought* you would not..."

"Succumb to Lord Lindhorst's charms?"

There was humor in her tone, and James screwed up his mouth in a grimace that made him seem younger than his years. "That you would never be any man's mistress."

"Your mother is not my mistress," he said.

She freed an arm from her wrap, and he felt her fingers tuck around his arm.

"Quite right," she said. "You have won the wager, James. Lindhorst and I have spent a long night together after looking fruitlessly for you and Gordon. And how the four of you appeared here this morning is a story we will get from you before the day is out. Our night together was not a matter of dallying but of keeping ourselves from freezing to death." She paused for a breath. "And shame on you Fitzhenry Lovelace for glaring at Lindhorst so."

She wagged a finger at her son, the baron, as if he were still a toddler in skirts, and then she turned a smile up at Lindhorst and went on. "And though Lindhorst is lovely and has protected me and been a perfect gentleman, and though we've become quite good friends on this adventure, I have no interest in becoming his mistress."

"I should think not," Fitz muttered.

"However, Lindhorst *has* asked me to become his wife, and I am saying..." She beamed a smile up at him. "Yes."

Warmth bubbled up, draining away the chill, not just of the mouldering manor, but the chill that had settled around his heart since his sons died and his first marriage fell completely apart.

"*Mother.*" Shock was written upon Fitz's and James's faces, but Gordon's mouth had dropped open and Swillingstone seemed to be fighting a grin.

Lindhorst gathered her into his arms. "Yes?"

She nodded.

"My dear, be assured, there will be no more wagers in the betting book with my name attached to them."

"How can you possibly control the gambling of nodcocks like these?" She swept a hand toward the four intruders.

"I suppose I can't, but my behavior will be impeccable. Let us say, this will be the last wager regarding Lindhorst and any lady."

"The last wager?" she asked, raising an eyebrow.

"The very last. I shall endeavor to bring you nothing but happiness and to never cause you regret."

"You'd best be certain of that," Fitz growled.

"They're still here," she whispered, and then said more loudly, "Boys. Out."

"Mother…"

"Shoo," she said flapping her hand. "Go and start the water for tea. We shall be down in a moment."

Swillingstone took charge, ushering them out the door and casting a quick grin over his shoulder.

When the door snicked shut on the four intruders, Lindhorst let out a long breath and then a hearty laugh which faded away when he saw her watching him, a look on her face which he could only describe as… thoughtful, perhaps doubtful.

Was she comparing him to the late Lord Loughton?

"Neda? My dear?" He held his breath, waiting and praying that she was not going to change her mind.

"Orson," she said.

No one had called him by his Christian name in years. He leaned in to kiss her, but she pushed him back.

"This is the last wager for me as well," she said. "I must know… My age…You are certain—"

He stopped her words with a kiss but lingered only a moment on her lips before pressing his forehead to hers. "I am certain. I admired you, Neda, and then I grew to love you from afar, and now… We will suit, I am sure of it."

Her gaze searched his face, her blue eyes glistening.

"Now," he said. "We've slept, we've found the boys, and we must marry directly. What say you?"

"You're forgetting Gordon's sister—does she have a name? She must be rescued from school. And there's also Christmas to be celebrated."

"Her name is Lucy. We'll fetch her on our way. Swillingstone may host our wedding. A common license, I think. Though I'd rather not wait a whole seven days… Perhaps… Does Swillingstone have a heated summerhouse?"

"I don't know how much more scandalous behavior my sons can endure." She lifted her chin, grinning. "Let us finish that last kiss while we still have a moment alone."

EPILOGUE

"You're certain about this, mother?"

The question had come from her eldest, of course. Fitz could not seem to reconcile himself with the thought of her marriage.

Outside the carriage window, fog shrouded the passing landscape.

"You know we all wish you well, Mother," Rupert said. "But, if... well, you shall always have a home with any one of us."

If only she'd been allowed this short journey alone, or better yet, in Orson's company. Instead, three of her four elder sons had insisted on escorting her. The fourth, Selwyn, would have squeezed himself in, except that he was out of the country seeing to his business interests.

She glanced at George, who'd not yet spoken. Seated across from her, he smiled. Her only dark-haired child, he was the one who most resembled Henry.

It was true, she'd had some doubts—none that she'd ever admit to any of them—but that smile reassured her.

"I've told you I like Lindhorst," George said as the carriage rolled to a stop. "I approve of this match. I think you both will be very happy."

The words warmed her. In the short space of mere days, she'd watched Orson, talked with him, spent hours with him. She liked him as well.

Was in fact, a bit giddy about him, to the point that she'd admitted to herself, that even before their very cold December adventure, Orson's patient wooing begun in the spring had won her heart.

She'd fallen in love.

A familiar squabble ensued about who would escort her down the aisle, Fitz insisting it was his prerogative, the others saying he was so opposed to the groom, he must forfeit.

She glanced out the window and saw Orson walking back and forth in front of the church door, her son-in-law, Simon, Duke of Swillingstone keeping pace with him.

When the carriage door opened, she brushed Fitz aside and stepped out first, going directly to Orson and taking his arm.

"You may all go in and take your places," Orson said. "My bride and I will enter together."

They shared a smile, having planned this ahead of time.

George and Simon nudged Rupert and Fitz forward. Inside the vestibule, Neda shooed the ladies gathered there off to their seats, pulling Lucy and Fitz's daughter, Mary Anastasia back.

She'd all but raised little Mary herself until Fitz remarried. This granddaughter was especially dear to her, and she had high hopes that Lucy would soon be as well. The two girls would be their only attendants, scattering petals from hot house flowers as they processed in before them.

She sent them off with their baskets and then, sharing another smile with her groom, squared her shoulders and walked into this next chapter of her life.

LATER THAT EVENING, while the Twelfth Night revelry proceeded downstairs, Orson led her as far as the first-floor landing and then hoisted her into his arms and made his way up another flight of stairs and into an unfamiliar wing of the grand ducal house.

"You know your way unassisted," she said.

"I had a footman lead me on a scouting mission."

They stopped at a door that was already ajar, and he shouldered it open, setting her on her feet inside.

"We have a grand suite, a sitting room and two bedchambers, good fires, and all of our things have been moved here."

The kiss that followed that quick speech left her breathless.

"We'll only be using one of the bedchambers," she said, watching his eyes darken. "Are there servants lurking?"

He shook his head.

"I suppose I shall have to make do with your services. Again."

He smiled and then joined her in laughter and led her into a surprisingly cozy chamber, warmed by a roaring fire. On a nearby table, covered dishes had been set out alongside bottles of wine, spirits and glasses. The bed loomed large, covers turned back revealing pristine white sheets, with her nightgown laid out.

She leaned into his chest, and his arm came around her, stroking her back. Truth to tell, she was the tiniest bit nervous.

"Let me pour us some wine," he said.

She looked up. Was he nervous too? In the last several days, they'd stolen some intimate time together, though they hadn't had the privacy to anticipate their vows.

"Just one sip for courage," she said. "You will need it dealing with all the hooks in this dress. It took my maid forever to do me up."

"Is that a dare, Lady Lindhorst?" His eyes gleamed with dark mischief. "I'll wager I can get you undone in no more than the blink of an eye."

"I should like to see you prove—"

She choked out a laugh as he spun her around and set about a skillful, thrilling, most welcome undoing.

THE END

Lady Loughton has appeared in earlier stories shepherding her children into happy marriages, most recently in *A Wallflower's Midsummer Night's Caper*, the tumultuous romance of Nancy and Simon, Duke of Swillingstone:

Determined to make the Duke of Swillingstone regret ruining her first season, Nancy Lovelace has one thing in mind at her family's Midsummer Night's Masquerade: *revenge*. But as the night unfolds and passions rise, will Nancy be caught in her own game?

Find A Wallflower's Midsummer Night's Caper here https:// books2read.com/aWallflowersMidsummerNightCaper

About Alina K. Field

USA Today bestselling author Alina K. Field earned a Bachelor of Arts Degree in English and German literature but prefers the happier world of historical romance fiction. Her roots are in the Midwestern U.S., but after six very, very, very cold years in Chicago, she moved to Southern California where she shares a midcentury home with a golden-eyed terrier and a feisty chihuahua and only occasionally misses snow.

Social Media Links:

Website: https://alinakfield.com/
Facebook: https://www.facebook.com/alinakfield
Twitter: https://twitter.com/AlinaKField
BookBub: https://www.bookbub.com/authors/alina-k-field
Goodreads: https://www.goodreads.com/author/show/7173518.
Alina_K_Field
Newsletter signup: https://landing.mailerlite.com/webforms/landing/z6q6e3

MISTLETOE & MIDNIGHT WISHES

SHERRY EWING

MISTLETOE & MIDNIGHT WISHES

BY SHERRY EWING

Can the magic of a midnight wish dispel the dark clouds of the past?

Mr. Joseph Morledge has taken on an almost impossible task. He has purchased the manor house that came to his family in his mother's dowry. But his father's deeds have left it haunted with memories best forgotten. Determined to fully renovate the house and reclaim the future, he sets Christmas as his target. But the woman he has long held in his heart has plans of her own.

For more years than she can count, Miss Charlotte Darby has hidden her feelings for Joseph Morledge, her brother's best friend. Some untold code of honor between men has made him keep her distance. But when the opportunity comes to help him redecorate his house, she won't take no for an answer.

As Joseph and Charlotte work to remake the manor into the home it should be, Joseph begins to realize that his house will not be a home without Charlotte as his wife. Has he left it too late to declare his love? Or will mistletoe and midnight wishes work their magic?

CHAPTER 1

London, England
July 1821

Joseph Morledge stared out his carriage window at the passing London scenery as though seeing it for the first time. He had spent the last several years investing in projects that some might consider a risky business adventure but thus far, his hunches had paid off and he had amassed a large fortune. A fortune that had allowed him to purchase his mother's old manor house. It was on the outskirts of town but considered in the rolling countryside. He still had enough to live comfortably until the next allotment rolled in.

Memories flooded his mind making him question if this had, in fact, been a wise decision. Before he had put in an offer, he had discussed the prospect with his mother, who still resided in a small house in the country, living a simple life. She had been shocked until he had voiced his reasoning. The manor would have been his inheritance if his mother hadn't sold the place. Given to her by her grandfather as part of her dowry when she married, the manor had nothing but horrifying memories for her. When his father died after falling down the stairs, she could do nothing else but sell it. As a boy of only twelve at the time, Joseph could only abide by her decisions.

The haunting memories of what his father had done to his mother caused Joseph to doubt again his reasons for purchasing a house that would only bring his mother pain. The few memories Joseph had of Captain Sander Morledge were not ones he wished to dwell on. But as the scenery changed from city to country, the manor house finally came into view. The carriage slowed, and unwanted visions of the deceased man came rushing back to his mind. Sander hadn't been a kind man. He had hidden his wife away on the third floor and pretended she was dead for years while he searched for a new bride, which caused Joseph to wonder if his mother would still be alive if events hadn't occurred as they had. His mother never talked about what brought about her leg being amputated, leaving her wheelchair bound, but Joseph had no doubt Sander had been the cause behind it. And now this... what had he been thinking?

"Are you certain this is a good idea?" his brother Michael asked, breaking into Joseph's thoughts.

"Whatever Destiny has in store for me has already been put in place, Michael. I've bought the place and plan to bring the manor back to life."

A snort left Michael. "You best bring a priest, then, to exorcise the place. There's going to be a ghost or two haunting that old house, including the previous owners."

"The previous couple who owned it didn't die, Michael. They went bankrupt. There's a difference," Joseph replied, with a grunt of annoyance.

"That, in itself, seems like a sign that the place is meant to remain empty and left to rot. You're going to have to make some major renovations to the place if you hope to convince mother to spend any time here by Christmas," Michael replied as the carriage door opened and a footman let down the step. "I think the place is cursed. You might just need a miracle to make this manor habitable again."

"Along with a few midnight wishes and a whole lot of prayers,"

Joseph muttered beneath his breath as he left the carriage and slowly walked toward the front door. He pulled out the brass key and placed it into the lock. Turning the key, he heard the click, pulled out the key and turned the knob, opening his past to confront his future. Michael strode in behind him and made his way toward the back of the house but Joseph stood where he was and gulped back his apprehension of the mistake he had possibly made.

Sunlight hadn't seen the entry hall in years, or so it seemed as dust bolts danced before his eyes while he gazed at the staircase across the marbled tile. He walked into the front parlor, inspecting the white-linen-cloth-covered furniture. Dust covered his leather gloves and he briefly rubbed at the fabric, knowing he'd be covered in white specks as he went through what now belonged to him. Joseph began wondering if the previous owners had made any changes to the décor. He would find out soon enough once the servants arrived and began cleaning. The hearth and chimneys would need to be inspected, as he witnessed a small mouse scurry to hide beneath the half-burned log. In fact, the carpenters couldn't arrive soon enough in order to make the changes he had planned for the place. The first floor was to be the start, but could he honestly have it ready by December?

"Hello? Is anyone here?"

Joseph raised his head at the sound of a female voice coming from the foyer. He'd know that voice anywhere and, for the first time this morning, a smile crept across his mouth. He came from around the corner of the parlor to see Miss Charlotte Darby looking very fetching in her riding habit. She was in the process of taking off her gloves.

"Good morning, Miss Charlotte. May I say how lovely you look today," Joseph declared, crossing the space between them.

She reached out her hands and took his. Giving them a gentle squeeze, she let go and stepped back with a smile. "Joseph! I thought I recognized your carriage."

He peered over her shoulder to see his friend Garrett tying the reins of his horse to a hitching post. "I see your brother is with you," he murmured knowing her reputation would remain intact.

"Of course, you know Garrett. And Michael? Where is he?"

Joseph nodded toward the rear of the house. "In the back, inspecting the rest of the manor. Are you here to see him?"

Something briefly flashed across her blue eyes before she gave a light laugh. "Garrett told me you bought the manor back. Knowing what I do of your history with the place, I would have thought any other house might suit better."

Joseph shrugged. "It would have been mine if our lives had turned out differently." Charlotte was well aware of his past, considering the amount of time he had spent with her brother. Garrett was his best friend, after all. Yet Charlotte had always held a certain place in Joseph's heart after Sophie Templeton had married her husband. Not that he blamed Sophie for not returning his affection. They had been raised together, so he supposed it was only natural Sophie would have thought of him more like a brother than husband material. Still… he always kept Charlotte at a distance, since she was his best friend's sister which by an undeclared gentleman code of honor made Joseph feel she should be off limits. And then there were Michael's feelings for the lady. He could never act against his brother's possible happiness even if it cost Joseph his own.

Her hand came to rest on his arm. "You're lost in thought, Joseph. Are you sure this was a good idea?" she asked softly.

"Everyone keeps asking me that and it's the same thing I'm beginning to question. But the answer remains the same. The deal is done and the manor is once again with my family," Joseph stated, as he began ushering her from the house. "I would prefer if you don't come inside. I'd rather you see the place once the renovations are complete."

"But we came to help, didn't we, Garrett," she replied, as they met her brother outside.

"Any way we can," Garrett said, slapping Joseph on his back.

"And I appreciate your offer but I've got this in hand," Joseph answered, even as a wagon began making its way up the drive. "Besides, won't you be busy with your charge this summer?"

Charlotte waved her hand in the air. "Lola and her father the Earl of Stanhope are off on an extended holiday together. Father, daughter time I suppose."

Garrett chuckled. "The earl will have his hands full without Charlotte as the girl's governess, and only a nanny to help him manage the child for the summer."

"Lola won't need lessons in reading and writing or any of the other academic studies I have planned for her upon their return," Charlotte answered. "So, you see, Joseph. We have more than ample time to help you in any way we can lend assistance."

"We can discuss this more at a later date. First, I need to access the manor and voice my plans with the workmen for the refurbishment. Garrett, we can talk later about how you might help. Charlotte will need to abide by my wishes." Joseph watched as Charlotte took on a look that said an argument was forthcoming.

"Really, Joseph, I am not some delicate flower that cannot withstand a bit of hard work. Why, I'll have you know—"

"Charlotte!" Michael's voice called from the doorway as he hurried to reach her side. "How wonderful to see you... and Garrett, too." Michael beamed staring at the young lady who was of the same age.

The adoration his brother felt for Charlotte was more than evident, and Joseph stepped back as he always did. But he did not miss the brief glance the lady bestowed upon him, causing his heart to flip end over end in his chest. Joseph wasn't sure if he imagined the whole encounter but he kept the memory in his heart until their paths would cross again.

CHAPTER 2

Outskirts of London
October 1821

Charlotte adjusted the blanket on her lap to keep her warm as the carriage rounded a curve in the road. Although the sun was shining, the brisk autumn air had her wishing for the warmth of the afternoon summer sun. She only had snow to look forward to in the months to come.

She ignored the other occupants inside the carriage while lost in thought over how she might be received at this impromptu visit to see Joseph and the progress he had thus far made on his home. Her brother Garrett had tried to warn her to stay away until a formal invitation had been given, but she was never one to listen to his advice once she had her mind made up. She shifted in her seat, feeling her brother's gaze upon her. She lifted her head and found she was right... he was silently watching her as if waiting for her to tell him she had changed her mind. *That* was never going to happen.

She gave a sigh of relief when his attention returned to his friend,

Lord Pierce Hartwell, who was sitting beside him. The two gentlemen began to quietly converse amongst themselves leaving Charlotte once again to her own thoughts. The carriage was crowded, since her own friend, Miss Florentia Eddowes, and Charlotte's chaperone Mary sat with her on the forward-facing seat. Garrett had insisted Mary travel with them. Never let it be said her brother would risk his sister's reputation when she entered an all-male household.

With London's busy streets stretching away to a less-traveled country road, Charlotte began doubting her decision and the welcome she might receive. If Michael was in residence, and she was certain he was, she knew she would be brought into the front parlor and a tea service would be placed before them, as if they knew she had been invited for a visit. Michael had been a dear friend for years but Charlotte was also uncomfortably aware that he had at one time held an affection for her she would never be able to return. Not when her heart had always longed for his older brother Joseph to notice her. But though Joseph had always been polite, she wondered if he would ever think of her as anything else but his best friend's sister or his brother's crush. Joseph always put everyone else in front of his own desires. This was an admirable trait, but she worried that, when it came to her, he would never think of himself first.

"There's no sense in doubting your decision, Charlotte. You'll know shortly if you'll be welcomed or not," Florentia quietly murmured. "Unless, of course, you'd like to turn around and return to London. Your brother can make that happen with a short rap on the roof."

"I still think this is a bad idea," Garrett grumbled. "Bringing ladies to a man's house unannounced is never a good idea."

Charlotte gave a sniff of aggravation. "Pish, posh. Joseph won't mind and we can again offer to help with whatever needs to still be done. Christmas will be here before he knows it and I can only imagine what still needs to be done with the manor."

Pierce turned his attention from the passing scenery to the women seated across from him. "I can only imagine the house is in a sad state of repairs. Didn't you say, Garrett, that Joseph planned to have the place completely remodeled so nothing of the original architecture remained the same?"

Garrett nodded. "So, I was told. Basically, he's renovating everything he can. He doesn't want his mother to be reminded of the past nightmares that occurred within those walls."

Florentia shook her head. "From the little Charlotte has told me, he has his work cut out for him, then, especially if he wants to host a Christmas holiday party." She gave a shudder.

"Joseph will see that, if nothing else, the first floor will be ready. I have faith in him," Charlotte replied, with a smile of confidence.

She watched one brow on her brother's forehead rise as if quizzical about her knowledge of his friend. "You haven't been sneaking over to see what progress Joseph has been making since July, have you?" he asked, in a warning tone.

"Are you questioning my common sense, Garrett?" she returned sarcastically.

"If I had any sense of my own, we would be anywhere else instead of trekking out to the countryside uninvited," her brother grumbled again.

The carriage rounded another curve and began the short ride to the front of Joseph's manor house. She began to fold the blanket on her lap. "Well, it's too late to further debate my impromptu decision. We've arrived."

And arrive they did, as the carriage wheels now smoothly rolled over a well-maintained easement to the house where the previous potholes had been filled in. The red bricks of the four-story manor had been cleaned of the moss along with the ivy that had threatened to overtake the windows. Charlotte's eyes roamed over the lawn, which had been neatly manicured since her last visit. Trees and shrubbery had been skillfully pruned. Roses would most likely bloom in a variety of shades come the spring and she wondered if the gardeners had had a chance to make the back of the house look as appealing as the front. She smiled in pleasure, knowing how satisfied Joseph must feel at the transformation taking place.

But, as the footman let down the step for the occupants of the carriage to descend, her smile quickly faded when she observed Michael bolting through the front door. Concern was etched upon his brow.

"Now isn't a good time for a visit, dear Charlotte," he uttered, before a resounding crash came from somewhere within the manor.

"What the devil is going on?" Garrett questioned as he held onto to his sister's arm to prevent her from running inside.

"It's Joseph… exorcising some demons on the third floor is the best way to describe it," Michael warned as he swiped at the hair falling over his forehead.

A growl of rage echoed in the air as another crash came from inside. Charlotte wrenched her arm from her brother's grasp.

"You can't go in there, Charlotte," Garrett bellowed, as she ran toward the front steps.

"Watch me," she replied, never once looking back before she ran through the front door, across the entry way floor, and lifted the hem of her dress to take the stairs two at a time. This was hardly a time to be lady-like. Not when Joseph needed her.

She didn't think how inappropriate this might appear to anyone other than her brother, Florentia, and Lord Hartwell. Once she reached the third-floor landing, she tried to get her bearings on where exactly Joseph was located. Hearing what sounded as though an ax was being taken to some furniture, she raced in that direction and swung open the door.

"I told you to leave me alone, Michael!" Joseph's voice was full of rage and Charlotte ducked in time to miss a vase being thrown toward the doorway. Her gasp of surprise caused Joseph's grey eyes to grow wide in alarm. "Charlotte! My God! What did I almost do?"

Her eyes took in the sight of him. She had never before seen him so disheveled. His black hair was sticking up on end, but that was hardly what drew her attention to the young man she had been attracted to for many a year. His linen shirt was open to his waist, giving her a view of a dusting of dark hair on the muscled skin of his chest. A chest that heaved after the exertion of destroying the room.

She gulped at the sight of him as he came rushing across the room to take her hands.

"Are you injured?" he asked, with a worried frown etched across his tormented face. "I will never forgive myself if I inadvertently caused you harm."

She shook her head no before noticing he was the one who was injured, if the scratches on his cheek and hands were any indication of the damage he had unknowingly done to his own body. Her eyes scanned what was once a bedroom and the destruction told her much. This room held plenty of unwanted memories that Joseph wanted to eradicate from his house. He had done a good job of destroying anything of value that remained in the bedroom. Glass from a mirror was shattered on the floor, the furniture hacked to bits. Even what she could see of the multicolor floral print wallpaper had been torn from most of the walls.

She clucked her tongue and reached into the reticule dangling from her wrist to pull out a handkerchief. She held the linen up and gently dabbed at one of the scratches dripping blood down his cheek.

"I don't know what demons from your past you were trying to get rid of in this room, Joseph, but I should tell you I believe they are now gone," she murmured softly. "Perhaps if you told me about them, it might help erase such unwanted memories."

He glanced back at the mess he had created. "I wouldn't wish to burden you," he replied so quietly she almost missed his words.

Her hand reached up to caressed one cheek. "Dearest Joseph... Telling me something that upset you in your past is no burden when I know confiding in me would help someone I care for. I am a very good listener." She hoped the smile she showed him was one that elicited confidence. Something terrible had happened in this room, enough so that Joseph wanted no part of the memories in his future.

He turned from her as if remembering his appearance and began putting himself back in order. He found his waistcoat and shook off whatever debris had found its way onto the garment. His cravat came next and he tied the linen efficiently before at last turning around to face her. A lock of his black hair fell over his forehead and she crossed the distance between them. Impulsively, Charlotte reached up to brush the thick locks back into place.

"Tell me," she urged, taking hold of his arm.

"Not here," he muttered before leading her from the room. He ushered her to the end of the hallway where an alcove near a window had a seating area overlooking the rear garden. He waited while she sat down before joining her. He gave a heavy sigh and his face portrayed all the anguish he must have been holding in. She had never seen him look so vulnerable.

She scooted closer to him and he took her hand and raised her fingertips to his lips. He had always kissed the air between them but this time she felt his mouth touch her gloved hand. She only wished he was kissing her skin instead.

"Tell me," she repeated, waiting for him to confess what had happened in that room.

"I wouldn't want you to think less of me," he said.

A small smile lit the corners of her mouth. "Joseph... I am confident that whatever happened in that room was not of your doing."

He let go of her hand and slumped in the seat, leaning his head back on the edge of the settee. "The room was my mother's," he began as a tear slid down his cheek.

She frowned in confusion. "But I've always known you and your mother to have a lovely rapport between you."

He gave her a sideways glance before he focused on the ceiling above him. It was as though, if he looked at her, he would never be able to get through the conversation. "My mother was never the problem." He took another heavy breath before sitting up and placing his forearms on his thighs. "It was my father. He was the very devil. Locked her away in that room for years and then tried to find himself another bride while he pretended she was dead. Michael and I hid ourselves in the room with her for days on end just to give her some form of comfort. Being wheelchair bound on the third floor, she never had freedom to roam her own house. The abuse she suffered both verbally and most likely physically..."

She reached over to clasp his hand again. "Oh, Joseph! How terrible!"

"She never confided to Michael and myself how she lost her leg. We were too young at the time of the incident. But it wasn't hard for me to surmise my father had something to do with it. An accident, he called it, but neither of them would ever say more."

Charlotte turned away from Joseph to gaze down the hallway to the room they just left. "I'm surprised you didn't start hacking away at that room from the start. But I cannot help but be concerned that, for all your efforts to remodel this house… will your mother be mentally prepared to actually step foot in a place that most likely still holds such nightmares for her?"

He raised tormented grey eyes to her. "That, my dear Charlotte, is the same question I've asked myself daily since I bought the place." He sat back up and ran his fingers through his hair. "But it was important to me to purchase this house so it was once more in our family. It was part of my mother's dowry. I thought, if I changed the interior enough, maybe, just maybe, it would be enough that we could make new memories together to outweigh all the bad things that happened in the past."

"That might be a lot to ask of your mother, Joseph," Charlotte replied softly.

"Yes, I know, but I'm trying my best. This is why I wanted to have the lower floors ready to celebrate Christmas. The holiday would be the perfect time to put the past where it belongs, and start a brand-new future." His smile was weak at best, as though he was doing his utmost not only to convince her of the wisdom of his words, but himself, too."

She clapped her hands together and stood. "Then let us redouble your efforts and let us help you get prepared for a Christmas event the like of which this old house has never seen."

Joseph shook his head and also rose to his feet. "Such an offer is completely unnecessary."

She began marching down the hallway with Joseph at her side. "Nonsense. We are friends, are we not? Garret will be only too happy to lend assistance and we can all move in so we are not running back and forth wasting time between residences."

He quickly took hold of her arm to halt their progress down the hallway. "You cannot be serious, Charlotte. You can't possibly move in here."

"Of course I can," she said brightly. "I'll bring my chaperone, if that soothes your manly pride, to put any doubt to rest about the respectability of the situation. Besides, with my brother along, who would even care about the living arrangements? It's not as though we're an integral part of Society."

"Maybe I care, Charlotte. Won't your employer have some say about you living under the roof of a man you are not related to?"

"Lord Stanhope is still abroad and has messaged me that he has no plans to return anytime soon. He has paid me a large settlement to see me through the coming winter until I can find another position as a governess."

"Charlotte... I won't have your reputation ruined because—"

"I won't hear another word on the matter, Joseph. We're moving in and that's the end of this conversation. Besides... this place needs a woman's touch." She tapped her finger to her chin. "As a matter of fact, let's send a message to your stepsisters. I think Margaret and Sophie can liven up this place and, as married women, they will also put to rest any issues as to what is *not* happening under this roof."

Charlotte began making her way towards the stairs and heard a curse being muttered from Joseph. But, as she put her hand on the banister, she felt the warmth of Joseph's fingers over her own.

"You're not going to take no for an answer, are you?" he asked and she saw the hint of a smile that was encouraging.

She gave a light laugh. "What do you think?"

CHAPTER 3

December, 1821

THE MONTHS that had swept by in a whirlwind of activity left Joseph feeling grateful to Charlotte, his stepsisters, and even his brother, who had worked alongside Joseph and the workmen to ensure the manor was ready for the holiday festivities. When Margaret and Sophie arrived with their husbands and children in tow, he should have also realized that this old house might trigger some unwanted memories for the ladies as well. Margaret, in particular, had been the focus of his father's infatuation with marrying her. But her heart had already belonged to Frederick and in the end everything worked out as it should. Margaret had been leery, when she first stepped foot into the entry way. That was until she had seen the changes he had thus far made.

Months later, there was nothing visual that reminded Joseph of the old manor and the changes his father had once made to make the place his own. There was still much to do on the upper floors but that would continue after the holiday. As he descended the main stairs to where he would soon greet his guests, he couldn't help but be pleased at the progress. The house had taken on a miraculous transformation, Joseph was overjoyed that the manor was finally a home. Each room was now bright and airy. Instead of the wood paneling leaving a darkness that always seemed to suffocate him, the walls had either been painted in pleasing light colors or wallpapered according to his, and Charlotte's, tastes.

In fact, the place had taken on so many characteristics of the young lady, he wondered how he would ever let her go home. After working with her side by side all these months, he had to finally admit he was in love with her, even though he had yet to admit it aloud. She seemed to belong here, though he still kept his distance due to his brother's love for her and the fact she was his best friend's sister. It was quite the conundrum.

The sound of carriage wheels arriving outside brought Charlotte from one of the back rooms as though he had called out for her to join him. She had a speck of flour on her nose and more on her apron. There was no doubt in Joseph's mind she had been in the kitchen.

"She's here?" Her excited tone caused Joseph to smile. He went over and couldn't resist wiping the flour from her nose and she gave a short gasp. "Oh dear! I must look a fright."

"You are beautiful, as always, Charlotte," he murmured, while she quickly untied her apron. He began heading toward the door, waving off the butler who then disappeared to perform his other duties. He turned back when he realized the lady wasn't behind him. "You won't join me?"

"I don't want to overstep any protocol. Maybe it would be best if you went greet her by yourself," she said, in a hushed tone.

Joseph went back and took her hand, pulling her forward. "Nonsense, Charlotte. You know how pleased she'll be to see you."

Before he could say anything further, reinforcements arrived in the form of his brother, Margaret, and Sophie. It seemed only fitting that those he cared most about would be with him as he greeted the new arrival. Opening the door, he made his way toward the carriage. Joseph rushed forward to assist getting his mother into her wheelchair.

"Welcome to Fairfax Manor, Mother," he said, as he settled her into the chair.

He watched when he eyes widened in surprise. "You renamed it."

He knelt down beside her and took her hands. "I restored it to the original name. It should never have been changed in the first place."

Jennette nodded her approval. "Your grandparents would have been proud of you, Joseph."

"Wait until you see what we've done with the inside. I think you'll be pleased," he began as he stood and went behind her to wheel her forward. "At least, I hope you will."

She gripped the arms of her chair. "You know I have my apprehensions about what this place did to me."

He stopped rolling her chair to once again stand before her. "It wasn't this house that did anything to you, mother, but a beast of a husband who abused you for years. Let us make new memories here and let the past remain where it belongs."

Jennette was greeted by Michael and the ladies she considered family, and when Joseph slowly maneuvered her wheelchair up the few stairs, he held his breath as the door was once more opened and he wheeled her inside. Suddenly the women took over the conversation, chatting away to tell Jennette of all the changes that had been made, as though she couldn't see them for herself. Margaret took over wheeling his mother and they made their way through the lower floor of the house.

"I think she likes what you've done with the place, brother," Michael beamed.

"Either that or she's in complete shock," Joseph returned, as they followed the women through the manor.

Michael gave a shrug. "It's probably a bit of both. She may need a bit of time to adjust to all the changes we've made." As they entered the ballroom, Michael held Joseph back. "When are you going to tell Charlotte you're in love with her?"

Joseph muttered a curse beneath his breath before he turned to face his brother. "I never said I was in love with Charlotte."

An amused smirk swept across Michael's features. "I know you've

MISTLETOE & MIDNIGHT WISHES

been worried about my own feelings for the lady but there is no need. Charlotte is a dear friend to me and there is nothing more between us, even though there was a time I wished the opposite. And just because she's your best friend's sister, doesn't mean you can't have feelings for her. Garrett knows how you care for her."

"He does?" Joseph whispered in a shocked tone.

Michael laughed, causing the ladies to turn to stare at the two brothers still standing near the entryway. They returned to their conversations as did his brother. "Of course he does. Now the question is, when will you admit your feelings to Charlotte. She's been in love with you for years, if you didn't know that, too."

"I've wasted so many years..." His voice trailed off as he watched the lady of his musings, who was excited in telling his mother of all the renovations that had been made. Michael left Joseph and went to his mother's side, taking over to wheel her from the room.

Joseph held his breath as they began making their way down a hallway toward an area he had specifically designed for his mother's use. Charolotte opened the door as Michael pushed the wheelchair into a suite of rooms.

Charlotte waved her hand around a beautiful sitting room with wallpaper featuring tiny blue flowers. "Joseph made these room specifically for your use, Mrs. Morledge," she began before his mother reached out to take hold of her arm.

"Charlotte, dear... I've known you since you were a little girl. I think you can call me by my given name," Jennette said with a smile.

Charlotte appeared humbled, if her face mirrored whatever she was feeling. "Jennette, then..." She began taking her through the rest of the rooms. Vanities had been lowered to meet the height requirements of Jennette's wheelchair, along with all the other amenities she might have use for. "Joseph was brilliant when he asked the builders to adjust everything so you wouldn't have any issues reaching anything you might need. He also had a ramp built going outside to the back garden, so you can have full range of its use. There's even a paved pathway for you."

Joseph stepped forward. "I wanted to ensure you never felt like your freedom was taken away, mother," he said, as he waited for her reaction. He wasn't prepared for her to burst into tears. Alarmed, he quickly lessened the distance between them and once more knelt down in front of her. "Mother, I'm so sorry if you're not happy with the place. We can change anything you want or need."

Jennette shook her head and wiped away at the wetness of her cheeks. "These are happy tears, son. I wouldn't change a thing."

A huge sigh of relief filled Joseph's heart. He looked over his mother's shoulder to see Charlotte beaming with pride. There was so much he wanted to tell the lady but this moment belonged to the woman who gave him life. He smiled and leaned forward to kiss his mother's cheek. "Welcome home, mother."

CHAPTER 4

Charlotte took her redingote from the maid and donned the garment. She picked up the sprigs of greenery and a bright red bow before heading toward the door.

"It's chilly outside and snowing, Miss Charlotte. Won't you want your bonnet?"

"It won't take me long to place this on the front door. I don't think I'll need a bonnet," she called over her shoulder, before the butler opened the door for her. With a quick word of thanks, she went to work on the decoration for the front door to the manor. Once everything was to her satisfaction, she went down the steps so she could get a complete picture of Joseph's home.

The place was... *perfect*! With her last added touch, she inspected other red bows and greenery beneath each window that Joseph had asked the servants to attend to. Even the lanterns coming up the drive were decorated for the holiday season, making Charlotte excited for all the festivities.

But that was only the beginning of the problem as her sudden happy mood plummeted. There wasn't much left to decorate for the party that Joseph and his family would be giving within the next two weeks. Guests who would travel farther than from town would soon be arriving to occupy the second-floor bedrooms. Once the party was over, there would no longer be any reason for Charlotte to remain at Fairfax Manor. She had been so certain that, given the last two months of close proximity to Joseph, he might see for himself that she was in love with him. She certainly couldn't blurt out her feelings for him without some sign that they might be returned. She had been patient but still... nothing.

She swore she saw something in those grey eyes of his whenever she caught him watching her. Desire... maybe even love... but how could she be sure, when they never spent any time alone together. Not that that would be proper with his mother and stepsisters here but still... she wanted a moment or two with him without all the responsibilities that he carried on his broad shoulders she wanted to wrap her arms around. Time was running out and she wasn't entirely certain that all the wishes she made at midnight each night would be answered.

"You've done a wonderful job making this old manor a home again, Charlotte." His deep baritone voice coming from behind her made her heart flip end over end, as she quickly twirled around to face him.

"Joseph! You shouldn't sneak up on a lady," she teased, realizing he was closer than she expected.

He chuckled. "You appeared lost in thought. Am I disturbing your brief moment of solitude? I know it's hard to find a moment of privacy as the day to the party gets closer," he said, with what looked like a mischievous twinkle in those mesmerizing grey eyes.

Good heavens... was he actually flirting with her? She decided to test her theory by stepping closer. "You're more than welcome to interrupt my solitude... well... anytime... Joseph." She realized that her voice had become a breathy whisper of anticipation of what might happen between them if only...

"Will you walk with me?" he asked holding out his arm.

"Yes," she answered, without a second of hesitation, knowing she was safe with him. This was the moment she had been waiting for, and she would take full advantage of the opportunity.

They began strolling toward the trees and away from any prying eyes, and she could only ponder what might happen next. He didn't take her far before he turned to face her and took her hands. He rubbed his thumbs across her skin, as she came to the realization that neither one of them had gloves on. His fingertips were warm, and chills that had nothing to do with the cold December air began to race down her spine.

"I cannot begin to offer my thanks for all you've done to make Fairfax Manor a home again," he said quietly, but this wasn't what she had been expecting him to voice aloud.

What had she thought he would say? That he would suddenly declare his love for her? Clearly this wasn't going to be the case, and disappointment filled her soul as never before. She meant nothing to him other than a friend.

She attempted to keep her voice steady and offered him a smile she was certain appeared weak at best. She shrugged. "It was only what anyone would do to help someone who..." She couldn't finish her sentence, because apparently she cared more for him than he cared for her. She gulped hard trying to swallow the bitter taste of unrequited love.

His head cocked to one side as if he was trying to determine what she hadn't said. "You went above and beyond what any friend would have done, Charlotte. How can I repay such a kindness?"

And there it was... He had said the words she had dreaded for months. She was only a friend to him. Nothing more. She raised her head to stare at the face of the man she had loved for so many years. She tried to memorize every line and feature, knowing she would somehow need to move on with her life.

"There is nothing for you to repay, Joseph. I did it gladly and willingly as any friend would do," she finally managed to whisper, before she shook off her disenchantment over what she had wished for with all her might. Apparently midnight wishes were for fools who thought such miracles might actually work. "We should return to the manor. There's still so much to do," she managed to reply, before she did the unthinkable and actually break down and cry in front of him.

"Yes… of course… We should return to the house."

He seemingly shook himself out of whatever further thoughts might be running amuck inside his head. What else was there to say? They were friends. Nothing more, and as Joseph began to escort her back through the woods, her brief moment of happiness that he might declare himself was at an end. So much for finding love…

CHAPTER 5

Joseph's gaze searched the ballroom for the one woman he couldn't get off his mind. She wasn't hard to find. Indeed, she was impossible to miss. She stood out like a diamond amongst all the other women who were attending the ball. Her tawny hair was swept up in a pleasing coiffure and, as she twirled to the patterns of the dance, tiny diamond pins reflected in the candlelight of the room. The dark green gown with a red ribbon below her breasts was becoming, and he wished he was the one to be at her side during the dance. He knew his hand would fit perfectly on her waist if he was able to waltz with her. He might need to ask the musicians to play a waltz and ask her for the privilege of her company.

His mind ran back to that day he had asked her to walk with him. *Fool!* That conversation certainly hadn't gone as he had planned. He had watched her face fall in what he could only term sorrow when he had mentioned they were friends. *Friends.* Good Lord! He wanted to be so much more to her, but he couldn't seem to find the words to voice his thoughts aloud. What the devil was the matter with him?

For the last week during the house party, he had watched her move about as any hostess would do to ensure his guests were entertained and the staff was keeping everything in order. He had never asked her to perform such a function, but she took it upon herself to do it without question. He had the distinct intuition that she did it to please him and, if he didn't act soon, he would lose her forever. The festivities would conclude tomorrow. If he didn't tell her he was in love with her tonight, she and her brother would be gone in the morning, and he would have lost his opportunity to finally tell her how he felt about her.

The music ended and he watched as she curtseyed to Lord Hartwell. Hartwell began escorting her from the dance floor and he reached for a fluted glass of champagne from a passing servant. He handed her the glass and she took a sip. Joseph's eyes met hers across the space of the ballroom and his heart soared before she broke contact and replied to something Hartwell was saying.

The female voice that interrupted his thoughts was a familiar one. "You're about out of time, Joseph. You best declare yourself tonight, before you miss a prime opportunity and let that wonderful lady slip from your grasp."

Joseph turned to stare down into the face of his stepsister, Sophie. Her green eyes appeared to sparkle in mischievous delight that she had read his mind.

"I've been a fool not to do so sooner," he confessed to the one person who most likely understood him better than anyone. After all, he had been infatuated with Sophie in their youth, even though he knew deep down nothing would ever happen between them. With those thoughts crossing his mind, it was as though everything fell into place. He had been wrong about his brother being in love with Charlotte. Garrett was aware, apparently, that Joseph was in love with his sister. So, the only person holding him back from the one person he loved was himself.

Sophie gave a bright laugh. "Finally!"

"What?" he asked with a frown, wondering what Sophie was talking about.

"You've finally realized what we've all known all along. It took you long enough, Joseph." She gave him a knowing smirk of satisfaction.

"Someone should have come along and knocked some sense into

me months ago," he replied, as he continued to watch Charlotte from across the room.

Sophie gave him a nudge. "Margaret and I thought with us hanging mistletoe at every entryway to a room would have been a clear indication that love was in the air for you."

He looked down at Sophie. "I thought it was just a family tradition that Frederick and Margaret started."

"They may have started it, but even I've continued such a tradition. Joseph… you are family and we wanted to ensure you always remain that way, too. I have to admit Margaret and I thought for certain we would have caught you and Charlotte kissing beneath one of the boughs in the past couple of weeks. Don't disappoint us now. Go and declare your feelings for the lady!"

He gave his stepsister a short bow. "I'll do my best to not further disappoint you." Without further delay, he left Sophie to make his way to the lady that owned his heart. "Charlotte, might I have a moment of your time?"

"Excuse us, Lord Hartwell," Charlotte murmured, before taking Joseph's arm.

He began escorting Charlotte through the ballroom and down a hallway toward his library. Once she was standing beneath the mistletoe above the doorway, he placed his hands upon her waist.

"Charlotte… would you please forgive this fool who wouldn't tell you how he felt about you before now?" he asked watching her blue eyes go wide in what he thought was disbelief.

Her hands trembled when she placed them on his arms. "Joseph… I—"

One of his arms wound around her bringing her closer while the other reached up to caress her cheek. "I have to confess I've been in love with you for more years than I can count, Charlotte. But fool that I was, I thought Michael was, too, and I couldn't let my feelings for you get in the way of my brother's happiness."

"Surely you must know that I never had feelings for Michael in that way," she answered, as her hands went to rest upon his chest.

"And then there was Garrett. He was my best friend and there's a certain code of honor among men that you don't come to care for your best friend's sister."

She gave a huff of humor. "That's silly. Garrett has known all along of my feelings for you."

"Then you do care for me?" he asked in awe, as he hugged her tighter.

"Joseph... I've been here loving you for as long as I can remember. I've waited for you to come to the same revelation. I had just about given up hope."

"I'm sorry I took so long before I told you I was in love with you."

"Finally... the words I've longed to hear. I'm in love with you, too, Joseph." Her smile was infectious as she wound her arm around his neck. Her eyes traveled to the mistletoe bough hanging above them. "Perhaps you should follow your family tradition and kiss me, Joseph."

"You know about that too?" he asked, already knowing the answer.

"Your mother told me, along with your sisters. Honestly, Joseph, you should know women can never keep secrets amongst themselves." She gave another bright laugh. "Tell me again that you love me."

"I love you, my dearest Charlotte."

"As I love you, my darling. Now kiss me under the mistletoe so I'll know that my midnight wishes have come true."

He gave her a smile before lowering his head to kiss her lips. Years of yearning for this lady could have easily overtaken him as he held her against his chest and deepened their kiss. It was as though everything in his life began and ended with Charlotte. He would never forget to tell her each and every day how much she meant to him.

He broke off their kiss and gladly took her back to their guests. He went to the musicians and asked them to play a waltz. As the chords of the music struck up, he escorted Charlotte to the dance floor. His life was now complete and he knew, with this lady in his life, he had found his home!

EPILOGUE

One Year Later

CHARLOTTE MINGLED among her guests as they celebrate the second Christmas at Fairfax Manor. Micheal and her mother-in-law raised their glasses in a silent toast from across the ballroom. Her marriage to Joseph had occurred in June after a courtship that had swept her completely off her feet. Balls, carriage rides, the theater, ices at Gunters, and anything Joseph could think of to basically woo her had finally made her ask him if they could just get married. The expression on Joseph's face when she had said the words aloud was still etched in her memory. Shock. Disbelief. And then pure joy. It was something she would never forget, and he did everything in his power to see that they were wed as soon as the banns were read.

The man of her dreams strode across the room to come to her side. He held out a glass of champagne but she declined with a knowing smile. She had news to tell him and now was a good a time as any. She pulled his arm as they left the ballroom and when she finally found a quiet room without any guests, she went into his arms. He bent down to kiss her lips.

"What mischief are you up to now, wife?" he asked nuzzling her neck.

"The worse sort, husband, but we have guests so we need to make this brief liaison quick," she teased, pressing her body into his. She heard a groan from deep inside his chest.

"Keep this up, and we will be leaving our guests to fend for themselves while I whisk you up to our bedroom, my love."

She caressed the nape of his neck. "Before we leave our guests, I have news for you."

"I'm certain it can wait. Let me kiss you instead, while we're still alone," he murmured leaving a trail of kisses down her neck.

"Behave for a moment, darling, so I can tell you my news," she begged with a laugh.

He raised his head, but she could see he was barely holding back on what he really wanted to be doing. "Very well, but be quick. I have other plans in store for us tonight."

She gave him a smirk before reaching for one of his hands and placing it on her stomach. "Congratulations, my dearest love. You're going to be a father."

His eyes widened and he stumbled back. "Are you serious?"

She nodded. "Are you happy?"

"Happy? Why, I want to shout for joy from the rooftop. Of course, I'm thrilled with such news," he declared, before coming back to lift her up and begin swinging her around. And then he remembered himself. "I didn't hurt you, did I?"

Her laughter filled the room. "You could never hurt me, Joseph."

His lips pressed against her own and for several minutes they had thoughts only of each other and the baby that would enter their lives in the months to come. But laughter coming from their guests broke the spell. They both looked upward to see the mistletoe bough over their heads.

Joseph's gaze returned to hers. "I really must say I do so enjoy this family tradition."

"We'll pass it down to our own children one day," Charlotte declared, with another smile.

"Let's go tell our guests of our news... that is, if you agree we should celebrate our child that will bless our lives in the coming year," he said awaiting her approval.

"I couldn't think of a better time than while we are with our family and friends," she said in excitement.

They returned to the ballroom and Joseph signaled for the attention of their guests. Applause erupted at the news of their forthcoming child. Charlotte and Joseph were surrounded by family and friends who came to offer their congratulations. The holiday party had become a different sort of celebration, and Charlotte was thrilled with the child that grew inside her.

When Joseph and Charlotte finally took leave of their guests far into the morning hours, Joseph's lovemaking look on a whole different meaning that night. And as she lay next to her husband after he had fallen fast asleep, Charlotte could only be thankful for the miracle of mistletoe and midnight wishes that had made all her dreams finally come true.

THE END

AUTHOR'S NOTE

Book reviews help readers to find books, and authors to find readers. Please consider writing a review for *Mistletoe & Midnight Wishes* within the Bluestocking Belles boxset *Merry Belles*. Even a few sentences telling people what you liked about the story is helpful. Reviews can be posted on eRetailer sites including BookBub and Goodreads.

I hope you enjoyed this novelette with Joseph and Charlotte and their journey to finding love. Hopefully you remember Joseph from my other novellas with the Belles where he was the secondary character in *Under the Mistletoe* and *A Mistletoe Kiss*. You can learn more about all my work that includes my medieval, time travel, and Regency era stories on my website at https://www.sherryewing.com/

Sherry Ewing picked up her first historical romance when she was a teenager and has been hooked ever since. An award-winning and bestselling author, she writes historical and time travel romances to awaken the soul one heart at a time. When not writing, she can be found in the San Francisco Bay Area at her day job as an Information Technology Specialist. You can learn more about Sherry and her books on her website where a new adventure awaits you on every page

You can learn more about Sherry Ewing at these social media links:

Bluesky: https://bsky.app/profile/sherryewing.bsky.social
Bookbub: www.bookbub.com/authors/sherry-ewing
Dragonblade Publishing: https://www.dragonbladepublishing.com/team/sherry-ewing/
Facebook: www.Facebook.com/SherryEwingAuthor
Goodreads: www.Goodreads.com/author/show/8382315.Sherry_Ewing
Instagram: https://instagram.com/sherry.ewing
Pinterest: www.Pinterest.com/SherryLEwing
Threads: https://www.threads.com/@sherry.ewing
TikTok: https://www.tiktok.com/@sherryewingauthor
Tumblr: https://sherryewing.tumblr.com/
X: www.X.com/Sherry_Ewing
YouTube: http://www.youtube.com/SherryEwingauthor
Newsletter Sign Up: http://bit.ly/2vGrqQM
Facebook Street Team: www.facebook.com/groups/799623313455472/
Facebook Official Fan page: https://www.facebook.com/groups/356905935241836/

MAGGIE'S WHEELBARROW

JUDE KNIGHT

MAGGIE'S WHEELBARROW

BY JUDE KNIGHT

A year ago, Maggie's husband marched out of Spain with his regiment to invade France. She hasn't heard from him since, and when she followed him, the battles were over and his regiment was gone. Letters to the army, him, and his family have brought no answers, so she and her children are off to find him, even if they have to walk the length and breadth of England.

CHAPTER 1

September 1814

THE SHIP DOCKED in Portsmouth on the morning tide. The passage from Spain had taken most of the money Maggie Parker had been able to save, and had not included food. Buying enough to keep the children from hunger during the voyage had depleted her slender reserves even further.

She did not have to carry Billy and Eva far from the wharf to the coach stop. However, she discovered that passage to the Midlands on a coach would cost more than she could afford, so they were facing another long walk. Two hundred miles, at least, and that was if the first village was the correct one.

Maggie was certain, however, that she would be able to earn money along the way. She was willing to turn her hand to any honest work, and it was now autumn, so there would be crops to harvest in the countryside, and extra hands might be needed even in the towns, when inns or great houses had busy times.

As she walked, she was looking for a hand cart or something similar. Ah, yes! Outside a general store was a sturdy wooden wheelbarrow. That was what she needed. Maggie went inside to find the price. "Three shillings, ma'am," said the shopkeeper. After some haggling, she bought it for two shillings, popped Billy inside, and pushed it back to the wharf.

She was determined to be out of town before nightfall so she would not have to spend her last few coins on accommodation. In summer, a woman, a toddling infant, and a baby could make themselves comfortable for the night in a hedge or under a tree—and she had done so many times during their long treks through Portugal, Spain, and even the south of France. Even if it rained—and in the England she remembered from her childhood, rain was always a possibility—she might find barns or abandoned cottages that would give them a little shelter from the elements.

Yes, they would not need to rent a room under a roof in the country. Towns, though, were not safe places for those without a stout door between them and the predators who would take even the little that Maggie and her children owned.

To her relief, the boy she had paid to watch her possessions was still waiting on the wharf, and so were her bags, her small trunk, and the bag with all the things she needed for the baby. She gave the boy another threepence and an extra penny to help her load the wheelbarrow. Then, with Billy perched on the trunk and Eva still in the shawl tied tightly to her back, she set off to walk to Ashton.

"It will take us most of September, I expect," she told her two children as she walked. Chatting to the children helped to pass the time as the long miles rolled away under the single wheel and her shoulders ached. Her feet, too, for it had been months since their last long trek across the Pyrenees, and through Spain to San Sebastián.

Once she had arrived at the Spanish port town, she had found work cleaning floors and making up rooms at an inn, so she could save enough money to buy passage for them all. Between that and the time on the ship, it had been more than three months since she walked long distances, and Eva had grown heavier—it felt like much heavier.

Eva was happy in her shawl. Soothed by her closeness to Maggie and rocked by the movement, she made no complaint. Maggie supposed she slept some of the time, and for the rest, watched the world pass with those wise six-month baby eyes.

Billy, who was never still even in his sleep, kept asking to get down from the wheelbarrow to walk and then to get up again a few minutes later, for he was tired of walking.

A steep hill perhaps two hours out of Portsmouth proved to be the biggest challenge of the day. Reaching the top, she found a safe place to rest her legs and change Eva's clouts. Then it was Billy's turn, and it was, as always, a struggle. Billy kept trying to wriggle away, but she soon had him clean and reclouted.

"You may run to that tree and back, Billy, while I get you a drink and something to eat." She had purchased a bottle of barley water and some buns with currants in them. Billy had his own metal cup. Eva's feeder cup, with its long spout, was of china. It was wrapped in rags, packed in a little box just a fraction larger than the wrapped cup, and tucked into Maggie's bag, where it was well padded by her clothing. It was one of the little family's least-easily replaceable possessions.

The barley water had been flavored with sugar and fruit juice. Maggie crumbled one of the buns into a plate and splashed it with barley water so that it softened and Maggie could feed it to Eva a spoonful at a time. She would have to find milk before the day was out. Her own had dried during the last long walk. Billy ate most of a bun and asked for a second cup of barley water. Between the three of them, they almost finished the bottle.

Once they were on their way again, Billy fell asleep in the wheelbarrow. Eva lay relaxed against Maggie's back—probably, she was also asleep.

The road trended down again, and then back up, but none of the hills they encountered were as steep as the first. Maggie sang a marching song, altering some of the words so that they were less profane. Billy was fond of repeating the sounds he heard.

They made another stop when they passed through a village in the late afternoon. The baker was putting up her shutters, and Maggie asked if she had any leftovers she did not plan to keep for the next day, and that Maggie could buy for half price.

They feasted on pies, sitting on a bench outside of the shop and the only price the woman asked for her bounty was Maggie's story. Maggie told her about growing up as the daughter of a sergeant, following the army with her Mama and then marrying a sergeant of her own and having her son. "When the army invaded France, I remained behind. Billy was very ill, and once he was well again, I was close to my confinement. Eva was born in February, and by the time we could travel again, the war was over. I should have been with him. If I had been with the army, I would know what happened, and I would have been with people who knew that Will and I were married."

The woman's eyes softened with pity, as if she was thinking that Will had abandoned Maggie and Billy. It was not true. He loved Maggie, and she loved him. Something was wrong, for Will would have returned for them if he could. Perhaps he was dead. Surely Maggie would know if Will was dead?

Her eyes filled with tears, and she turned away to pour the last of the barley water into the children's cups.

"You could do with some milk for the little ones," said the baker, and she hurried into the shop. When she came back, she had questions. What did Maggie do when she realized Will wasn't coming for her? How did she get to England? Where was she going?

Eva had been five weeks old when news of Napoleon's surrender and of the victory at Toulouse filtered through to the remnants of soldiers' families left behind in Spain. She and Billy joined the band of wives and children who crossed the Pyrenees in the hopes of joining the army's embarkation. "By the time we got there, Will's regiment was already gone, overseas to Canada, they told me. They wouldn't send me there or even back to England, because I didn't have my marriage papers." The precious document had been lost in a river crossing where she'd had a choice between saving Billy or saving her bag.

"The other wives that the army rejected decided to return to Spain.

I went back with a group of my friends, since I spoke more Spanish than French, and the French didn't want us there." Most of the wives were Spanish, and some of them were only wives by the most generous interpretation of the term. But they were Maggie's friends.

"When Will didn't answer my letters—" she had sent them both to the regiment and to 'Ashton, the Midlands'— "I found a job in an inn at San Sebastián in Spain to earn enough to pay for our passage. And now I am walking to the Midlands. I know Will comes from a village called Ashton. I am going to visit all of them if I must, and find Will's family."

It was only after several letters had gone unanswered that a kindly Englishman who was in San Sebastián on business explained that Parker was a common surname and that many villages in England were called Ashton. Even in the English Midlands, which was all she knew about where Will's family lived, there were several Ashtons. She had addressed her next letter to every Ashton village she could find on the businessman's map, proclaiming her intention to leave Spain and come to England. More precious coins were spent on sending those letters, and she hoped one of them had reached Will's mother.

"You're a brave woman, Mrs. Parker," said the baker. "Do you not have family of your own?"

Maggie shook her head. Ma and Pa had been all the family she had. Both were orphans and both were gone, Ma of a fever in Portugal when Maggie was a child and Pa at Badajoz two and a half years ago. She had admired Will for some time, but it was not until Pa died, when the officer of their regiment said that she must marry or go back to England, that Will had spoken of his own regard for her. Once they were wed, admiration had swiftly deepened into love.

"If Will's family don't want me, at least I'll know," she said, more to herself than to the other woman. "I can make a life for myself and the children, but I need to know what happened to their Daddy."

The baker stood up. "Wait here." She bustled off along the street and disappeared into another shop. A few minutes later, she came back, smiling. "You and the children will sleep here tonight, Mrs. Parker. You can have my brother's room." Her eyes filled with tears, which she blinked away. "He died at Talavera, he did, and I know he'd want me to help a fellow soldier's wife."

She gave a decisive nod. "And then, in the morning, the carter will take you on your journey. He is not going far, but he'll save a day's walking, I reckon."

Maggie accepted, and tried to offer money for bed and board, but the baker said that Will had fought to save England, and the least she could do was help his little family. The carter said the same. "I was in the Peninsula, ma'am. If I cannot help the family of one of our own, what is the world coming to?"

She spent a pleasant ride sharing memories of funny or heartwarming things that happened during the wars, each of them—by silent mutual agreement—avoiding mention of all the tragedies they had seen.

When their ways parted, he left her with an innkeeper's son who had been in his company in the army, and the son insisted that his family would be glad to have her and the two little ones to stay for the night. Maggie went to sleep as soon as the children, and dreamt of Will.

In the morning, a friend of the innkeeper's son drove her north, but he proved to be not quite so charitable, and in the end, Maggie had to produce the pistol that her father had given her long ago. It was not loaded, of course. Loaded guns could not be carried in pockets and were, in any case, not safe around children. Maggie judged that the man would not know the difference, and she was right. He unloaded her wheelbarrow and her possessions from his cart, called her some unpleasant names, and went on his way.

And so it went through the rest of September and into October. Maggie and her children found safe refuge some nights and on others slept outside under the stars. Sometimes they were offered lifts and sometimes they walked. Three times, they stopped for several days while Maggie harvested vegetables, picked fruit, or stacked hay. Twice more, Maggie had to use her pistol to discourage someone with quite the wrong idea about camp followers.

Most of those who offered them help were ex-soldiers or families who had lost someone to war. They all proved to be trustworthy. In a little over three weeks, Maggie and the children arrived at the first village of Ashton on her list.

Her heart warmed by the kindness of so many people, she called first on the innkeeper and then on the vicar to find out whether the neighborhood held a family called Parker, whose son William had been in Spain with the army.

But the answer at both places was 'No.' This was the wrong Ashton.

The vicar and his wife were kind enough to give her and the children a place to sleep. Maggie assured them that she was not discouraged. Disappointed, of course, but it had been too much to hope that they would strike lucky at the first try. Tomorrow, the little family would begin their journey to the next Ashton on the list.

Ashton-on-Dove, England, September 1814

Will Parker had largely recovered from the injuries that had nearly killed him at Toulouse. He would walk with a limp forever, but at least he still had his leg, even if it was scarred from multiple shrapnel strikes and twisted from an ill-set bone. He had a long deep scar across his shoulder and back where he'd apparently been hit by a sword. But the worst thing was the hole in his memory.

More than two years had disappeared from his mind, leaving a blank. His mother said he'd had a blow on his head during the fighting for Cuidad Rodrigo, and the doctor said that explained it, for he'd apparently had a second blow in exactly the same place at Toulouse.

He remembered the beginning of the siege at Cuidad Rodrigo and then nothing else, until he had woken up more than two years later in a surgery tent in France. Woken and slipped back into unconsciousness over and again through more than a month until at last he found himself in his own familiar boyhood bedroom back in Ashton-on-Dove, under his mother's care.

With enough memories of the war up until his first injury, Will didn't mind that he had forgotten another two years of the same. Except that he was bone-deep certain that something important was hidden in that hole. Something he desperately wanted to remember. Something that left him uneasy and unsettled.

But trying to force the memories to surface only gave him a headache, and he had work to do. Since he managed to get back on his feet again, he'd been keeping accounts and records for most of the merchants in their little village, using skills he must have developed during the two missing years. How odd to keep the skill but lose all memory of acquiring it.

He was good at the work, but something was still missing. He didn't fit into the life he'd had before he joined the army, and the life he was building felt wrong, somehow. The old familiar places no longer felt like home.

If only he could remember the important matter he was certain hid somewhere, deep in the shadows of his memory.

CHAPTER 2

The hope of soon being reunited with Will, or at least reaching his mother, had kept Maggie moving along the winding roads from Portsmouth to the first village of Ashton. When that proved to be the wrong place, she changed her strategy. Winter was coming. Even now, the heat was gone from the long evenings as soon as the sun dipped below the horizon. If she had to find lodgings for herself and the children during the winter, then she must make more than the few coins she had picked up on her way north.

Having made the decision between one village and the next, she put it into practice at the first opportunity, asking at both inns and the three major houses if there was any work available.

One of the inns took her on to clean rooms and empty slop pails. For one week, she told them. After that, she said, she must be off once more on her search. With Eva on her back and Billy tagging behind, she managed the heavy work with ease, and a week later set off the next Ashton with several more shillings in her purse and a warmer coat for each child to keep them comfortable in the sometimes-cold wind.

The second Ashton was as disappointing as the first, but Maggie got two night's work at the inn, and moved on the third. Thus it went through the autumn and on into early winter. When the snow came, she would have to be settled, but meanwhile, she moved from village to village, stopping to work whenever her money ran low, and at every village called Ashton or something similar, asking for the Parker family. All to no avail.

She was between Ashtons in early December when, on the strength of a stint as a maid at yet another inn, she was offered temporary work at the local great house, where they needed extra servants during a house party. At first, she thought she'd have to turn the job down, though the wages were excellent. But another woman overheard her telling the hiring steward about her children.

"I reckon they could stay with Ma," she said. "She's looking after me own young uns, while I earn a few coins, so two more wouldn't matter to her none, and she could do with the pennies." The woman introduced herself as Frannie, and offered to take Maggie to visit "Ma" immediately.

"If she could put you up at night," said the steward, "I shall add two shillings a day to the wages, for where I could find you a bed, I do not know. Mind you, you'll have to be at your post by five in the morning, and will not be home until after the guests have had their dinner."

Frannie's mother proved to be a kind woman whom Eva took to straight away, and the other children were twins of Billy's age, so Maggie went off to work the following morning with a light heart. If she saw out the two weeks of the house party, she would earn the princely sum of eighteen shillings! Four shillings of that would go Frannie's mother, but fourteen shillings would feed her little family for weeks, if she was careful.

It was hard work, but in some ways, it was also a holiday. No walking for hours with Eva on her back and the wheelbarrow before her. No need to find dry spaces through the day to feed the children or to change a wet clout. And she enjoyed the walks with Frannie in the pre-dawn quiet and the velvet dark of the late evening.

After the first three days of the house party, the servants settled into a routine—those who belonged to the house, the temporary hires, and servants of guests all learning what they could expect from one another. Hearing how some of the guests behaved toward the servants, Maggie was pleased to be working where she didn't see them. In the morning, she was one of several maids assigned to the drawing room, the little parlors, the billiards room, and other gathering spaces before any of the guests were awake. They tidied, cleaned, laid fires, and set the rooms up for whatever use the mistress of the house had planned for the day.

After that work was finished, she was sent wherever she was most needed, one day helping in the kitchen, the next cleaning the rooms of the senior servants, the third ironing a great pile of linen that had come back from the wash.

They were long days, and she missed the children, for she was gone before they were awake and home late at night. But the camaraderie of the servants' hall was pleasant. And if some of the menservants were inclined to regard her with lustful eyes, Maggie had been putting soldiers in their place ever since she first began to develop a woman's shape. Those who did not desist at a pleasant refusal soon found themselves outmatched, though she only once had to resort to stern measures.

The man she kicked in the crotch, a visiting valet, complained to the butler when he had uncurled from the ball he'd made of himself as he cradled his injured parts. Maggie, nothing cowed, told them she had refused the man and he had ignored her warnings. "I do not like to hurt people," she said, "but I've spent the past twenty years at war, first with my father and then with my husband. I've been taught to defend myself from men who think women are playthings. He got what he deserved, and if you disapprove, sir and madam, I'll take my wages for the past three days, and leave."

"That will not be necessary," said the housekeeper, and she told the butler that Maggie was a good worker, and got on well with the other servants—even the men who had approached her and been refused.

They sent Maggie back to her work, and she heard no more about it.

Then, on the fifth day, a lady's maid of one of the guests fell down the stairs and broke her arm. The housekeeper, looking harried, called the temporary servants together. "Do any of you have any experience as a lady's maid?" She asked the question, but did not sound hopeful.

Surely, this would be a chance to earn a few extra coins? "I have acted as maid to the wives of several officers," Maggie said. "I can dress hair and press fine garments without damaging them. Mend them, too." And the wives had always given her a vail for her efforts—sometimes a shilling, sometimes half a crown, on one red letter occasion, a third-guinea worth seven whole shillings. Not that she expected such bounty to happen again, but just imagine!

"You will be serving two ladies," said the housekeeper. "They are sisters and share both a room and a maid. You will need to sleep in the suite's dressing room to be available to them at all hours."

Maggie didn't like the sound of that. Not seeing her children at all for more than a week? But then, they were not seeing her now, even though she slept with them in the same bed but left before they woke. And Frannie's mother assured her they were well and enjoying their time with Frannie's children.

"There will be another five shillings in your wage packet for the extra duties," said the housekeeper, and that decided it. Maggie nodded, and the housekeeper took her upstairs to meet the ladies. She soon decided she had made the right decision. Lady Clara and Lady Eugenie seemed to be pleasant ladies, ready with a thank you and a smile when Maggie did something for them.

Maggie was needed immediately to dress their hair for the first activity of the day. After they had left the room to go downstairs and join the other guests, she found her way to the room on the fourth floor where their poor maid had been carried after the accident. The woman greeted her with a surly, "And who might you be? I am not a raree show."

"I am Mrs. Maggie Parker, and I am helping your ladies while you are laid up, Miss Brown. I came to see if there is anything I need to know about being their maid, and also, if there is anything I can do for you."

Miss Brown regarded her steadily and then thawed a little. "Might as well come in, then. Mrs. Parker, is it? Don't see many married women in our position."

"I cannot claim to be a proper lady's maid, Miss Brown. Not like you. That's why I'd be grateful for any advice you can give me. I am a sergeant's daughter and a sergeant's wife, and have served a few officer's wives during my time in the army. But something like this grand house party is beyond anything I've known."

With a frown, Miss Brown asked, "Where is your husband, Mrs. Parker?"

"I do not know," Maggie replied, with a sigh. She launched into the often-told story. "Will disappeared at Toulouse...." ending with, "I'll go to all of them if I must. I need to know, you see."

Miss Brown looked more puzzled than either condemning or sympathetic. "I don't understand," she complained. "I assume you are a housemaid here. Where is your daughter?"

"I am a temporary servant," Maggie explained. While she spoke, she was dusting and tidying, for it wasn't in her nature to sit still when there was work to be done, and Miss Brown must be uncomfortable having to look at dusty surfaces and clutter. "Hired for the house party. Eva and her older brother Billy are staying with a local cottager, who is also looking after her grandchildren. Once the party is over, we shall be off to the next Ashton on our list." With a twinkle in her eye, she added, "Us and our wheelbarrow," for Miss Brown looked as if she could do with a laugh, and she might be amused by the idea of Maggie trundling a baby and an infant along the lanes of England in a wheelbarrow, on top of their worldly possessions.

It worked. "Why do you have a wheelbarrow?" asked Miss Brown. So, Maggie told that part of her story, and a few anecdotes about her little family's adventures along the lanes and byways of England, and Miss Brown thawed still further and explained the idiosyncrasies of 'her' young ladies, and the dangers of a house party to willful heiresses who were not as sophisticated as they thought. Part of Maggie's job would be to win their trust and keep them safe.

By the time Maggie returned to the young ladies' room, she was as ready as she might be to fulfill her duties, though keeping them safe might be beyond her. Still. She would try.

Being a ladies' maid was a pleasant job when the ladies were nice. Maggie had served a few officers' wives who were right cows! The two sisters continued to be appreciative, if demanding. She and Miss Brown became friends, of a sort, as Maggie continued to visit the maid every day. The work was easy for a woman whose daily life was usually much more physically demanding.

As for keeping the young ladies safe, that was a little more problematic. The best she could do was share the servants' observations of the gentlemen who clustered around the pair. Some were what Maggie thought of as "real gentlemen." Some, like the master of the valet who had attacked her, were wolves in sheep's clothing, with a black reputation for bothering the maids and wandering at night into the bedrooms of people to whom they were not married.

Whether the young ladies took any notice of her was another matter, but they at least allowed her to tell her stories—not just those told by the other servants, but also tales of her experiences as the daughter and wife of a soldier.

They particularly loved the story of how she and Will came to marry. "When my father passed away, I thought I would have to go home to England. 'Home,' I say, but until a few months ago, I have only childhood memories from when Pa's regiment was briefly posted here. I was born on campaign, and my mother and I followed my father until I was eight, which is when a bad ague went through the camp. By the time it was finished with, hundreds were dead, including Ma."

She would carry on with her work while she talked—mending a slipper, or pouring water for them to wash, or dressing their hair, or taking it down and brushing it. One hundred strokes each and not a stroke more or less.

"And so, I grew up in a tent with Pa, or in the baggage train of the army. Then, all of a sudden, I was a single woman alone. Pa's savings would have been enough to take me to England, but I had no family there. Where would I live? What would I do?"

She would pause, then, her hands busy, continued the current task, waiting for one of the young ladies to say, "What happened, Mrs. Parker?"

"The soldiers who didn't have a wife began to bring me presents and ask me to marry them. All except the one I wanted. Corporal Will Parker watched me from afar, and I waited for him, but he didn't come. Then our officer told me that I had to choose or I had to leave, for half of the bachelors were squabbling over who had my favor, and the other half were writing poetry or picking flowers, and not a single one of them was remembering we were meant to be fighting the French."

She chuckled, and the ladies giggled with her. "I was still waiting for Corporal Parker, but my time had run out. So, I picked a bunch of wildflowers and took it to him. I told him I was a good cook, an excellent seamstress, a competent laundress and would make him a faithful wife, but he need not count on me for any poetry, for I was a practical soldier's daughter."

Her hands stilled as she remembered his shocked expression and how it changed to dawning delight. Half lost in the dream of that day, she finished her story. "He said he had always wanted to marry me, but he never thought he had a chance. We went to find the chaplain, and were married that very day. And we had more than a year together before we were separated. Happy, even if there was a war on, because we were together. I loved him, and he loved me."

The ladies sighed. "I do hope I can find a man I love," said Lady Eugenie, and Lady Clara agreed.

The days were long. Maggie started as early as the housemaids, and stayed up later. But she also had time during the day to run over to Frannie's house and see her children, who were thriving, but—or so Frannie's mum said—all the better for seeing their ma.

It was while returning from one such excursion three days before the end of the house party that she heard a lady's voice say, sharply, "I said no, Lord Clement." Surely that was Lady Eugenie's voice?

Maggie pushed through the screening hedge, and there, in a small private garden, Lady Eugenie was fighting in the arms of the arrogant young sprig whose valet had attacked Maggie. The little garden was lamentably short of weapons. Maggie, stuck with a last-resort action, put her hand between the villain's legs, grabbed, and pulled.

He screamed and let go of Lady Eugenie, but his shriek had not gone unnoticed. Maggie could hear voices approaching. She had to think fast. The upper classes had some odd ideas, and she didn't want her charge to be compelled to marry such a wicked man.

"We shall say he attacked me and you arrived just as I kicked him," she whispered to the lady. The man was still curled in a ball, clutching his groin and whimpering. He was not in any fit state to disagree with their story, and even if he did, who would believe him?

She could only hope Lady Eugenie would follow her lead, and sure enough, when a group of guests rounded the end of the hedge and came through the rose arch toward them, Lady Eugenie turned to Maggie and started smoothing the garments that had been disarranged in pushing through the hedge and bending over to deal with Lord Clement.

"Mrs. Parker, are you sure you are unhurt," Lady Eugenie was saying when the plump matron who was the worst gossip of the lady guests sailed up saying, "Why, Lady Eugenie. What happened here? How did Lord Clement become injured?"

"I arrived just in time to see that horrid man attack my maid," said Lady Eugenie. "Mrs. Parker kicked him. I must say it was very effective. Lord Clement let go of her immediately. Well done, Mrs. Parker."

Of course, it was not as simple as that. Indeed, there was a huge fuss. Lord Clement was a younger son of a marquess, and his father demanded that Maggie be punished. "The chit should be whipped," he declared. "No doubt she led my poor son on, thinking she would get money out of him."

The host and hostess of the house party were in a difficult position. It seemed to Maggie that they knew perfectly well who to blame for the assault, but they did not want to offend the marquess.

For a short while, Maggie was afraid that she would, indeed, be whipped, but Lady Eugenie took her brother the earl to one side for an earnest conversation, and after that, the earl demanded that everyone wait while he had a private word with the marquess.

Whatever he said, the marquess changed course entirely. He told the host and hostess that he was leaving the situation in their hands, ordered his carriage, and marched his son off upstairs. Within half an hour, they were gone.

As for Maggie, she was on her way, too. Dismissed, but with her full wages for the fortnight plus a bonus from the hostess, "for your trouble, Mrs. Parker, and for your husband's service." Even better, when she said farewell to the two sisters—and recommended Frannie to replace her for the two final days of the house party—they insisted on giving her a half-sovereign as a vail for her services.

"We are grateful for your stories, Mrs. Parker," said Lady Clara. "We learned a great deal." Lady Eugenie added, "And I am grateful for your quick thinking, and sorry that defending me cost you your job."

"You need not be concerned," Maggie told her. "I have been paid for the fortnight, and I shall be back with my children two days earlier than I expected. It is fine weather, too. Tomorrow morning, we shall be on our way, and who knows? Perhaps we shall find Will's family in the next village of Ashton."

That was not the end of the largesse, for the earl insisted on escorting Maggie back to Frannie's mum's house. "My sister told me what that scoundrel tried to do, Mrs. Parker. My family owes you a debt. I trust you will accept this purse and its contents as a token of our appreciation, and if there is anything I can do for you, please let me know."

The purse contained the almost unbelievable sum of a whole guinea. Together with what she had earned and what the ladies had given her, Maggie now had more than enough to find somewhere safe for her and the children to spend the winter, and she might not even have to find a job right away. It would be good to be settled by Christmas. The winter had been mild so far, but that could not last.

She could also spend a bit on letters to the remaining villages of

Ashton. Or… There was something she had heard. Would the earl think her impertinent if she asked? Well, and what if he did? At worst, he would say no, and he might say yes!

"My lord, there might be something. Is it true that lords do not have to pay to send their letters?"

"It is, Mrs. Parker. Or, to be more precise, members of Parliament do not have to pay to use His Majesty's royal mail. Do you have a letter you wish to send?"

"Several, sir. I am looking for my husband's family." Maggie explained all about being separated from Will, and how she knew only that he came from a village called Ashton, which was somewhere in the Midlands. "I wrote from Spain, my lord, and a diplomatic gentleman helped me make a list of the villages named Ashton and sent the letters for me. But if one of those letters arrived, and if they responded, I never heard."

"Write your letters, Mrs. Parker—you can write?"

Maggie nodded.

"Very good. Then write your letters, and I'll send a servant down to collect them."

Where would Maggie get paper? From the general store, she supposed. It was probably still open at this time.

The earl must have seen her hesitancy, for he said, "I shall send my valet down with some paper. Is this the house, Mrs. Parker? I shall leave you, then. God bless you on your way, ma'am, and thank you again."

Gracious. An earl had blessed her and thanked her. Maggie felt as lofty as the queen! Wouldn't Will laugh when she told him? If Will was still alive. If she could find him.

CHAPTER 3

Will had spent most of the day preparing for quarter day, which was on the twenty-fifth of December, but would be observed in this village in two days' time, on the twenty-fourth. Almost all the places he worked for held their shops or workshops by tenancy from one of the local landowners, and quarter day was traditionally not only the time to present a request for necessary repairs and improvements, but also to pay the quarterly rent.

The roof of the general store needed reshingling. The wall between the bakery and the bookshop was crumbling where a shifting spring had undermined the foundation stones. The smithy, which had been owned by the same family from time immemorial, had no rent to pay, but was seeking a small loan from the local viscount to install a puddling furnace to make wrought iron.

Will had spent much of the day making fair copies of his reports that presented the arguments for each. The little spare parlor the baker let him use as his office backed onto the bakeries brick ovens and was always warm, but the winter had arrived with a vengeance, after weeks of mild weather.

Outside, the wind was bleak, and the odd icy drops of rain threatened sleet before nightfall. Which was not far off, so he needed to hop to it and get home. He stretched his cramped hand several times, spreading and clenching, before pulling on his coat and gloves, and winding his muffler around his neck before putting on his cap.

"I'm off home, Davey," he called to the baker.

"Gibbon at the tavern has a letter for your Ma," Davey shouted back. "He told me when he picked up his stew."

"Thanks!"

Will turned his steps toward the tavern. Somewhat reluctantly, for Mary Gibbon, the tavern keeper's daughter, had shown a recent tendency to bat her eyelashes at him. Since she was a virtuous maiden, he had to assume she was angling for a wedding ring.

Will had only recently recovered enough to find the female half of humanity of any interest at all, and he certainly did not wish to acquire a wife. And that was leaving aside the chance that he'd somehow picked one up in his two missing years. Unlikely, true, for if that was the case, where was she?

Presumably, if he tried, he could find someone from his old regiment who could give him answers on the matter, but he'd need more than a vague and easily ignored male stirring to provoke him into making the effort.

Sure enough, when he pushed open the tavern door, Mary propped the broom she had been using against a table and rushed up, standing too close and smiling with shining eyes. "Why, it is Mr. Parker! What may I get you, Mr. Parker? Some stew? It's a good one today."

"Your Pa has a letter for me, Miss Gibbon," Will told her, resisting the urge to push her away and taking a step back instead. "I'll just have that, please, and get home before the storm sets in."

She blinked rapidly, looking up at him through her eyelashes and moving closer again. "No need go home through the cold. You can stay here in the warm, Mr. Parker."

Gibbon came to Will's rescue, entering from the kitchen with the mailbag over his shoulder. "Leave the poor man be, girl," he said. "He doesn't need you clambering all over him, and that floor won't sweep itself."

Mary sniffed and tossed her head but obeyed, stomping her way to the broom. Gibbon handed Will the letter. He glanced at it. The mark said it had been franked by some lord in London, but it was addressed to his mother, sure enough. Will shrugged.

"Thank you, Mr. Gibbon. I'll wish you a good evening, then."

Back out into the rain, which was becoming more persistent and, if possible, even icier. But it was only a five-minute brisk walk home, and he was soon turning in at the gate and crossing the little front garden to let himself into the house.

"It's me, Ma," he called, as he stopped in the hall to take off all his outer layers. He walked through the little house in his stockinged feet, for his slippers would be warming by the kitchen fire. And sure enough, there they were. He stood on the threshold and breathed in the wonderful smells of baking. Mama had been preparing for Christmas, when his sisters were expected with their families. All of them lived not much more than an hour away by cart, so they could come for the day. It would be good to see them all.

That two-year blank had apparently been eventful for the family he left behind in England. His two younger sisters had married—the eldest of the three was already wed and had a child before the hole in his memory. He'd come home to two new nieces and a nephew. New to him—two of them were already walking, and the youngest two were born in marriages that he didn't remember hearing about.

And his father had died in those two years, too, so his mother was left in the cottage by herself, except that his sisters took turns month by month about to stay with her so she would not be alone in her grief.

Once he was back on his feet again, they had heaved a collective sigh of relief and left the cottage to him and Ma. Ma seemed pleased to have her only surviving son back home again, even if not quite in one piece. "I love my daughters, Will. Don't doubt it. But they should be organizing their own homes, not mine, and it is good to have a man to do for again."

"I've a letter for you, Ma," he told her.

"Who is it from?" she asked, without turning from the pot she was stirring.

"It doesn't say on the outside," Will said. "It has been franked by a Lord Somebody-or-other. I can't quite make out the name. In London, Ma."

"Get along with you," Ma said, tickled. "A lord from London, writing to me? Open it and read it for me. There's a dear."

Ma could read printing, if the words were simple, but she much preferred Will to read to her. He used a knife to pry up the seal and opened the sheet of paper that comprised the envelope and letter.

As he read it through for the first time, he heard a buzzing in his ears, and his knees turned weak. He sat in the nearest chair and read it again. The words hadn't changed. Will's world had, though. He stared at the words as if a third reading would give a different meaning.

"Well? Go on. Has some duke found out I'm his long-lost daughter?" Ma chuckled.

Will couldn't manage even a weak smile.

"What is it, Will?" Ma asked, turning away from the pot at last and giving him a searching look.

"I'll read it to you.

"Dear Mrs. Parke

You may have wondered why you have not heard from me in the past year. I have been writing letters to Ashton in the Midlands, but I have recently learned that there are seven villages with that name, and I fear my letters have not reached you.

Or they have found their way to you and you do not wish to know me or your grandchildren, but that I do not wish to believe. Will spoke so often of how you would welcome us when he brought us home. I can only hope you will want us even though we come without him.

As Will may have written to you, I was not able to go with the army to France, as I was having some trouble with my second pregnancy. I had two letters from Will, and then nothing more. As soon as I could after Eva's birth, I followed the army to France, only to find that Will's regiment had shipped out.

Perhaps you know what happened to Will. I have been unable to find out.

I do not have the papers that proved our marriage, so the army would not talk to me. I am so sorry for your loss, and for my own.

I am in England, and in the Midlands. I have been going from one village of Ashton to another, but I recently had the good fortune to assist a lady with a difficulty, and her brother proved to be an earl. To return the favor, he has offered to frank my letters for me, including this one. I have written to every village of Ashton that I have not yet visited, and I can only hope one of my letters will reach you.

I shall make my way to each Ashton in turn, so I cannot say when I shall arrive, but if this letter has found you so shall I. I am so looking forward to introducing you to your grandson, Billy, and your granddaughter, baby Eva, who was born after Will left for France.

I hope you will be able to welcome us, but you must not worry that we shall be a burden. I am well accustomed to working to provide for myself and my children, and will happily continue to do so.

We send you our affectionate and respectful regards

Margaret, William, and Evangeline Parker."

While he was reading, he was aware of his mother sinking into another chair, but he had not looked directly at her. He did now.

Her eyes were filled with tears but she was smiling. "Thank God," she said. "I have been so worried."

"You knew I had a wife and you didn't tell me?" Will couldn't help but feel betrayed.

"What could I say, Will?" his mother asked. "You had forgotten them, and I had no idea what had become of them. Had she deserted you? Had they all died? How would it have helped to tell you what little I knew?"

She scrambled to her feet and pulled out a drawer on the kitchen dresser. She handed him a package tied with ribbon. "Here. Here are your letters. When you've read them, you'll know as much about your wife as I do. Oh, my dear son, perhaps when you see her you will remember everything."

Or perhaps not. What would he do if he didn't know this wife of his? A thought occurred to him. "Margaret. Not... No, it couldn't be... I didn't marry Maggie Finch, did I? Sergeant Finch's daughter?"

Ma nodded. "That's it. Are you remembering, Will?" She sounded hopeful.

He shook his head. "Not from after Ciudad Rodrigo. From before. She... I doubt there was a man in the regiment who was not at least a little in love with Maggie Finch. Not that any of us would risk the sergeant's reaction if we showed her the least disrespect!"

He could feel his lips spreading in a grin as he remembered the cheerful pretty daughter of the formidable soldier. "I married Maggie Finch!"

"So, I should hope, Will Parker, since you had two children by her," said Ma, rather sharply. "Go and wash up for dinner, lad. You can read your letters after."

Will obediently got to his feet. *Maggie Finch.* Maggie Parker, now, and wandering the Midlands with his two children in tow. Wandering where? He checked the date and location at the top of the letter. It was dated two weeks ago, and she was not here yet. She had included a village name, as well, and he knew it. Not more than thirty miles hence, but he supposed a woman with two children might travel slowly. On the other hand, perhaps she was heading for a different Ashton.

As he washed his hands and face, he pictured her out in the cold and the rain and shuddered. He hoped she had found somewhere safe and warm to wait out the storm. She and the little ones.

He had a powerful urge to race out the door and start searching for them. In the dark and the rain, it would be pointless. Possibly even dangerous. He would leave in the morning, once it was light, riding in the direction of the village she had left weeks ago.

He'd have to tell his customers that he could not carry out his duties on quarter day, in two days' time. His records were all ready, so it would not be hard for them to present their own requests and pay their own rents. It made no difference if it *was* hard. His first responsibility was to Maggie Parker and her two children. No, not her. Their. Their two children.

Christmas was three days away. Could he find them in time to bring them home for Christmas? He was certainly going to try!

CHAPTER 4

The tinker's cart had a cover of oiled cloth that kept the rain off his wares, as well as off Maggie and the children, who were huddled together in the space the tinker had cleared for them. They had met him two nights ago, when they were about to eat their supper in a field by a little stream halfway between one Ashton and another.

Maggie had managed to catch some fish, and when the tinker saw her preparing to cook it over a fire, he offered to trade what he called twist bread for some of her fish. The tinker's wife rolled her bread dough into a long sausage shape then wound it around a stick, which she rested on two more sticks so it cooked above the embers of her fire. She turned it every few minutes so it cooked evenly, and it was delicious.

The tinker and his wife had a crock of butter and a handful of sweet carrots. Maggie added some apples to the joint meal. She had spent two days working in an orchard in return for food and a bed in the barn, and the farmer had given her a few pennies and a box of apples when she left.

Once the children were settled for the night, Maggie told the couple her story.

"Ashton-on-Dove," the wife repeated, when Maggie mentioned her next destination, the sixth Ashton on her list. "Fergus, it's not out of our way to go through Ashton-on-Dove on our way to Downwood Market." It was not a question, but a statement. "We can fit Mrs. Parker and the little ones into the cart."

"That we can, Ginny," said Fergus, and so they did.

Maggie was grateful. It meant she and the children would be in their sixth Ashton before Christmas. She had been spending snatches of time when they were distracted or asleep, or during the four days of storm when they could not travel, making little Christmas gifts. Surely, she would be able to find somewhere to stay in the village. Some place safe and warm where she and the children could rest and enjoy a holiday?

Yesterday's travel had been pleasant, until the evening when the rain began. Fergus had stopped at a farm whose owner was friendly to travelers, and offered some tinkering for a night in his barn for all of them, including the horse.

They made a late start in the morning, but Fergus said they were no more than an hour and a half from Ashton-on-Dove, and Ginny pointed out that none of them would melt. They set off in the rain, Ginny and Fergus in raincoats on the driver's seat, sharing a blanket, and Maggie and the children in the cart.

Her son found the confinement particularly hard. Usually, she could put Billy down to walk, or at the very least distract him by pointing out interesting things to look at, but under the cover, there was nothing to see beyond the interior of the cart.

Maggie sang songs, told stories, and invented adventures for Neddy, the wooden horse that Will had carved for Billy when he was a baby. The time slowly passed.

"I can see Ashton!" Ginny shouted, at last.

It was a good ten minutes later that the cart came to a stop. A few moments later, Ginny unlaced the flap at the back of the cart. "Come along, Parkers! We've arrived in Ashton. Fergus thought we might ask for your husband's family at the tavern.

Billy flung himself at Ginny, and Eva, who was dozing on Maggie's breast, woke up and blinked after him. Maggie could only move at a crouch, which was awkward while holding Eva, but she scooted toward the flap and was soon hurrying after Ginny, who was carrying Billy in through a door under a sign Maggie couldn't read from this angle. The rain had stopped, at least for the moment.

Inside, Fergus was waiting to speak to the tavernkeeper, who was busy with another man, anonymous in a long rain coat that sent a pang through Maggie's heart, for it was a soldier's coat, and that, and something about the man's shoulders, reminded her of Will.

Then he turned and took a step towards her and several thoughts collided in her mind, striking her speechless and freezing her in place. He could almost be Will, but this man was older, thinner, and moved with a limp, his leg stiff and awkward. He could almost be Will, but he looked straight at her without recognition. Of course, he probably could not see her face in the shadow of her bonnet as she stood with her back to the light. It had to be Will, for if he'd had a brother or cousin who was his double, would he not have told her?

He saw her looking as he walked toward her. She was in the doorway, so he stopped and lifted his cap politely. That removed all doubt from her mind, for there was the scar on his forehead from the blow on his head he'd taken at Cuidad Rodrigo.

"Will Parker?" Her voice made a question of it, though there was no question in her mind. It was Will, even if he did not know her.

"Yes," he said, inclining his head in a polite nod. "I am he."

Maggie responded to the nod with a slight curtsey, and pushed her bonnet back on her head so he could more clearly see her face. "Do you not know me, Will? I am Maggie. Maggie Parker."

"My wife," he said. His eyes focused on the child in her arms. "So, this must be Evangeline." He moved his gaze to Billy. "And William?"

"Eva and Billy, yes. Will? What is it? Where have you been? What is wrong?"

Will cast an eye over his shoulder at Fergus and the tavernkeeper. They were both watching, as was Ginny. He lowered his voice and whispered. "I was injured at Toulouse, Miss Fi... that is, Maggie." His tongue stumbled over her name. "I hit my head. I don't remember..."

In his eyes were despair, embarrassment, and the bone-deep decency for which she loved him. "I'm sorry, Maggie."

She sat Eva onto her hip to free one hand, which she put on Will's arm. She kept her own voice low. "We shall work it out, Will. That is, if you want to."

His eyes cleared and he spoke at normal volume. "I was just hiring a horse to come and find you. Ma received your letter last night, though the date on it was more than two weeks ago." He turned his head to call across the room to the tavernkeeper. "It seems I won't be needing that horse after all. Here is Mrs. Parker come to find me before I could go to look for her."

The tavernkeeper's eyes widened, but Fergus and Ginny looked relieved. "Will, these are Ginny and Fergus Fleming, who gave me and the children a lift in their cart," Maggie told Will.

"Thank you for bringing my family safely home," Will told them, politely.

IT WAS JUST a form of words, and yet Will felt the deep truth of them. This was his family. The girl he had admired (as had half the regiment), had matured and was even more beautiful than she'd been three years ago, and the two sweet children were adorable. The boy had something of the look of Will's sister's boy, who had recently turned two. Will judged that Billy, as Maggie called him, was a little younger than his cousin. Eva, the baby, melted Will's heart completely, with her chubby cheeks and her cheerful smile.

The carter's wife went to hand the boy to him, but Billy buried his head on her shoulder and clung tighter. "He doesn't know me," Will explained.

"He was not much older than Eva is now when Will had to leave us," Maggie explained. "Say goodbye to Mrs. Fleming, Billy. This is your Da, and we are going home with him. Fergus, could I have my things from the cart?"

Fergus nodded, and they all went outside, where the man

offloaded—of all things—a wheelbarrow and then a trunk, a large bag and a smaller one, which he put into the barrow. Ginny put Billy into the barrow, and Maggie went to take up the handles, but Will said, "My job."

She glanced at his leg, but nodded. Quite right, too. He might be a bit lame, but he could handle a wheelbarrow. Before he could push the barrow on its way, Maggie thanked the Flemings, giving Ginny a hug, so Will released the handles to shake Fergus's hand. Then Billy shook hands with Fergus too, Ginny gave the boy and baby Eva a kiss on the forehead, and Maggie dropped a kiss on Fergus's cheek, making him blush.

"Thank you both," she said.

"We'll be around most of the day," Fergus told her. "Fixing things. If you need us."

Will's internal response was swift and possessive. *She's my wife. If she needs anything or anyone, I'll be the one.* He was astounded at the strength of the emotion over a wife and children he had still not remembered. Perhaps his heart remembered them though his head couldn't.

"We shall be fine," Maggie was assuring the Fleming. "You heard Will. We are home."

"When did you arrive in England?" Will asked as she strode alongside him on the way to Ma's cottage. She summed up the journey for him in laconic sentences, starting with the arrival in Portsmouth and her purchase of the wheelbarrow. A world of detail was buried in, "I was fortunate enough to find work enough along the way to keep us fed, and people like the Flemings have offered us rides from time to time."

His admiration for her courage and enterprise rose by leaps and bounds.

He pushed the wheelbarrow around the back of the house just as the rain started again. He offered Billy his hands to help him down, and then picked up the bags.

"Let's get you inside out of the rain," Will said. He strode to the back door, and Maggie followed, carrying Eva and leading Billy by the hand. After they'd taken off their coats and shoes, he said, "I'll leave the bags here. Come and meet Ma."

Maggie picked up Eva and the smaller bag. "The children need their clouts changed," she observed. "I'll keep this one, Will. Can you take Billy's hand?"

Billy made no objection, so Will led his little family through the scullery and into the kitchen, where Ma was working bread dough at the table, with her back to them.

"Is that you, Will? Didn't they have a horse to hire."

"No need, Ma," Will said. "Maggie and the children are here."

She spun around, her hands white with flour. "Here! My dear child, you've come all this way alone? And I've not even made your bed up with clean sheets, yet. And these are my grandchildren! Oh, how splendid they are! What a wonderful Christmas this is going to be!

Some thirty minutes later, with the children changed into clean dry clothes and the bread set to rise, they settled in the parlor. The adults had a cup of tea each, and the children had milk, though they had currently both abandoned their mugs in favor of the little feast Ma had produced from her biscuit tins. Eva was sitting on her grandmother's lap, with a piece of biscuit in her hand, and Billy was, rather cautiously, perched on his father's knee.

Will had lost his heart to them both, and so had Ma, and if he still had no memory at all of marrying Maggie, he was certain it had been the best decision he had ever made.

"Billy wants Neddy," the little boy announced, suddenly.

Without interrupting the story she had been telling Ma about Eva's birth in a Spanish convent, Maggie dug into the little bag full of the children's things, which she'd kept beside her. Her hand came up empty, and her voice trailed off. She pulled the bag onto her lap and looked inside.

"Excuse me, Ma," she said. "I need to check the other bag."

"I'll get it for you," said Will. He set Billy on his feet and fetched the bag from the porch. She went through that, while Billy clambered back on Will's knee and watched, his thumb in his mouth and his eyes somber. The muffled word he said around the thumb was probably Neddy.

"It is his wooden horse," Maggie explained. "It isn't here."

Billy's eyes brimmed with tears. "Neddy?" he asked.

"When did you last see it, dear?" Ma asked Maggie.

Maggie was certain. "He had it in the Flemings' cart." She got up from the floor where she'd been sitting to search the bag. "I'll have to catch them. Billy loves that horse." Billy wriggled down from Will's knee and ran to his mother to clasp her around the knees. By now, he was wailing.

"I'll go," Will said. "Mr. Fleming said they would be working in the village today. I'll find them."

"It's pouring with rain," Ma protested.

"We've marched in worse," Will said. "Fought in worse, too, Ma. Billy, I'm going to get Neddy. I will be back as fast as I can."

The Flemings were easy to find. The cart was gone from outside of the tavern, but when Will poked his head inside to ask which way they had gone, they were both there— Mr. Fleming sharpening knives on a whetstone and Mrs. Fleming examining the holes in a couple of pots. "We can mend these as soon as we can set up our stove," she was telling the tavernkeeper.

They all looked around when Will opened the door further and stepped inside. "Mrs. Fleming, gentlemen. Mrs. Fleming, Billy has lost his wooden horse. May I look in your cart to see if it is there?"

"I will check for you," she replied. "Wait here," and a moment later, she was back, with the little toy in one hand.

She beamed as she held it out to Will. "You are a good father to go out in the rain to make your little boy happy," she told him.

But Will could not reply. As he took the horse, his hands remembered the shape and he could feel it taking its current form under his knife. It had taken several nights, sitting by the fire in the cottage they were sharing with another two couples, Maggie sitting next to him with baby Billy in her arms.

That memory unlocked others, and for a time he was blind and deaf to his surroundings as nearly three years' worth of experiences tumbled out of the suddenly unlocked part of his mind and filled the hole in his memory.

He suddenly realized that the Flemings and the tavernkeeper were talking to one another about him. "Never knew him to have fits." That was the tavernkeeper, sounding anxious and a tad irritated.

"Yes, put it there, Fergus. Now, Mr. Parker, sit down." That was Ginny Fleming. She had hold of his arm and was trying to encourage him to sit in a chair that had appeared in the middle of the room where no chair had been before he touched the horse.

"I am well," he assured her. "My memories came back, all at once. It was the horse, you see. I remembered carving it for Billy, and just like that, everything I had forgotten since the bump on my head at Toulouse came crowding back in. It blinded me for a moment, there. I'm right again, now. I need to get home and tell Maggie! My Maggie. I can't believe I couldn't remember her."

"Fergus and I will see you home," Ginny declared, and would not take no for an answer.

He invited them in at his mother's, but perhaps they understood that he wanted to be alone with his family, for they said they had to get back to work. "We'll pop by tomorrow before we leave town," Ginny promised.

"Stop in for a cup of tea," he asked, grateful to these people who had helped Maggie, but having to use all his discipline to remain calm and polite when all he wanted to do was close the door in their faces and hurry through to the kitchen and see his beloved wife and precious babies.

Ma had Eva tucked against her shoulder and was walking the floor with her, crooning as she went.

Billy was so big! Will could not believe how much he had grown. Changed, too, from a babe in arms into a harum scarum broth of a boy, clambering or running everywhere and never still.

But it had been more than a year. Children of that age grew fast. Will would have to be patient and loving. Billy would get to know him again. He crouched down and held out the wooden horse. "Neddy," the child cried, and threw himself across the room to retrieve the toy. "Da made it," he informed Will.

"Yes," Will agreed. "I made it. I carved it with a knife in the winter of the year before last, while we were in winter quarters, and you were a baby." Billy ignored the long explanation and Will tried something simpler. "I am your Da."

Billy looked up from his close examination of Neddy to cast Will a look redolent with disbelief.

Maggie and Ma had similar expressions. Ma spoke first, asking Maggie, "Did you tell him that, about the winter quarters?" Maggie shook her head without taking her eyes off Will.

"I remembered everything," Will told her. Told them both, but most of his attention was on Maggie. "As soon as I was holding Neddy, my memories flooded back." He chuckled. "The Flemings thought I was having a fit. I couldn't wait to get back to my little colonel and the recruits."

Laughing, while tears streamed down her cheeks, Maggie told Ma, "He has always called me his little colonel, and the children are the recruits, of course."

She walked into the arms that Will had opened to receive her. After a moment, he stretched one of them out to Ma.

Tears running down her face, Ma said, again, "It is going to be a wonderful Christmas."

Even as she stepped gladly into his embrace, Billy pulled on Will's trousers, demanding, "Up!"

"I haven't a free arm, Billy-boy," Will said. "Your Ma will pick you up, and we'll all have a hug."

So that was what they did, Maggie holding Billy, Ma holding Eva, and Will holding them all. And at last, Will Parker, a year after leaving the battlefields of Europe, felt he had come home.

CHAPTER 5

Ashton-on-Dove, 1857

"WILL," Maggie called. "Bill's family will be here soon." Bill, or Billy as she sometimes still called him, had come up from London on the train with his family, covering in three hours the distance that had once taken months for him, his sister and his mother.

Maggie's grandsons Ethan, George, and Albert had gone to meet the train at the station in Daventry, taking a cart each, for Bill had a sizeable family.

Will emerged from the shed where he had his workshop. His hair was white now, and his steps were slower, especially on cold days like today—the old injury pained him more in such weather. He still stood straight and tall, and—though his face showed the wear of many years —to Maggie, he was still the handsome young man she had married forty-seven years ago.

"All done," he said, as he walked toward her. "Christmas is more complicated now than it used to be!"

Indeed. Their six children all had children of their own, and many of their grandchildren were already adults. Liam, Bill's eldest son, had recently married, and was bringing his wife to a family Christmas for the first time, and Angie, his next in age, was bringing her betrothed for the family's inspection.

"It will just be Bill and his family tonight," Maggie reminded Will. "Eva said she and Harold will drive over tomorrow morning, in time to join us for church." She went on through the children, reminding Will of the expected arrival time of each of family. He knew the arrangements perfectly well, of course, but—bless the dear man—he also knew that Maggie felt the need to recite the details again, relishing the fact she would soon have most of her nestlings back under her roof.

Most, but not all. Peter was an officer with the British army, and had been posted to India earlier this year. Maggie worried about them, of course, but India appeared to be peaceful now, after the dreadful events a couple of years ago. And Catherine had married a Canadian, and lived with her husband and children on the other side of the Atlantic. They have been back to visit twice, but it was a very long way to come. Perhaps, in time, steam ships would make travel across the ocean nearly as easy as trains had made land travel.

Ernest was the son that Will called their reunion baby, since he was born nine months after that memorable Christmas when Maggie first came to Ashton. He lived just down the road, in the big house that Will had built when his business thrived. When Ernest left school, he had joined his father, managing accounts and other business details for local enterprises, farms and estates, and when Will was appointed churchwarden, Ernest had taken over the day-to-day management of W. Parker and Son. He and his wife Susan had moved into the house, and Will and Maggie into the cottage, when Susan's fourth child was born.

Vicky, Will and Maggie's baby, was also a local, having married the son of a prosperous farmer ten years ago. They and their four (and counting) children would meet everyone for a Christmas lunch at Ernest's tomorrow after church, though they would return to the farm for dinner with Vicky's in-laws. Still, there would be many visits between the houses during Bill's stay.

Maggie could hear their darlings approaching. The clop of hooves, the jingle of bells on the harnesses, the rumble of wheels, the excited chatter of adults and children, the high voices of the latter a melody atop the deeper tones of the former.

She waited on the porch, and Will came to stand beside her, his arm around her waist. He pressed a kiss to her hair. "I replaced that broken board on the wheelbarrow," he said.

To others, the comment might have sounded out of place, with their loved ones just turning in at the gate, but Maggie knew what her grandchildren were sure to ask, probably as soon as they tumbled off the cart.

And sure enough, once they were all inside, and Bill and his wife Anne had hugged her, the new granddaughter-in-law and prospective grandson-in-law had been introduced, and the other grandchildren had all been greeted, Bill's youngest child said, "Gran, Gran, can we see the wheelbarrow?"

Anne chuckled. "Bill has been telling them the story again," she said. "How their Gran walked twice as far as we have come today with their father and Aunt Eva in a wheelbarrow."

"Gran and Grandpa still have the wheelbarrow," said the youngest child to his new sister-in-law, puffing out his chest with pride.

"It is in the shed, Liam," Will told the young man, and Liam went to fetch it, and was soon back inside pushing the barrow that had done her family such good service. Will had known this would happen and had cleaned it.

"Of course," said Bill, "Pa has replaced every board at least twice and the wheel three times, so it is really not the same wheelbarrow at all."

The grandchildren didn't agree, and regarded the object with awe. "That," said the youngest child to Liam's wife, "is Gran's wheelbarrow."

THE END

AUTHOR'S NOTE

Maggie's Wheelbarrow was first written as a short story for my newsletter subscribers, and was revised and extended for this collection. Subscribe to my newsletter for a free short story once every two months.

Jude always wanted to be a novelist. She started in her teens, but life kept getting in the way. Years passed, and with them dozens of unfinished manuscripts. She had a successful career in commercial writing, but the fear grew. What if she tried, failed, and lost the dream forever? The years since 2014 have seen more than 25 novels, more novellas, 5 volumes of short stories, 3 awards, and thousands of positive reviews. The dream is alive.

Website and blog: https://judeknightauthor.com/
Subscribe to newsletter: https://judeknightauthor.com/newsletter/
Bookshop: https://shop.judeknightauthor.com/
Facebook: https://www.facebook.com/JudeKnightAuthor/
Pinterest: https://nz.pinterest.com/jknight1033/
Bookbub: https://www.bookbub.com/profile/jude-knight
Goodreads: https://www.goodreads.com/author/show/8603586.Jude_Knight
LinkedIn: https://linkedin.com/in/jude-knight-465557166/

FOREVER HOLD YOUR PEACE

RUE ALLYN

FOREVER HOLD YOUR PEACE

BY RUE ALLYN

A Regency Era Christmas Short Story

Home from the wars, Captain Prescott Drake is shocked to learn that his fiancée plans to wed someone else. Can he reach her in time to prevent the nuptials? Will she want him, or has their treasured love died the slow death he nearly suffered in a French prison? Desperate and believing the man she loved is dead, Miss Elizabeth Feddleston seeks rescue in the form of marriage to a kind friend. He knows she does not love him now but has hopes that once she has mourned the man who first won her heart that she will turn to him. Three friends, one wedding and the storm of the century. Will the right couple triumph or will nature put love to death?

PART I
THE RETURN

"She can't marry him! Betts is my fiancée." The news wasn't just unwelcome. It capped a series of mishaps and disasters that had begun years ago with Captain Prescott Aelfwyn Drake's capture by the French.

Less than an hour ago, in the gray winter dawn, Prescott had stood outside the Earl of Trehallow's townhouse, knocked on the door, and waited, pacing. He stamped his feet in his worn boots. Beneath his thin cloak he rubbed his arms. Icy cold burned his ears and froze the tip of his nose. He wished he'd had a hat or better yet, a muffler. With each turn he coughed.

Where's the cursed footman?

Prescott banged a bare fist on the door once more, pounding the wood until the portal opened. The august personage on the inside of the door stood only as tall as Prescott's chin. Nonetheless the man looked down his nose at the scruffy person who dared assault the door of Major Lord Arthur Trevor PenRhydderch, twenty-first Earl of Trehallow.

Prescott didn't care. He barreled into the foyer, forcing the servant aside.

"I beg your pardon, sir! His lordship is not at home to the likes of you." The man's lip curled.

"Lord Trehallow is the 'likes of me,' and I know he is at home."

The shorter man straightened to his full height. "I must ask you to leave, sir."

Prescott had warmed enough to be able to move faster and raced up the stairs, calling, "Bollocks to that."

"Smithe, Fortes, I need you," the doorman yelled.

Prescott ran on, reaching the door at the far end of the corridor at the same moment pursuing footsteps sprinted behind him. A fit of coughing seized him as he pounded on the wooden surface.

A man in banyan and a face full of shaving cream opened the door opened. "Carruthers, what's going on out here?"

Prescott swallowed a cough, shoved past his friend and stumbled toward the hearth. "Trehallow, tell your man you are expecting me."

"All is well, Carruthers. You may go." The earl shut the door on the servant then turned, wiping lather from his cheeks and chin. "Prescott. By all that's holy, I thought you were dead."

Prescott reared backward, tucking his chin. "Dead?"

On the far side of the room, a door opened.

"I've brought the gray superfine as you requested, my lord. I thought the burgundy cravat…" The earl's valet broke off in surprise. "Ah, I did not realize you have a visitor. Please excuse me."

He made to depart, but Trehallow stopped him. "Leave the clothes. Pour two brandies, then send for my physician and bring breakfast for two here. After that, wait for the physician's arrival and bring him to me the instant he arrives."

"Of course, my lord." The valet bowed.

While waiting for the man to go, Prescott removed his cloak and hung it on a stand near the fireplace. He stood on the hearth warming his hands and letting heat seep into every chilly bone and fiber. He tried not to cough, but the inflammation in his lungs defeated his efforts. The fit bent him nearly double.

As the door closed on the valet, Trehallow began to dress. "You look like hell. Sit, before you fall down, man."

A gentle push was all that was needed. Prescott nearly fell into a hearthside chair.

"Sorry, I came straight from the ship." He paused to clear his throat. "I knew you would be here. Nothing to do on shipboard except read old issues of the Teatime Tattler. One of them reported that you had remained in London, but intended to leave within the week."

His friend pulled on a shirt and tucked it into his trousers.

"Town is nearly empty," Trehallow said. "Everyone who could return to the country for the holidays has done so. The weather has been the very devil, but that is neither here nor there."

The earl handed Prescott a tumbler of brandy then sat in the opposite chair.

"Bit early in the day, don't you think?" He eyed the drink, forcing back a cough.

"Drink it," Trehallow ordered. "Then tell me what happened to you. Last I heard you were declared missing presumed dead at Leipzig in October 1813."

"I was carrying letters from General Sir Charles Stewart to the Crown Prince when I found my way blocked by a squad of ten soldiers wearing the insignia of the imperial guard. They were facing the road, and I was in the trees. I chose to burn the letters, which of course drew their attention. A fight ensued in which the enemy attempted to stop the destruction. They succeeded in disarming me and beating me to a pulp, but the letters were destroyed. I was captured and sent to the dungeons of Charlemont at Givet."

"Odd. That prison was not known to hold officers."

"I was in uniform but, to avoid significant torture, wore no insignia. For that reason, the French decided I was a deserter and my treatment was worse than that of a common seaman or private."

Trehallow nodded. "That explains why you appear to be a ghost of yourself, but not why you remained in prison after the war ended, last June."

"I can only guess. My jailer hated the English. I suspect he would never have released me had Bourbon troops not taken over the prison. I was transferred to a hospital and was there several months before I decided to leave and damn the sawbones who kept telling me I was dying. More time passed while I made my way to the coast and found a vessel to take me to Dover. By then the weather began to worsen. Getting to London was a challenge. I went first to the Feddleston home, but the knocker was up. I came here next."

He ran out of breath as he finished, and a coughing fit defeated his every effort to resist.

"They've gone to the country," Trehallow explained.

"Miss Feddleston. I've not been able to write to her or anyone. I..." coughing seized him once more. "I have missed her greatly. We are to wed as soon as I sell my commission. She needs to know that our plans can move forward."

"Oh." Trehallow's facial muscle's tightened, and his shoulders bunched.

"Oh? What is it? Has something happened to Betts? Tell me." A cough welled in Prescott's chest. He refused to permit himself to succumb.

"She's marrying Lord Tellus Leigh at St. Martin's church in Leicester on December 25th. Percy and I were invited, but with Percy increasing and the weather, we declined."

"Tellus Leigh, the Duke of Leigh's seventh brother and my good friend?"

"I know of no other Lord Tellus Leigh," Trehallow remarked.

"She can't marry him! Betts is my fiancée. Tellus and everyone in society knows that. Devil take it, the man agreed to stand up with me when Betts and I married."

Had Tellus always wanted Betts or is this some new start because I was reported dead?

PART II
THE RACE

London
December 14, 1815

Before dawn the next morning, Trehallow's horse master closed the stable doors as Prescott mounted, then set off for Leicester. The earl had not wanted to lend a horse. He had consented, however, once Prescott agreed to spend the night at the Trehallow townhouse and submit to the physician's examination.

"Let me send a messenger," the earl argued. "Stay here. Recover your health. You'll not do Miss Feddleston any good if you kill yourself to get to her."

Prescott had refused every argument. "I need to see her, Trev."

"And you will."

"You don't understand. My love for her kept me alive when all seemed lost. I can't count the occasions, when I tried to escape and was caught. Betts is the reason I never gave up. If you won't help, I'll find a mount on my own."

The earl had yielded, but insisted that his friend would take warm clothing from the earl's own wardrobe and a Trehallow groom would accompany him.

Prescott might have declined out of pride, but he was smart enough to know that both demands increased his chances of arriving in Leicester before the wedding.

Five days. In good weather and with good roads the journey to Leicester took five days—six if a man wasn't in a hurry. However, the snow had been falling for weeks, and he was in a great hurry. How long would it take to get to Leicester? A week? Two? More? He'd ridden in worse weather over worse terrain with cannon smoke and screams of the wounded in his ears. He could do this. A snowstorm was nothing compared with the mud, blood and fog faced by battlefield messengers.

Trehallow had not been able to tell him much about Betts' decision to marry Lord Tellus Leigh save that the announcement of their nuptials had been published in early November. What had happened to the woman he loved, who, he believed, loved him? She'd written to him while he was fighting. Letters of dreams about how their lives would be. The number of their children. The wedding they would have at the tiny church near her home. The honeymoon she longed for in the wilds of Scotland. The home she knew they would make at his small estate near the Yorkshire coast. The days she longed to spend with him well into old age.

He'd laughed, as she no doubt intended, when she told him of the argument between her young twin sisters about which of them should toss petals before the bride and which of them would move into her room. Fortunately, she'd been able to intervene before hair pulling escalated into wrestling.

She would be a wonderful mother. She'd had plenty of practice, raising her one brother and two sisters after their mother died. Their father, Squire Feddleston made a reasonable income from two large farms he leased to crofters. However, Betts too often was forced to strict economies. The squire enjoyed games of chance entirely too much. He favored London over provincial gambling hells. Too often he left his children on their own to carry out his responsibilities in Wigston.

Prescott swayed in the saddle. Fog was creeping in.

"You need to stop and rest, Captain," Jamie O'Bryan, the groom, said, coming up on Prescott's right.

"There's an inn a few miles further on. We'll stop there to rest the horses and eat." He trotted ahead, hoping that O'Bryan wouldn't hear the coughing that plagued him. Every fit burned his lungs and caused a cold sweat to break out beneath the borrowed fur-lined cloak. 'Twas naught to be done for the cough or the chills. He had to get to Betts.

The snow and fog faded and Betts' smile filled Prescott's vision. While home on leave and awaiting orders, he'd attended a provincial assembly at the request of his good friend Lord Tellus Leigh. Curse the man who was wedding Prescott's beloved. Someone, he could not recall whom, had introduced him to a brown-haired, green-eyed young woman.

He'd thought her pretty enough, in her elegant ensemble of ecru muslin sprigged with green ribbon that matched her eyes.

He'd bowed over her hand and asked. "May I have the honor of a dance, Miss Feddleston?"

"Yes, thank you Captain." She'd smiled at him.

Charming, he'd thought.

"What do you think of Napoleon's strategy at Austerlitz?" She'd asked as they performed the opening steps of the waltz."

He'd been taken aback by a question not common to young ladies. Did she seriously want to know his thoughts, or was she simply hoping he would fill the conversational gap until she could dance with someone else?

"I believe Boney's strategy at Austerlitz showed the advantage of having superior intelligence during battle."

"Interesting. No doubt you are correct. Had the Allied army possessed better information, they would have seen Bonaparte's withdrawal from the Pratzen Heights as the feint it was and perhaps not have been fooled into weakening the center of their line by sending more troops to Pratzen than was wise."

The urge to know how she'd learned of the strategies used became irresistible. "Are you a student of military strategies, Miss Feddleston?"

She'd tossed back her head and laughed. "Strategies of all sorts, Captain."

"For example?" Intrigued he'd prompted her for more.

"Do you know Lady Beatrix Sandrow?"

"I've heard the name. I do not believe I have had the pleasure of her acquaintance."

"Her father is a recently elevated life peer, and his ambitions for his daughter's marriage to an ancient noble house are well known."

"Does the lady share her father's desires?"

"You tell me. She attends nearly every social event and appears completely cowed by her overbearing papa."

"I'm not certain how I see this as an example of strategy?"

"I spoke with her once or twice and discovered she has a predilection for Greek and Latin philosophers."

"Unusual for a tonish young lady, but not unheard of."

"She finds entertainments such as this assembly to be boring."

"Ah, I begin to understand. She has developed some stratagem for escaping the social events her papa insists she attend."

"In a manner of speaking. She attends as her father insists. However, at the earliest opportunity—usually when Lord Sandrow is occupied in the card room—she escapes to her host's library or the ladies' retiring room, if the affair is held at a public venue. She always brings a book with her, usually brought by her maid who meets her in the chosen retreat to give Lady Beatrix the book. The maid also stands guard and warns her mistress if Lord Sandrow returns to the ballroom."

"Ingenious. She knows her opponent well enough to take advantage of the available terrain and deceive her opponent into believing that she is compliant with his wishes."

"In other words, she strategizes to get what she wants."

"Do you have stratagems that you employ, Miss Feddleston?"

She'd fluttered her eyelashes and smiled that enchanting smile. "All women strategize, Captain. However, revealing those strategies to a stranger would be unwise, don't you think?"

"Any soldier would have to agree."

They had spun into a turn as the music rose to a crescendo.

A wave of dizziness struck Prescott. Sleet pelted his face. Fortunately, he righted himself before he took a spill into a snowbank.

"Captain?" The groom cantered up to his side. "Are you well?"

Pay attention to the present, man. "Well enough, thank you for your concern."

"Perhaps we should stop for a bit?"

The fellow could not possibly understand the urgency. "Stop if you wish. I'll continue without you."

The man fell back.

Watching the road ahead, which was disappearing rapidly beneath an icy coat, Prescott pressed his mount to a faster pace. As they pounded down the king's highway, the trees, the road faced and Bett's face filled his vision. Howling wind and beating hooves became the dulcet rhythms of her voice. He shivered not with cold but with the warm delight of her company.

Once more the groom drew near. "We've arrived, sir."

Prescott blinked, and finally saw the snow-screened shapes of a village on either side. Short moments later, he and the groom clattered into the courtyard of the Edgeware Cock & Bull.

PART III
THE INNER DEBATE

Leicestershire,
December 14, 1815

A treasured locket open in her hands, Miss Elizabeth Eloise
Feddleston sat by the window of the elegant sitting room—part of the
suite assigned her at Leigh Chase. She stroked the pad of one thumb
across the miniature within.

The handsome soldier depicted stared out at her with an intent
moss-green gaze. His square chin framed a generous mouth. The
resolute set of his broad shoulders spoke of the strength of his
courage and determination. Captain Prescott Aelfwyn Drake had
given her the locket as a remembrance on the day she accepted his
proposal of marriage. A marriage that would never be, for darling
Prescott was dead.

Betts sniffled back a tear. She had cried too much already. 'Twas
past time to lay Prescott and his memory to rest.

Outside the December day was gloomy and dreary, entirely too close a match to her thoughts. The wind howled as it battled with the branches of the trees which more often than not fell to the snow, ice and cold of the windy assault. In Betts' heart, fear and worry did battle with her every attempt at the calm control she relied on to deal with disasters big and small, since the day of her mother's passing. That had been sixteen years ago. She'd been seven when she'd made her way from the nursery to her father's study and found him mumbling into a glass, which she later learned was Scotch whisky. Strathnaver's best—nothing but the best for Squire Feddleston, regardless of what economies were necessary to acquire said best.

"London gentlemen won't respect a man who wears shoddy clothes, serves second rate whisky, rides ill-bred hacks..." the list went on.

She pushed painful memories aside and tried to concentrate on the future. Tried to convince herself she was doing the right thing. The only thing. To save her brother and sisters from soul-killing lives planned by their cousin and new guardian, marrying Lord Tellus Leigh was the right thing, the only thing.

In a few short weeks, on Christmas Day, she would be married. Her future husband, a kind, warm, generous man, like Prescott, yet Tellus Leigh was not the man of her dreams. He was a dear a friend who deserved better than the half measure of love that had been all she could promise him in exchange for the protection he offered her and her family.

She knuckled away a second tear. It should have been Prescott standing beside her in the church. However, Prescott Drake was dead, as were all of the dreams they had shared. In the wake of the news that he was missing and presumed dead had come a string of disasters that had led her to this moment.

It was imperative she marry quickly. Her lips twitched with a failed smile. No, she wasn't *enceinte*. It was her siblings' welfare that necessitated her quick nuptials.

They'd lived at the Feddlestone Grange for her entire life. She'd foregone a come-out to save money and keep a roof over their heads. Her father, if he knew of the difficulties his gambling caused, never acknowledged that sacrifice or any of the myriad others. Phillip had not gone to Eton like every other Feddleston son. No, he'd been educated by the local vicar whose kindness and generosity had been repaid with vegetables, eggs and mutton or pork from the Feddleston home farm. The nursery maid had been let go before Betts was eight. She'd raised her twin sisters, and her brother to the best of her ability.

Had it not been for the kindness of Tellus' older brother, His Grace of Leigh, Betts was not certain how she would have managed. The duke, his aunt, ten brothers and two sisters had taken the motherless Feddleston brood to their hearts.

She and Lady Blythe Leigh, now Marchioness of Cynedroit, had been friends from the cradle. They'd shared lessons with Blythe's governesses and other tutors. The duke had even kept those employees on to teach the younger Feddlestons. The brothers, most of them older, had tolerated Betts and her sisters. They'd taken her brother into their manly fold.

Not until 1811 when Betts made her first social appearance at a Leicester assembly did she and Tellus find a common bond over the tediousness of such functions. Afterward, she'd begun to feel comfortable in company. They had both confessed to being shy of strangers and agreed to help each other in difficult situations. They'd even had a signal—a forefinger resting against the cheek would send one or the other to the rescue. Then, a year or so later, Tellus had introduced her to Captain, Sir Prescott Drake.

Weeks afterward, when Tellus had called on her shortly after Prescott's proposal, he'd confessed to a small jealousy. He feared he'd be losing his friend.

"Nothing of the sort, Tellus dear." Betts had said. "Prescott and I owe you much. You will always be our friend."

Tellus had celebrated with them at the private betrothal. They'd agreed not to announce their engagement until Prescott sold his commission. When he'd left to join the allied armies against Napoleon, Tellus had been the one he'd charged with watching over Betts and family.

It had helped, having a friend who missed Prescott nearly as much as she did. The letter from one of Prescott's fellow officers informed her he had vanished while carrying classified messages. Evidence of a struggle had been found along with the charred remains of the letters and the corpse of his mount. If Prescott had survived the fight he was most likely a French captive and his chances of survival were not good. If he had evaded the enemy, he had been unable to return to his regiment. Either way, he was presumed dead.

Tellus had been with her when they learned of Prescott's fate. He'd held her hand and supported her in her grief. Later, after her father had died in a hunting accident—at least that's the story that had been put about—Tellus had been a stalwart source of advice and wisdom. The truth was that her father had made a bet that he could make a nearly impossible jump. Of course, he'd been drunk when he'd made the bet and more drunk when he made the attempt despite every effort by friends to stop him.

Betts wore mourning for Prescott, though nominally for her father. That time had been fraught with demands for payment from creditors. She'd sold furniture, paintings, her mother's jewelry, anything that would keep the house and give them food and clothing.

The day her father's heir and their guardian had ridden into the courtyard at Feddlestone Grange had been the last straw. He'd made clear that she would no longer manage anything. She would marry a man of his choosing—a wealthy old man willing to take her and pay off the family debts for the privilege. Her brother and sisters would be sent to a parochial school and have the "nobility" beaten out of them if they refused to learn to be good Christians.

She'd considered taking her siblings and running away. She had neither the funds nor the means. The idea of marriage to an ancient sanctimonious stranger terrified her. The fate awaiting her brother and sisters horrified her. She'd escaped to the garden one day, and Tellus had found her there. She'd poured out all her troubles and woes to him.

"I don't know what to do, Tellus. Cousin Hector is the exact opposite of father, but completely unyielding. I cannot allow him to send my siblings to that horrid school. I've read about it, asked about it, and the place is infamous for its strict treatment of children. It usually only takes in orphans and other children without resources. Which Cousin Hector believes makes it perfect for my brother and sisters who have been raised with, to his mind, unwonted privilege and must be properly instructed in humility and industry before their souls are steeped in evil. He has doubled the rents on the home farms and decreased the amount paid to laborers and local shop keepers. He dispenses justice in the form of transportation, hanging or beatings. He is intolerable, but I have no alternative."

"Marry me." Tellus had blurted.

"Oh, sweet Tellus. Thank you, but you know my heart died with Prescott."

"Yes." He'd taken her hand. "I do know. I miss him too. Hear me out, please."

"Very well."

"Prescott charged me with looking after you."

"Yes."

"And you are in danger from your cousin's machinations."

"My guardian would not see it that way."

"Nonetheless. What better way for me to honor Prescott's wishes than to marry you and protect you and your family from your cousin? I have a modest estate from a distant uncle and enough income from investments to be able to provide for you. I can send your Phillip to school and hire a governess for your sisters. I understand you. The Leigh name and the Duke's authority will be yours. You will have the life you should have had with Prescott."

She blinked back tears. "I am honored, Tellus. However, you are not Prescott. How can you wish to marry a woman whose heart is in the grave? A woman you know cannot love you."

"Love comes in all sorts of forms and perhaps with time, you will be able to give me a morsel of the affection you had for Prescott."

"And if that never happens?"

"Then I will count myself lucky to have a dear friend as my wife. You can be that without betraying Prescott. You can help me manage the properties and businesses of the Leigh family. You wouldn't have to go to London and be involved in the ton. Blythe will gladly take on all of that social responsibility, especially where your siblings are concerned. Phillip would have ten older brothers to guide him. The girls—Grace and Joy—will have dowries and all the opportunities given the nieces of a duke."

"I don't know…"

"Think about it."

She had nodded. "I'll tell you my answer at next week's assembly. I'll save you the first waltz."

She'd said yes. It really was the only reasonable solution. Her cousin had protested until the Duke of Leigh had summoned him. That conversation had been short and effective. What the duke had said to Cousin Hector she did not know. However, within the week she, Grace, Joy and Phillip had moved to apartments at Leigh Chase.

The marriage had been announced in the papers that November when the banns were first called and the wedding, a small—by ducal standards—family affair would take place at the St. Martin's church in Leicester with the bishop presiding. The wedding breakfast would follow at Leigh Chase.

Then she and Tellus would be off on a honeymoon of sorts. They would make stops at all the various properties owned by the Leigh family, including the brewery in Scotland, recently acquired by the Duke. She'd always dreamed of visiting Scotland. However, the dreams had included Prescott at her side. How would it feel to have a different man sharing the moments that should become cherished memories? A different man fathering the children who should have been Prescott's.

Such questions were pointless. She must live in the world as it was. Her sisters and brother were already adjusting to their new situation.

"We love the new governess," Joy—the more vocal of the twins—had said while Grace nodded enthusiastic agreement at her side. "We cannot wait to begin dancing lessons."

"Oh, the tutor's a good enough fellow," her brother admitted when pressed for his feelings. "He'll prepare me right properly for Eton, and that's what I'm truly looking forward to."

She should follow their example and put the past into the past.

And I shall in a few moments.

She closed the locket and gathered her skirts, preparing to leave, but continued staring out the window, her thumb caressing the locket.

She did not see the snowy blanket beyond the window. She did not hear the crackle of wood in the hearth. Instead, she saw the moment Prescott had spun her round as the music of their first waltz together had risen to a crescendo. Her breath quickened, as it had then, and she'd taken moments to steady her breathing as the dance had ended.

"Thank you for a most entertaining dance and conversation, Captain Drake." she'd said when she could. She had smiled, extending her hand.

He'd bowed, kissed the air above her gloved fingers. "It was a pleasure, Miss Feddleston. Might I call on you? I would enjoy continuing our discussion and perhaps expanding into other topics of mutual interest."

Her heart had thrilled, and she had consented.

They had spent the next two months in each other's company. By the time his orders came, he had spoken to her father, then proposed. She had accepted. They agreed to share the news only with close family and friends, but hold any announcement until he sold his commission.

PART IV

OBSTACLES

Daventry, Northhamptonshire
December 20. 1815

They'd spent entirely too much time at the Cock & Bull. The innkeeper's wife had heard Prescott coughing and insisted he take her personally prepared physic of honey, mint and whisky. When he'd tried to refuse, the groom had become stubborn and declined to have the horses brought round until he'd finished every bit of his stew and drunk all of the potion.

The groom had continued to urge Prescott to stop, citing fever that might confuse him as to the path. He'd volunteered to carry word to Leicester.

Swaying in the saddle, Prescott considered his options.

"Have you been to Leicester before?" he asked of the groom.

"No, sir, but I'm in better shape than you and can ask the way whenever I stop for food."

"Aye you could." *Would he ride with the same urgency and*

determination as me? Would Betts or even Tellus believe the word of a groom? If I kill myself in the effort to reach Betts, then my failure won't matter. She'll wed a good man, and I'll be gone. However, as long as I have breath in my body, I must try. Sending the groom ahead increases my chances.

Wisdom said the groom was right. Sending him would not stop Prescott.

"Very well," he finally conceded. "I'll write a note for you to carry when we next stop."

"Thank you for your trust, Sir Drake. You'll not regret it."

Coughing racked Prescott with every mile. His mount didn't care, by now the horse had become used to the shifting of muscles required for Prescott simply to stay in the saddle. The gray, snowy days blended into darker snowy nights. For the past four days, they would canter into town long after sunset or a solitary farm yard and beg assistance for their mounts, food and rest for themselves. Prescott resented each moment when necessity forced a halt. However, his own experience and training told him that without some rest, some sustenance, he would be unable to continue.

The snow had deepened enough to hide the mile markers. Only when they passed a town or village could he measure his progress. North Watford, Bricket Wood, Slip End, Tingrith, Broughton all came and went in a blur of stable yard, brief warmth as he ate, and the ever-colder resumption of his ride.

None of it mattered. Not until they approached an inn at Daventry, where Prescott would write the promised note. The innkeeper had ordered the entry to the yard kept clear of snow. All would have been well, had not the ice that built up beneath the snow gone unnoticed.

On the evening of 20 December, Prescott cantered into the yard, holding his horse together by sheer will as the valiant steed slid on that unseen sheet. As he pulled to a stop before a waiting stable-hand they both heard an equine scream blending with the groom's shout.

Prescott leapt to the ground tossed the reins to the waiting stablehand and raced back to the entrance. Thuds and popping crunches drowned out his footsteps. The sight was horrifying. The groom lay pinned beneath his grunting mount. The horse, its upper foreleg twisted at an impossible angle, had fallen so that its entire body blocked the narrow space of the entry.

People surrounded Prescott. Exclamations and screams created a symphony of pain and dismay.

Prescott's hand went to his sword and came away empty. Along with refusing to carry saddle bags, he'd chosen not to wear a blade or pistol to lighten the load on the horse.

"A dirk. Hand me a dirk!" He'd shouted and extended his hand. He used the voice of command that even in the face of roaring cannon would calm panicked troops.

The surrounding crowd fell silent.

The haft of a long knife filled his palm. He strode forward, steadied the horse's head against his thigh, crooning to the beast. As the mare calmed, he slit its throat.

Hot blood gushed over his ice-covered gloves and thawed his hands a small bit.

"Clear this beast away," he ordered, resuming his command tone. "Beware the rider. Send for a physician."

He went to the groom, who looked up at Prescott glassy eyed. "I'm sorry, sir."

"Not a bit of it. You've naught to regret. We'll have you inside in a trice with a physician to tend you."

Fortunately, the man fainted at the first attempt to move the body of the horse.

Hours later, the physician left the groom, joining Prescott in the public room where he forced himself to eat.

"Well?" He looked up at the man as he sat across from him.

The physician motioned for food and drink.

"Your groom is a very lucky man."

Prescott raised a brow.

"He has a clean break of his right femur and a sprained right ankle," the physician continued. "With proper rest and care, he should make a full and complete recovery."

"Th…" a coughing fit seized Prescott.

The doctor waited patiently until the fit ceased and Prescott managed to down some ale.

"You, I believe, are in a much worse case than your groom, sir."

"I cannot allow that to matter. I must be in Leicester before Christmas Day."

"In this weather and with the lung infection that I can hear as you breathe, I doubt you'll make it as far as Dunton Bassett."

"I will make Leicester before Christmas day or die trying."

"Hmm. Most likely." While the server brought his meal, the physician studied Prescott.

"What unit did you serve with?" the man asked.

"Rocket Brigade."

"You saw battle at Leipzig."

"Captured there. Spent the rest of the war in the dungeons of Charlemont at Givet."

"That's where you acquired this lung infection."

"Yes," Prescott said though he knew it wasn't a question.

"Why is it so important that you get to Leicester quickly?"

"My fiancee is about to marry another man."

"I assume she is not being forced, so why would you care. She's rejected you, clearly."

Prescott resisted the pain squeezing his heart at the thought that Betts' affections had changed. "She thinks I'm dead."

"Ah," the doctor said. "Unless you get to her before the vows are said, you will have no opportunity to change things."

"Precisely." Prescott spooned up the last of his stew and rose. "I must speak with the innkeeper regarding care for my groom."

"I urge you to spend the night here. I may be able to help reduce that infection enough for you to continue tomorrow in much better case."

He was tempted. He could progress faster if he coughed less, had less fever. However, he couldn't afford the time.

"How far have you come?" the doctor asked.

"Left Mayfair early on 14 December."

"You've done well to come this far in six days, given your condition and the weather."

"Hence the need to continue on. I can rest and recover once I get to Leicester."

"I served with Wellington throughout the Spanish and French campaigns. Believe me when I tell you that you will not get to Leicester alive without some rest and care."

"I do not doubt you, sir. I witnessed the death of too many fellow soldiers who'd refused to stop due to the urgency of their missions. I might have been one had I not been captured. Yet the chances had been equally good I could have died in Charlemont. So many captives did. How many of those men would ride through a blizzard, risk freezing to death just to see a beloved one last time? Can you blame me for that?"

"Not at all," the doctor confessed. "Nonetheless, all my experience tells me your chances of success improve with even a single day's rest and care."

"What sort of care? Would you dose me with laudanum until my body heals itself?"

"No. Juice of the poppy would not help you. However, a course of alternating steam baths, tinctures of honey, lemon and whisky, compresses of flax and mallow sprinkled with a small amount of mustard applied back and chest. Afterwards sleep of at least eight hours."

"All that and I shall be cured?"

"No, but your chances of surviving to reach Leicester increase greatly."

"I don't know." Prescott could not believe he even considered halting.

"Give me thirty-six hours. You've come more than seventy miles on sheer determination. You cannot keep up that pace for the thirty more miles it will take you to get to Leicester in this weather. Your body will give out."

"By the morning of 22nd December you will have improved your odds of traversing those miles and surviving to plead your case with your beloved. In addition, your horse will be well rested."

Prescott pushed away from the table. He stood, about to refuse the doctor's kindness despite the logic of his argument. The room spun. He moved to take a step and crashed to the floor—his legs too weak to hold him.

"Help!" the doctor yelled.

The innkeeper came at a run. "What's to do?"

The physician did not stop to explain the obvious. "Help me carry this man above."

Still lucid, Prescott protested. "I can walk."

Both men ignored him. He was lifted and toted up the stairs into a chamber where he was laid on a bed.

"I need a very hot bath," ordered the doctor, and mint as well as...

The man's voice faded as Prescott succumbed to the involuntary relaxation of his muscles now that he no longer supported himself but lay on a feather mattress.

Wait for me, Betts. Please.

His eyes closed, and his mind wandered into dreams of the woman he loved more than life.

PART V
MEMORIES AND DREAMS

Leigh Chase, Leicestershire
21 December 1815

Candles on the side table added to the dim light of morning. Still, Betts held the powder blue satin close to her face as she tacked the overskirt of snowflake sprinkled lace to the bodice. Over the objections of the Duke of Leigh—soon to be her brother-in-law--she was making her own wedding gown.

As the future bride of one of his nine brothers, he had already gifted her with a complete trousseau. Trunks in which to carry said trousseau to her new home. A maid to tend to her both here at Leigh Chase then at Yorkshire where she and Lord Tellus Leigh would live. The duke had settled an annual income on her. A far too large income, in her mind. He had housed herself, her brother, and two sisters for the past three months. He would continue to pay for the governess and tutor who would journey to Yorkshire with them. They only things the duke had not paid for were her new home—which had been in Tellus' possession since birth—the honeymoon, and this dress.

She had purchased the satin herself. The snowflake lace had been a gift from her siblings, soon after they arrived at Leigh Chase this past September.

Tellus, who grieved Prescott's loss nearly as much as she, had proposed in late October. She'd thought about it for one week before accepting. The banns were read in mid-November, and the date of the ceremony was set for December 25th. From then on, the duke had made almost every decision regarding the wedding. She hadn't minded too much, save when it came to her dress. That was when His Grace of Leigh learned just how stubborn Miss Elizabeth Feddleston could be.

It had been Tellus who finally convinced His Grace to yield on this one point.

She hadn't wanted a winter wedding. The plan had always been for July. She would be married from her childhood home to Sir Prescott A. Drake on a warm summer day. A day that echoed in every way the warmth and easy comfort she felt with Prescott.

They'd made that decision on a July day years ago.

Prescott had driven up in a rented barouche drawn by four matched grays. He was there to take Betts and her siblings on a picnic. The carriage was spacious for four but crowded with five or more passengers. After loading picnic trappings, her brother, two sisters as well as a maid and footman, no room was left for Betts.

She'd smiled at Prescott as he'd assisted her onto the driver's perch. He'd grinned back. No words were needed to tell her the arrangement was deliberate. The drive would be entirely appropriate, but she and Prescott would have an opportunity to share some personal conversation.

They'd been engaged for all of three weeks. Prescott had visited nearly every day. On that sunny July day, he'd asked her when she wanted to marry.

"Today." They'd both laughed. They had agreed not to wed until after Prescott sold his Captain's commission. "Let us wed in July on a day so like today it would feel the same." She'd explained.

"And how is it that today feels to you?" Prescott had asked.

"Like freedom."

At that moment the breeze had attempted to steal her bonnet.

She'd neglected to tie the ribbons in her hurry to join her beloved.

Prescott performed an act of extreme dexterity. Reins all in one hand, he stood, and reached out with his free hand, snagging the end of one ribbon. Then he'd reeled in the bonnet and offered it to her as he sat.

She took it.

He resumed guiding the horses with both hands. What an excellent driver he was, she recalled.

The rest of the day had been the same. She and Prescott had played at hide and seek with the children. They'd stolen a kiss while waiting for her brother Phillip to find them.

He would have been a great father.

The food he'd brought was perfect and thoughtfully chosen with small hands in mind.

He would have been the perfect host.

However, Prescott was dead and gone. Tellus, a somewhat more sober and staid man would host parties with her, would father her children. Try as she might she could not see Tellus at hide and seek. Oh, he was kind to Phillip, Joy, and Grace. He would never hurt them. He would teach Phillip how to manage estates, if that was what her brother wished. He would see Joy and Grace well-prepared for their come out. He would be generous and patient with her. The one thing he could not do would be to replace Prescott. Thank heaven Tellus understood. He'd said when proposing, "I do not want to supplant Prescott. I love him, not in the same way, but with the same depth of feeling as you. I hope that our marriage will bring us both comfort with our memories of a truly good man."

That wisdom had played a great part in her decision to accept Tellus' proposal. That and knowing her siblings would never want or worry as she had for the past several years. She'd accepted with her eyes open to the realities of marrying a man she called friend rather than beloved. What she'd failed to consider was the consequence of marrying into one of the oldest, wealthiest, and most influential families in Britain. She would live in comfort and ease beyond belief. However, along with that comfort, came a degree of status and celebrity which she found far from comfortable. Tellus and even the duke had assured her that her obligations as a Leigh would be minimal, but they wished her to be aware of what might be required, especially on State occasions. She'd understood, and promised to do her duty. 'Twas the price she would pay, she'd told herself, to ensure her siblings' futures. A small price, compared to the sorrow she would carry for the rest of her life.

PART VI
TOO LITTLE TIME

Five miles past Kirby Muxloe, Leicestershire
December 24, 1815

As the sun rose behind the cloudy sky, flurries of snow swirled in the breeze, and Prescott guided his steed from the stableyard onto the Leicester road.

The innkeeper, who had learned from the doctor of Prescott's purpose had forced on him a packet of hard biscuits.

"I made 'em with oats, so you can share with your horse. My stable boy's been feeding that horse up. That gelding's as ready as can be. God keep you Captain."

"And you," Prescott had replied as he left. He'd appreciated the kindness of the doctor and the innkeeper. When he succeeded in his current quest, he'd find a way to return and reward those generous folk.

Within moments the flurries became sheets, driven near sideways by the increasing wind. Prescott could see nothing but white. He slowed from a trot to a walk.

He leaned close to his mount's neck. "I must trust you, now. You'll follow the easiest path, I know. I believe you'll get us to Leicester in time. When you do, I'll buy you from Trehallow, and you shall never have to carry another rider, you shall always be warm and well fed. I promise."

With that he fell silent and rested against the horse's warmth.

He drifted in and out of sleep. His chest ached, still, but the physician's intense treatment had lessened the infection enough that Prescott rarely coughed. Usually, it was his stomach's grumbling that would stir him into wakefulness. He'd take the time to break off a piece of snow softened biscuit and feed it to his horse before taking his own bite. Pausing just a few chilly moments, they would set off again

Night fell, and he passed through the silent village of Dunton Bassett without even looking for an inn. He'd long ago lost sensation in his feet and hands. Thank heaven for the horse's heat or he'd have frozen to death. Kirby Muxloe passed in much the same way. As the sun rose on December 24th, peeking through occasional breaks in the clouds, Prescott's horse rounded a bend in the road and came to a complete stop.

The lack of motion stirred him from a snooze. A coughing fit seized him. Thus, it was some moments before he could take in the scene.

Simultaneously, two coaches, one curricle and one stagecoach, had tried to cross a narrow bridge over a frozen stream. No doubt the snow had blinded each driver to the presence of the other vehicle. The wind would have masked any sound until much too late to prevent the disaster.

One of the curricle's lead horses lay still on the road, the remaining seven horses, were inextricably tangled in the conjoined harnesses. A man stood at the head of the remaining lead, attempting to calm the beast.

The stage coach lay on its side. The driver and a coachman stood on the upward side with the door of the coach open, and were trying to extricate a screaming woman.

Prescott did not stop to think but brought his horse up to the coach. "Hand her to me," he shouted above the howling wind.

"Aye," the driver shouted back.

The screaming woman filled his arms. Prescott turned his horse, made for the end of the bridge where a few pines offered some small shelter. It took precious moments, but he spoke calmly to the woman, crooning assurance as he would to a child.

When he at last set her down near the trees she was quiet, if still shaken.

"My husband, my child, please...."

"Fear not, madam. I'll return with them anon."

Back he went, and received a lad of about eight from the driver.

"That was sparking great fun," the boy burbled. "I want to do it again. Are you the sheriff? You're not going to nab the driver, are you?"

Prescott ignored all the questions handing the boy to his mother and returning to the coach.

"Oww! Watch what you do, you fool of a driver. You're hurting me."

"I'm sorry, sir. But we have to remove you from this coach. Just a bit more."

The driver and coachman pulled. The man should have pushed, helping to move his bulk, but he didn't.

"You there with the curricle," Prescott shouted. "Get these horses untangled and out of the way.

Then he dismounted, tied his reins to the canted boot of the coach and clambered up to help.

"Who are you? If you've come to rob us, you'll find nothing of value."

Prescott shook his head, and grabbed the man beneath one shoulder. Pulling with the driver and coachman he succeeded in lifting the corpulent gentleman. They lowered the man to the ground where he shook off their hold as if their touch would harm him somehow.

The shrug upset the balance of all three.

Prescott fell, but managed to catch onto a coach wheel and lower himself the rest of the way to the ground. The coachman toppled into the coach. The driver tilted backward, his arms pinwheeling but could not save himself. He went over the edge of the coach landing with a sickening crunch on the ice-covered bridge.

Prescott raced to his side.

"What about me?" the rescued man hollered.

The driver lay still as death.

Prescott checked for breath and a pulse. Finding them, he shouted orders.

"Coachman?'

"Aye sir. I am here." His head stuck out of the coach door opening.

"Can you help me rig a travois from pieces of the coach?"

"Aye. I'll get me axe from the boot."

"I say this is most improper. I'm a paying customer and should be tended to first," uttered the fat man. "I insist you leave these malingerers and take me and my family to the nearest inn."

Prescott ignored him.

The man from the curricle came over. "What can I do to help?"

"Have you a knife? Prescott asked.

"Aye."

"Start cutting up the harnesses for a travois."

"Well, I never." The fat man stalked off. He could be heard arguing with his wife.

How long it took, Prescott could not have said. By the time the unconscious driver had been strapped onto the travois and one of the horses harnessed to the makeshift sledge, he was sweating despite the chill that slowed his fingers and the more frequent coughing bouts.

The coachman had mounted the harnessed horse. "I'll get him to the last village. Thank you for your help, sir."

"Thank you and God keep you from more snow."

"Aye, I'll second that," the curricle driver said.

"What about them," Prescott murmured.

The two men looked over to where the woman and her son huddled next to the screen of pines. Her husband was slipping and sliding his way in the same direction as the travois.

"Can you help them get to the nearest village?" Prescott asked.

"Aye. But you seem to be in bad case, sir. Come with us."

Prescott shook his head. "I've an urgent need to be in Leicester by Christmas Day.

The curricle driver cast a glance at the sky where clouds were crowding out the sun.

"There's more weather on the way. I'll pray for you."

"And I you."

The man walked off, and Prescott fed his horse a piece of biscuit before mounting and threading his way through the remnants of the accident.

On the far side of the stream, he urged the gelding to a slow trot until the snow once more flew too thick for sight.

The day darkened, and he coughed more and more. The sweat continued. Most likely he had a fever. He swayed in the saddle so much that he took time to lash himself in place. Night fell. He'd no idea how long ago he passed through Kirby Muxloe or even to what village the dark shapes of buildings he rode by belonged. It had to be sometime close to midnight because he heard snatches of a choir raised in song when the wind would let up for a moment.

"...Born this happy morning, Jesus, Lord at last..." lingered in his ears just beneath the scream of the icy wind.

He returned to leaning against the gelding's neck.

"You're a fool, Prescott," Betts' teasing replaced the choir. The windy howls faded from his hearing.

"I am more sane than any other man," he'd joked in return.

"I don't believe you, for you have just begged me to marry you. Me, the poorest of ladies, daughter of a ne'er do well squire who will bring a brother, two sisters and a mountain of debt into any marriage she might make. Only a fool would propose to such."

"Nay," he'd insisted. You are not simply beautiful, you are kind, generous, industrious, thrifty, have experience as a mother and in many wifely duties. In addition, you are tremendous fun to be with. I could wed no better woman, for no better exists."

"Are you sure," she sobered.

"Certain as the channel separates England from the continent."

"Hmm. That's fairly certain. Very well. We will marry. Just as soon as you return from the wars and you sell your commission."

The horse stopping once more brought him round. The sun had come out. Buildings crowded the street. A boy pulling a sled loaded with wood approached.

"Say, you there." Prescott motioned the lad closer. He cast his arm out toward the shops lining the street. "What place is this?"

"Why Leicester, sir."

"Are you sure?"

"Lived here all me life, so I should know."

"And St. Martin's church, how do I get there from here?"

The lad shook his head. 'Are you daft? 'Tis St. Martin's right there."

Prescott lifted himself up and followed with his eyes the line of the boy's pointing finger toward the left. His head swam.

I made it.

"What..." coughing seized him.

The boy stepped away, fear on his face.

"What d...day?"

But the boy had run off.

Prescott pried at the knot of the rope keeping him in the saddle. It refused to come loose. He tore at it. Dug in with his fingernails. Watching carefully because he could not feel. His nails broke. His fingers scraped raw, bled into the hemp. It was enough to soften the knot, and it slipped loose with a speed that toppled him into the snow beside the gelding. Pain exploded as his head struck something hard.

PART VII
GET HER TO THE CHURCH

Leicester
December 25, 1815

Long brown hair around her shoulders, Betts frowned at her reflection in the mirror. The dress had turned out better than she had expected. She had her mother's veil to hand and would don it at the church. However, her reflection did not please her. She eyed the satin slippers on the bed. Those too she would put on at the church. Beside it lay the fur lined cloak gifted her by Ladies Blythe and Bella Leigh. A smile broke her frown for a moment until she turned back to the mirror.

She raised her hand and ran her fingertips over the three stranded choker of pearls and its pearl crusted blue topaz. One of eleven different pieces the duke had sent for her selection along with a personal note.

Each of these belonged to a Leigh bride. Neither Tellus, nor I could decide which would suit your tastes best. I should tell you that there were originally twelve pieces. However, as the first to marry in our generation it fell to my sister Blythe to choose first.

Tellus is the next to wed, hence you must choose from the remaining jewels. Once you decide, the piece is yours to keep. The family's gift to you for the happiness you bring our brother. Your maid will return the remaining ten to me."

With kind regards,

Leigh

She'd folded the note and put it in her escritoire but had taken most of the previous day to make her selection. She'd sent an innocuous note with the returned pieces, thanking His Grace for his kindness and generosity.

She wasn't certain she would ever become accustomed to such luxuries or the comfort and level of service that most of the Leigh family took for granted. She wasn't certain she wanted to become accustomed.

Her maid answered a knock at the door.

"Lady Cynedroit and Lady Bella, miss," the maid announced.

Gowned, coiffed and ready with cloaks over their arms, the two rushed into the room.

"You've not had your hair dressed, yet." Blythe exclaimed. "You do recall we are expected at the church at noon?"

"'Tis quarter before the hour now," Bella added. "The drive alone will take more than a half an hour."

"Then I shall be late," Betts stated calmly, refusing to add to the panic."

Her tranquil statement had the desired effect.

"Then we'd best get busy with your hair. Please fetch the hair dresser," Blythe, Lady Cynedroit, instructed the maid.

"How can you be so calm? Bella queried. "I swear were I to be wed, I would be prostrate with nerves."

"When the time comes, sister. I suspect you will be too eager for that sort of anxiety."

"I swear Blythe you take all the fun out of imagining my future."

Betts ignored the quibbling until the hairdresser arrived.

He minced into the room followed by a child of perhaps ten.

"If miss will sit, please." Said the little man who affected an Italian accent. He gestured toward the low chair before the dressing table.

In the mirror Betts watched him examine her hair, picking up a few strands, pulling it away from her face.

"*Hai dei capelli bellissimi, signorina.*"

"I beg your pardon. I do not speak Italian."

"He said you have beautiful hair," Blythe translated.

Betts' face heated. "Thank you."

"It is my pleasure to serve you. What style do you wish?"

"I...I...ah...I don't know. What do you suggest?"

"I thought you might not be certain. I have drawings." Snapping his fingers, he turned to the boy. "*Figliolo, perfavore i desgni.*"

Four drawings of faceless women, each with a different hair style were placed before her on the dressing table.

Betts blinked. "They are lovely and, ah, very intricate."

"I show you La Grecque," he pointed to the first image. The others are in order, La Madonna, La Sévigné, and La Chinoise."

The drawings were all lovely, but Betts could not imagine herself in such styles. She looked the hair dresser in the eye. "I do not wish to offend, sir. However, I prefer something simpler. Perhaps a chignon at my neck with no part on the crown."

He smiled at her. "*La signorina is*...how do you say... most wise. Your face is perfect. You have no need of intricate tresses to distract from a weak chin or a lazy eye. *Va bene*, we begin.

She sat watching as he brushed and combed. She felt his fingers separating then weaving at her nape.

Not too much later he stepped back. "*Basta. Abbiamo gle spilli?*"

All three women looked at him in confusion.

"*A bah, figlio, come si dice for cine in inglese?*" He addressed his son.

"Hair pins, Papa."

"Si, si. Have we pins for the hair?"

"Oh," Bella spoke up as she fumbled in her reticule then pulled blue topaz encrusted hair pins. "I nearly forgot. Here."

The hair dresser took them from her. Studied the chignon he had created then added the pins at strategic points. He took up a hand mirror, positioning it so Betts could see the chignon.

"Oh, my." Her fingers went to her lips. "Thank you."

"*Prego, signorina. È stato un piacere*. I leave you now."

The boy began to gather up the tools and drawings.

"Wait." Betts insisted. "I must pay you."

"*No, grazie, il duca mi ha già dato il mio compenso.*"

She wanted to argue but the man was rapidly walking out the door followed by his son. There really was no time, given how late she was for her own wedding.

The maid answered the door once again. "Your Grace," Betts heard the servant say before sinking into a low curtsey.

"You will forgive the intrusion, Miss Feddleston, sisters. I am come on a mission of mercy from Tellus."

"Oh, I am sorry," Betts apologized, striding in the direction of her cloak. "We will leave immediately."

His Grace of Leigh smiled. Tellus was afraid you had changed your mind."

"She had not even had her hair dressed," Bella piped up.

"A bride's style is most important," the duke acknowledged.

"No, no, your grace." Betts added. "I was… simply…er… woolgathering and lost track of the time."

"Quite understandable. You must become used to calling me Lovis, since you are to be my sister."

Betts put fingers to lips.

The duke extended his arm. "Shall we to the church?"

"Yes, of course." She snatched up her cloak then took his arm.

They had stepped into the hall when she halted. "Wait."

The duke raised a brow in question.

"My…my prayer book. It was my mother's and is all I have left of her. I must take it so I can feel she is blessing this union. 'Tis why I decided not to carry a bouquet."

"Then we must fetch the prayer book."

They returned to her suite and she hurried to the bedside table. Opening the drawer she found it empty.

"Oh dear. It's gone." She turned to the duke. "I don't know what to do?"

"Do you recall the last time you used the book?"

"I carry it with me always. I think, I might possibly have used it in the library. I wanted to check a reference and compare a phrase from your copy of **The Rime of the Ancient Mariner** with that in the prayer book."

His Grace gestured to the maid. "Go to the library and find Miss Feddleston's prayer book. Then meet us in the vestibule/foyer."

The maid hurried away.

The duke took Betts' cloak from her and settled it over her shoulders before fastening the clasp at her neck.

"Have you your veil?" Blythe asked.

"Yes, in my reticule." Betts lifted the purse.

"Then let us leave. I gave the coachman orders to walk the horses close by so he could come as we left the house." His Grace of Leigh said, offering his arm once more.

The prayer book in her hands, her soon to be sisters seated across from her and the duke by her side, the coach set off at a careful pace. Even though the snow had momentarily stopped, the road from Leigh Chase to St. Martin's church was still treacherous.

The duke and his sisters spoke softly to each other.

Betts took little notice. Her surroundings faded and she saw with her mind's eye Prescott's smiling face.

"All will be well, my love."

The silent words eased the regret in her heart. Prescott really would approve her union with his best friend.

She kept his image at the forefront of her thoughts until the coach stopped at the church steps. She made her way into the narthex on the duke's arm then stepped into a small room with his sisters. There they arranged her veil. Bella took her reticule.

"I'll hold this for you."

"You're sure you don't want us to precede you as attendants?" Blythe asked.

Betts straightened and raised her chin. Prescott would want her to be joyful in this moment. "I am certain."

"Then we will be off," Blythe said.

"Lovis is just outside the door. He'll wait until you are ready." Bella closed the door as the two left.

Betts was alone.

"I will always love you. I will always be with you." The mental image of Prescott whispered.

She could wait an eternity and never be ready to marry another man. She must do so, however. For herself, for her family. She squared her shoulders once more and opened the door to the narthex.

The duke offered his arm.

She took it and wordlessly they walked to the entrance of the nave.

They passed the uniformed ushers standing at the door of the nave. As she made her first step onto the carpeted aisle, the organist struck the first chords of Jesu, Joy of Man's Desiring, and the congregation stood.

The bishop waited before the altar in the center of the apse. To one side, stood Tellus and his brother Voltunus.

Her fingers trembled on the duke's arm until he placed his free hand over hers and she was able to still herself.

She could not say how long it took to walk the full length of that aisle but all too soon she stood a few feet away from the bishop. "You are doing the right thing."

She prayed that voice in her head spoke true.

The prelate began the ceremony. His Grace of Leigh stepped back. Tellus took her hand and led her closer. At his touch the voice in her head fell silent. She heard the bishop state clearly.

"...into which holy estate these two persons present come now to be joined. Therefore, if any man can show any just cause ..."

PART VIII
FOREVER HOLD YOUR PEACE

Leicester
December 25, 1815

"'Ere now sir. You're injured."

"No," Prescott protested, struggling against the hands lifting him from the ground. He was unspeakably cold and a thousand blacksmith's pounded iron in his head.

"We're just trying to help. You been lying in the snow for the lord knows how long."

"The snow? I was on a horse. Where's my horse?"

"Be this your mount?" a second voice asked.

He turned his head toward the sound and nearly toppled back into the snowy road.

The gelding spun crazily nearby.

Strong arms steadied him.

"Go gentle sir. You got big bump on your forehead and hair's all matted with frozen blood. Probably a blessing or you might a bled to death before we found you."

"Yes, my horse."

"You just come with us, now. We'll get you to the infirmary. 'Tis but a short way from here."

"No." Prescott struggled again and this time broke free. "I must get to St. Martin's Church."

"Well, you're standing beside it." The first man gestured to a wall bordering one side of the alley.

"Excellent. Thank you. Hold my horse, and I'll give you a crown when I return." He stumbled toward the front of the building.

"Here, you can't go in there. Duke of Leigh's got a wedding's in progress." The men caught him one on each side where the alley joined the street.

"Even if you got inside, the servants will toss you back out again."

"You don't understand. I'm the groom."

Two faces peered at him, looking him up and down. "Your loony. Groom's been in the church for more than two hours. Bride just got here. Folks was beginning to wonder if she changed her mind."

Prescott blinked, and finally recognized the blurred shapes lining the street for a crowd of onlookers. As he watched the organ could be heard playing Jesu Joy of Man's Desiring.

I can't delay longer.

Strength born of determination allowed him to throw off his captors and he pelted up the church steps. At the top he hit a patch of ice and hurtled unbalanced toward the closed door. The force of impact with the portal, pushed it open. Prescott along with a heavy gust of wind flew into the nave.

"You there, get out of here."

He was running down the aisle passing the last of the pews when someone's foot shot out in front of him and tripped. Momentum lifted him into the air and he spun, his entire world spinning. In the moment before he landed, Betts' face, her beautiful face, filled his vision.

The prelate stopped speaking.

Then his back hit the carpeted marble and all the air in his lung whooshed out. He opened his mouth trying to breath but his muscles seemed frozen. Like a landed fish he flailed his arms and legs in a vain attempt to right himself.

"Hold him," said a voice.

How many manhandled him he could not say. Indeed, he had no time to say before a fist thumped the center of his chest and he sucked in air.

"You can let go now," the voice said.

Prescott lay there breathing. In, out, in, out until he felt steady enough to gain his feet.

The prelate resumed speaking. "Therefore, if any man can show any just cause…"

He stood, but a hand reached out from the nearest pew and drew him to a seat.

"You're supposed to be dead."

Prescott turned his face and looked into the eyes of His Grace of Leigh.

"As you can see," he coughed. "I am not yet departed."

"…Why they may not lawfully be joined…"

Behind him quiet murmurs filled the air.

"Are you ill?" the duke asked.

"Explanations can wait. I must…" Prescott stood but swayed his head still spinning. He hoped he would not empty his stomach at this solemn moment.

"…Together let him now speak, or else…"

"I can show just cause," Prescott shouted. At least he though he shouted, but the prelate continued.

"…Forever hold his peace."

His Grace stood beside Prescott, a steadying arm around his shoulders. "My Lord Bishop, stop!"

The command echoed through the nave. A silence nearly as loud followed.

"Come with me."

The duke took Prescott's arm and approached the altar.

"Now say your piece, Captain Drake."

"Prescott," Betts whispered, but he heard her.

"Drake, by all that's holy," Tellus murmured.

He too was heard.

"My Lord Bishop," Prescott said. "I can show just cause why this man and this woman should not lawfully joined."

"Your Grace," the bishop gave Prescott a scathing glance. "This is most irregular."

"Agreed," the duke said. "However, I believe this gentleman, Captain Prescott A. Drake, has a prior claim to Miss Feddleston's hand."

"Harrumphf. Is that true young man?"

"Yes, My Lord Bishop. Miss Feddleston and I were betrothed three years past in July."

"Miss Feddleston?" The bishop turned to Prescott's beloved.

"It is," she confirmed.

"Do you wish at this time to dissolve your betrothal to Sir Tellus Leigh?"

"Yes. I'm sorry Tellus."

He grinned at her. "I'm not. I have ever wanted your happiness and now you shall have it."

"You are still willing to marry me?" Prescott asked.

Her once quiet smile broadened. "With all my heart."

Nearby by the duke conversed with the bishop.

"Since the Bishop approves, I recommend," the duke said. "That we continue with the ceremony, but exchange Captain Drake for my brother. Will that meet with your approval?"

The entire group nodded.

His Grace turned and made the announcement to the congregation. Then he and Lord Voltunus Leigh returned to the family pew.

Tellus stood beside Prescott, in bedraggled coat, worn shirt and trowsers, who joined hands with Betts before the bishop.

When the time came for the rings, Tellus offered the one he had intended to use, but Prescott shook his head. From an inner pocket of his torn, weathered coat he withdrew a small gold circlet.

"With this ring I thee wed with my body I thee worship, and with all my worldly goods I thee endow…."

Soon they knelt before the bishop who instructed the congregation. "Let us pray…

They held hands throughout the prayers, the psalms, the recitational, the readings of saints Paul and Peter and at last the blessing.

As man and wife they rose and faced the congregation then made their way from the church. The Duke's carriage awaited them. Prescott handed Betts in and sat beside her.

"Now you can kiss me properly," his wife said.

He replied with action. The bliss of that kiss sustained them through the long wedding breakfast, but Prescott began to cough. First a little, then deeper and longer.

His Grace noticed and sent them to the apartment set aside for their use. "I will send for the doctor then explain to our guests.

By the time the doctor arrived, Betts had Prescott tucked into bed with a compress on his chest.

The doctor sent her from the room and spent a great deal of time examining her husband.

Ladies Blythe and Bella came to sit with her joined later by Tellus and his grace.

Finally, the doctor emerged.

Betts stood to hear his diagnosis.

"Mrs. Drake," he spoke solemnly. "I believe your husband to be dying."

"No." Her hand went to her chest. She could feel the blood drain from her face and the room spun, but she forced herself to steady.

"There is a slim chance that with careful nursing he might recover. The problem is not so much the infection in his lungs but rather that his exhaustion is so great he has no strength left to fight the inflammation."

"Surely with rest, he can recover."

"Possibly. I will write out instructions for his care before I leave then I will return every day to check on his progress. We should know within the week if he will survive or not."

The doctor left with the duke who promised to deliver the instructions once written.

"I will not let him die." Betts stamped her foot and fisted her hands.

"We'll help you," Bella said.

"Everyone at Leigh Chase will help," Blythe confirmed. "Though Cynedroit and I will return home as soon as the weather permits."

"Then we'd best get to work. I know from experience with my mother that plenty of hot water is needed as well as herbs for the best compresses."

They planned carefully. Bella and Blythe left to order all that was needed for the sickroom. Betts went to sit beside her sleeping husband, tucking her hand into his.

"I've just gotten you back. You cannot leave me again." Then she bowed her head in prayer.

EPILOGUE

Aelfwyn Manor, Yorkshire coast
Date July 1817

Betts sat on a blanket beneath the old oak atop the hill that sheltered the manor house from the Channel. The day was sunny, the breeze light. Whitecaps rolled in the waters, building, crashing on the beach below then disappeared as water rushed away from the shore. She loved her home, and thanked Heaven every day that she would soon celebrate the birth of her first child instead of mourning the death of her only true love.

"I've never seen a sight more beautiful in my life," Prescott spoke from behind her as he approached.

She looked over her shoulder at him. His gaze was fixed on her. Then turning to the view once more she lifted her chin in the air. "Indeed, the prospect of the channel from this vantage is truly stunning," she spoke with studied archness.

"Minx." Prescott dropped down beside her. "You know very well I meant you and not the scenery."

She smiled at him. Pleased that he could smile and joke again. For months after his illness, he was somber, almost depressed until finally she'd managed to lead him to speak of his time in the French prison.

She'd been horrified, but the telling purged some deep sorrow from Prescott. He began to laugh, plan, and make love with a sweetness that thrilled her to her toes. The day she'd told him she was increasing he'd danced her around their sitting room. That night he'd wined her, dined her, and bowed to every request she'd made. That hadn't changed in the past eight months. He was her beloved Prescott once more. Yes, there were shadows on his soul. War did that to men. However, he shared those dark moments as much as he shared the more plentiful moments of joy. She was truly a part of him, and he a part of her.

How blessed I am. She fingered the pearls he'd given her to replace the Leigh heirloom choker when she insisted that it be returned.

"Here, my dear," he said, placing an arm around her shoulders then dropping an envelope into her lap.

She leaned her head against his shoulder and tore open the paper.

They read the letter together.

"This is wonderful news," he remarked. "I wish Lady Bella and Glenlewis will be as happy in their marriage as we are.

"Indeed, the news is most welcome after the dreadful time they've had."

"Shall I accept the invitation on our behalf?"

"Oh yes. Our babe should be old enough to travel by then, and summer is the perfect time for a journey."

"I agree. I'd not wish a winter ride on my worst enemy."

"I should be sorry that you nearly killed yourself to prevent me marrying Tellus Leigh. Somehow I cannot find a smidgen of regret in any corner of my mind or heart."

"I would do it again, my love." He drew her to him for a kiss.

One thing led to another, and the sun was setting before they, hand-in-hand, at last strolled into the house.

The End

If you enjoyed Betts and Prescott's story, and would like more about the Leigh siblings, try A *Waltz for the Wallflower*, the tale of Tellus's sister Blythe.

Since her first stumble during her first season, she hasn't been able to live down her reputation as an accident waiting to happen. You can get A *Waltz for the Wallflower* here https://books2read.com/u/bOPdAo

ABOUT RUE ALLYN

Award winning romance author, Rue Allyn has a life long passion for happy ever after. She lives south of the border with her husband of more than forty years and their cat Tanto. She has two sons and is a proud veteran of the US Navy. She writes heart melting romance in all sub-genres, but her favorite is historical romance, especially medieval.

Subscribe to Rue's News, https://www.rueallyn.come/subscriber-entered-from-online-profile/ where you may learn more about Rue and receive a FREE download.

Website: **https://RueAllyn.com**
Facebook: **https://www.facebook.com/groups/**
rueallyndaringdamsels
BookBub: **https://www.bookbub.com/authors/rue-ally**

ABOUT THE BLUESTOCKING BELLES

MEET THE BLUESTOCKING BELLES

The Bluestocking Belles (the "BellesInBlue") are a group of very different writers united by a love of history and a history of writing about love. From sweet to steamy, from light-hearted fun to dark tortured tales full of angst, from London ballrooms to country cottages to the sultan's seraglio, one or more of us will have a tale to suit your tastes and mood.

Learn more about the Bluestocking Belles at:
Website: www.BluestockingBelles.net/
Newsletter: https://bluestockingbelles.net/subscribe-to-our-newsletter/
Teatime Tattler twice-weekly gossip magazine: https://bluestockingbelles.net/category/teatime-tattler/
Free books: https://bluestockingbelles.net/teatime-tattler-free-books/
https://www.facebook.com/bellesinbluex.com/BellesInBlue
https://www.pinterest.com/bellesinblue/
https://instagram.com/bellesinblue

THE BELLES WOULD LIKE YOUR HELP!

Book reviews help readers to find books, and authors to find readers. Please consider writing a review for Merry Belles, even a couple of sentences telling people what you liked (or didn't like) about the stories. Reviews can be posted on Goodreads and on most eRetailers websites.

MALALA FUND

The Bluestocking Belles have chosen the Malala Fund as the charity they support, and to which they donate some of their royalties. Periodically, they take on projects intended to directly support this cause, which exemplifies their personal values and intentions: the right of girls and women to do whatever they choose with their lives.

How can you help?

Make a donation at https://malala.org/donate

OTHER BOOKS BY THE BLUESTOCKING BELLES

Find buy links and story blurbs for all the following books on our website at https://bluestockingbelles.net/belles-joint-projects/

Love's Perilous Road (2025)

Travelers, a house party, smugglers, spies—and a mysterious highwayman. Who is the infamous Captain Moonlight? And how many lives will he change--for good or for ill?

A Christmas Quintet (2024)

Five charming stories of love for your holiday season.

Christmastide Kisses (2023)

Six gentlemen and the ladies with whom they discover the power of a Christmastide Kiss.

Under the Harvest Moon (2023)

As the village of Reabridge in Cheshire prepares for the first Harvest Festival following Waterloo, families are overjoyed to welcome back their loved ones from the war.

But excitement quickly turns to mystery when mere weeks before the festival, an orphaned child turns up in the town—a toddler born near Toulouse to an English mother who left clues that tie her to Reabridge.

With two prominent families feuding for generations and the central event of the Harvest Moon festival looming, tensions rise, and secrets begin to surface.

Belles & Beaux (2022)

Eight charming stories of love, family, and miracles. Each Belle has contributed a tale set in the festive season—one just long enough to fit in between tasks at this busy time of the year. The tales are unrelated, except by the festive season.

Desperate Daughters (2022)

The Earl of Seahaven desperately wanted a son and heir but died leaving nine daughters and a fifth wife. Cruelly turned out by the new earl, they live hand-to-mouth in a small cottage. The young dowager Countess's one regret is that she cannot give Seahaven's dear girls a chance at happiness.

When a cousin offers the use of her townhouse in York during the season, the Countess rallies her stepdaughters. They will pool their resources so that the youngest marriageable daughters might make successful matches, thereby saving them all.

They their adventures in York, amid a whirl of balls, lectures, and alfresco picnics. Is it possible each of them might find love by the time the York horse races bring the Season to a close?

Storm *&* Shelter (2021)

When a storm blows off the North Sea and slams into the village of Fenwick on Sea, the villagers prepare for the inevitable: shipwreck, flood, land slips, and stranded travelers. The Queen's Barque Inn quickly fills with the injured, the devious, and the lonely—lords, ladies, and simple folk; spies, pirates, and smugglers all trapped together. Intrigue crackles through the village, and passion lights up the hotel.

One storm, eight authors, eight heartwarming novellas.

Holiday Escapes (2020)

Holidays, relatives, pressure to marry—sometimes it is all too much. Is it any wonder a woman may need to escape? The heroines in this collection of stories aren't afraid to take matters into their own hands when they've had enough.

Fire *&* Frost (2020)

In a winter so cold the Thames freezes over, five couples venture onto the ice in pursuit of love to warm their hearts. Love unexpected, rekindled, or brand new—even one that's a whack on the side of the head—heats up the frigid winter. After weeks of fog and cold, all five stories converge on the ice at the 1814 Frost Fair when the ladies' campaign to help the wounded and unemployed veterans of the Napoleonic wars culminates in a charity auction that shocks the high sticklers of the ton.

Valentine's From Bath (2019)

The Master of Ceremonies announces a great ball to be held on Valentine's Day in the Upper Assembly Rooms of Bath. Ladies of the highest rank—and some who wish they were—scheme, prepare, and compete to make best use of the opportunity. Dukes, earls, tradesmen, and the occasional charlatan are alert to the possibilities as the event draws nigh.

But anything can happen in the magic of music and candlelight as couples dance, flirt, and open themselves to romantic possibilities. Problems and conflict may just fade away at a Valentine's Day Ball.

Follow Your Star Home (2018)

Forged for lovers, the Viking star ring is said to bring lovers together, no matter how far, no matter how hard.

In eight stories, covering more than half the world and a thousand years, our heroes and heroines put the legend to the test. Watch the star work its magic, as prodigals return home in the season of good will, uncertain of their welcome.

Never Too Late (2017)

Eight authors and eight different takes on four dramatic elements selected by our readers—an older heroine, a wise man, a Bible, and a compromising situation that isn't.

Set in a variety of locations around the world over eight centuries, welcome to the romance of the Bluestocking Belles' 2017 Holiday and More Anthology.

It's Never Too Late to find love.

Holly and Hopeful Hearts (2016)

When the Duchess of Haverford sends out invitations to a Yuletide house party and a New Year's Eve ball at her country estate, Hollystone Hall, those who respond know that Her Grace intends to raise money for her favorite cause and promote whatever love-matches she can. Seven assorted heroes and heroines set out with their pocketbooks firmly clutched and hearts in protective custody. Or are they?

Eight assorted heroes and heroines find more than they've bargained for when they set out for Hollystone Hall for a charity ball.